THE
RESORT

SIGNET
Published by New American Library, a division of
Penguin Group (USA) Inc., 375 Hudson Street,
New York, New York 10014, U.S.A.
Penguin Books Ltd, 80 Strand,
London WC2R 0RL, England
Penguin Books Australia Ltd., 250 Camberwell Road,
Camberwell, Victoria 3124, Australia
Penguin Books Canada Ltd, 10 Alcorn Avenue,
Toronto, Ontario, Canada M4V 3B2
Penguin Books (NZ), cnr Airborne and Rosedale Roads,
Albany, Auckland 1310, New Zealand

Penguin Books Ltd, Registered Offices:
80 Strand, London WC2R 0RL, England

First published by Signet, an imprint of New American Library,
a division of Penguin Group (USA) Inc.

ISBN 0-7394-4569-3

THE
RESORT

Bentley Little

A SIGNET BOOK

For David Hernandez,
cocreator of
"Death Is Not an Option"

THURSDAY

One

"Where *is* this place?" Lowell wondered aloud, but Rachel, tiredly fanning herself with the AAA map as she sat next to him, did not respond, and the kids in the back were too busy fighting to even listen. They'd left the Biosphere after lunch and had been driving ever since. The sun was bright overhead, neither sunglasses nor the windshield visor able to keep out its potent rays, and Lowell had long since shut off the air conditioner to keep the car from overheating. There'd been no signs for the resort at all, nothing in over thirty miles, and he was starting to worry. These single lane roads that crisscrossed the desert all looked the same and were all poorly marked, and it was more than possible that they had taken a wrong turn somewhere and were quickly on their way to some ill-tempered cattle baron's ranch or some crazy survivalists' compound.

But at least they were away from California.

It was the weekend of his twentieth high school reunion, and that was one of the reasons they were out here. They'd been planning this vacation anyway, but when he learned that the reunion was going to be taking place at the same time, he made *sure* that they were going to be out of state.

It was not that he was ashamed of his job or anything, it was just that . . . well, he *was* ashamed of his job. He liked it, the pay was good, and truth be told there was nothing he'd rather be doing, but whenever someone from his youth wandered into the supermarket and saw him behind the register with his name tag that touted his fifteen years of service, he cringed inwardly, praying that he would not be recognized.

That didn't happen too often these days. He'd remained in his hometown of Fountain Valley after graduating from college and getting married, but five years later Ralphs transferred him to a new store in Brea, twenty miles away. While a few of his former classmates had moved to or worked in the northern part of Orange County, they seldom if ever dropped by the store or the shopping center it anchored. Of course, there were a few friends from both high school and college whom he still saw on a regular basis and they knew exactly what he did for a living, but that was different. They understood him, and with them he didn't feel like the abject underachiever he did when meeting people he'd known only peripherally.

Divorced from his past, taken on its own terms, his work was both enjoyable and surprisingly fulfilling. No, he wasn't finding a cure for cancer or writing the great American novel, but neither was he sitting in a cubicle looking at a computer screen all day, juggling meaningless numbers as were so many of his fellow business majors. By his own reckoning, he performed a practical and valuable service as assistant manager of Orange County's highest grossing Ralphs supermarket, making sure that the people of Brea and surrounding communities had fresh meat and produce, guaranteeing that customers wanting ethnic foods or health-conscious products would find the goods they desired on the store's well-stocked shelves. He was friendly with his clientele, knew many of his customers by name, and he took pains to ensure that the supermarket's checkers, boxboys and stock clerks had a pleasant environment in which to work.

Still, he didn't relish the thought of meeting ex-friends and ex-girlfriends and old acquaintances and comparing lifetime achievements.

If he was embarrassed about his job, though, he was proud of his family. Rachel and the kids were far and away the best things that had ever happened to him—much better than he deserved, truth be told—and there was no way he could be anything but happy, content and eternally grateful when it came to his personal life.

Ahead, the road wound around a small hill of white limestone that was dotted with innumerable ocotillos, nearly all of them blooming, their long octopus branches green with leaves and tipped with red flowers.

"Dad?" Ryan whined from the backseat, echoing a phrase he'd heard on a commercial. "Are we there yet?"

Lowell smiled. "Very funny."

Although they were far too old for it, the twins took up the chant. "Dad? Are we there yet? Dad? Are we there yet? Dad?"

"We're there," Lowell said. "We're in our hotel room and you're asleep. You're just *dreaming* that you're still in the car."

That threw them.

"Are you just joking?" Ryan asked tentatively.

"Of course he's just joking," Rachel said, giving Lowell a poke in the side.

The twins ran with it. "Don't listen to Mom," Curtis said. "She's part of the dream." "You can't believe a word she says." "We're all part of the dream," Owen elaborated. "Our whole family. You don't really have a family at all. You're not even a boy. You're just a stray pup at the pound who's dreaming that you're a human."

"Mom!" Ryan cried.

"Knock it off you two," Rachel ordered. "If I catch you torturing your brother on this trip . . ."

Lowell smiled.

Hot air blew in from the window as he drove, causing his hair to whip around wildly, and he found himself wondering why cars didn't have wings anymore. When he was a kid and they'd go on family vacations, the station wagon had had no air conditioning, and his dad used to open the wings, two small triangular windows in front of and adjacent to the driver's and passenger windows, to direct the outside air where he wanted and to create a flow through the car.

Ahead, Lowell could see that the road passed between two hills, and he vowed to himself that if he didn't see the resort or a sign for it, he would turn around on the other side of those hills and backtrack until he found a street that actually had a name and could be identified on a published map.

They'd learned about The Reata from Rachel's sister Pam, whose family had spent a week last summer at Tucson's Westward Look resort. Ordinarily, a hotel in the middle of the desert would not have been their first choice for a summer vacation destination, but Pam had learned that many of Arizona's best resorts, which in the winter catered to wealthy Easterners looking to escape the snow, dropped their rates considerably during the summer months, when very few Easterners dared brave the heat, in order to attract locals and others who could not usually afford to stay at such luxury accommodations. Westward Look had been wonderful, Pam said, but she'd heard from a fellow guest about another, even more exclusive resort with rates during the summer a full seventy-five percent cheaper than those at peak season. The only drawback was that it was way out in the desert, all by itself, and far away from Tucson's nightlife and shopping. To Lowell and Rachel, that made it seem even more attractive, and Rachel had immediately gotten online and looked up the Web site for The Reata.

They were sold instantly. Photos of The Reata showed a gigantic lagoon-shaped pool ringed with tall palm trees, around which bathing-suited guests reclined on lounge chairs under shady umbrellas, their drinks set on adjacent small tables. At one end of the pool was a snack bar cabana. At the other was a small, patently fake Disneyish cliff from which a waterfall fell into the pool. Next to the waterfall, built into the fake cliff, was a long winding slide. Photos of the rooms showed expensive Santa Fe décor and spectacular desert views through floor-to-ceiling windows. The restaurants looked luxurious, the displayed Sunday brunch was a smorgasbord, and the elegant high-ceilinged lobby resembled nothing so much as the great hall of a southwest San Simeon.

All for little more than the price of a Motel 6.

They made reservations online, and a few days later an acknowledgement arrived in the mail in the form of a confirmation letter and two full-color brochures.

The brochures were where they'd gotten their directions to the resort—which was what had led them way out here, miles from nowhere.

Lowell sped down the road, between the two hills, fully prepared to turn around at the next wide spot in the road.

And there it was.

If anything, The Reata exceeded the expectations raised by the brochures and Web site. Nestled at the foot of the Santa Clara Mountains, a low-slung range of rocky desert peaks, the collection of two-story adobe and ranch-style buildings was terraced over several acres of land and looked like a small city. Palm trees and cottonwoods lined the lanes and the parking lots that connected the various sections of the resort, and deep green lawns gave the landscaped grounds the appearance of an oasis in this rough and rugged country.

The bumpy sun-faded road segued into smooth fresh pavement, and a few yards beyond that, a western-style guardhouse with an attached iron gate marked the entrance of The Reata. Lowell slowed the car as they approached. "Exclusive," he said.

Rachel nodded. "To keep out the riffraff."

"The hoi polloi," he countered.

"The rabble."

"The masses."

Curtis groaned. "Knock it off, you guys. You think you're cute, but you're not. You're just annoying."

Lowell laughed and stopped before the gate. A uniformed young man stepped out of the guardhouse, clipboard in hand. "May I help you?"

"We have reservations," Lowell explained. "Under 'Thurman.'"

The guard glanced down at the sheet of paper on his clipboard. "Lowell Thurman?"

"Yeah."

"Welcome to The Reata." The guard handed him a green parking pass the size of a postcard. On it was printed a number and the logo of the resort: a sun setting behind a stylized saguaro cactus. "Hang this from your rearview mirror or keep it on your dashboard at all times. Vehicles that do not display a parking pass will be towed at the owner's expense. Enjoy your stay." He stepped back inside, and a second later the gate swung open.

Lowell drove through and headed up the road toward the cluster of buildings on the hillside. "Cheery greeting. Threatening your customers."

"Don't start," Rachel groaned.

"I'm just saying."

"We're having fun now!" Owen piped up from the back.

"We *are* having fun," Rachel told him. "We're all going to get along and have a good time on this trip. Okay?"

Lowell grinned. *"Jawohl!"*

The road wound through a veritable cactus forest landscaped with the prettiest plants Arizona had to offer, an idealized version of the desert southwest, before passing between two sentrylike boulders that stood at the entrance to the lower parking lot.

"Cool," Curtis said admiringly. It *was* cool, Lowell thought as he pulled the car into a parking space close to the lobby entrance. He unfolded a cardboard sunscreen, and placed it inside the windshield as the rest of the family got out and stretched.

The lobby was housed in what looked like an adobe mansion, the main building on a Mexican millionaire's cattle spread perhaps. The Reata had started out as a dude ranch in the early 1920s, and Lowell assumed that this had been the structure originally used to house guests. A stone walkway covered by a spreading bougainvillea with bright magenta flowers led to a pair of double doors that looked like they had come from an old Spanish mission. On either side, planters made from native rock boasted the desert's flashiest flowers, a rainbow array of succulents and cacti that seemed even more arresting against the dull brown adobe.

The lobby doors were opened from the inside by two clean-cut young men wearing vaguely western uniforms consisting of black pants, white shirt and turquoise bolo tie. The one on the right smiled at them as they passed by. "Welcome to The Reata."

"Thanks, dude," Curtis said, and Rachel pinched his shoulder. "Knock it off."

The air conditioning in the lobby felt wonderful after the dry heat outside. Though he hadn't noticed it until now, Lowell was sweating, and he used a finger to wipe away the drops of suddenly cold perspiration that were dripping down the sides of his face from under his hairline. The lobby was huge, much larger than the outside of the building would indicate, larger even than it appeared on the Web site photos and in the brochure. A tinted skylight in the center of the thirty-foot ceiling provided discreet illumination to an expansive sitting area consisting of several leather chairs and two long couches that looked as though they had been lifted from Ethan Edwards's ranch. To the left was a long mahogany front desk that, down to the ornate mirror on the wall behind it, resembled nothing so much as the saloon bar in an old western movie. To the right, a wall of floor-to-ceiling windows and glass double doors overlooked a broad flagstone patio. Below the patio, afternoon sun glinted off the water in the enormous pool, where quite a few people appeared to be swimming. Straight ahead was a rough-hewn fireplace, obviously not in use at the moment, and, next to that, an open doorway that led into a gift shop.

"I'll check in," Lowell said. "You guys can look around."

Rachel and the kids headed straight for the gift shop, and he walked up to the front desk. The pretty, happy-faced clerk behind the counter was named Tammy, and according to her name tag she was originally from New Haven, Connecticut, and had been working at The Reata for six years. Lowell found it odd that the resort's name tags contained such detailed information about employees, but it was strangely comforting as well, knowing that people from all over the United States worked here. It made the place seem less provincial and less inbred than would be expected from its remote location.

"Reservations for Thurman," he told her.

"Are you with a group or convention?" she asked.

"No."

The young woman typed something on a keyboard below the counter in front of her and then looked at the connected computer screen. "Lowell Thurman?"

"Yes."

"You'll be staying with us for five nights, departing on Wednesday?"

"Yes."

"Two connecting rooms, one with a king-sized bed, one with two full-sized and a foldout?"

"Yeah."

"Excellent. May I see your driver's license and a major credit card, Mr. Thurman?"

He handed both to her.

She smiled as she ran the Visa card through a scanner. "So, is this your first time at The Reata?"

He nodded.

"You're really going to enjoy your stay. Southern Arizona has so many wonderful places to visit. In fact, here's something you might find helpful." She reached under the counter and handed him a folded, slickly printed map. "It has everything from Tombstone to Tubac, and lists mileage from The Reata. You'll also find several magazines in your room that detail day-trip destinations. Should you desire reservations for any of Tucson's many cultural events or fine restaurants, our concierge desk is open twenty-four hours a day. It's number two on your room phone."

"How far *is* Tucson from here?" Lowell asked.

She laughed. "It's only forty miles to civilization. Although if you're planning to drive there, give yourself at least an hour and a half to get to I-10. Those desert roads are tricky if you're not used to them."

"We found *that* out."

Rachel and the kids emerged from the gift shop. "It's a rip-off!" Owen announced. "Thirty bucks for a T-shirt!"

"And two-fifty for a can of Coke." Curtis shook his head.

Lowell smiled. Sensible shoppers already. He and Rachel were doing something right.

He finished checking in, and Tammy gave him two keys for each room—or rather magnetized cards that could be used to open the electronic locks on the doors of the rooms, the hotel industry's modern equivalent of keys.

"Would you like a tour of the facilities?" the clerk asked.

"We'd love it," Rachel said instantly, obviously knowing after all these years that he would have declined and instead asked for a map of the resort so that they could explore on their own.

"I'll be happy to show you around."

Another young woman emerged from a room behind the front

desk, a section of wall next to the mirror opening to reveal the hidden doorway through which she passed. *Samantha. Juniper, Arizona. Four years,* her name tag read. The two uniformed sentries once again opened the lobby's front doors, and an elderly couple entered the cool lobby from the heat-blasted world outside. Samantha smiled at them as they approached the front desk. "Hello. May I help you?"

Tammy disappeared into the same hidden room from which her coworker had come and a moment later walked out from an unseen hallway to the left of the gift shop. "Let's start out here," she said, and led them onto the patio. It was like stepping into an oven, and the pool below them suddenly seemed even more inviting than it had before.

"I want to check out the pool," Curtis announced.

"Yeah," Ryan seconded.

Tammy laughed. "All right. Let's go." There were several round tables with umbrellas protruding from center holes and four or five chairs around each, but the patio was empty save for themselves. Tammy explained that while quite a few people came up at dusk to take drinks and watch the sunset, it was a little too hot in the midafternoon for anyone to sit out here. They followed her down a wide flagstone staircase that led past terraces alternating between kinetic metal sculptures and exotic cacti to the enclosed pool area, a space easily the size of two suburban homesites.

The pool was crowded. Nearly all of the chairs and lounges were taken, and several kids were lying on beach towels spread out on the cement. More children and adults were in the pool itself, yelling, splashing, playing. Top forty music blared from loudspeakers hidden in the palm trees, and waiters wearing western uniforms that looked none too cool could be seen hurrying between relaxing guests and the bar, trays of iced drinks in hand.

"We have two pools," Tammy explained as she unlocked the gate to let them in. "The big pool, here, and our indoor lap pool, which is adjacent to the weight room and spa facilities for the convenience of our more health-conscious guests. There are whirlpools in both areas—two here by the big pool—and, as you can see, there's a waterfall and slide. Inside the rock, behind the waterfall, are restrooms and a shower area. Towels are on that cart next to the cabana, and rubber rafts and floaties are available free of charge on a first come first served basis."

"They sell snacks there?" Curtis asked, pointing to the open serving window in the cabana.

"Snacks, soft drinks, cocktails and sandwiches. You can order at the window or from one of our waiters, who are usually pretty conscientious about canvassing the poolside area for hungry and thirsty guests."

There seemed something comical to Lowell about the overdressed waiters sweating in their tightly buttoned uniforms while catering to bathing-suited tourists, and he chuckled.

"What's so funny?" Tammy asked.

"Nothing. Those waiters. They just look like something out of a Monty Python routine."

The young woman smiled politely. "Who's Monty Python?"

Lowell shook his head, not wanting to explain. More than his growing children or the appearance of gray strands in his hair or the hardening of laugh lines into wrinkles, what made him realize he was growing old was the passing of his cultural touchstones into irrelevance, the knowledge that his frames of reference were no longer recognized by the younger generation. The other day, he'd been at Tower Records and absently picked up a Ravi Shankar CD, remembering how his older brother used to listen endlessly to *The Concert for Bangla Desh,* and how he'd always hated that droning sitar music. A heavily pierced salesclerk stocking CDs next to him said, "Wow. Ravi Shankar. I didn't know we had that."

"You like him?" Lowell asked, surprised.

"I read about him. He's the father of this female singer."

"Norah Jones," Lowell said to show that he wasn't completely unhip.

"Yeah." The clerk motioned toward the CD. "So what does he play? Jazz?"

Lowell realized that the boy knew nothing about Ravi Shankar other than the fact that he was Norah Jones's father. Any joke he might have made about interminable sitar solos or Indian music would have gone right over the kid's head.

Mick was right. What a drag it is getting old.

Tammy led them around the side of the pool, past one of the spas, past the waterfall, to a long low Santa Fe–style building that faced the upsloping mountain rather than the resort buildings situated down the hillside and winding toward the flat desert below. They walked inside. There was a maitre d's station next to the entrance, and round tables with white linen tablecloths took up the center of the large room. Plush comfortable-looking booths lined both the windowed wall facing the pool area and the series of glass alcoves that backed against the brown rocky mountainside.

"This is the Saguaro Room, our five-star restaurant. It was recently featured on the Food Network's *Best of the West* and specializes in gourmet Southwest cuisine. Our chef, Roland Acuna, has won numerous awards and apprenticed with Bobby Flay in New York. He's really amazing, and we're very lucky to have him. On Saturday mornings, he gives tours of his Gourmet Garden, which is located just behind Building Five—your building, actually—and they're really a lot of fun. If you'd like to sign up, just let me know or call the front desk before Friday night."

"That sounds wonderful," Rachel said.

"It is, it is."

They walked through a side door next to the maitre d's station and into a darker adjacent restaurant dominated by a large bar. "The Grille offers a more informal dining experience," Tammy explained. "It can get a little loud late on weekend nights, but before ten and during the weekdays, it's a great place to take the family. Oh, and room service can be ordered from either of our restaurants."

After exiting through another door, Tammy led them outside. "We'll drive the rest of the way," she told them. An electric golf cart, its white sides emblazoned with the resort's logo, was waiting under the shade of a cottonwood tree in a small parking lot on the side of the restaurants. Tammy got into the driver's seat, Lowell and Rachel climbed into the seat behind her, and the kids crammed into a backward-facing bench that hung over the rear of the vehicle.

Tammy pulled out of the parking lot and drove at a steady speed down a single-lane road that wound past the metal fence that enclosed the pool area before passing through an empty stretch between buildings. She pointed toward a narrow dirt pathway that led past a copse of desert brush. "That's one of our numerous nature trails. We have a birding trail, a cactus trail, a rock trail and assorted other jogging and hiking trails that traverse the desert within The Reata's boundaries. There's even the Antelope Canyon trail, which goes over two miles into the Santa Claras to a beautiful picnic spot and natural hot spring. Maps are in the welcome pack in your rooms and additional copies can be obtained at the front desk. A word of caution, though: the desert is dangerous. There are snakes, poisonous plants and insects, and slippery unstable slopes. So if you do decide to go hiking, always stay on the marked trails. And always carry water with you wherever you go. It's hot out here."

Rachel laughed. "We noticed."

"There's a helicopter?" Ryan exclaimed from the back.

Lowell looked to the right, saw a small section of concrete square and part of a chopper blade behind what looked like a service building.

"Very observant!" Tammy said appreciatively. "Yes, indeed, we do have our own heliport in case of emergencies."

"What kind of emergencies do you get out here?" Lowell asked.

"You'd be surprised," she said cheerfully but did not answer the question. "Behind Building One up ahead is our driving range. By next summer, we expect to have our new eighteen-hole golf course in place. By the way, let me know if you want to stop anywhere."

"I think we'd just like to see our rooms," Lowell said, and was glad when Rachel didn't disagree.

"Okay then. We'll take the short tour. Tennis courts to the left. Spa, weight room, lap pool in the building to your right. More information? All in the welcome pack." She maneuvered past a parked pickup truck filled with groundskeeping tools and stopped to allow a heavyset housekeeper pushing a cleaning cart cross the lane. Finally, Tammy turned left at one of the two-story structures housing the hotel rooms. "Here we are. Building Five." The cart slowed to a stop, pulled into a parking space. "This will be yours. After I take you back to the lobby, just drive your own car down the same way we came and park right here." She clapped her hands enthusiastically. "All right! Everybody out!"

The kids leaped off the back of the cart onto the hot asphalt and Lowell awkwardly climbed down from his seat before helping Rachel out. The heat was scorching, and all of their faces were red. Despite the breeze generated by the movement of the open-air vehicle, Lowell was sweating, and he wiped his forehead on his shirtsleeve and followed Tammy down an outside corridor past several room doors, past an ice machine, to room 522, their room. Room 523, the kids' room, was right next door.

Tammy stepped aside. "After you," she said.

Lowell used the magnetic card to open the door. There was a split-second of hesitation, an almost unconscious flinching at the unoccupied space in front of him. He was not sure what instinct caused him to freeze, but it snapped when Rachel walked past him into the cool air-conditioned room. He followed, and any trace of trepidation was forgotten as he looked up at the frosted skylight in the center of the high vaulted ceiling, saw the large picture window overlooking a gorgeous desert landscape. There was a couch, chair and coffee table with tastefully arranged magazines in the sitting area, a wide-screen television within a customized armoire, and a bathroom that was nearly as big as their bedroom at home. In the open closet he could see complimentary bathrobes and slippers. The coffeemaker on the vanity next to the small built-in refrigerator, was an espresso machine.

Nice, Lowell thought. He could get used to this.

Curtis and Owen opened the door to the adjoining room and rushed in. He heard shouts of "Cool!" and "Killer!" and "Our own TV!!"

"Where am I staying?" Ryan asked.

"With your brothers," Rachel explained.

"No! They're going to scare me!"

"They won't," Lowell promised. "Don't worry. Now why don't you go check out your room."

Ryan ran next door.

Tammy smiled. "How do you like it?" she asked.

"It's perfect," he said.

Two

This place was off the hook, Curtis thought. It was like the secret hideout of some James Bond villain, a fancy palace way out in the middle of nowhere with all of the best babes and food and technological luxuries money could buy.

Curtis loved James Bond. Especially the old movies from the 1960s, the ones with Sean Connery. They were way before his time, but there was something about their clean happy view of the world that appealed to him, something about the simple purity of the villains that spoke to him. He'd tried to read a few of the books—his dad was a big fan and told him they were great—but they seemed so boring compared to the movies, and no matter how hard he tried he could never seem to get into them.

Owen, he could tell, was not quite as impressed by the hotel. He liked the girls hanging out by the pool, liked the fact that they had their own room and their own satellite TV, but he didn't like the fact that the resort was so isolated, so far from any city. He hadn't said anything about it—Owen never did—but Curtis could tell that the remoteness made his brother uncomfortable. That was one of the things that *he* thought was so cool. It was the contrast between the no man's land around them and this posh resort with its pools and waterfalls and tennis courts and golf course and fancy restaurant that was so fresh.

He and Owen were nothing like each other when you came right down to it. They should have been as alike as two peas in a pod, as their grandmother would say, but even physically they were light years apart. Curtis was tall and thin with thick wavy black hair and a dark complexion. Owen had black hair as well, but his was straight, and he was a good head shorter and a good ten pounds heavier. He was also, like their brother Ryan, extremely pale. Curtis wasn't sure either of his two brothers had ever had a tan. Burns, yes. Tans, no. They were like their dad that way. Curtis was more like his mom.

He and Owen were very close, the best of friends really, but he wondered more and more often lately if that was not due to the fact that they were twins, and that fate and biology had thrown them together and made them partners. If there had not been that connection, if they met each other on the street right now and weren't related, didn't know each other, would they even have anything to talk about?

Curtis wasn't sure.

"I'm coming down!"

He looked up to see Owen at the top of the slide, arms upraised. Before anyone could stop him, before their parents saw him and told him to sit, Owen pushed off, standing up as though he were skateboarding down the wet slippery slope. He fell halfway, landing hard on his butt, nearly tumbling head over heels, but he was unhurt and splashed into the pool laughing.

In books and movies, Curtis thought, there was always a good twin and a bad twin.

He wondered which one he was.

"I saw that!" their mom called from the far edge of the shallow end, where she, their dad and Ryan were rearranging lounge chairs. Her voice carried over all of the other voices and conversations around the pool area, causing strangers to turn around and look. Curtis felt his face redden in embarrassment. "You two are forbidden to use the slide! Do you hear me? You are forbidden!"

They nodded their acknowledgement, not daring to shout back, not wanting to draw any more attention to themselves.

"That was stylin'."

Curtis glanced over to see another boy treading water right behind them. He had spiky hair and an earring and what looked like a small blue tattoo on his right upper arm.

"Thanks," Owen said.

"How long're you guys staying here?" the kid asked.

"Five nights," Curtis told him. "What about you?"

"Came yesterday. We'll be checking out Monday morning."

"Five nights," Owen said. "Just like us."

The other boy's name was David and he was a local. He was also sixteen, two years older than they were. He went to *high* school, and he could even drive, although he was here with his parents and didn't have any wheels. The three of them chilled for a while by the side of the pool, checking out the hot chicks and the MILFs and anyone between thirteen and thirty wearing a bikini, before jumping back into the water to cool off.

David was on the swim team at his high school, and he sped

across the length of the pool several times, turning around at different destination points before finally returning with a report. "Woman in the white one-piece," he said, nodding toward the crowded cabana area. "Bush."

Curtis swam across the pool and pulled himself up over the side. Directly in front of him, at eye level, was a lounge chair perfectly positioned to lend a view of the woman's partially spread legs. Sure enough, he could see a few small strands of short black pubic hair sticking out from the edge of the bathing suit by her left thigh.

He was instantly erect, and he popped back down in the water and swam over to where David and Owen were kicking back by a fake rock outcropping in the deep end. "Boner time!" he announced.

Owen swam over to check it out. He returned, grinning.

"Rumor is," David said, "that people go skinny-dipping here at night. Especially in that hot tub. I'm going to come back out around ten or so and see what I can see."

Curtis glanced over at his brother; neither of them said a word. There was no way that their parents would let them out alone after dark. Hell, they'd probably be in bed and asleep by ten. On the other hand, they did have their own room. And if they closed and locked the door between their room and their parents' . . .

But Ryan would be sleeping with them. And there was no way their little brother would keep his mouth shut about something like this.

David watched them, waiting for a response. When he saw that none was forthcoming, he shrugged and paddled over to the slide, pulling himself up. Sitting on the edge, he looked up at the top of the fake rocks where a father and his young toddler were about to go down.

"Excuse me!" the man called.

David ignored him, pretended not to hear, insolently kicked his feet in the water.

"Young man!"

David looked up at the sky, seemingly examining the desert clouds, humming a song.

"Will you please get off the slide so we can come down?" the man yelled.

Lazily, David got to his feet. Standing on the bottom edge of the slide, he paused for a good long minute. "Shi-i-it!" he yelled at the top of his lungs, jumping off. He hit the water hard, causing a noisy splash. Around the pool, adults glared at him with disapproval.

Curtis looked at Owen and grinned. Neither of them would have had the balls to do such a thing, not even if they were David's age. But now they were friends with someone who did. They'd finally met someone cool. And he actually liked them!

This was going to be one badass vacation.

Laughing, the three of them quickly swam to the opposite side of the pool before the father and his son slid down.

David's parents were in their room—*Fucking,* David said—but he'd commandeered a poolside table with an umbrella and four chairs, and there was a big bag of Doritos, a six-pack of Coke and a stack of towels on the table. They hopped out of the pool and sat around the table making fun of passersby while they drank the cola and ate the chips. Ignoring their mother's admonitions about eating and swimming, they jumped right back into the water afterward, paddling hard in a race to the waterfall. David won by several lengths.

They treaded water for a few moments, catching their breath. Suddenly David, peering down beneath his kicking feet, frowned.

"What is it?" Curtis asked.

"There's something under the waterfall. I think it's a dead body."

"Nuh-uh," Owen told him.

"Look for yourself."

Curtis didn't want to look. They were in the middle of a crowded pool on a hot summer day, surrounded by kids and adults and a virtual army of hotel staff, but he felt cold suddenly and as alone as a little boy in a haunted house. Still, he and Owen both stared into the water, and beneath the foam and the bubbles, in the dark blue of the pool's deep end, there *did* appear to be a dark sunken figure, an unmoving shape with the appearance of heft.

A body.

"I'm out of here!" Owen said, paddling over to the edge and pulling himself out of the water, his voice filled with panic.

Curtis followed his brother. He was just thankful that Ryan wasn't there, that their younger brother was staying with their parents somewhere by the far shallow end of the pool. He clambered onto the concrete, wondering if he should find someone from the hotel and tell them or wait until he found his dad. He knew he shouldn't start yelling; that would cause a panic.

"Wait a minute, you two!" David, laughing, was swimming after them. "Hold on!"

Owen, already ten feet away, stopped. Curtis turned around.

"It's not a dead body. It's just a patch on the floor of the pool. What a bunch of pansies."

They looked again, and sure enough, from this vantage point, it was obvious that there was no body, that there'd been some sort of work done beneath the waterfall and the vaguely human shape was merely a replastering job.

Curtis laughed, pretending to enjoy the joke, but the laugh was too forced. He knew what he'd seen, and when he looked into his brother's eyes, he knew that Owen felt the same. There *had* been something there. At the moment they'd looked down into the water below them, they'd seen a form far more solid than the flat shape now on the pool floor and much more clearly defined.

He would be dreaming about that figure tonight.

They swam around for a while longer, but then David's parents came to get him—*Must be all fucked out,* he muttered as they entered through the gate—and Curtis and Owen swam over to where their parents and Ryan had staked out several lounge chairs.

"So what are our plans for tomorrow?" their dad asked. "There's a lot to see around here." He held up the magazine he'd been reading, and Curtis saw that the cover story was "101 Things to Do in Tucson."

"We're *tired* of driving around," Curtis said. He kicked his brother under the water.

Owen nodded in agreement. "Yeah, why don't we just stay around here? Swim and stuff."

"Yeah, we're tired of driving around," Ryan whined.

"See?" Curtis said. "Even Ryan's tired of it."

"If we *do* stay," their mother said, "you're going to have to play with Ryan. No ditching him. No ignoring him. No teasing him."

"No problem!" Curtis looked over at Owen, who grinned.

"I'm tired of driving around, too," their mother admitted.

Their dad nodded. "All right, then. We'll stay here. What the hey. We're at an expensive resort. We might as well take advantage of it."

"Yay!" Ryan said, bouncing in his chair.

Curtis was about to make fun of his brother but thought the better of it and smiled at his parents. "Yay," he said.

Three

The meal was amazing. Almond-crusted catfish in lemon herb sauce with cayenne grilled vegetables and garlic mashed potatoes for him, mesquite-broiled chili-dusted chicken breast with chipotle rice, black beans and summer squash soup for her—and hot dogs for the kids.

They didn't go out very often, especially since Ryan had come along, and when they did, it was generally at a Mexican or Italian restaurant that was family friendly and noisy enough that their children didn't disturb anyone. So the Saguaro Room was a real treat. They wouldn't be able to afford it more than this once—it was homemade sandwiches in the room and burgers at the Grille for the rest of their stay—but Lowell was glad they'd come, and having such a fine meal in such a fine restaurant was almost enough to make him forget that the opening mixer of the reunion was going on at the same time.

Almost.

Rachel even took pictures of their dinner. It looked too beautiful to eat, she said, and she quickly reached into her purse, whipped out her trusty Canon Sure Shot and photographed the table so she'd be able to remember their foray into the world of gourmet cuisine. Lowell often made fun of her penchant for documenting every moment in their lives on film, but the truth was that he admired her dedication. He sometimes wished he had that sort of focus, no pun intended, but he was terminally lackadaisical about such things, and if Rachel hadn't been so committed to recording their trips and gatherings and family milestones, the entire pictorial depiction of their life together would have consisted of a roll of honeymoon photos and a few blurry baby snapshots.

He'd been afraid that they would be underdressed for the occasion in their shorts and light summer shirts, but to his surprise everyone, save a few elderly couples, was similarly attired. The food was formal but the atmosphere was not, and he decided that he could get used to resort living pretty easily. There seemed to be none of the pretensions of city life—it was like upscale Orange County without the emphasis on appearance—and that appealed to both the epicurean and egalitarian impulses within him. Though there were only a few other children in the dining room, neither he nor Rachel felt out of place here with their kids, and that too was nice.

Afterward, they walked back to their room along a winding gravel path outlined by low solar-powered lights. The sun was down, but the western sky retained a trace of orange that delineated the far horizon. Big black beetles tottered on too-thin legs across the path before them, attracted by the lights, and here and there could be heard the staccato scuttling of lizard feet on sand.

Rachel snapped a photo of a silhouetted saguaro, then made the four of them pose before a burbling Mexican fountain at the junction of two trails. It was night, but the temperature was still high, and Lowell was sweating as they made their way down the path. Below on the desert plain, he could see the glow of occasional ranch houses, and far away across the open country were clusters of lights of the towns they'd passed through on their way here. Somewhere to the south, behind the black bulk of the Catalina Mountains was Tucson.

They met an elderly couple walking arm in arm just past the tennis courts who greeted them with a friendly "Lovely evening, isn't it?" but other than that they were alone, and Lowell found himself wondering if there were bobcats out here. Or coyotes. There were undoubtedly rattlesnakes, and probably a whole host of nocturnal predators with which he wasn't even familiar.

Next time, he thought, they'd skip the trail and take the paved sidewalk. At least after dark.

The path ended at the small paved lot where the guests of Building Five parked their vehicles. They passed between a Suburban and a Land Cruiser, then walked along the open corridor toward their rooms. Bugs flew in and out of the light, moths and assorted flying insects bumping arrhythmically against the glass of the porch lamps next to each room door. Lowell took out his key card, ran it through the reader. A green light winked on, and he pushed open the door.

Or tried to.

The door gave less than an inch before stopping with a loud metallic rattle. The interior bolt lock was engaged.

"Who's there?" a man's gruff sleepy voice shouted from inside.

Lowell nearly jumped in shock.

Rachel *did* jump, and the panicked kids ran back down the corridor to the relative safety of the parking lot.

Lowell pulled the door shut, an action that sounded absurdly amplified in the still night air.

"I'm calling security!" the man yelled.

Lowell didn't know what to do. "You're in our room!" he called out. He glanced over at Rachel, who looked back at him with confused, frightened eyes. He expected the door to open and to be confronted by an enraged Broderick Crawford look-alike, but instead his announcement was met with silence. Had the man gone back to sleep?

"This is our room! You're in our room!" Lowell repeated.

"It's my room!" the man yelled.

Silence again.

Lowell stepped back from the door, taking Rachel's hand. Without a word, they retreated to the parking lot where the boys were huddled next to their car with anxious faces. "That guy stoled your room," Ryan said.

"What about our room?" Curtis asked. "Is someone in our room, too?"

"I don't know," Lowell told them. "Come on."

All five of them took the sidewalk directly back to the lobby. It was getting late, but there were couples on the lobby couches, cuddling under the low lighting, talking intimately. Lowell strode up to the counter, where a lone young woman spoke quietly on the phone. When she saw them approach, she promptly hung up and smiled. "Good evening."

"There's someone in our room," Lowell declared.

The young woman—*Eileen. Socorro, New Mexico. Two Years*—was suddenly concerned. "A prowler?"

"Sort of. We went out for dinner, and when we came back and started to open our door, a man was in there and yelled at us, threatened to call security. He seemed to think it was *his* room."

"He got in there *somehow,*" Rachel said pointedly. "I made sure the door was locked when we left."

The desk clerk seemed to be at a loss. Her smile was back but it seemed strained, false. "Let me look it up." She positioned her fingers on the keyboard. "What's the room number?"

"Five twenty-two," Lowell told her.

"Room 522?" she said, looking at her computer. "That's Mr. Blodgett's room."

"It's *our* room," Rachel said, exasperated.

Lowell showed her the keys. "And so is 523."

"Let me check. What's your name, please?"

"Thurman. Lowell Thurman." He glanced at Rachel and saw in her expression a mirror of the annoyance he felt.

The desk clerk typed his name into her computer. "This will just take a moment." She smiled up at him then looked back down at the monitor. Her smile disappeared instantly and Lowell thought that the blanched expression on her face owed more to fear than embarrassment, though that didn't seem to make much sense. "You're right," she said. "You were assigned rooms 522 and 523."

"I know we're right," Rachel snapped. "What did you think? We were lying?"

"No, ma'am. Of course not. I didn't mean to imply—"

"We just want our rooms back," Lowell said.

"And we want to know how something like this could happen in the first place," Rachel said pointedly.

"I'm very sorry. I don't know *how* it could have happened. What I can do is upgrade you to a deluxe suite. Two bedrooms, sitting room, luxury bath with sauna shower. It's much nicer than the adjoining rooms you have now. And you'll be closer to the pool."

"Am I going to have to pay extra for this?" Lowell asked.

"Oh no, sir."

"All of our things are still in there," Rachel said. "Our luggage, our personal items . . . everything."

"Like I said, we're very sorry for the inconvenience. Let me call Mr. Blodgett, and we'll get this straightened out." She picked up the phone, punched in the room number and the pound sign. "Hello . . ." she started to say.

They could hear Mr. Blodgett's tirade even from where they stood.

The desk clerk attempted to placate the man, but it was clear that he was in no mood to be pacified. "I understand," the young woman assured him. "Yes, that is why I'm calling . . . yes, I understand . . . yes, it is our fault . . . I know exactly how you feel . . . yes . . . yes."

Listening to Eileen's side of the conversation, Lowell felt sorry for the young woman. True, it was The Reata's fault and such a thing should never have occurred, but at the same time everyone made mistakes. This wasn't the person who had checked them in; she might not have checked in Mr. Blodgett. Yet she was taking the heat for it.

Rachel, he saw, shared no such sympathy for the girl.

After a too-long conversation filled with almost constant apologies and a promise to halve Blodgett's room rate, Eileen finally got the man to agree to open his doors and let them take out their belongings. She gave them card keys to their new suite and said that a porter would meet them in front of their old rooms to help them move. "Again," she said, "we're really sorry for the inconvenience."

"You should be," Rachel told her.

The porter was waiting for them outside of the room when they returned, a clean-cut young man who looked like he should be a cast member at Disneyland (*Lance. Las Vegas, Nevada. Four Years*). He'd brought along a luggage cart and parked it next to the door, and when they walked up, he nodded politely, then knocked on the door. "Mr. Blodgett?"

"Give me a minute!" Blodgett yelled roughly. "Jesus Christ!"

The porter smiled at Lowell apologetically.

A moment later, they heard a muffled "All right! Hurry up and do it, then!"

There'd been no click, no sound of a disengaging latch, but Lowell tried to open the door anyway. As he suspected, it was still locked, and the porter had to let them in with a passkey. They stepped inside. The bed was unmade, as though Blodgett had been sleeping in it, and a single suitcase was lying open on the dresser. Otherwise, everything was as they'd left it. The man himself was nowhere to be seen in the bedroom/sitting room area or the large open bathroom, but the door to the small alcove housing the toilet was closed. "Make it quick!" Blodgett said from inside.

Lowell opened the door separating 522 from 523 and told the kids to get their things together. He and Rachel started gathering their belongings. He glanced at the closed door to the toilet. It seemed increasingly suspicious to him that the man had taken the room as his own without asking any questions of the resort staff. Hadn't he noticed the wet bathing suits hanging from the shower rod? The clothes in the closet? The bags of food on the table? The luggage? Blodgett was either singularly unobservant, a complete moron or some type of psycho. Lowell was beginning to suspect the latter. There seemed something very odd about the way the man was hiding in the toilet closet. Even if he slept in the nude, it would have taken him only a moment to pull on a shirt and a pair of pants. On the other hand, maybe he was embarrassed and didn't want to face them.

Although he didn't seem like the type to be easily embarrassed.

"Are you through yet?" Blodgett demanded.

No, there was definitely something weird going on here.

In the adjoining room, the boys had gathered all of their bags and suitcases together and were carrying them out into the corridor, piling them on the luggage cart. This had become something of an adventure for them, and he could tell that though they were moaning and complaining under their breath, they were relishing the experience and would be reliving this moment endlessly in their conversations for the next week and retelling it to their friends for the rest of the summer.

Rachel had finished shoving the last stray paperback into a tote bag, and the porter helped them carry their suitcases and ice chest and plastic sacks out of the rooms and onto the cart. The second they brought out the final load, the door slammed shut behind them. There was a loud angry click as the security lock was engaged. He had not seen Blodgett, although the man must have been right behind them as they headed out the door, and when he met Rachel's eyes, he saw that she had not caught a glimpse of him either.

Something about that made him uneasy.

They had no idea where they were going, but the porter—*Lance*—obviously knew the way to their new suite, and they followed him up a winding cement pathway, past occasional couples and families out for leisurely evening strolls, past other hotel workers hurrying through the darkness to provide for guests' needs.

This building was smaller than the one housing their previous rooms and was in the shape of a V. It contained only four suites—two up, two down—and the porter led them to the upper right, where Lowell slid his card into the reader and then opened the door. If their previous room was the largest and most luxurious he had ever seen, their new lodgings made that look like ship's quarters. And the view was breathtaking. They were slightly higher than they had been previously, and in addition to the panorama of the desert, they could see much of The Reata laid out before them, its buildings and tennis courts and lighted pathways looking like an oasis of civilization against the vast darkness of the wild.

With the porter's help, they unloaded their belongings from the luggage cart. Lowell was unsure whether he was expected to tip the man or not—he *had* helped them move, but then again there would have been no *reason* to move had The Reata not screwed up and double booked their room—but when he made a move to reach for his wallet, Rachel stopped his hand and gave a quick angry shake of her head. So Lowell merely thanked the man and closed and locked the door behind him.

"There's a TV in the bathroom!" Ryan called.

"You can take a dump and watch cartoons!" Curtis said, giggling.

"Curtis . . ." Rachel warned.

It *was* a great suite, the type ordinarily seen only in the glossy magazines in their mundane little hotel rooms. Each of the bedrooms had walk-in closets and large Santa Fe–style dressers with overstuffed earth-toned couches big enough to sleep on, a fact that the boys picked up on instantly. "Can Ryan sleep on the couch?" Owen asked. "I don't want him in my bed." There were two queen-size beds in the room.

"Me either," Curtis echoed.

"It's up to Ryan," Rachel told them.

"I want to sleep on the couch!" Ryan announced.

The phone rang, and Rachel answered. "Hello? Yes, we did . . . yes . . . okay . . . all of it? That's great. . . . Yes . . . yes . . . okay. Thank you." She hung up and grinned. "Everything in the minibar," she said. "Comped."

They turned the key to open the small refrigerator. In addition to cans of beer and bottles of liquor, there were soft drinks, orange juice and a selection of candy bars.

"The Milky Way's mine," Curtis called.

"After we unpack," Lowell said. "Put everything away and then you can have candy bars."

The boys dragged their bags and suitcases into their room and started putting their clothes in the dresser while he and Rachel did the same in their room. Suddenly Rachel paused, stopped. A funny look came over her face, and she started digging through each piece of luggage and then searching the tote bags and the plastic sack with the wet bathing suits.

"What is it?" Lowell asked. "Is something missing?" He thought of Blodgett's angry complaints and gruff shouting.

She looked at him, her face flushed, anxious. "Yes."

"What?"

She glanced out the open door to make sure the kids weren't outside and couldn't hear. "Panties," she said quietly. "A pair of my panties is gone."

Four

Rachel heard the thunder and got up from bed to look out the window, cracking open the louvered shutters just enough to be able to see outside. Lowell was dead asleep, sprawled over half the bed, and the kids were in the next room, zonked out from the heat and the swimming and the generally chaotic events of the day. She knew this was the monsoon season in southern Arizona from reading the *Tucson Living* and *Southwest Lifestyle* magazines provided by the resort, and indeed the weather forecast on the local news that they'd watched had predicted a thunderstorm somctime after ten. Tomorrow, however, was supposed to be clear and over a hundred degrees.

Humidity really did make a difference, she thought. People were always joking about the cliché "it's not the heat, it's the humidity," as though the phrase were false or inane, but this afternoon, lying out by the pool in hundred-degree heat, it honestly had felt cooler and more pleasant than a typical eighty-degree day in Southern California.

Not that she would ever want to live here.

It was a nice place to visit, but . . .

The truth was that it wasn't even that nice of a place to visit. She couldn't say why exactly, couldn't put her finger on anything, but ever since they'd arrived at the resort, even before the mix-up with the room, a part of her had been thinking that she'd rather be back home, back at work.

That was silly, though. This place had everything. Gym, spa, pool, hiking trails, tennis courts, luxurious air-conditioned rooms with satellite television, a wonderful restaurant. So why would she rather be at work? She didn't even like her job all that much. It was just a stopgap position, something to do until . . . until . . .

Until what?

She realized suddenly that she had a job rather than a career, and she wondered when that had happened. Lowell had always had that attitude, had always considered a job to be merely something one did in order to make enough money to support a family and a lifestyle, but she had started out more ambitiously, more optimistically. She'd always loved art and drawing, which was why she'd earned her degree in graphic design in college. And the first few years after graduation, she'd worked at a local design firm, rising upward through the ranks. When the company went under, she'd been forced to take a day job at a bank, although she continued to apply at various graphics houses, even doing a couple of freelance jobs that led to additional contract work. Somewhere along the line, though, she'd gotten derailed, had stopped freelancing, stopped applying, made friends with her coworkers and settled in at the bank. When, though? When the twins came along, perhaps. With kids and a full-time job, she simply hadn't had the time or energy to pursue her own career goals.

Did she resent Lowell for this? No. Well . . . maybe just a little. Deep down. But she never thought about it, and she didn't know why she was thinking of it now. They were on vacation, for God's sake. She should be enjoying the luxuries surrounding her instead of creating dissatisfaction where it didn't exist.

Lightning suddenly flashed, illuminating the billowing storm clouds, and her heart jumped in her chest. She had never been one of those people afraid of thunder or lightning. On the contrary, she'd always enjoyed storms, found them to be curiously appealing, almost soothing, particularly at night when she was safely ensconced indoors as the weather raged outside. But it seemed as if the overarching cloud revealed by the lightning had the clear contours of a face.

A heavy masculine face filled with uncontrollable rage.

She tried to tell herself that she had just imagined it, but lightning flashed again, and the visage was still there, closer, the deep-set eyes trained directly on her as though looking across the distance through the window of her room, into her eyes. She stepped back from the shutters, frightened. Maybe she was still asleep, she thought. Maybe this was all part of a nightmare. It did have that sense of foggy surrealism usually associated with dreams, but somehow she knew that this was really happening.

Feeling alone, feeling afraid, she picked up the remote control from her nightstand and turned on the television, but the storm must have affected the satellite reception because only two stations came in. The first was showing a horror movie. *Children Who Won't Sleep* was the title, according to the ID bar that appeared temporarily on top of the screen, and Rachel saw a spooky wide-eyed girl in a windblown camisole standing atop a desert bluff at night. That was too close for comfort, and, chilled, she flipped through the channels until she found the only other station on air—something called AdultVue. The bar said this film was called *Return to Beaver Valley,* and in it one woman had her face buried in the hairy crotch of another woman who was moaning in ecstasy, eyes closed and lip-sticked lips parted sensuously.

She shut off the television before one of the boys heard anything.

Outside, thunder rumbled.

Rachel thought of that fierce cloud countenance and the terrible rage she had seen there. She considered waking up Lowell but decided that was stupid. What was there to be afraid of? A random convergence of clouds that happened to resemble a scary face? How old was she, ten?

Still, she looked toward the shuttered window with dread. Between the slats and around the edges, the flash of lightning shone through, a blinding white that made the surrounding darkness even deeper. It reminded her of a scene in a horror movie, and she was unable to make herself move forward to once again look outside, scared that the cloud face would now be right next to the glass, glaring at her with its terrible expression of rage and hate.

She stood there for a moment, trying to think through the situation logically. What else could it be other than a chance coalescence of storm clouds? God? A demon? It made no rational sense for any sort of supernatural entity to manipulate water vapor so that it resembled an evil face, and there certainly wasn't any sort of monster that was made out of cloud. Not that she believed in that sort of stuff to begin with. No, she was upset, her brain was tired and her mind was simply putting a morbid spin on perfectly natural events.

She forced herself to move forward across the darkened room, sidling next to the slightly open shutter slats, looking down this time instead of up. Below, the grounds of the resort were bathed in darkness, low lights along the pathways combining with the occasional flash of lightning to create a shifting world of shadows. The lights of the tennis court were off, as were those on the building housing the spa facility. The palms and saguaros and landscaped bushes seemed menacing and out of proportion, and made her think of the living trees that attacked Disney's Snow White.

A figure walked across the grass below, a dark shape that had been lurking near the edge of the building beyond her sight line but now moved suspiciously across the open expanse of lawn like a thief on his way to rob a house. Rachel could see only a silhouette, no details, but she could tell it was a man not a woman. A gardener. He was carrying a rake but something about the way he held it made it seem more like a weapon than a tool, and there was in his carriage and bearing the suggestion of violence, as though this was a man used to physically intimidating people.

The figure reached the head of a lighted pathway where he stopped, turned, looked up. Though she could not see the features of the shadowed face, she could see the eyes, bright and wide and trained on her.

Immediately, instinctively, she stepped away from the window, hid in the darkness of the room. There was no way he could see her through the slats. He probably wasn't even looking at her, was probably just checking out the trees next to the building to see when they needed to be trimmed. But she was creeped out nonetheless, and she remained in the darkness for a few moments, away from the window, waiting, giving him time to leave and get to wherever he was going at—she glanced over at the clock—one fifteen in the morning.

Where *could* he be going? While he was carrying a rake, it was highly unlikely that he would be doing grounds work in the middle of the night. True, resorts and other high-end businesses sometimes made their hired help work in the wee small hours so as not to disturb guests. But while custodians could buff lobby floors thanks to inside lights, it was pretty close to impossible to prune flowers or trim bushes outside in the dark.

She thought of going back to bed, wanting to just put this night behind her and wake up when the world was fresh and sunny, but she had to look, she had to know, and once more she moved next to the window.

He was still in the same spot, looking up at her, and the second she peeked down through the slats at him, he raised his weaponlike rake as if in greeting.

And then . . .

he danced.

It was a strange little jig, lasting only a few seconds, but it was clearly for her benefit, and she held her breath as lightning flashed and the man danced crazily, feet stomping furiously on the grass, hands twirling the rake. Then he was gone, disappearing into the night.

Rachel exhaled, unaware until that moment that she'd been holding her breath. She scanned the ground below, looking for any sign of the gardener, but he was gone. Glancing into the sky at a fading flash of lightning, the clouds were once again just clouds. The show was over.

She didn't like The Reata. From the guy who'd stolen their room to the psychotic gardener, it seemed to her that everything was going wrong; this place was turning out to be the antithesis of everything they'd expected, and the thought of staying here another four nights made her feel more than a little apprehensive.

But there was nothing they could do about it now. Even if they took off tomorrow and canceled the rest of their stay, they would still have to pay for all five nights, and she knew Lowell would not be willing to write off that kind of money—even if she did somehow manage to convince him that a spooky gardener had been prowling the grounds at one in the morning and a demonic cloud face had been looking at her through the window.

She was overreacting, she told herself.

Tired and emotionally exhausted, she climbed back into bed. Lowell stirred next to her as she settled into place. "What is it?" he asked groggily.

"Nothing," she said. "Go back to sleep."

FRIDAY

Five

It was after eight when Lowell awoke. Curtis and Owen were already at the pool. Rachel and Ryan were seated at a table in front of the television, drinking orange juice from the minibar and eating Entenmann's muffins that they'd brought with them in the ice chest. The room was full of children's show chatter and bright desert sunshine, and Lowell realized that he must have been pretty damn tired to stay asleep through all that.

He put on one of The Reata robes from the closet and grabbed a muffin, sitting down. A copy of *USA Today* had been delivered to their room and was lying on the table in front of him. "I was thinking of going to that lap pool," he told Rachel. "Swimming twenty minutes or so each morning to get some exercise while we're here. Maybe checking out the weight room."

She reached over and stuck her hand between the folds of the robe, pinching the roll of fat around his middle. "That's a fine idea."

He patted her stomach. "Feel free to join me."

Laughing, she squirmed away. "I'm on vacation."

Neither of them mentioned what had happened last night—*panties* —and he wasn't sure if that was because Ryan was here or because they wanted to pretend that it hadn't occurred. Both, probably. But he was acutely aware of the fact that beneath their surface jocularity, a darker layer had been added on to the vacation and no matter how hard they tried to maintain the carefree innocence of the past two days, it was ruined, gone, and the rest of their trip would be tainted by the events of last night.

Damn that Blodgett.

Lowell wondered what the asshole looked like. In his mind, he imagined a heavy, beefy man with a jowly angry face and a bulbous alcoholic's nose, a man not unlike Mr. Mack, his high school science teacher. Mean, petty and vindictive, Mack pretty much had it in for any student who wasn't a member of the geology club or whose life didn't revolve around the physical sciences, and Lowell and his friends had hated the teacher. Hell, half the school had. And although Lowell hadn't been in on the senior prank that had resulted in sugar being poured into Mr. Mack's gas tank, ruining the engine of his brand new Buick LeSabre, he had secretly applauded the incident from afar.

Mr. Mack. Jesus, he hadn't thought of that old bastard in years.

Lowell wondered if he was still alive.

Rachel stood and walked over to one of the bathroom sinks to wash the muffin crumbs off her hands. "Are you really going to try and exercise?"

"Yeah. Why not."

"Then take your key," she told him. "Ryan and I are going out to the big pool to keep an eye on the twins. We probably won't be here when you get back."

"What's the plan for lunch?"

"Snacks. We have the chips and salsa that we brought, and I think there's one of those cheese samplers in the minibar. Besides, it's hot. You don't eat much when it's hot, you just drink a lot."

"Speak for yourself."

"We'll have a real dinner. Maybe we should check the menu at that Grille."

"That's the one disadvantage of this place. We can't just drive over to some take-out place or something. We're stuck with the food on hand."

She looked at him meaningfully. "The *one* disadvantage?"

"We just got off on the wrong foot," he said, for his own sake as much as hers. "It's all uphill from here."

"Maybe we'll reverse it tomorrow. Go to Tucson or one of the tourist destinations, have a real, reasonably priced lunch, and then snack for dinner by the pool."

"Yeah!" Ryan said. "Burger King!"

Lowell smiled at them. "Sounds like a plan."

He couldn't remember where the building that housed the pool and weight room was located, so after changing into his bathing suit and slipping on a pair of sandals, he opened the leather Welcome binder next to the phone on the end table and turned the pages until he found a map of the resort. A walkway led from their building to what was referred to as the "Exercise Center" two parking lots down. As long as he stayed on course and didn't take any of the forks or side paths, he'd be there in three minutes. He slammed the binder shut, took another muffin to eat on the way, grabbed a bottle of water and picked up his key card.

"See you later." He gave Rachel a quick kiss, then ran a hand through Ryan's close-cropped hair. "Meet you at the big pool, buddy. Tell Curtis and Owen they have to let you play or they can't swim. Tell them I said so."

Ryan grinned.

Outside it was hot already. Eight thirty and the temperature had to be well above eighty. Lowell was not the most heat-tolerant man on the planet—one reason he was grateful to work in an air-conditioned environment—but there was something very pleasant about vacationing in a spot where a person could swim comfortably in the early morning or late evening. It was humid, though, much more humid than yesterday, and he could tell from the wet gravel and the leaves on the ground that the predicted rain had arrived sometime last night. Despite that, today's sky was clear, cloudless and an impossibly deep blue almost cheery enough to make him forget the debacle of last night.

panties

Almost.

He thought of Blodgett, which made him think again of Mr. Mack. One of the reasons they'd taken this vacation now, at the end of June, was so that he could generate a legitimate excuse—to himself if no one else—to avoid his high school reunion. But his brain had been strolling down memory lane ever since they'd come here, and he was not really sure why. He was certainly not one of those pathetic middle-aged men living off former glories and pining for those idyllic teenage years. Yet he could not deny that he had spent quite a bit of time lately recalling his own past. Even now he saw a quasi-punk teenager dashing through the parking lot without shoes or sandals, yelping "Shit, shit, shit, shit . . ." as his feet hit the hot asphalt, and he found himself thinking about some of his old friends from high school and college, realizing that he could not imagine them middle-aged. They were frozen in his mind at their most carefree and irresponsible, and doubtlessly they had succumbed to the pressures and responsibilities of life to become respectable citizens—everyone did—but he still could not see it and hoped it wasn't true. Toby and Russ and Carlos from high school, Dennis and Lu from college; he still saw them playing hackeysack in the park, partying all night long, and it was sad to think of them balding and in business suits, running in the rat race. He'd rather imagine them as beach bums or professional students, refusing to grow up and grow old, living on the fringes of society in rented apartments filled with strewn CDs and tacked-up posters.

In a way, he supposed, he was glad that he had not kept in touch with them.

And he was definitely glad that he'd avoided the reunion.

But what about himself? How had he turned out? What would they think of him?

Those were questions he did not want to examine too closely.

The pool room was empty. He'd half expected it to be filled with jocks and health fanatics, all getting in their two hundred morning laps, but the pool area was unoccupied, the cement floor dry, clean towels all folded on a cart, and he saw no one exercising as he passed through the weight room. He had the entire building to himself—luckily—since the rules posted above a bench along the side wall stated that all swimmers must shower before entering the water and he clearly hadn't bathed this morning. He quickly jumped in and dunked his head before someone else entered and saw his wild uncombed hair.

The water was bathwater warm and remarkably free from the strong chlorine smell of the outdoor pool. He'd read somewhere that chlorine did not really smell, that the scent everyone associated with swimming pools and ironically thought was a "clean" odor, was actually caused by the interaction of chlorine with sweat and urine and other bodily fluids. Which meant that this pool was relatively uncontaminated.

The pool was divided into five lanes by ropes and buoys stretched across its length. He was in the first lane, and he paddled back and forth aimlessly for a few moments, acclimatizing himself, before backing against the wall of the shallow end and shoving off.

Lowell could not remember the last time he'd swum for exercise, and it felt good to be swimming so swiftly, with such purpose. Ordinarily, on vacations, he'd horse around with the boys, make a few halfhearted runs across the pool of whatever hotel they were staying at, then join Rachel for some sunbathing and reading. Other than vacations, he never swam at all these days. He had always liked the water, though, and it was invigorating to be doing laps, feeling the liquid sliding sensuously against his skin as he propelled himself toward the deep end of the pool.

He reached the far side, flipped over, pushed against the wall, and with swift kicks and broad, even strokes sped back down his lane, feeling the satisfying stretch of muscles in his arms and thighs and stomach.

He was halfway across the pool when someone grabbed his left foot.

Lowell kicked out, flailing wildly, shocked more than anything else, but the grip on his foot tightened, bony fingers digging into the thin flesh, holding firm. For a brief moment he was swimming in place like a cartoon character, then the hand let go and he floundered in the water as he fought against a force that was no longer there. Twisting, sputtering, trying to keep himself afloat and determine who had grabbed him at the same time, Lowell looked down into the bubbly choppy water beneath him, then scanned the surface of the pool. It was empty. There was still no one in the room but himself.

Someone had grabbed his foot.

He remembered that back in high school, Tony Sherman used to do that to him in P.E.

But Tony Sherman had been killed in a drunk driving accident their senior year.

Tony had been the drunk driver.

A chill passed through him, making the water seem icicle cold. Even if he was superstitious—which he wasn't—there could be no possible connection between what he thought he'd felt and a twenty-year-old accident. Still, the coldness remained, and he pulled himself out of the pool, hopping onto the side. He sat there for a few moments, feet dangling in the water, as he continued to search for his unseen assailant. It was clear, however, that he was the only one in the building, and he decided that he had simply overreacted to a perfectly logical, explainable, natural incident. There was no mystery here.

no ghost

His foot had probably just caught on the lane rope and his brain had misinterpreted what he'd felt.

He forced himself to believe it and slid back into the water. Once again, everything seemed normal. He was in a pool in the resort's Exercise Center, not in the basement of some haunted house. He took up where he'd left off, swimming to the shallow end. Pivoting at the wall, he headed back into the deep water.

Fingers grabbed his right foot.

They were weaker this time, as though they'd used up all of their strength with the first attack, but they still clutched the middle portion of his foot with clear purpose, and the assault was nonetheless shocking for its familiarity. He kicked out hard, trying to hurt whoever—*whatever*—was at the other end of those hands, but he connected with nothing save water. When he stopped swimming and spun around, the pool was empty. There was no one here except him.

For the first time since he was a child, Lowell felt that deep primal fear of the boogeyman that had made his boyhood nights a living hell, a terror that he had never been able to make his parents understand. He gripped the edge of the pool and started pulling himself up.

The hand was back, grabbing him, attempting to draw him into the deep water. Whatever was in the pool wasn't strong enough to drag him down—but it clearly wanted to. The invisible fingers clutching his ankle were pulling at him, but they simply didn't have the strength.

He freed himself from the unseen grip and flopped onto the cement, trying to catch his breath. Reflections of light off the still rippling water shimmered on the wall and ceiling. Feeling he was still too close to the edge, he quickly stood and moved away from the pool, taking refuge on a bench against the wall, ready to run out of the room at the slightest sign of anything unusual. He was panting hard, not so much from the physical exertion as from fear.

What the hell had just happened?

He'd had a supernatural experience. There was no doubt about that. If he had formerly considered himself skeptical but open-minded when it came to the paranormal, he was now a firm believer. But what should he do about it? Should he rush back and tell Rachel? Let someone on the hotel staff know so they could . . . could . . . what? Hire a ghostbuster? Keep people away until the haunting stopped? The practical aftermath of such an incident never seemed to be addressed in horror movies, and he was unsure of what step to take next. Logic told him to keep quiet, not say anything to anyone, wait and see if something like this happened to anyone else before sticking his neck out and exposing himself to ridicule. At the same time, didn't he have an obligation to protect others? This wasn't just some shadow on the wall, this was a physical force that had attempted to pull him into the water, that could have drowned him. Shouldn't he warn others to keep them from harm?

But would anyone listen? Would anyone believe?

The lap pool sat there, light blue under the fluorescent lights, water once again calm, looking as modern and innocent as that in any fitness club.

Taking a deep breath, Lowell slid on his sandals, inching sideways toward the door, keeping his eye on the pool, prepared to run at any moment should the lights in the room go off or the water start to roil mysteriously. As he reached the exit, he was suddenly aware that there were other noises in the building, that his were not the only sounds in the Exercise Center. He walked through the doorway, past the showers and lockers. From the weight room up ahead, he heard the regular clang of metal on metal, as though someone were in there working out. This, too, seemed spooky under the circumstances, and his first irrational thought was that he would walk in only to find the place empty, none of the machines in use. He shivered—and not just from the air-conditioning on his wet skin.

. . . *Clang* . . .

. . . *Clang* . . .

. . . *Clang* . . .

He paused in the weight room doorway, overcome with the certainty that there'd be no one there. Or that he would catch a peripheral glimpse of someone in the mirrors lining the walls but the room itself would be empty. Thankfully, though, he saw through the overlapping rows of exercise equipment an overweight bald man sitting at one of the weight-lifting machines, heard the man's very real grunts of exertion. As he drew closer, however, walking toward the exit, preparing to give a friendly greeting as he passed by, he saw that the bald man was not just overweight but grossly obese—three hundred pounds at least.

And wearing no clothes.

The sight was disconcerting, and alarm bells started going off in his head. Lowell wanted to glance away, but his gaze was drawn by the huge symmetrical folds in the pale sweaty skin, the rounded rolls of fat that jiggled with each grunting lift and subsequent dropping of weights. The man was not only enormous but fearsome looking, his shiny shaved head and ferocious countenance giving him an almost inhuman appearance, and Lowell slowed, stopped, not wanting to walk past the man.

Afraid to pass by him.

. . . *Clang* . . .

. . . *Clang* . . .

. . . *Clang* . . .

He scowled at Lowell, continued to press weights, and, horrifyingly, his penis trembled and grew until it was fully erect. The man lifted the forked bars up to his shoulder level then let out a tremendous guttural grunt as he shoved them above his head.

Lowell did not stay to see the finish but quickly exited the building, practically running as he made his way down the short corridor.

A closed door to his right said SPA. He did not even want to think about what could be in there.

Outside . . . everything was normal. A family of four was heading down one of the gravel paths on a nature walk, the younger boy complaining that his feet hurt. On the road connecting the parking lots, a Reata staffer drove by on an electric cart piled high with clean towels. Lowell stood there for a moment just to reacquaint himself with the real world. He heard the shouts of children playing at the big pool, heard the thump of music from within a passing Lexus. The air was hot and still, but it felt real, it felt good, and in the space of a few moments what he had experienced within the Exercise Center seemed unreal even to himself. He turned around, looked at the door, but though it looked perfectly normal and he felt no vibe, he was not about to go inside again.

He started walking back to the room.

"Dad!"

Rachel and Ryan were walking up the sidewalk toward him, on their way to the big pool. He purposely slowed his gait as he saw them approach, waving.

Ryan ran over. "We're going swimming!"

He ran a hand through his son's hair. "That's great, sport. Have fun."

"Are you coming, too?"

"In a while."

"That was quick," Rachel said.

"Yeah."

"So how was your swim?" she asked.

He thought for a moment, unsure of what to say.

She frowned. "Lowell?"

He forced himself to smile. "Fine," he told her. "Fine."

Six

"Check out that one. I bet her snatch is a snack and a half."

Owen casually glanced to his left, following David's subtle nod, and saw an older girl, probably seventeen or eighteen, walking toward them, the thin material of her white thong bikini clinging to her lithe form, revealing jutting nipples and a visible cleft between her thighs.

They were sitting in the Jacuzzi, drinking Cokes, feigning a sophistication only David actually possessed. Originally, David had wanted to go swimming, and Curtis would have gone along with it even though he didn't want to, but Owen had put his foot down. They'd been the first people to the pool this morning other than the staff, and when he'd glanced into the water of the deep end next to the waterfall, he had spied a shape at the bottom. The same human shape he and Curtis had seen yesterday. He didn't think his brother had noticed it because Curtis had been scoping out a hot resort worker in a one-piece who was scooping bugs and leaves out of the shallow end with a net, but he could tell from Curtis's reaction to David's suggestion that they get in some serious swim time that the figure was still in his mind.

The dead man.

That's what it was. It wasn't a *figure*. It was the drowned body of a man, and the fact that it had disappeared and turned into something like a stain on the light blue bottom of the pool made him think that it was probably the ghost of someone who'd died there. Not that he really believed in ghosts—not exactly—but he was still open-minded enough not to discount things he saw just because other people said they weren't true.

So he'd suggested that they hang out in the Jacuzzi, check out the chicks. Going on babe watch automatically trumped swimming, and David and Curtis readily agreed to his plan. They'd been here for nearly half an hour now, watching as the pool area filled up, even scaring away an elderly couple who wanted to use the whirlpool.

The girl in the white thong passed by, and all three of them casually turned their heads to check out her ass.

"I'd love to sniff her suit," David said, and Owen could not help giggling.

Curtis finished his Coke and tapped his plastic cup on the raised ring of cement encircling the Jacuzzi. David tossed him the two-liter bottle and Curtis poured himself a refill. Suddenly the whirlpool's timer went off, and the jets stopped, bubbles ceasing. David stood. "I don't know about you two, but I'm sweating like a fucking pig here. I think it's time we hit the cool water."

Curtis nodded. "I'm with you."

Even Owen had to admit that a half hour in swirling warm water beneath an increasingly hot sun was more than enough. The three of them got out, carrying their drinks and walking over to the edge of the big pool. In front of them, two young boys sped down the slide together.

"Fags," David said disdainfully. He sat down on the edge of the pool, putting his feet in the water. "Jesus Christ!" he cried out. "That's cold!"

It *was* cold, Owen discovered as he dangled his own toes, and though he knew the best and quickest way to get used to the water was to jump in all at once, the three of them opted for a more gradual approach, sitting there and allowing their legs to slowly stir the water in an effort to acclimatize themselves.

A moment later, David's parents passed by on their way to the restaurant for a late breakfast or early lunch or brunch. Owen was amazed by how casual and unconcerned they seemed about their son. They'd both been under the impression that David was back in their room watching television and were surprised to see him here, but aside from a perfunctory greeting, they didn't stop to talk, didn't even seem to give a shit where he was or what he was doing, and the second they were beyond the shallow end of the pool, David was on his feet facing their retreating backs, both middle fingers raised high in the air.

Owen and Curtis looked at each other. Their parents might have been incurable doofuses who embarrassed them more often than not and put far too many restrictions on them in comparison with the parents of their friends, but at least things had not deteriorated to this extent. David was grinning, as though the whole thing was hilarious, but Owen thought it was kind of sad. He remembered an antidrug commercial he'd seen where a bunch of kids pissed and moaned about their too-strict parents, recited a litany of offenses, said "I hated you," and then looked into the camera and said, "Thanks." He'd always kind of felt that way himself—angry at his parents for their micromanagement of his life, yet at the same time grateful that they cared so much—and this split-second glimpse into David's family dynamics only reinforced his feelings.

"Hey," David said, fingering his earring, "why don't we see who can get kicked out of the pool the fastest?"

"I don't want to get kicked out," Curtis told him.

"Me either," Owen admitted.

"Okay. Let's see who can do something outrageous and be the first to get a warning." He glanced around. "They must have lifeguards around here someplace. Or some kind of hotel worker who can lecture us."

"And it has to be on the slide," Curtis said, getting into the mood. "No harassing people or yelling at kids or splashing old women. It's for a trick or something you do on the slide."

David nodded. "Deal."

The slide.

Owen watched an over-the-hill jock careen down on his ass, hands in the air, whooping all the way, before landing above that irregular spot on the pool floor.

The body.

"Pussyboy?" Curtis prodded. "You in?"

"Yeah." Owen nodded. "I'm in."

David went first and, as agreed, Owen and Curtis sat on the edge of the pool and watched from the sidelines. At the top of the slide, David stood for a moment, then shouted "My balls!" at the top of his lungs and, melodramatically clutching his groin, slid face-first all the winding way down to the water.

No one even noticed. There were no reprimands over the loudspeaker, outraged security guards did not meet him at the pool's edge, and the swimmers and sunbathers surrounding them did not look up at David's cry.

"Strike one," Curtis said as David swam up. He dove in and with long even strokes headed for the recessed steps in the faux cliff, which he climbed quickly. Reaching the top, Curtis stood for a moment at the head of the slide in a classic surfer's pose—knees bent, arms stretched out for balance—before shoving off and riding to the bottom, standing all the way.

Suddenly the piped-in music stopped, and an echoing voice came over the hidden speakers: "Please remain seated on the slide. Any guest who stands on or misuses the slide will be barred from using the pool for the rest of the day."

"Son of a bitch," David said.

Curtis laughed, swimming up. "Works every time."

"You win," David admitted. "You have mad skills, man." He looked at Owen. "What were you going to do?"

Owen shrugged. "Wave my weenie at the crowd."

"Brought a pair of tweezers along, did you?"

"You're thinking of my brother."

Curtis splashed him. "Loser."

"Ten o'clock," David said under his breath.

Owen and Curtis casually turned their heads; Owen to the left, Curtis to the right. A good-looking girl of approximately their own age was walking lazily toward them through the shallow water, using her arms to help propel her forward.

"Breast stroke," David muttered.

The girl reached them and stopped, looking from one to the other before letting her gaze settle on Owen. "Hi," she said. "I'm Brenda."

"Owen," he managed to get out.

"These your friends?"

"Brother," Curtis said, introducing himself. "My name's Curtis. No one calls me Curt."

"David," David said suavely. "No one calls me Dave."

"You can call me Owe if you want," Owen said lamely.

Brenda laughed. She had one of those inviting, infectious laughs that you usually only heard in movies or read about in books, an inclusive full-throated expression of mirth that was at once hearty and supremely feminine. "I saw you guys on the slide. What in the world were you thinking? Was that some sort of dare?"

"A bet," Curtis corrected.

"A bet? What for? Money?"

"Nothing. It was more like a contest," Owen explained.

"Well you must've won. You're the only one who didn't completely humiliate himself."

"He was up next," Curtis said. "He was going to stand up there and flash the pool."

Brenda raised an eyebrow. "The full monty?"

Owen reddened, splashed his brother in retaliation.

"I'm sorry it didn't get that far."

They let that one hang there.

She was definitely a hottie, Owen thought. And for some ungodly reason, she seemed to have taken an interest in *him*. He had no idea why. Back in the real world, back at his school, none of the girls were interested in him at all. He wasn't some freak like Kyle Hendersen, wasn't completely ostracized and rejected by society, but he wasn't in the winner's circle, either. He was just part of the nameless rabble whom no one noticed and whom girls chose to ignore. Curtis, too, although at least Lisa Bowen seemed to be interested in him.

"So what are you guys doing?" Brenda asked. "Want to check out the Jacuzzi?"

They looked at each other.

"Sure," Owen said, and though he was starting to sweat just *thinking* about that hot water, he forced himself to smile.

"All right," "Okay," David and Curtis acquiesced.

She waited for them to get out of the pool first, probably not wanting them to check out her ass as she pulled herself out of the water— or maybe wanting to check out *their* asses as *they* got out. Owen suddenly felt self-conscious, and he quickly hoisted himself onto the cement and hurried over to the Jacuzzi. David cranked up the timer and the jets kicked in just as Owen was sitting down.

Brenda padded across the hot concrete toward them, and Owen was acutely conscious of the fact that her crotch was just about eye level. He immediately looked away, not wanting to be caught staring, and she sat down in the Jacuzzi next to him. She sat slightly closer than was polite, their thighs practically touching even though there was plenty of room for everyone.

"So where are you all from?" she asked.

You all, Owen thought. She was probably from the South. His heart sank a little. Although he knew it was stupid and childish, he'd held out hope that she lived somewhere near him, that they'd hit it off here at the resort and go back home as boyfriend and girlfriend. Curtis would laugh outrageously if he knew his brother had such sappy thoughts, and David most certainly would too, but Owen couldn't help it.

"Tucson," David said, tugging at his earring. "I'm a local boy."

"We're from California," Curtis offered.

"Me too! Where?"

Owen's heart speeded up. "Brea."

"Fountain Valley! We're practically neighbors!"

He had a chance. Fountain Valley was at the opposite end of Orange County and still seemed pretty far to him, but he'd be getting his learner's permit in five months, be able to drive in a year and a half, and then the distance wouldn't matter. He felt absurdly elated, and he vowed to do everything he could to get to know this girl. It might lead nowhere—she was definitely out of his league and would probably discover that in about a minute—but his vacation suddenly seemed about a thousand times better.

"How long are you staying?" he asked her.

"Five nights."

Five nights. The same as them. The same as David. Something about that made him feel vaguely curious about the coincidence, but overriding that was the exciting realization that they'd all be here together for several more days. It seemed too good to be true.

"You hear about the dive-in movie?" David asked.

Brenda shook her head.

"Saturday night. They're going to drop a screen over the area where the waterfall is and let people watch the movie while they swim or float on rafts or just sit on the edge with their feet in the water. Sounds pretty cool."

"We'll be there," Owen offered.

"What's the movie?" she asked.

"I don't know. Some old family flick. *Toy Story* or something. I don't know. But it'll be kind of fun just to hang out in the pool, watch the movie." He grinned. "Snorkle between people and scare them. Pull down their bathing suits."

Brenda laughed. "*I'll* be there." Under the cover of bubbles, she put her hand on Owen's thigh, gave his leg a small squeeze.

Shit like this didn't happen to him.

The pool area was *really* crowded now. There were long lines at the snack bar and the raft booth, and all of the chairs and tables seemed to be taken. Several parents had put down blankets on the cement for their kids to lay out on. So many people were clustered in the shallow end of the water that a young girl, apparently lost and confused, paddled around in a circle crying. From somewhere within the cacophonous din of the crowd, they all heard a faint voice call out, "Brenda!"

Brenda stood. "I have to go. My dad's calling me."

"Uh, nice to meet you," Owen said awkwardly.

"I'm busy this afternoon, but why don't we meet out here tonight," she said. "About nine?"

"Where?" Curtis asked.

"Right here. At the Jacuzzi."

It would be tough to get out, and they'd have to come up with something pretty damn good to convince their mom that they should be allowed to roam around the resort by themselves after dark, but one look at Brenda's warm inviting smile made Owen realize that, whatever it took, he would do it. He thought of her hand squeezing his leg and imagined what might happen under the cover of darkness. "We'll be here," he said.

Involuntarily, he glanced over at the big pool. A father waited in front of the slide for his little boy to come down. His heart skipped in his chest. What would that shape on the pool floor look like at night? Would it appear as benign as it did now? Or would the heft return, the sense of three-dimensionality?

He pushed the thought from his mind, focused on Brenda.

She smiled at him. "See you later." She waved to Curtis and David. "Bye, guys."

They watched as she climbed out and padded across the cement, disappearing into the throng of guests.

Curtis was jealous, he could tell, but David high-fived him. "Way to go, bro!"

Owen grinned.

"Don't get too cocky, though."

"That's *exactly* what I'm going to get."

"Cock?" Curtis snickered. "I always had my doubts about you."

"Asshole." He kicked his feet, splashed water on his brother.

Suddenly, Curtis grimaced. "Oh no," he groaned, his eyes focused on a point past Owen's shoulder.

He turned around to see their mom marching toward them, Ryan out in front of her.

David grinned. "Looks like it's babysitting time for you fine young ladies."

The three of them looked at each other, then, without speaking, simultaneously leaped out of the Jacuzzi and sprinted to the big pool.

Owen dived in. "Cur—" he heard his mom call out in the split second before his head hit the water, and then the three of them were speeding through the pool as quickly as they could away from Ryan.

Seven

I was misinformed.

The line from *Casablanca* kept going through his head as Patrick Schlaegel checked in. Around him in The Reata's spacious lobby he saw old couples and young families. Through the glass doors and picture window that overlooked the main pool, kids were playing in the water while middle-aged Middle Americans lay whitely on the padded lounge chairs soaking up sun or idly flipping through mass-market magazines.

Where were the singles, the hot babes, the scenesters? He'd been under the impression that this resort catered to a young hip crowd, had been led to believe that he would be among *his* people here rather than stuck staying with a bunch of refugees from Branson and Orlando.

I was misinformed.

Townsend had been the one to put that idea in his head, and Patrick would not be surprised to learn that the misconception had been intentional. It was just like the editor to play a joke like that on him, and Patrick vowed that if that was indeed what had happened, he would pay the man back in spades.

It wouldn't have been so bad if he'd at least been somewhat close to Tucson. He'd come out west for the Tucson International Film Festival, and his plan had been to spend the week alternately checking out the films and getting in a little R and R. At the paper's expense, of course.

But The Reata was way the hell out in the Far Country, the Big Country, the Wonderful Country—his mind supplied endless descriptions from the golden age of westerns—and that pretty much ruled out the flexible schedule he'd had in mind. After the hellacious trip out here, just attending the festival seemed like far too much work. He dreaded the thought of driving fifty miles through the desert to watch some pretentious art film, then driving fifty miles back here to sleep at night. There was nothing more excruciating than sitting through a bad avant-garde movie. At least with a failed comedy or a crappy genre flick a viewer could be distracted and sometimes entertained by the plot, as simplistic, predictable and pedestrian as it might be. But when you were stuck with something like *The Depth of Aphis,* which he'd seen at the Cutting Edge Festival last month and which consisted entirely of a grotesquely overweight woman stacking and restacking building blocks in a badly lit room while an infuriating piano played the same note endlessly, there was very little entertainment value to be had.

And from everything he'd heard about the new organizer for the Tucson festival, that's exactly the type of movie he was likely to encounter.

An elderly man in an embarrassing hat and plaid Bermuda shorts nodded at him in greeting on his way out to the patio.

I was misinformed.

The desk clerks were all cute, though. Three young women obviously chosen for their smiles and sex appeal who exuded the sort of professional demeanor that he found very attractive. The one taking care of him—Tammy, according to her name tag—offered to give him a tour of the resort after presenting him with the keys to his room, but he could think of nothing more pointless and he declined, asking instead for a map so he could find the room himself.

His car was parked out front, but, map in hand, he walked onto the patio and started down the steps that led to the swimming pool, attempting to get the lay of the land. He glanced down at the humongous pool with its fake mountain, waterfall and slide, then around at the perfectly maintained desert landscaping.

The Shining.

He didn't know what made him think of that. This long low Ape City conglomeration of buildings bore absolutely no resemblance to the single epic-scaled structure of the Kubrick film. But the vibe was there, that lurking sense of dread, like a low-level hum, and not for the first time he wished that he wrote for *Rolling Stone* or *New Times* or some other countercultural publication so he'd be able to incorporate his impressions and experiences in a virtuosic gonzo piece that deconstructed not only the film festival but his entire Arizona trip, instead of turning in the staid linear article required by a mass-market daily.

He paused halfway down the steps. There was something about this place that made him supremely uneasy . . . but he liked it. Suddenly the thought of spending the next few nights way out here in the middle of nowhere didn't seem quite so boring. Feeling better, almost cheery, he bounded back up the steps and through the lobby, declining the staff's offers of help as he made his way out to the rental car.

The first thing Patrick did when he entered his room was to crank down the thermostat to sixty. The second thing was to check over the television listings to make sure he had some type of movie channel like HBO or Showtime. To his surprise, he had both—as well as IFC and Sundance. Apparently, the place wasn't as culturally barren as he thought.

He didn't bother to unpack but simply put his suitcase on top of the low dresser and opened it. This first day was his, there were no film festival events scheduled, so he put on his bathing suit, grabbed a *Premiere* magazine, his cell phone and a V8 from the minibar, and headed out to the pool. Taking a towel from the cart next to the gated entrance, he spread it out on one of the lounge chairs. To his left was a family of four, all rubbing each others' backs with suntan lotion and talking loudly. To his right, a pair of middle-aged women raked their MIA husbands over the coals. The view across the width of the pool was of several elderly couples, their chairs pushed close together.

He wasn't in the mood to strike up a conversation with any of these people or interact with them in any way, so he pulled his lounge chair back a few feet so that it was not aligned with anyone else's, and sat down silently, not meeting anyone's gaze. He closed his eyes, leaned back. From hidden loudspeakers issued a familiar song at a refreshingly audible level. The Sundays. It was followed by Jill Sobule. Darden Smith. Downy Mildew. Suzanne Vega. Alterna-folkpop from the early 1990s. He loved those songs, but he hadn't heard them for a long time and listening to them now made him feel unaccountably sad. He had loved the music of that time, the music of his college years, but all of those groups and singers had fallen by the wayside, not lived up to their potential, and the excitement of hearing something new and different and alive had turned to a melancholy nostalgia for a musical future that had not come to pass. It was an indication of how shallow he was that if he could go back in time he would not avert tragedies or prevent horrific political disasters but would work to ensure that the music of that era grew into the cultural juggernaut it should have been.

Politics changed. Art lasted.

It was why he was a film critic instead of a White House correspondent. Well, that and the fact that he had absolutely no aptitude for or interest in government affairs or current events.

His cell phone rang. It was Townsend, checking on him. The editor gave him a quick rundown of the day's events back in the real world, then said, "So," and he could almost hear the man's smile. "How's The Reata? The joint jumping? I tried to find you a hotel as close to the hub of Tucson's nightlife as I could—"

"Oh fuck you," Patrick told him.

"That man said a bad word!"

Patrick looked to his left and saw a towheaded boy pointing at him in shock.

"Hey!" the boy's father said angrily. "There are kids here, mister!"

Townsend was still chattering away on the other end of the line, but Patrick ignored him and held up his hand in apology to the father, a beefy bellicose man who looked like he could have been a lumberjack or a trucker.

"Why did that man say a bad word?" the boy asked.

"Because he's a fairy," the man answered, looking purposely at Patrick.

Patrick didn't know what to say, didn't know whether he should even try to defend himself. He *had* used foul language within earshot of children, and while back in Chicago that would not have rated even a raised eyebrow, here it was obviously an egregious faux pas. He glanced about him and suddenly discovered that this little contretemps was the focus of attention for nearly all of the guests around the pool. Mothers and fathers were glaring at him, two teenaged bathing beauties looked at him with disgust. A group of young boys were whispering and giggling.

"I'll call you back later," he said to Townsend, and clicked off the phone.

He faced the father, sporting what he hoped was an appropriate look of contrition. "I'm sorry," he said. "I was talking to my boss and I got so caught up in it that I forgot other people could hear what I was saying."

"Yeah?"

"I wasn't thinking," Patrick said, knowing he should give it up but unable to walk away. "I apologize."

He was hoping for an acceptance of his apology, some sort of absolution, but the man just stared at him angrily.

Why should he even care what this Neanderthal thought? *Fairy?* What the hell was this, the 1950s? He had a lot of gay friends, and he'd never felt embarrassed about being seen with them or worried about being mistaken as one of them during one of their frequent nights out. He didn't care if someone *did* think he was gay.

But surprisingly, shockingly, he didn't want any of the people here at the pool to think he was anything but heterosexual. For some unexplainable reason, he cared about the opinions of his fellow guests—and not just because he was hoping to bag a bim while he was here. He wanted them to respect him. More than that, he wanted the people here to think that he was like them, that he was one of them, although he had no idea how such a ridiculous aspiration had taken root. He was not and had never been a conformist, was one of those contrary people who had always taken great pride in his willingness to go against the grain, but he felt himself folding like a house of cards, and he didn't like himself for it, didn't like himself one little bit.

Fuck the pool. He had to get out of here, get back to his room.

The father was still glaring at him.

"Sorry," he said again, moving away.

The towheaded boy looked up at him as he passed. "Fairy," he said quietly.

Patrick strode purposefully toward the gate. In back of him, people started giggling. He did not turn around but continued to look forward, and by the time he had exited the pool area, everyone behind him was laughing loudly.

Eight

Rachel sat on the lounge chair watching the boys in the pool from behind her dark sunglasses. Ryan had wanted to play Marco Polo but had been overruled by the twins, who were now happily engaged in some aquatic variation of volleyball with their new friend David while Ryan tried in vain to keep up.

She felt sorry for Ryan sometimes, and she knew that Lowell did too. The twins were a team, a unified force, and in any endeavor, play or conflict, Ryan was always the outsider. Smaller, younger, quieter, shyer, he always seemed to be at a disadvantage, and Rachel supposed that was why she and Lowell were easier on him, even favored him in some ways. Not that they didn't love all three boys equally, but Ryan needed a little affirmative action, a leg up just to be able to stand on a level playing field with his more aggressive brothers.

Curtis purposely smacked the beach ball far above Ryan's head and than laughed as the younger boy jumped for it and missed, splashing into the water. Rachel wanted to intervene, but then it was Ryan's turn and he spiked the ball at Curtis's face, causing his brother to duck and cry out in surprise. *Good for you,* she thought.

It was nearly noon, but she found that she wasn't hungry. The heat made her thirsty—she'd gone through three bottles of Dasani since coming out here—but it seemed to suppress her appetite. From beneath her sunglasses, she peeked down at her stomach, at the slight bulge that was visible above her bikini bottom even while lying down. She could afford to skip a few lunches. She glanced over at Lowell. So could he.

She'd wait until the kids complained, then feed them.

Rachel closed her eyes, let the warmth of the sun hit her face. This was old school, she knew. Today's conventional wisdom said that she should cover herself while in the sun and spend the hottest part of the day indoors, but there was something sensuous and strangely gratifying about soaking in the rays, feeling the taut sweaty heat of her skin bronzing. Lowell had on a shirt and hat, his lounge chair pulled under the partial shade of an umbrella, and the kids were slathered with 45 SPF waterproof sunblock, but she enjoyed basking in the sun in her favorite carcinogen aid, baby oil. She may have been closing in on forty, but right now she felt like a teenager again. And it felt *good.*

She started to doze. The clearly differentiated sounds of her kids in the pool and the conversations of the people around her and the clink of drinking glasses and the slap of sandals from servers passing by gradually coalesced into a single gently oscillating drone. The reddish tinged background behind her closed eyelids darkened into a monochromatic black.

And then . . .

Something suddenly seemed wrong.

She had no idea what it was at first, but she sat up, her eyes snapping to attention behind her glasses. Her initial impulse was to find the kids and make sure they were all right. She spotted them immediately—they were in exactly the same spot they had been minutes previously, before she'd started to nod off—and they were happily playing their game.

So that wasn't it.

But something still seemed off. She had never really believed that cliché about being able to *feel* eyes on the back of your neck, had never thought it was possible to sense when you were being watched, but that was exactly the feeling she had right now, and she turned her head to the right. A gardener was pulling weeds on the small square of grass between the Jacuzzi and the cabana bar. Dark and weathered, he resembled an old bitter farmer. A resort this big had to have more than one gardener, had to employ a whole team of landscapers, but she was sure this was the same man she had seen at night, during the thunderstorm, and though she did not know *how* she knew it, she did.

And he was looking at her.

The man met her eyes, smiled, and that smile made her flesh crawl. It was the creepiest, dirtiest stare she had ever encountered, and she quickly looked the other way, back toward the pool. She suddenly felt naked, exposed, and wished she were wearing her one-piece. And a long shirt. In her mind, she tried to determine what he could see from his vantage point. She raised her right knee to make sure her crotch was covered and adjusted the height of her right shoulder in order to block any view of her breasts.

The disturbing sensation that she was being watched still remained, and it was all she could do not to turn her head again and look. But she refused to give him the satisfaction. He was there, though, she could feel it, and she imagined Mr. Blodgett selling the gardener her panties, the two of them greedily and disgustingly pawing the material like wild animals.

She'd seen the gardener, but what did Blodgett look like? She hadn't gotten a clear view of him, but she'd remember his voice for as long as she lived, that gruff angry growl unexpectedly yelling at them from inside their own room as they tried to get in. Barking orders as they attempted to remove their belongings. There seemed something odd and rather ominous about the fact that he had gone to such lengths to keep himself hidden from them.

Maybe he and the gardener were the same person.

That was hardly likely, but for some inexplicable reason, the two were connected in her mind.

That seemed ominous as well.

In the pool, the kids continued playing. Next to her, Lowell read a novel, oblivious.

She glanced up at the sky, an inverted sea of pastel blue in which were suspended great billowing clouds of white, but quickly looked away, bringing her gaze back down to earth. She did not want to recognize shapes in the contours of the clouds, afraid of encountering a fierce face filled with rage and hate glaring back at her from above. Instinctively, involuntarily, her head turned to the right.

The gardener was gone.

She did not know how that was possible. Unless he hopped the fence, the only way he could have exited the pool area was to pass by the bar and then her chair, or walk around the front of the Jacuzzi and out the side gate, which she would have seen in her peripheral vision. It was as if he had simply disappeared, and if she hadn't seen him so clearly, if his presence had not been so concrete, she might have thought she'd imagined the whole thing.

But she hadn't.

There was a pile of pulled weeds on the small square of grass to prove it.

Rachel adjusted the back of her chair to a full sitting position and scanned the areas both inside and outside the fence but saw no sign of the gardener—which made her feel both relieved and nervous.

"Anything wrong?" Lowell asked, looking up from his book.

"No," she answered, putting her chair back down and closing her eyes. "Nothing."

This time she did fall asleep, and she awoke some time later with a full bladder. Not too much time could have passed because the sun was still at approximately the same location in the sky, but it had been more than a few minutes because the kids were no longer in the pool, and next to her Lowell had a drink in hand. She scanned the now very crowded pool area and saw Curtis, Owen and Ryan crammed together with David on a single lounge chair several yards away, Cokes in hand, a bag of pretzels between them. Nutritious lunch, she thought wryly. What a good mom she was.

She turned toward Lowell. "I have to go to the bathroom," she told him. "Watch the boys."

He grinned. "I have been, Ms. Van Winkle."

"Very funny." She got up and started toward the restrooms, pulling out her bikini where it had ridden up and surreptitiously looking around for any sign of the gardener. Thankfully, he did not seem to be around. She passed by the boys, waving as she walked by, but the twins were too cool for the room and were in that phase where they liked to pretend they didn't even have parents, so they ignored her. Ryan smiled and waved back.

The door was locked when she reached the women's restroom, and there was a CLOSED FOR CLEANING sign on it. She could go back to their suite, but it was getting to be an emergency and at this point the lobby was much closer, so she let herself out through the iron gate, hurrying up the steps.

She found a bathroom, making it just in time, and quickly rushed into the nearest stall, pulled down her bikini bottom and sat on the toilet.

She heard voices through the wall as she peed, a man's deep badgering baritone delivering an indecipherable lecture to an obviously distraught young woman who kept interjecting in a frightened unintelligible voice.

What was on the other side of this wall? She tried to visualize the layout of the building but could not determine if it was one of the conference rooms, the gift shop or an office behind the front desk.

"I'm sorry!" the woman screamed, and her voice was suddenly much louder and clearer. "I won't do it again!"

There was a loud thump against the wall, and Rachel jumped, nearly falling off the toilet. She stood hastily and pulled up her bathing suit.

"Not me!" the woman screamed.

Rachel stood in the stall, unmoving, not sure what to do. She felt outrage, yes, and she knew she should immediately report this abuse to, if not the management, then whatever law enforcement authorities had jurisdiction over this area of the desert. But she was also

afraid, and the fear kept her from moving, kept her even from flushing the toilet, an action she was sure would alert the people on the
other side of the wall to her presence.

So what? she asked herself. But she already knew what. She was
afraid if that angry man knew she was here he might come into the
bathroom and . . . what? Hurt her? Beat her?

Yes. That was exactly what she thought. And that was exactly
what she believed was happening in the other room. That thump had
been the man throwing the woman against a wall. She was being
physically abused, assaulted, and it was quite possible that Rachel
was the only one aware that it was happening.

There was silence after that, and somehow the silence seemed
more horrible than the voices and the noises had. She imagined a
young woman slumping to the floor, her head bashed in, leaving a
smeared trail of blood on the wall behind her while the man wiped
his hands and hurriedly left the room.

What should she do? What *could* she do? The logical move would
be to go up to the front desk and report what she'd heard, to demand
that resort security find the attacker and turn him over to the police
or sheriff. But for all she knew, the person behind the front desk
might *be* the attacker, and then he'd grab her and pull her into his secret little room and throw her against the wall. Or worse.

She knew that the likelihood of that happening was practically nil,
but she was still scared, and even a ridiculous thought like that did
not seem nearly as ridiculous as it should.

That last thump had been *loud.*

She flushed the toilet, then ran out of the bathroom as quickly as
she could, not bothering to wash her hands. She sprinted past conference room doors and through the wide corridor, then out through a
side exit, avoiding the front lobby.

Outside, the gardener was clipping dead buds from a drought-re-
sistant flowering plant. He looked up at her as she passed by.

And smiled knowingly.

"That's what I heard," Rachel insisted. She eyed Lowell suspiciously. He was questioning her story as she knew he would—as he
should—but there was no conviction behind it. His inquiry was perfunctory; as though he knew what she said was true and had some
sort of inside knowledge he was loath to reveal, which, if anything,
made her more perplexed than would have simple disbelief.

He nodded, acknowledging that he'd heard what she said but giving no indication that he had an opinion one way or the other.

"I just want you to come in there with me so we can figure out what room is behind that wall. I'm not going to make a scene, I just . . . want to know." She lowered her voice so they wouldn't be overheard by the other guests at the pool. "If someone really *was* hurt, it would be wrong of me to just ignore it."

He sighed. "And there's the psycho gardener . . ."

"You don't believe me? I'll show him to you!"

But he *did* believe her. She could see that. She just didn't know why. There was something going on here to which she was not privy, and it left her feeling off-balance and uneasy. This wasn't like him. This wasn't like *them.* But she said nothing, did not challenge him, did not acknowledge that his behavior was at all unusual.

Which wasn't like *her.*

"Okay," he said. "Let's go. Curtis!" she called. "Owen! You guys stay out of the pool until we get back. And watch Ryan!"

Curtis ignored him, but Owen gave a dismissive wave of acknowledgement and Ryan shouted, "Where you going?"

"To the lobby!" he responded, and added loudly, "Did you hear me, Curtis Thurman?"

"I heard!" Curtis said quickly, attempting to ward off future embarrassment.

Lowell looked at her, smiling. "Lead on."

They walked up the stairs and into the lobby. Rachel felt out of place in her bathing suit amid such formal surroundings. Before, she'd had such a desperate need to go to the bathroom that she hadn't noticed, but this time the discrepancy between their attire and the environs seemed glaringly obvious, and she was embarrassed to be parading past uniformed members of The Reata's staff in her bikini while down the wide corridor at the far end of the lobby, business-suited men with drinks in hand and white name tags affixed to their lapels wandered in and out of a conference room.

She led Lowell to the restroom doors, explained where the stall was located, and then the two of them backtracked through the building until they found the room that would seem to be behind the appropriate wall. "It must be here," Rachel said, stopping, and there were goose bumps on her arms. Lowell had suddenly gone quiet.

The plaque on the door read: MANAGER.

"What do we do now?" Rachel whispered.

Lowell was about to answer when the door to the office opened, and it was only the grounding of his hand instantly grabbing her wrist that kept her from screaming aloud. Instead, she merely let out a quick hard gasp as the manager stepped out. A rotund man in a beige suit, with a thick beard and a jolly face, he smiled at them. "Hello," he said. "May I be of assistance?"

"No," Lowell said, and she was surprised by the calmness of his voice. "We're just wandering around."

The manager chuckled. "Enjoy yourselves." He strode away from them, turning the corner and heading toward the front desk.

"I didn't see anything in there. Did you?" Lowell looked at her.

She'd been so rattled and startled that she hadn't had the presence of mind to peek inside the office before the door swung shut. "I didn't look," she admitted.

"So what do you want to do?" They were both whispering, as if afraid of being overheard, and she realized that he had caught her fear. He made a move toward the door, and she grabbed his arm, holding him back, not afraid that he would find something incriminating in there—

a blood-stained wall

—but that he would be caught trespassing.

And beaten.

"We'll just take a quick peek inside."

"No," she said. "Let's go."

"But what if you're right? What if someone was injured? Or worse?"

She pulled on his arm, looking toward the corner where the manager had disappeared. "Let's get out of here."

He peered into her eyes, and for a second she thought she was going to get one of his moralistic lectures about Doing the Right Thing. But then he allowed himself to be led away, and the two of them walked in silence around the corner, past the front desk and through the lobby, absurdly conspicuous in their bathing suits. At the concierge's station near the door, the manager stood talking to the elderly man behind the desk. He smiled at them as they passed by. "Enjoy your stay," he told them.

As they stepped outside into the blinding sunlight, Rachel tried to imagine what the manager would sound like if he were yelling angrily, attempting to determine whether he could be the one she heard from inside the bathroom.

And tried to forget the panicked, terrified cries of the girl.

And the thump of her body against the wall.

Nine

Gloria Pedwin stared out the dusty windshield of the car at the unin-habited wasteland before them. This was, without a doubt, the worst and most depressing vacation they'd ever taken.

And she blamed Ralph.

For the past three years, they'd spent their summer break in Southern California at a resort in Laguna Beach that overlooked the ocean and gave them breathtaking views of the sunsets. But this year Ralph had read an article in an in-flight magazine about the "Indian Loop," a historic and supposedly spectacular trip that triangulated between the scenic wonders of Arizona's Navajo nation and the Grand Canyon. He'd been so excited and enthusiastic that, against her better judgment, she'd allowed him to prevail in his choice of vacation destination.

They'd flown into Phoenix and rented a car, a comfortable Cadil-lac, and for a few brief moments she thought everything was going to turn out well. But the vacation went straight downhill from there. Canyon de Chelly had been windy and outrageously hot, and the adjoining town, Chinle, was a poverty-stricken nightmare where the only restaurant was an overcrowded Taco Bell and theirs were the sole white faces in sight. Monument Valley was more of the same, and while the accommodations at the Grand Canyon were much nicer, the place was overrun with tourists: obnoxious Germans and Japanese who insisted on shoving their way through crowds of mild-mannered Americans to photograph the same stationary geologic formations that their countrymen had been capturing on film for decades.

Thank God she'd had the good sense to insist that Ralph book a week at The Reata. It was quite far out of their way, down in the southern portion of the state, but she'd read about it in *Sunset* maga-zine's "Great Hotels of the Southwest" issue and had instantly been captivated by the contrast between the barren desert landscape and the opulent accommodations plunked right down in the middle of it.

The Reata was a luxury resort catering to wintertime visitors from the East, and in the summer months rates were discounted tremendously, as no civilized people would dare brave the heat. Of course, she used both the lowered price and the exoticism of the desert's outrageous summer temperatures to entice Ralph into agreeing to a five-night stay—although she'd been more than prepared to battle it out and insist that since he'd gotten to choose the first half of their trip, she should choose the second.

But where *was* The Reata? Ralph had been mumbling to himself for the past half hour, and this rough primitive road hardly seemed like the way to a luxury resort. They were clearly lost, but Ralph had gotten them into this and he could damn well get them out. Gloria lifted the folded newspaper from her lap and began perusing the front page. At a lobby shop in the Grand Canyon's El Tovar, she'd picked up several of the most prominent papers from around the country—including her own beloved *New York Times*—in order to have something to read on the long trip south, and she'd been parcelling the sections out over the past six hours. She was now on the *Los Angeles Times*, and she frowned in disapproval as she read an article that described an event taking place several years prior as occurring "back in the day." She was astounded that a newspaper of record allowed its reporters to incorporate slang into legitimate news articles, particularly such an ungrammatical phrase as "back in the day." Hadn't newspapers at one time been the bastions of linguistic correctness, holding the fort against the storming hordes of nonsensical vulgarisms that threatened to overwhelm the English language?

Of course, what did one expect from a *California* newspaper?

"I think that's it," Ralph said, nodding at the windshield. She looked up from the paper, followed his gaze and saw a sight for sore eyes: a beautiful oasis of lush green vegetation and welcoming Southwest buildings set against the monochromatic brown rock of a low desert mountain. *This* was the exotic vacation getaway she had seen in her *Sunset* magazine, and she supposed the difficult access was needed to weed out the riffraff and the lookiloos. Some guests, she seemed to remember from the article, coptered in and landed at the resort's heliport. Maybe that's what they should have done. It didn't matter now, though. They were finally here; that was the important thing.

The cracked potholed asphalt turned to smooth new pavement as they pulled next to a guardhouse adjacent to a gate that blocked the road. Already she was feeling better, and while Ralph paid the parking attendant or showed his confirmation letter or did whatever it was he had to do, Gloria scanned the rows of vehicles, feeling vaguely reassured by the sight of so many high-end sedans and SUVs. The gate opened, and they drove up to the lobby entrance, stopping beneath a shaded overhang. A smartly dressed valet opened her door and helped her out while another attendant took the keys from Ralph to park the car.

They stepped into the lobby, past the two handsome young men who held open the double doors . . . and it was as if the whole first half of their trip had never taken place. The memory of those five wretched days was erased as they stepped into the posh regional furnishings of the air-conditioned lobby. *This* was what a vacation was supposed to be. She relaxed into the familiar arms of comfort. A very helpful young woman behind the massive front desk checked them in, and a team of bellboys and attendants unloaded their luggage and drove them in a golf cart to their deluxe suite overlooking a desert that no longer seemed quite so barren and ugly but, through the picture window of their well-appointed, climate-controlled bedroom, looked almost pretty.

Gloria availed herself of a mineral water from the minibar and leaned back on the love seat to rest. The suitcases still needed to be unpacked—Ralph refused to have hired help do *that* for them—but the unpacking could wait. It had been a hellishly long trip, and she deserved a little me time. She picked up a magazine from the coffee table while Ralph went into the bathroom.

"Jesus Christ!" he exclaimed seconds later, and she heard him gagging.

Gloria jumped up from the love seat and hurried into the bathroom. "What is it?"

"Stay out!" he ordered, but it was too late. The toilet seat was up, and in the bowl she could see spattered blood and what looked like a clotted clump of dark tissue floating in the stained water.

A fetus?

The mess in the toilet certainly did not resemble anything even remotely human. But the image of a young woman forcefully expelling fetal tissue in a spontaneous miscarriage was forefront in her mind, and she backed away in shock.

"Gloria?" Ralph said.

She held up her hands, shook her head, continued backing off.

A fetus.

She knew exactly why she'd thought of such a scenario. Her mother. Her mother had had a miscarriage, although by the time she learned of it Gloria was an adult and her mother was practically on her deathbed. It had been a girl, three years before Gloria had been born, and she'd felt sadness and also anger at her mother for depriving her of a sister with whom she could have grown up and shared secrets, and whose advice she could have sought during those troubled teen years. She knew intellectually that it was not her mother's fault, that her mother had no doubt felt far worse about it than she did, but the anger was still there, and the only way to dissipate it was for her to imagine the gruesome circumstances of the miscarriage. Gloria had received no details from her mother—she had not asked for any—but she'd invented a whole mental tableau to which she had returned repeatedly over the years.

And the end result always looked like the scene in their bathroom: a blood-spattered toilet.

Ralph seemed confused. "What should I do, do you think? Flush it?"

His indecision brought back her resolve, and Gloria was suddenly able to function again. "Don't touch anything," she snapped. "It might be a crime scene for all we know."

"Then—"

"Call the lobby and tell them to send someone over here right now. Then help me with our bags. We are *not* staying in this room another second."

"I'm very sorry," the girl at the front desk was saying. She was obviously extremely dismayed. Her face was red, the space above her upper lip wet with sweat, but Gloria didn't care. Something like this should not occur in a Howard Johnson's, let alone The Reata. It was inexcusable.

"I want to speak to the manager," she said coldly.

"Right away, ma'am." The girl picked up a phone hidden just below their sight line and pushed a button. "Mr. Cabot? We have a guest emergency. Could you come immediately to the front desk?" She hung up the phone. "The manager will be right here."

Seconds later, a portly bearded man of obvious breeding strode around the corner and into the lobby, greeting Ralph with an outstretched hand and offering Gloria a courtly bow. He immediately looked familiar, though it took her a moment to place him.

Mr. Cabot?

He looked just like Sebastian Cabot, the actor who had played a butler on that god-awful television show *Family Affair.*

For a brief instant, she thought that this might be the actor's son or brother, but then a more sinister idea came to mind, and she was suddenly certain that this man was a fake and a phony, modeling himself after Sebastian Cabot and even going so far as to steal the man's name. But why and for what purpose? Imitating a long-dead character actor was hardly the way to earn the trust of staff and customers. The feeling persisted that the manager was not what he seemed, and the banality of his disguise unnerved her, putting her on the defensive when she had come to excoriate The Reata's staff for that horror back in her suite.

"What seems to be the trouble?" the manager—

Mr. Cabot

—asked.

Ralph looked to her, and she shoved her unfounded concerns aside to angrily describe what they'd found in their bathroom and demand to know how such a thing could have gone undetected in a resort that was supposed to have such a sterling reputation. She pointed to their suitcases, piled high on a luggage cart. "This is completely unacceptable. There is no reason my husband and I should have to vacate our room, particularly not for something as outrageous as this."

"I understand completely," the manager said in a smooth reassuring voice, "and I can assure you that a full investigation will be conducted not only to determine how this occurred but how it could have gone unnoticed by our cleaning staff."

"Someone had a miscarriage or performed an abortion in our bathroom. How could this happen without anyone noticing?"

"I would like to know the answer to that question just as much as you do, Mrs. Pedwin. Believe me."

Ralph chimed in. "What happens if there's some sort of medical emergency here? The Reata is *very* far from the nearest city."

"We have our own medical staff: a doctor and two nurses on-site and on call at all times. In the event of an extreme accident or medical exigency, there's also a helicopter to take guests to Desert Regional Hospital in Tucson. We are, I daresay, prepared for every eventuality."

The reassurances were logical, proper and should have made her feel better, but Gloria still didn't trust the manager and found that his pat answers made her very uneasy. There was nothing specific to which she could point, nothing he said that was wrong or even unusual. But he himself was unusual, and that colored everything he said.

They were transferred to another suite, this one inspected by Mr. Cabot himself before they entered, and though it was clean and well-appointed, in her mind it carried the taint of their previous room. This first night's stay was free, comped as a result of what they'd experienced, and the manager assured them that for the rest of their visit, they would receive a free night for each night paid. Originally, their plan was to remain at The Reata for five days, but now she wasn't sure she wanted to stay more than one. She had a bad feeling about this place, and while she wasn't some young New Age nitwit or superstitious old hippie, she would definitely feel a lot more confident if they finished out their vacation at another resort.

Why couldn't they have just gone to Laguna Beach the way they usually did?

They unpacked, settled in, waited to find out the verdict on that bloody mass from the toilet, but when Gloria hadn't heard back from anyone on staff after an hour, she dialed the front desk, irritated. "This is Mrs. Pedwin," she said in a voice meant to convey her dissatisfaction. "My husband and I—"

"Mrs. Pedwin! I'm glad you called." She recognized the voice of the unhelpful girl behind the front desk. "We just got a report from Dr. Randolph." There was a long pause.

"And?" Gloria prodded.

"The doctor says it *was* a fetus. A dog fetus."

A dog fetus? Somehow that was even more disturbing, and she tried to figure out by what strange confluence of circumstances an unborn animal could end up in the toilet of their hotel bathroom. She recalled the scene in her mind, and what troubled her most was all of the blood on the side of the bowl. It looked as though the miscarriage had taken place by someone sitting on the toilet, not by a person tossing the dog fetus into the commode. The only scenarios she could come up with were someone holding the dog above the toilet as it miscarried; a large dog such as a Saint Bernard actually sitting on the pot; or a pregnant woman expelling the dog fetus from her womb.

It was the latter that seemed to her most likely.

What in God's name was she thinking? Her mind was concocting wild impossibilities, and the fact that she was seriously entertaining the idea that a woman could have been carrying a dog fetus—

and that the resort's manager was a Sebastian Cabot impersonator

—spoke to her state of mind. This entire trip had been nothing but an unmitigated disaster, and she seemed to be reacting to it by going off on gruesome flights of fancy. The girl from the front desk was still prattling on, but Gloria wasn't paying attention, and she said a short "Thank you" and hung up the phone.

Like the rest of this hellish vacation, their stay at The Reata was not working out as planned, and she turned toward Ralph. "I—" *think we should go home,* was what she had intended to say. But her husband was dead asleep on top of the covers, mouth open, and after the long trip from the Grand Canyon and all they'd been through since, she didn't have the heart to wake him and tell him that they were going to pack and drive all the way to Tucson in order to find another hotel to spend the night. No, they'd stay here tonight and to-morrow they'd talk about cutting their stay short and heading back east.

She looked out the window.

She'd had enough of this damn desert to last her a lifetime.

Ten

Ryan didn't like the indoor pool.

The outdoor pool was fine. In fact, it was great. Bigger than any pool he'd ever seen, with a fast slide and cool waterfall that looked like something from Disneyland, it had a huge shallow end big enough for him to swim across and not worry about drowning. He loved it. But the indoor pool, the lap pool, the pool reserved for health freaks and athletes was . . . well, creepy.

Their dad had told them to stay away from it, which he supposed was why his brothers had made him come, but now that they were here, Ryan wished he had stayed with his parents. There'd been something weird, something off, about their dad's warning, as though he was concealing information from them, and they'd all picked up on it. Curtis and Owen, of course, had been intrigued, but Ryan had not liked it from the start, and if his brothers hadn't threatened to cut him off for the rest of the vacation and not play with him, he would not have come with them.

But he had come and he was here, and he didn't like it one bit. The weight room had been eerie enough with its rows of unused exercise equipment and fun house mirror walls, but the pool room beyond was even worse. The ceiling lights were dull and dim, the deep end of the water murky. There was about the chamber the aura of a tomb or temple, and even the twins' usually loud voices were quiet and subdued.

He wished David had come with them. It wouldn't seem so creepy with someone else here.

The cleaner was the spookiest thing. It slid slowly over the floor of the pool, ticking strangely, an odd-shaped blue object several shades darker than the pool bottom. It was tethered by hose to a machine hidden behind a low wall in the room's southwest corner, the machine emitting a low buzzing hum. He imagined trying to swim in that pool with the ticking cleaner methodically gliding past him, and just the thought of it gave him goose bumps.

"How come dad didn't want us to come here?" Curtis wondered aloud, although he must have had some idea because his voice was nowhere near as loud as usual.

"Maybe it's deep and he thought we'd drown," Owen said doubtfully. "There's no lifeguard or any other people."

"Maybe," Curtis said. "Come on, let's go."

He's scared, Ryan thought, and the realization left him feeling strangely energized; frightened but at the same time excited.

His brothers turned and started out of the pool room but Ryan remained behind for a moment, taking everything in, trying to understand exactly what it was that scared him about this place, that scared his brothers, and, possibly, their dad. Then he, too, turned away.

"Ryan."

He stopped.

"Ryan."

There were a whole host of noises in the room: the snick-click of the pool cleaner, the mechanical hum of its hidden motor, the low lapping of the water, the background vacuum of the air-conditioning system. By themselves, they seemed innocent and ordinary enough, but they masked another sound, a secret sound, a voice, and it seemed to Ryan that that was the reason those noises existed, to throw others off the track, to keep them from hearing what he was hearing.

"Ryan."

Or perhaps the mechanical sounds themselves were creating the whispered name, each contributing an element, a syllable, to the word that he heard.

"Ryan."

He looked around the room and saw . . . pictures. Images. Like a movie that was playing over the concrete reality before him. They weren't transparent like the ghostly figures in movies but they weren't fully realized and three-dimensional either, and he could definitely tell that they were not part of the physical world.

In the pool were naked men and women, good-looking well-fed individuals who did not look as though they'd ever had a day of adversity in their lives. Against the wall, other men and women, skinny and starved, shivered in terror. He knew it wasn't real, but he had the feeling that it had been . . . or could be. This was ESP, he thought, and there was no shock or disbelief in the discovery, only an interested sort of bemusement. No one would believe him, he knew. His brothers always made fun of him for reading books about UFOs and psychic phenomena and unexplained oddities of nature. If he told them, they'd just think it was his imagination working overtime.

But it wasn't his imagination, and he was surprised by how calm he was about the whole thing. Maybe all of those books and comics and magazines had prepared him for this, had opened his mind enough about the paranormal that he wasn't completely thrown when he finally encountered it.

He turned his head slightly and the scene shifted, like one of those 3-D cards where you moved the card to a different angle and the figure changed to a different position. Now the pool was filled with blood rather than water, and sickly candles lined the walls of the room. He couldn't smell the candles but he could tell from the dirty glow of the flames and the issuing black smoke that they gave off a foul stench. It looked like something out of the Middle Ages, but the pool cleaner was still moving methodically from one end to the other, looking black beneath the red liquid, its long snaking hose stretching back to the humming machine behind the small wall in the southwest corner.

As a test, he moved his head yet again, and once more the scene shifted. This time, the pool water was black, so black that its surface was shiny, reflective. The walls of the room were moldy and dripping with fungus. Only one light was on above the shallow end of the pool, and the rest of the room was engulfed in an inky darkness. Things were moving in that darkness, although whether they were animal, human or monster he could not tell. Whatever they were, they were scary, and he moved his head in an effort to get rid of them, but the scene held. Quickly, he swiveled his head to the left and to the right, trying to dislodge the view before him and shift to another less threatening picture, but it was of no use.

White figures emerged from the murk in front of him, skinny wraithlike forms with no discernable faces, only blurred blank visages. They were walking—or rather gliding—across the top of the shiny black water, and he didn't know how he knew this but he did: their touch meant death.

He stumbled backward, trying to get away, but there were too many of them and they were moving too quickly.

One of them reached for him.

Grabbed him.

And then he was looking into Owen's puzzled face. His brother had seized his arm, and was pulling him through the doorway. "Are you all right?" Owen asked, and then, almost as an afterthought, "What were you looking at? Did you see something?"

A certain quality in his brother's tone of voice made Ryan want to tell him, made him think Owen might understand and believe him, but at the last second he shook his head. "No," he said. "Nothing."

"You sure? You looked like . . ." He didn't finish the sentence.

"No," Ryan said.

"Come on, then. Let's go. We're hungry."

In the room, Ryan retrieved his notebook from where he'd hidden it beneath his underwear, and brought both it and a pen into the bathroom with him, locking the door. He'd thought of an idea on the walk back. He was going to write his own book: *Haunted Hotels of the United States.* Maybe someone had written one like it already, but no one had written the book *he* was going to write. No one had had the experience he had just had, and he quickly jotted down a record of what had happened by the indoor pool.

He was going to be a psychic investigator.

Never before had a career seemed so attainable to him—and so right. He'd toyed with the idea of being an archeologist when he grew up (he liked dinosaurs) or a director (he liked movies), but neither of those had been realistic aspirations. This, though . . .

This was real.

He knew about psychic phenomena. Knew a *lot* about it. And now he had ESP besides. He'd study The Reata while they were here, write a chapter about it, then move in to another haunted hotel. If he could just get his parents to take vacations at resorts and motels and inns that had a history of ghostly disturbances, he could use his own psychic powers to pinpoint the reasons for the disturbances and then write about them. He'd probably be the youngest author ever of one of those books, and he imagined himself going to Borders or Barnes and Noble for a book signing, autographing the hundreds of books that his fans would buy.

And why stop at hotels? He could do haunted restaurants, haunted national parks, a whole series of haunted vacation books.

The fear he had felt by the indoor pool, that overwhelming feeling of dread and mortal danger had disappeared with distance, replaced by an excited anticipation. He still remembered what had happened, though, and he knew that he would have to be careful while he was here. They all would.

That meant that they needed to stay away from the exercise pool. His dad was right about that.

What had his father seen in there?

And there were probably quite a few other places on the resort's grounds that should be avoided. But he had faith in his ability to pick out those trouble spots. The Reata might be a full-fledged spook house, but he and his family would be safe here.

As long as his ESP worked.

Eleven

This was preposterous. They had made reservations ahead of time and should have been able to walk to an open table immediately upon arriving. Instead, they were stuck in a cramped antechamber waiting for a group of diners to vacate the table that should have been saved for them. If they were not stranded here in this remote corner of the wilderness, Gloria would have taken her business elsewhere and let the management know exactly how she felt about being treated so shabbily. But the Saguaro Room was the only real restaurant for perhaps hundreds of miles, so they were obliged to comply with its chaotic reservation system and put up with its disrespectful conduct.

She shifted in her seat, looked about, and found that she was being stared at by a rather handsome middle-aged man standing to the side of the closed door who was obviously waiting for a table as well. He smiled as he caught her eye. "Did you call ahead, too?"

"This is absurd," Gloria said loudly, hoping the wait staff could hear. "Apparently they don't know the meaning of the word 'reservation' here."

The man chuckled as he walked over. "No, they don't." He nodded at her, held out a hand to Ralph. "Phillip Emmons," he said.

"I'm Ralph Pedwin. This is my wife, Gloria."

"Pleased to meet you." He remained on his feet next to their bench, his focus on the hostess standing like a sentinel at her podium between the waiting area and the dining room. "I've been here for a half hour already." He made a slight motion to the left. "That family was here before me. They didn't make reservations, though, and if they get in before I do, I am going to be royally pissed." He smiled slightly at Gloria. "Pardon my French."

"Our reservations were for six thirty," she said. "We got here exactly on time. That was fifteen minutes ago."

"Mine were for six twenty."

There was an awkward pause.

"So what do you do?" Ralph asked.

"For a living? I'm a writer."

A writer? That piqued Gloria's interest. "What do you write?" she asked. "Maybe I've read something of yours."

"Suspense novels. Thrillers." He correctly read the reaction on her face and smiled. "Probably not up your alley."

"I generally read biographies," she admitted.

Ralph chuckled. "So are you here for a little R and R?"

Emmons continued to smile but suddenly there seemed to be very little amusement in it. "Not rest and relaxation. But if you mean research and review, then yes I am."

"Research? You mean for one of your books?"

"Not exactly."

Gloria looked at him. "Well, what *are* you researching, Mr. Emmons?"

This time he did not smile. "You don't want to know."

A shiver passed through her, and in that brief second she reflected on all that had happened since their arrival. He was right. She *didn't* want to know. But she had to know. If it was something to do with The Reata, something that might impact their stay here—however short that might be—she needed to find out. "Why?" she asked.

He crouched down next to their bench and looked at them quite seriously, lowering his voice. "Get out," he suggested. "As soon as you can. Tomorrow morning, check out of The Reata, drive to Tucson and book a room at Westward Look or Ventana Canyon. Anyplace but here."

Ralph snorted.

"Why?" Gloria asked again, both intrigued and a little frightened. This man was a stranger, and she wasn't sure she should believe anything he had to say, but he obviously had the same trepidation she had about The Reata.

"Trust me," Emmons said. "This is a bad place."

"Bad how?"

"You don't want to know," he said again.

"Pedwin," the hostess announced, picking up two menus and a wine list from the shelf behind her podium. "Party of two?"

"That's us." Ralph stood, nodding at Emmons. "Nice to meet you."

"Maybe we'll see you tomorrow," Gloria tried experimentally.

"You won't see me. I'll be gone. And I'd advise you to do the same."

She wanted to talk to him more, wanted to ask him why exactly he was leaving, but the hostess was walking away from them and Ralph was ushering her into the dining room, and Phillip Emmons stepped aside to let another couple take the bench seat they'd vacated.

The Saguaro Room was crowded and they were led to a small table for two in the center of the floor. The décor was nice, the ambience casual, the menu surprisingly eclectic. She wasn't quite sure it was worth the wait, but being seated and served mollified her a bit, and she ordered shrimp and crab meat enchiladas (*when in Rome*) while Ralph requested prime rib with potato leek soup.

She wanted to talk about The Reata while they waited for the food to arrive, about what was wrong with this place, about the dog fetus in the toilet and Sebastian Cabot and the writer's suggestion that they leave, but Ralph immediately changed the subject when he saw where the conversation was headed, and it occurred to her that Ralph was *afraid* to talk about The Reata. At least out here, in public. His attitude made her more apprehensive, and when he switched the topic to another, blander, subject she willingly and gratefully went along.

Their meals arrived, beautifully presented and smelling heavenly. Color-coordinated Fiesta plates were placed before them filled with generous helpings of artistically prepared food, and though they hadn't ordered any drinks, had merely been sipping water with lemon from the crystal goblets provided, Ralph decided to order one of the rare imported lagers from the beer menu on the flip side of the wine list. The waiter left to get Ralph's drink, and Gloria picked up her fork, preparing to cut into her enchilada.

When she noticed something out of the corner of her eye.

A small puddle of blood between the steak and mashed potatoes on Ralph's plate.

She froze, her gaze moving quickly over the rest of the dishes, and saw a dark blotch of thick liquid at the bottom of his bowl with a few bubble-like spots floating higher in the translucent soup. She looked down at her enchiladas and saw that her fork had sliced through a pool of liquid that was slightly redder and less viscous than the surrounding sauce. She tried not to gag but she couldn't help thinking about that clotted horror in the toilet, and, clutching her handkerchief to her mouth, she ran for the ladies' room. She made it just in time, regurgitating today's meals and snacks all the way back to her Grand Canyon breakfast, a seemingly endless spew of vomit issuing from her mouth in great retching spurts. Still hunched over, she grabbed a handful of toilet paper from the roll and used it to wipe

her lips and chin before flushing the toilet and stumbling over to the
sink, where she splashed water on her face and rinsed her mouth.

How on earth did blood get into their food? And why weren't any
of the other patrons complaining? Had the chef accidentally cut his
hand while preparing their dishes and then decided to let the plates
go out as is instead of remaking the meal? Or had he not noticed that
he was bleeding, only discovering it after the fact, after the food had
gone out and it was too late to recall it? She thought of what that
writer, Phillip Emmons, had told them—

Get out.

—and could not help thinking that the blood in their food had
been placed there intentionally, and that it was connected to that dog
fetus in their toilet.

There was entirely too much blood on this vacation.

If the attempt was to frighten her or cow her, the individuals behind this grotesque act had severely miscalculated. The more she
thought about it, the angrier she became, and when she reflected on
the fact that she had been humiliated in front of the entire restaurant,
made to dash out of the dining room in order to vomit in a toilet
stall, it made her furious.

They'd picked on the wrong woman.

Gloria straightened, fixed her face and looked herself in the eye,
satisfied by the firm resolve she saw there. She returned to the dining
room and scanned the sea of diners' faces for Phillip Emmons but he
was nowhere to be found. A glance toward the waiting area showed
only a young couple and a family of four.

Maybe he'd gotten fed up with the wait and left, opting for room
service.

The dishes were gone when she returned to the table. "I told them
to take everything back and cook us a new meal," Ralph said angrily. "What do you think that was? Blood? It looked like blood
to me."

Gloria remained standing. "Waiter!" she called out at the top of
her voice.

All eyes in the restaurant turned to her, and their waiter came hurrying over. "I'm very sorry," he said in a voice filled with apologetic
subservience. "I don't know how such a thing could have happened . . ."

"I want to speak to the manager!" Gloria demanded.

The waiter started to say something, speaking softly in a vain attempt to get her to keep her voice down, but the manager had heard
and was already there, apologizing profusely, assuring them that

such a thing would never happen again, that he didn't know how it had occurred this time.

"I want that chef fired," she commanded. "There is absolutely no excuse for something like this. It's not only a health code violation, it's an affront to human decency."

"I understand, madam."

"There was blood in our food!"

"We're still not sure if—"

"Blood!"

"Yes, madam," the manager said.

"Naturally, I do not expect to be charged for this meal, not after the horrific ordeal your restaurant put us through."

"Of course not," the manager agreed. "And rest assured, whoever is responsible for this prank—"

"It's a little more serious than a prank!" Ralph said.

"Quite so, sir. Quite so. But I just want you to know that the person or persons responsible will be held accountable."

Once again, the words were right, but there seemed something wrong with their delivery. As with Mr. Cabot, the intent behind the manager's placating promises was suspect, and despite her outward bravery and bluster, inwardly Gloria felt off balance and strangely scared. Beneath the surface normalcy were dark currents she could neither see nor understand but which she nonetheless knew were there.

"Please enjoy the rest of your meal," the manager said, as the waiter nodded solemnly next to him. "And once again please accept our heartfelt apologies for this unfortunate incident."

Gloria sat down, looked at Ralph, and the two of them waited in silence. There was nothing to say, and Gloria felt increasingly uncomfortable as the minutes dragged by. Around them, other diners ate their food and carried on casual conversations. To their left, a couple and their teenaged daughter got up and left, two elderly women taking their seats after the tablecloth had been replaced and the dishes and silverware replenished. Gloria kept glancing toward the waiting area by the entrance, hoping to spot Phillip Emmons—

Get out.

—but the writer was nowhere to be seen, and she found herself wondering exactly what the writer knew about The Reata, what he had learned in his research that made him want to get away from here so quickly.

Finally the food arrived, brought by their waiter and accompanied by the apologetic manager. Full plates and glasses were arranged on the table in front of them before the two men discreetly disappeared. A hush seemed to fall over the dining room, and though people kept talking, waiters kept waiting, hostesses kept seating customers, everything was lower, slower, quieter, and the rest of the restaurant seemed to fade into the background. Gloria remembered last year when a friend of hers had taken her to a concert of so-called "New Music," which for some pretentious and inexplicable reason was spelled "Nu Music" on the program. One piece had been titled "Expectant Silence" and consisted of a man sitting at the piano, playing nothing. Every once in a while he would extend his hands, place his fingers above the keyboard and look as though he were about to play something. Only he never did. Those moments when he seemed poised to play, however, did find her *waiting* for the advent of music, and against her will, she felt the difference in the type of silence in the concert hall.

Expectant silence.

It was what she felt here, now, and she understood that everyone in the dining room was waiting to see whether they would eat their dinner.

Why?

She could think of no answer to that question that did not make her feel profoundly discomfited. It was as though everyone but themselves was in on a joke—and they were the brunt of it. Gloria swiveled her head around. No one would meet her gaze, but no one exactly turned away either. All attention was upon them.

She and Ralph looked at the food, then looked at each other, afraid to eat. The imported beer suddenly looked an awful lot like urine, the soup was busy enough to hide gobs of saliva. A smear of artistically rendered white sauce on the blue-and-red corn enchiladas could have easily been ejaculate.

Suddenly Gloria was no longer hungry, and with a queasy stomach, she pushed her chair back from the table. Ralph followed suit. "Let's go," he said, and arm in arm, eyes straight ahead, they headed across the crowded restaurant toward the exit, as around them the other diners returned to their meals and conversations.

Twelve

The Grille was not quite what they'd been led to expect.

Lowell followed the miniskirted waitress to a table against a far wall, Rachel and the kids right behind him. In contrast to the casual classy quiet of the Saguaro Room last night, the Grille was loud, boisterous and defiantly crass. On initial inspection during daylight hours, it had appeared to be a typical burger and beer joint, albeit one slightly tonier than usual. Despite Tammy's assertion that the place could get a little loud and raucous on Friday and Saturday nights, they had not really believed the eatery would be this rowdy.

They were wrong.

"I'll be dipped in shit!" a drunken man yelled, and he was greeted with a chorus of wild laughter.

The odd thing was that the Grille's patrons did not seem to be people who could afford to stay at The Reata—even with the reduced summer rate. They were certainly not people he had seen around the pool or in the lobby or walking to and from the rooms. And they obviously couldn't be locals. There *were* no locals way out here. Perhaps they were part of the resort's staff . . . only that didn't seem right, either.

He didn't know where these people came from.

And that bothered him.

A gaggle of young women who looked like secretaries here for a good-time weekend were gathered around the front of the bar, doing shots, while half a dozen biker types watched them from two pushed-together tables. At a corner booth, a small skinny man with a Jackie Gleason mustache was groping a tube-topped Anna Nicole Smith look-alike.

He saw the look of disapproval on Rachel's face, saw inquisitive excitement in the expressions of the boys, but they were here, it was late, and if they wanted something for dinner they had no choice; they would just have to make the best of things and pretend this was a normal restaurant. The waitress passed out menus, then leaned forward over the table in a way that showed her implants to best advantage. "Could I start ya'll off with a drink? Margarita maybe?"

"Iced tea for me," Lowell told her.

"Just water," Rachel said shortly.

"Coke," the boys announced, eyes wide and staring.

The waitress grinned at them. "You got it. I'll be back in a mo for your order. If you need anything, just holler. My name's Bambi." She swiveled around and, with a flick of her pert miniskirted butt, was gone.

"Wow," Curtis said.

"Keep your eyes in your head," Lowell told him, smiling.

"You shouldn't even be in here," Rachel said. "If there was any other place to eat . . ." She shook her head. "Why would The Reata even have a place like this on its grounds?"

"I don't know," Lowell admitted.

Owen and Curtis were both grinning, but Ryan seemed subdued, a little nervous.

As they looked at their menus, there was a commotion at the opposite end of the room. Men and women were leaving their seats to stand by the small stage that had been set up to the left of the bar. A screen was lowered from the ceiling, and someone tapped a microphone. "Testing," a man said, his voice amplified through a series of hidden speakers. "One, two, three . . ."

Bambi returned with their drinks. "Have you decided on your order?" she asked as she slid the boys' Coke glasses across the table.

The twins knew what they wanted without even looking at the menu—they always ordered the same thing: cheeseburgers, hold the pickles—and Ryan asked for his usual grilled cheese sandwich. Rachel ordered a barbecued portobello mushroom burger. Lowell was the only one who hadn't decided, and he quickly scanned the menu before choosing a Mexican pizza.

By the time Bambi left with their orders, one of the secretaries was on the stage and singing off-key to a prerecorded backing track, her friends egging her on. It was karaoke night, apparently; although for all he knew *every* night was karaoke night at the Grille. He couldn't see the words on the screen from where they sat, but he tried to understand the lyrics. "I love the dead," the woman sneered into the microphone, and that sounded vaguely familiar. He thought it was an Alice Cooper song his older brother used to listen to when he was a kid.

"This is great," Curtis said, grinning.

"I don't like this at all," Rachel stated flatly. "Let's just hurry up and eat and go back to our room."

But the food did not arrive right away, and they sat there listening as a goateed, muscle-shirted man growled his way through Ice-T's "Cop Killer" and then a buxom, overly made-up young woman did a Betty Boop version of Marilyn Manson's "Antichrist Superstar" while around them the crowd got bigger and noisier and drunker.

The song choices seemed strange, Lowell thought, and there was something about the music the performers picked that made him uneasy. But then their food arrived and they started eating. They chatted as they ate, discussing what had happened today, what they were going to do tomorrow. In the background, the endless parade of karaoke singers continued, and when Lowell occasionally tuned in to the songs, they were not anything that he recognized.

He was looking around for the waitress in order to get a refill on his iced tea when he finally had the opportunity to listen to what the burly man on stage was singing. "Skin my daddy's hide!" the man screamed over an industrial backing track. "Steal his toupee! Fuck my momma's asshole! She likes it best that way!"

Bambi arrived, pitcher in hand, to pour his iced tea, but he hardly paid attention. His focus was on the man on stage and his outrageous song. "The Holocaust was a lie! Those Jews should fuckin' die!"

Were those the words appearing on the screen?

Rachel was listening, too. "Let's get out of here," she said.

"Miss!" Lowell called in an effort to ask for the check. "Bambi!" But the waitress was walking away and could not hear him with all of the surrounding music.

The song ended, the crowd screamed wildly. A trashy looking young woman got up to sing, and the karaoke started again. It wasn't only the words that were wrong now. It was the music itself—the rhythm, the melody, the harmonics—that was disconcerting, that spurred Lowell into chasing down the waitress, cornering her at the bar and demanding the check. He wrote down their room number, added an appropriate tip and signed for it, taking the carbon.

The Grille seemed to have suddenly become crazier. That maddening music was thumping in his skull as he passed a table of ugly dirty men pounding their fists on the wood in unison, shouting a phrase that he could almost—but not quite—understand. Unbelievably, Jackie Gleason and Anna Nicole were half-naked in their booth, rubbing ketchup on each other.

One of the secretaries jumped on stage and took off her top to the drunken cheers of the other patrons, her huge breasts jiggling in time to the music.

He reached their table. "We're leaving now," Rachel said, lips tight. He didn't know how he could understand her amid all of the noise and chaos, but he could, and he nodded his agreement. He pulled the twins' collars to get them out of their chairs while Rachel took Ryan's hand and led him away from the table toward the exit. The twins, no doubt, would have liked to stay and see where this was all going—he'd been young once himself, he knew how teenaged boys thought—but there was something not just unsavory but *dangerous* about the mood of the crowd here tonight, and when they were finally outside and he heard a young woman scream into the microphone, "Look! I'm on my period!" he was glad that they'd left when they did.

The night air was warm but felt clean and good after the stifling atmosphere of the Grille. Curtis and Owen asked if they could join their friend David and his parents, who were swimming at the big pool, but they asked in a restrained and hesitant manner, as though they already knew the answer to their question and accepted it. An angry Rachel told them they were staying in their room tonight, that she wasn't about to let them consort with those used pieces of white trash from the Grille, who no doubt would move their drunken revelry to the pool once they tired of karaoke.

Lowell agreed, telling the boys that they could watch TV instead, and the five of them started silently back down the path toward their suite.

Later, in bed, when the boys were in their own room and asleep, Rachel was all over Lowell, roughly yanking down his underwear and grabbing his penis, pulling on it with one hand while she cupped his balls tightly with the other. She made him erect, almost against his will, and then climbed on top of him, guiding him in.

"Fuck me," Rachel whispered in his ear. "Fuck me hard."

"The kids . . ." he whispered.

"Fuck me!" she ordered.

He didn't know what had gotten into her, and while ordinarily he would have been thrilled with such a command, he found it unnerving tonight—

Look! I'm on my period!

—and it took all of his powers of concentration to maintain his erection as she thrust lustily against him, trying to drive him in deeper.

Thirteen

Patrick awoke in darkness. Ordinarily, he slept all the way through the night, not stirring from the time his head hit the pillow until the sun rose in the morning. But the racket from the room next door had penetrated even his deep slumber, and he opened his eyes and groggily searched for the blue LED numbers on his nightstand alarm clock before realizing that he was not at home, he was at a hotel. He vaguely recalled seeing a clock somewhere in the room, but he could not remember where and, swiveling his head, could not seem to find it in the pitch black space.

He could see nothing, but he could hear plenty. It sounded like a group of rock stars were having a party next door. Through the wall, he heard breaking glass and loud thumping music and peals of raucous laughter that *almost* drowned out the shouted conversations. A dog began barking, a big dog like a Labrador or a Saint Bernard, and it kept barking, its baritone yelps constant through the seemingly paper-thin walls.

Patrick sat up, fumbled for the switch to the wall lamp next to his bed and turned it on. If anything, the noise from the next room seemed even louder in the light. He picked up the phone and immediately dialed the front desk. "Hello," he said. "This is Patrick Schlaegel in room 215. The people in the room next to me are having some kind of wild party, and it's so loud I can't even sleep. Is there some way you can make them tone it down?"

The female desk clerk seemed singularly uninterested in being helpful. "Which room would that be, sir?"

"The one next to me."

"I need the number."

"I don't know the number," he said, exasperated. The barking seemed to have grown louder. "Do you want me to put my clothes on and go outside and check? I'm sure you know the numbers of the rooms here. Even if you don't, wouldn't it be easier for you to just grab one of those maps in front of you and look it up?"

The woman sounded offended. "Is the noise coming from the room to the north of you or the south?"

"North."

"That's 217," she said curtly.

"Well, do you think you could tell them to knock it off? It's"—his eyes sought the clock—"after two."

"I'll see what I can do."

"They have a dog there, too. Are they allowed to have dogs in their room?"

"No. Pets are not allowed in rooms at The Reata," the woman said. "We discourage guests from bringing their animals here at all, but for those who are unable to travel without their dogs or cats, we provide a pet boarding facility."

"Well, the dog's barking right now. Can't you hear it?" He held the phone closer to the wall, the noise of the animal distinctly audible above the general din of the party.

"No, I can't, sir. But as I said, I'll see what I can do."

The connection was terminated, he was left with a dial tone droning in his ear, and Patrick hung up the phone. He waited a few moments, listening to the ruckus, then put his ear to the wall to see if he could make out any of the conversations. He frowned. What had sounded like party talk from a distance was now differentiated into more ritualistic sound lines. There was a deep low voice chanting the same unintelligible word over and over again while two shouting female voices punctuated the litany at regular overlapping intervals. He couldn't really tell what they were saying, but he thought one of them called out "Apples!" although that didn't really make any sense. Several male voices, less deep than the first, were talking loudly in cadences that suggested they were reading poems. The dog barked randomly.

He moved his ear away from the wall, and once again it sounded like a wild chaotic party. He heard laughter, screaming.

Patrick waited several more minutes—ten by the clock—and when it became clear that the resort's management was not going to do anything to quiet his neighbors, he dialed the lobby again. This time he got a busy signal.

The party grew louder.

He pounded on the wall with his fist, but the noise continued unabated and he doubted his knocks could be heard above the racket. "Quiet down in there!" he shouted, slamming both fists against the wall in a staccato barrage. There was an earsplitting report from the other room, as of a gunshot, and he backed away quickly. The laughter came again, louder, other voices joining in, and then *several* dogs started barking.

This time he walked up to the lobby, putting on his clothes, trekking up the deserted sidewalk all the way past the pool to the patio, letting himself in through the south-facing double doors, determined to *drag* someone over to the room if he couldn't find anyone who would believe him. Even walking past, he heard screams and laughter and loud conversation and the incessant barking of dogs, and he was surprised that none of the other guests were complaining. Yet the corridor was quiet, the surrounding landscape bathed in darkness, and the tranquil nighttime setting lent the raucous room a spotlighted focus it would not otherwise possess.

The Shining.

The lobby was empty, as was to be expected at this hour, but behind the front desk stood a pert fresh-faced young woman whose appearance and demeanor did not jibe at all with the voice on the phone. "Excuse me," he said, walking up. "I'm in room 215, and I just called to complain about a loud party in the room next door."

"Yes, Mr. Schlaegel!" The young woman smiled brightly. "How may I be of assistance?"

He stared at her, astounded by her cluelessness. "You can tell the people in the next room—217, by the way—to keep it down, other people are trying to sleep. Or, even better, you could transfer me to a different room so that I wouldn't have to put up with their noise any more."

She typed something into the computer in front of her and frowned. "Which room did you say the noises were coming from?" she asked.

"The one next to me. On the right. Room 217."

"Room 217 is closed for refurbishing," she said. "There's no one staying in that room. There hasn't been since last fall."

"That's ridiculous."

"It's true."

"I'm telling you, I heard them."

"I'm sorry, sir, but that's simply not possible."

"Yeah, well, I guess I made it all up. I woke up from a sound sleep in the middle of the night, put on my clothes and walked all the way up here just to play a practical joke on you, huh?"

"That's not what I'm saying, sir." There was defensiveness in her voice. *Good,* he thought. If his night was going to be ruined, he was damn well sure he was going to make someone else a little uncomfortable. It was going to take him forever to fall asleep now as it was; he'd probably end up dozing through one of the festival screenings in the morning. The least he could do was spread the joy.

"What *are* you saying?" he asked her.

"There is no one—"

"Yes there is."

"I can assure you—"

"How can you assure me?" he demanded. "Huh? You've been sitting here in the lobby all night. I was just *there*! They woke me up!"

"That room has been gutted. It's in the process of being remodeled. There's no furniture, no working lights, nothing."

"Maybe workers are having a party in there. I don't know. All I know is that there's dogs barking and screaming and chanting and laughing and what sounded a hell of a lot like a gunshot."

"Chanting?" The desk clerk looked pale. "A gunshot?"

He was being sucked into something that he didn't understand but that seemed awfully familiar. *What movie was it?* he thought.

"Yes," he told her. "Why?"

She shook her head, the mask of resort desk clerk pulled once more over the human face that had momentarily peeked through. "Nothing."

But it wasn't nothing, and it suddenly occurred to him that the reason the room was being gutted and remodeled when those to either side of it remained untouched was because a murder had occurred there, a ritualistic murder, and they needed to get the sprayed blood off the walls and floor and ceiling.

"What about a new room?" he asked. "Could I get a new room?"

"Let me check." She typed something into her computer, waited a moment, then shook her head. "I'm sorry. We're all booked up."

"Well can you at least send someone over to *check* on that room? A janitor or security or someone?"

"There's no one in room 217—"

"I'm not making it up!"

"I didn't say you were. I was just saying that there's no one in room 217, but I'll have someone look anyway, just in case."

"Fine," he said.

But it was not fine, and as he walked out of the lobby and back down the flagstone steps, there was a nagging thought at the back of his mind, a belief that whatever was going to happen could have been avoided had he done something differently.

Whatever was going to happen?

He'd seen too many movies.

Nevertheless, the feeling persisted, and as he walked down the darkened steps toward the lighted blue lagoon pool, he felt cold. Townsend may have booked him at The Reata as a joke, but that act had set in motion a chain of events that now seemed increasingly threatening. He thought of that little boy and his father—

fairy

—and the rowdy gathering in the room next door, and while he didn't know what it all added up to, he didn't like it, and it was starting to make him extremely nervous.

He walked around the outside of the fence that ringed the pool area and headed back toward his room. There were low-wattage ground-level lights lining the sidewalk, but in an effort to save money or simply to impart a sense of romanticism and class to the resort, there were no overhead streetlamps on the road and the end result was that the areas to either side of the walkway remained shrouded in a deep wild darkness. He passed the first building, and then the lights of the pool were blocked and the grounds before him were thrown into even deeper gloom, only those weak lights lining the walkway providing any illumination at all.

He began to walk faster, the sound of his footsteps lonely in the stillness, simultaneously loud and small. As he increased his speed, he began to imagine someone or something was behind him, following him, stalking him. It was a Lewton-Tourneur moment, and if it hadn't been so viscerally frightening, he would have slowed down to savor the delicious *frisson* of it.

He kept walking, passed the second building. His room was in the one behind the one ahead, and he quickened his pace even more.

There was a rattle from off to his left.

And right.

A quick snickering across the sidewalk behind him.

Patrick was already jumpy—nature wasn't his natural habitat—and these noises amplified his growing sense of unease. He cursed Townsend for booking him into a hotel with such a remote location. How different this night would be if he were in downtown Tucson, on a busy street, near a 7-Eleven and a Subway, down the block from a well-lighted gas station instead of out in the middle of the fucking desert.

But it wasn't just the desert that unnerved him. No, as much as he tried to restrict his imagination to the physical, biological world, that was not what frightened him.

He thought of the low chanting voice in the room next door, the poetic cadences.

Fairy.

There was something off about this whole place, something fundamentally wrong with the entire resort, and while he couldn't name the movie of which it reminded him, he was clear in his mind that whatever lay at the root of all this could not be explained away with a logical real-world rationalization.

There was movement on the sidewalk ahead, and he stopped cold, peering into the dimness. A pack of rattlesnakes slithered toward him, moving in unison, their undulations eerily synchronized. If he had not known it was a physical impossibility, he would have sworn they were remote-controlled and connected to the same command station. Behind them, spookily reflecting the dim illumination of the lights lining the sidewalk, he could see the eyes of what had to be a wolf or coyote, its furry bulk only a vague outline in the dimness. The animal growled savagely and, as if in answer, the snakes rattled in unison.

What the hell was going on here? He glanced from side to side, expecting to see bobcats flanking him, but the area beyond the sidewalk was so dark that he couldn't tell *what* was out there. In his mind's eye, he saw the wolf leap at him and rip out his neck while vultures and other desert scavengers came to feast on his gutted remains. He knew he should run, get out of the way of the beast, but he had no idea if he'd be jumping from the frying pan into the fire, and terror immobilized him.

There was sudden noise on the road up ahead: the hum of an electric motor, the clank of rattling metal. Low headlights illuminated the darkness, and the animals ran, the wolf dashing off into the night, the snakes slithering back into the shadows. A golf cart pulled up next to him, and painted on the side, above The Reata's logo, was the word *Security*.

A lamp went on in the small cab as the cart stopped. Patrick saw an overweight man with a buzz cut and a brown uniform. "Are you Mr. Schlaegel?"

"Yes," he said with relief. "Thank God you showed up. There was a wolf right here." He pointed. "And seven or eight rattlesnakes."

"Yeah." The security guard seemed underwhelmed. "Now, you complained about noise in the room next to yours, correct?"

Patrick nodded.

"Well, I checked out room 217, and if anyone was there, they're gone now. You're safe." It was hard to see the guard's shadowed face but it was impossible to miss the smirking derision in his voice. *"Fairy,"* was what the man was really saying, and Patrick felt not only embarrassed but defensive.

"I never thought I wasn't safe," he emphasized. "I just couldn't sleep because those assholes were making so much noise."

"Yeah," the guard said noncommittally, putting his cart into gear. "Good luck with your wolves. And your snakes."

He couldn't hear over the hum of the cart's motor, but Patrick imagined the guard chuckling to himself as he drove away.

He hurried down the sidewalk, passing by room 217 on his way back.

The party was still going on.

SATURDAY

Fourteen

There was a knock at the door.

Jarred from his sleep, Lowell squinted at the clock. Six a.m.

Jesus Christ. This was supposed to be a vacation.

Next to him in the bed, Rachel had kicked off the blanket and was asleep on her stomach, legs spread wide, bare buttocks exposed.

Fuck me! Fuck me hard!

Lowell covered her and sat up. The knock came again. Shorter, harder, more insistent.

He got out of bed, took one of the robes from the closet, put it on, and fumbled with the security lock before groggily opening the door. "Yeah?"

"Mr. Thurman?" The athletic looking man on the doorstep had the appearance of a football coach and the smile of a Realtor. "I'm the activities coordinator. I'm just here to remind you that we have a tour of the chef's gourmet garden this morning at eight, and then at nine is practice for this afternoon's pool volleyball tournament."

Activities coordinator?

He was having a difficult time concentrating, getting his mind around concepts that were no doubt simple and self-explanatory. "What?" he said.

"Your wife expressed an interest in taking the garden tour, and we were hoping you'd join us for a little fun in the sun. We're counting on you to help us out with our intraresort volleyball tournament."

It was too much information this early in the morning, a lot to absorb all at once. "I'm not really—" he began.

"Oh, you'll have a great time! It's something we do each weekend as a diversion for our more active guests, a little friendly competition to liven up your stay, and a memorable part of The Reata experience. There are three teams: the Roadrunners, the Coyotes and the Cactus Wrens. We play both days, pool volleyball on Saturday and basketball on Sunday, and the winning team receives drinks on the house at the Grille."

The Grille.

Now Lowell was awake. "I'm sorry," he said. "I'm not interested."

"Come on. The Wrens need you. The Roadrunners have a full team and so do the Coyotes. The Cactus Wrens are still one man short."

"Sorry. We have other plans."

"Too much of a pussy?"

Lowell blinked, unwilling to believe he'd heard what the director had just said. "Excuse me?"

"I just said that since the Cactus Wrens are one *man* short, that maybe I should be looking elsewhere for someone to participate."

Lowell slammed the door in the activities coordinator's face. He was too old to fall for that sort of jock talk, the simplistic rhetoric that attempted to goad guys into action by making them feel obligated to defend their manhood. That idiotic tactic hadn't even worked on him in high school, and it sure as hell wasn't going to work on him now. Ignoring the continued knocking at the door, he shambled back to the bed, took off his robe and fell back onto the mattress, but he was wide awake and no matter how hard he tried, he knew he would not be able to make himself fall back asleep.

He sat up. The knocking had stopped—the activities coordinator having given up and no doubt gone away—and Lowell looked at the telephone next to the bed, wondering if he should call the manager and complain. It was inexcusable that he should be harassed in his own room by a resort employee. Weren't workers at The Reata specially trained to pamper their guests? That's what their Web site claimed. And whatever happened to the once universally accepted motto, "The customer is always right?"

But then he thought of what Rachel had heard in the bathroom, a manager berating an employee and throwing her against the wall. He remembered the spectral hand in the pool and the horrific zoo that was the Grille, and refrained from picking up the phone. For all he knew, The Reata had sent the activities coordinator here to do exactly what he had done. At the very least, the resort was complicitous by not ensuring that its employees treat guests with respect.

There was movement on the bed behind him. Rachel was awake, but she looked groggy, stunned, almost drugged, and he had the unsettling feeling that if he mentioned last night's bout of lovemaking—

Fuck me hard!

—she would not remember it.

He turned away, looked toward the closed door that led to the boys' room. Why hadn't they all left? Why was he keeping his family here? It was a question that nagged at him but one for which he had no answer. The ostensible reason, the practical reason, was that they would still have to pay for the stay even if they left early. But the real reason was harder to pin down. By all rights, they should have decamped right after his experience in the exercise pool, maybe even after their encounter with the room-stealing Mr. Blodgett. And they definitely should have packed up and gone after that scene at the Grille.

But they hadn't.

Instead, they remained, and although these considerations troubled him intellectually, emotionally they didn't really register. It seemed entirely natural not to complain about abuse from the staff, perfectly normal to plan the day's itinerary assuming they would remain here through the end of their originally scheduled stay, and while he didn't feel the least bit dopey, he understood that his behavior was as passively accepting as Rachel's seemed to be.

He knew he should be worried about that.

But he wasn't.

Lowell reached over and gave his wife a quick kiss, ignoring her rather ferocious morning breath, then got out of bed, put his robe back on and went over to make some coffee in the coffee machine. A few minutes later, the boys came in to get muffins for breakfast, which they immediately carried back into their rooms so they could watch TV. "First shower!" Curtis called.

"Second!" Owen instantly announced.

"Last!" Ryan said, and Lowell had to smile. The kid had a sense of humor.

Obviously his brothers didn't think so. "What a dweeb," Curtis said derisively before the door slammed shut.

"Dillweed," Owen seconded.

Rachel, emerging from the bathroom, must have heard the exchange, too. "Do you ever think about how fast time is flying?" she asked.

"All the time," he admitted.

"It seems like just yesterday that we were changing the twins' diapers, and next year Ryan will be going to junior high school."

"How do you think he'll do?" Lowell asked seriously. "You think it'll be a tough adjustment?"

"Academically?"

"You know what I'm talking about."

"His friend Roberto will be going to Brea-Olinda, too," she said hopefully. "And Yung."

He shook his head. "I just don't see it being an easy transition."

"His brothers'll be there."

"Yeah," Lowell said sarcastically. "That'll be a big help."

"What exactly are you worried about? That he'll be picked on and bullied? That happens more in elementary than junior high school, and he's doing fine."

"Not that. It's just . . ." He sighed. "There's more social pressure. There's going to be girls and dances and dating."

"That's three, four years away. By the time he's in high school—"

"He'll be just as shy and awkward as he is today."

She put a hand on his arm. "You worry too much. Ryan's a lot tougher than you think."

"Maybe," he said, pouring a cup of coffee. "Hopefully."

"Butthead!" Curtis shouted from behind the closed door.

"I'm telling Mom!" Ryan announced.

The twins' voices were suddenly lower, frantic, as they engaged in last-minute negotiations with their brother.

He met Rachel's gaze. "Do you wonder sometimes if we're good parents, if we've done right by those boys?"

She smiled. "Every day of my life."

Lowell laughed. Rachel was right. He did worry too much. But it was hard not to. Especially with Ryan. The twins could take care of themselves. You could set them down anywhere and they'd come out fine. But Ryan was different, sensitive, more like himself in a lot of ways, and it made him overprotective to the extent that he sometimes underestimated his son's resiliency.

As if on cue, Owen and Ryan emerged from their room. There was the sound of water from their bathroom, where Curtis was taking a shower. "So, are we really going to Tucson today?" Owen asked.

Lowell grabbed a blueberry muffin. "That's the plan. There's a planetarium there. And a Spanish mission. They have a desert museum, which is supposed to be like a zoo but you can go underground and see the bats in their caves and the snakes in their holes."

"I'd rather stay here and swim."

"Not me," Ryan said, but his dissent was halfhearted. He probably wanted to stay, too, but the lure of a Burger King lunch was too strong.

"Get dressed and get ready," Rachel suggested. "The sooner we leave, the sooner we can get back."

Owen brightened. "Then we can swim?"

"Then you can swim."

The boys returned to their room, and seconds later Lowell heard the sound of fists pounding on the bathroom door. "Stop beating off and hurry up in there! We have to take a shower, too!"

Forty minutes later, they were dressed and ready to go. Rachel had her purse and her camera, Lowell was carrying a small ice chest filled with bottled water, and the kids had books and MP3 players to entertain them on the long drive to the city. As they walked down the short steps from the door of their suite, a fat man in a bathing suit passed by, carrying a volleyball to what was obviously practice for this afternoon's game. He wiped sweat from his oversized forehead and glanced at Lowell with an expression of disgust. "Pussied out, huh?"

"Excuse me?" Lowell said, a little too loudly.

The man kept walking.

"What did you say?"

A safe distance away, the fat man turned, walking backward. "The activities coordinator told us. You're the only male guest who refused to play in the tournament. He said you pussied out."

The activities coordinator.

Lowell's jaw clenched with anger, but when the man turned back around and headed up the sidewalk toward the pool, he let him go.

"What was all *that?*" Rachel asked.

He told her about the visit this morning, how he declined to participate in their volleyball tournament.

"How did that jerk even know who you are?" She lowered her voice. "Do you think the activities director gave out our room number?"

"Yes I do. And it's *coordinator,* not director."

"Whatever. The point is, we're busy, we have plans. So you can't play in their little game. So what? That doesn't mean he had the right to broadcast our room number to every loser on the planet and tell them to harass us." It was strange to see her get angry and worked up the way she usually did and then see it all dissipate and fade away. Ordinarily, her tirade would have escalated as she strode straight to the lobby to give the resort's management a piece of her mind, but now she simply shook her head. "I can't believe this."

Lowell smiled. "I guess now we'll be ostracized by our fellow guests."

"Hell with them," Rachel said. "Let's take a day trip back to the real world."

"Yeah!" Ryan cheered.

They walked down the sidewalk toward the lot where they'd parked. A short man with mismatched clothes had just slammed the trunk of his dusty Volvo. He pointed his key ring at the car, which emitted the familiar hiccuping chirrup of an activating alarm, then looked across the parking lot at Lowell. "Hey! Grocery boy!" the man shouted.

Grocery boy? Where the hell had that come from? No one here knew him and he hadn't talked to anyone about his job. How could—

"I'd like to squeeze your wife's melons!"

Lowell's fists clenched involuntarily at his sides, and he felt his face redden in anger and in embarrassment at the fact that Rachel and the kids had been subjected to this harassment. "Come here and say that!"

Rachel put a restraining hand on his arm. "Lowell," she warned.

"I bet *your* wife doesn't even *have* any melons!" Curtis shouted.

"I bet you don't even have a *wife!*" Owen called out.

The man did not respond but passed between two SUVs and started up one of the gravel paths, both middle fingers raised.

The twins looked sheepishly at Lowell, expecting a rebuke. "Sorry," Owen mumbled. "Yeah," Curtis said. Neither could bring themselves to face their mother.

Lowell had to smile. He knew it was his parental duty to be firm and strict and disapproving of such disrespectful behavior, but he could not help feeling a little proud of his boys and the way they'd stuck up for their parents. "Come on," he said. "It's getting late, it's getting hot, let's head to Tucson."

Again, there was a little voice in the back of his mind telling him this was wrong, he should not be having shouting matches with other resort guests as though he were still in high school, but once more the warning was muted, rational rather than emotional, and carried no impact.

They piled into the car, kids and their things in the back, ice chest next to Rachel's feet in the front seat, purse and camera on her lap.

And the engine would not start.

He turned the key in the ignition over and over again, but there was no noise, nothing, not even a click, and finally he stopped, realizing the futility of it. The car was clearly dead.

They'd been in their seats for only a few minutes and already they were sweating, the interior of the car smelling of body odor and failing deodorant. Lowell wiped his forehead to keep the perspiration from dripping into his eyes. "Everybody out!" he ordered.

The boys gratefully piled out the back doors, while Rachel opened her door and turned toward him. "What do you think it is?"

"The battery. I hope. If it's anything major . . ." He trailed off, sighed. "It's a long way to Tucson if we have to be towed." He reached under the dashboard, popped the hood and got out, walking to the front of the car to check the engine. He wasn't mechanically inclined, so unless something was glaringly obvious he'd have no clue if anything was wrong. Nevertheless, he inspected the battery posts and connections, examined the spark plug wires. He couldn't see anything amiss, and he stepped back from the car, staring at the engine, stumped and annoyed.

Rachel fidgeted. "If this is going to be a while, I wouldn't mind going on that gourmet garden tour. I think it starts in about ten minutes."

Lowell looked at her. "Our friend the activities coordinator suggested that."

"It's an activity," she pointed out.

"I thought you had to sign up ahead of time."

Rachel shrugged. "All they can do is kick me out."

He chuckled. "And you'd throw such a fit about it and be so loud and obnoxious that they'd beg you to stay."

She grinned. "That's not inconceivable."

"Go ahead," he told her. "Even if it is just the battery, I wouldn't trust dragging all of you across the desert until I'm certain that everything's fine."

"All right!" Curtis exclaimed. "Does that mean we can stay and swim?"

"I wanted to go to Burger King," Ryan whined.

"We'll go tomorrow," Lowell promised. "And yes, you can swim. But not until we find out what's wrong with this car so I can watch you."

"Dad!" Curtis said.

"We *do* know how to swim," Owen pointed out.

"Not unless your mom or I are there."

"Mom let us go yesterday—"

"Well, I'm not Mom and this isn't yesterday."

"They'll be fine," Rachel said in a tone of voice that suggested *You're being overprotective again.* "If you want, tell them they can hang around the pool but they can't swim."

"Mom!" Curtis cried, mortally betrayed.

"Then what's the point?" Owen asked.

"Or," she said, "you can stay here in the parking lot and help your father with the car."

Both sighed heavily.

"Go to the pool," Lowell told them. "But no swimming. Wait for me."

"How *can* we swim?" Curtis muttered. "We're wearing Levi's."

"Then no skinny-dipping." He gave Rachel a quick kiss. "Have fun at your garden tour."

"Are you sure?"

"See you later."

They split up, Rachel heading down to the lower end of the parking lot toward the section of the resort housing the cook's garden, the twins running off in the opposite direction toward the pool.

Ryan remained where he was, and Lowell looked down at his son, surprised. "You don't want to go with your brothers?"

"No. I'd rather stay with you, Dad."

That made him smile. Feeling happy, he put an arm around Ryan's shoulder, gave him a quick squeeze. "Good. Glad you're here." He looked at the dirty engine under the open hood. "Now let's try to figure out what's wrong with our car."

Roland Acuna, The Reata's head chef, was one of those hip and handsome young men so prized by televised cooking shows. Knowledgeable and telegenic, with a good speaking voice and a gift for making complicated procedures sound easy and doable, he made a grand entrance when he arrived in the garden, and for fifteen minutes that sped by like five, he regaled them with descriptions of how he came up with the menu each week at the Saguaro Room and how he utilized ingredients he grew in his gourmet garden.

Aside from Rachel, there were five women of various ages on the tour, as well as a middle-aged husband and wife, and two young, obviously gay men who appeared to be a couple.

"Mr. Acuna?" one of the women asked, an overweight elderly woman with the gypsy/bohemian air of an old hippie.

"Roland," he said. "Call me Roland."

"Roland. First of all, let me say that you have a beautiful garden here. But what I'd like to know is, is it organic or do you use pesticides and chemical fertilizers to get such a wonderful crop?"

He chuckled. "There's one in every bunch. No, it's all organic. No chemicals, no pesticides. We keep vermin away with various plants that are noxious or toxic to them, fight aphids with ladybugs and generally combat nature with nature. Does that mean that we some-times have spots on our tomatoes or holes in our apples? Sure." He grinned. "But that's what a paring knife is for."

The hippie woman nodded, satisfied.

"Let's go this way." He led them down a row lined with shoulder-high tomato plants bursting with clumps of yellow flowers and heavy green fruit just beginning to redden. "I'm sure you all recog-nize these. As you can see, it's not quite the peak season yet, but we're going to have a record crop, I think. We have Champion, Early Girl, Roma, a variety of yellow and cherry tomatoes. They seem to do very well in this climate, as do bell peppers and chilis." He pointed to the left where a variety of peppers were growing in a row behind the tomatoes and glanced back at the hippie woman. "I've planted basil between the vegetables to ward off whitefly."

From there, they went on to a wide open area across which spread a chaos of intertwining vines. "Zucchini, chayote, a whole host of squash," he said, and proceeded to regale them with mouth-watering uses for each. Mixed in with the various squash were melons—wa-termelon, honeydew, cantaloupe—and for these, too, he had unusual and creative recipes. "In my kitchen," he informed them, "melons are not just for dessert."

Rachel was enjoying herself. She loved cooking, loved gardening, and it was a real treat to be able to learn about both from one of Ari-zona's top chefs. His anecdotes were funny and fascinating, and he promised that after the garden tour he would invite them back to his kitchen for a hands-on demo. He'd brought a basket with him, and at each stop, he paused to pick a ripe fruit or vegetable to be used in recipes later.

The group continued past the squash and melons to a plot of wildly growing herbs. "Here we have teas and spices as well as some edible flowers native to the Sonoran Desert that I like to incor-porate into many of my dishes." Roland bent down, picked a handful of purple bell-shaped blossoms, broke off several branches covered with tiny water-conserving leaves. He grew visibly excited as they passed a patch of overgrown wildflowers. "Hemlock," the chef said, pointing to one herb that resembled white dill. "Dumbcane, poke-weed, nightshade. This, as you can see, is our poison patch."

Poison patch?

She felt the first faint stirrings of suspicion within her. Not for the first time, reality seemed to have subtly slipped away, leaving her in an altered unfamiliar universe where sinister intent and motivations lurked behind the mundane façade of everyday events. "These are particularly toxic," he continued, as though there was nothing unusual about growing herbs of death. "Don't even brush against them."

Rachel decided to speak up. "Why are you growing these plants?" she asked in a voice that she hoped sounded neutral but curious. "To keep away pests?"

"No," he said shortly but did not offer any follow up. He kept walking. Stopped. "See this little plant with the pink flowers? Buckleroot. An aphrodisiac that I like to incorporate into my chef's salad. How many of you women have husbands or boyfriends who can't keep it up long enough for you to get yours? May I see a show of hands?" He smiled at the wife. "You're excused."

"Thanks," the husband said.

"And us?" one of the gay men asked.

"You, too."

Several of the women giggled embarrassedly.

"Viagra's got nothing on this baby. Let me tell you. Ten minutes after consuming a pinch of this in, say, a nice salad of leafy greens with a piquant orzo vinaigrette, or a white bean and sweet potato soup with cranberry couilis, the penis will be at its peak and will remain gloriously erect for three full hours."

"Does it have any effect on females?" the hippie woman asked.

"No. But this little miracle worker over here"—he gently touched a leafy branch on a tall thin bush—"can make you so orgasmic that the slightest touch to any part of your body, even your kneecap, will make you come so hard you won't know what hit you." He picked several leaves, dropping them into his basket.

Her vague misgivings blossomed into a full-fledged sense of dread that made her think of that horrible cloud face she'd seen in the storm. This wasn't just a case of nebulous bad vibes but recognition that there was some sort of maleficent, perhaps cosmic, force influencing life here at The Reata. She made the determination then and there that they were going to leave this place immediately. They'd sleep in their car by the side of the highway if they had to, but they were going to get out of here today. She didn't know why they had waited this long. They should have left after that first night. But somehow the reality of the unreality here, the urgency of the potential danger, seemed to fade soon after it manifested itself. It was as though she suffered from short-term memory loss or some type of imposed ennui that kept her from acting on what she knew to be right, even kept her from communicating with Lowell about it.

But that wasn't going to happen this time. She was focused now, she could see clearly, and she wasn't going to let this place sap her resolve or trick her into staying.

This place.

She realized for the first time The Reata was haunted. She didn't know why she hadn't noticed before, but it was true. Although now that she thought about it, "haunted" seemed too weak a word for what was happening here, too limited and specific in its definition. This wasn't a set of buildings plagued by ghosts but was a location suffused with a corrupting power that influenced everything in its general vicinity.

The woman next to her nudged Rachel's arm. "He's the reason we came here," she confided. "I saw him on the Food Network and thought he was terrific. I even got some of his recipes off their Web site."

Rachel nodded, smiling. What the hell was she thinking? Cosmic forces? She was letting her imagination run away with her. So there were poison herbs and aphrodisiacs growing in the chef's garden. So what? Those things had been cultivated for centuries. The Native Americans who had once farmed in this place had probably made use of such plants as they did everything else that grew around them, and if Roland Acuna wanted to have an authentic Southwest garden incorporating as much indigenous vegetation as possible, naturally they would be part of his planting.

"His vegetarian meatloaf is out of this world," the woman said.

"Let's keep walking," the chef announced.

This part of the garden was on a slight downward slope, and they passed single file over two split-log steps embedded in the dirt. To both sides grew some sort of deep green ground cover. "New Zealand spinach," Roland said. "It's a little rough if you eat it raw, so I don't often use it for salads, but it's delicious when steamed."

He didn't stop to pick any but continued onward. "And this is the heart of my garden, its raison d'être." Roland led them between two overgrown bushes to what looked like a children's play area, a section of ground cordoned into a rectangle by four railroad ties.

"Come closer," he said enthusiastically, bending down.

They gathered around. In the dry open area, Rachel saw a little corral and a barn made out of papier mâché surrounded by bonsai pine trees. Nailed to the hard-packed dirt with skinny overlong spikes were rats. Dead rats that had been shaved bald and lacquered with some sort of clear glossy finish to make them shine. One of them was positioned on its hind legs in front of the barn, its pink pointy whiskerless face overlooking the scene before it. Another was situated next to the corral fence and dressed in a ragged piece of black cloth. Still others were arranged in a semicircle looking out at the bonsai trees. There was new blood saturating the dirt on which the barn was located, and what looked like an unborn kitten lying curled behind the papier-mâché structure, its translucent eyelids closed tightly. The entire scene was so sick and disgusting and out of place that she didn't know what to say. There had to be some sort of narrative to this tableaux, but she had no idea what it could be. Were the rats supposed to be farmers or townspeople or family? What was the point? She looked around at her fellow tour takers and was shocked to see not outrage and horror but only mild curiosity and an inquisitive interest.

She focused on the semicircle of dead shaved rats. *This* was the reason for the garden's existence? It didn't make any sense, and she found the irrationality of it unnerving. But no one seemed to be questioning the chef's statement. That bothered her, too. She didn't like their passivity. It was as if they and the chef were all on some mental wavelength she could not hope to access.

"This was the first thing I set up when I started the gourmet garden five years ago," Roland said, and there was pride in his voice. "I planted the rest of the fruits and vegetables around it."

Rachel excused herself, walking back between the bushes to the garden proper. Her chest felt heavy, her lungs filled with foul air, and she breathed deeply as she looked around at the squash and the herbs and the rows of tomatoes. She scanned the section of garden they had not yet visited, saw an apple tree, some citrus trees, tall stakes with climbing vines of various peas and beans, and, at the far end of the garden . . .

The gardener.

He was staring at her as he crouched down beneath an orange tree, and though she was only a foot or two away from her tour group, her mouth felt suddenly dry and her heart pounded crazily with fear. He was pulling weeds and had a perfect right to be there, but she knew instinctively that work was not what had brought him to this spot at this time.

She had.

He stood, and there was a dark stain on the left knee of his dirty work pants, a stain that could have been coffee, could have been mud but that she knew to be blood.

There was a bigger stain in the crotch of his pants. A wet spot that could only be one thing.

Rachel wanted to walk back behind the bushes to where Roland was showing off the sickening tableaux that was the heart of his garden, but she did not want to give that twisted bastard the satisfaction of knowing that he had scared her off, so she remained where she was, staring at the gardener at the far end of the vegetable patch.

And he started dancing.

It was the same strange capering jig he'd performed Thursday night, and once again it was for the benefit of her and her alone. If anything, it seemed more odd and incongruous in daylight. She felt unclean merely from watching it, violated in some strange indefinable way. His eyes remained fixed on her, a dirty knowing gaze that matched perfectly his sinister movements, and she finally forced herself to turn aside and hurry back to join the rest of the tour.

From down at the end of the garden she heard rough derisive laughter.

They were just finishing up with that sickening corral and its bald rat diorama. Whatever insights or information he had to impart had already been divulged, but she didn't really care. She was happy just to get away from the gardener. And when Roland led them out again and started down the dirt path toward the apple trees, the man was gone. It had been less than half a minute and as far as she could tell there were no gates in any section of the high iron fence that surrounded the garden at this end, but he had vanished and was nowhere to be seen.

Rachel spent the rest of the tour in a state of heightened anxiety, always alert for the sound of movement behind the trees or bushier plants, eyes constantly searching for any sign of the gardener. But he had really and truly gone, and when they finally came to the end, a part of her was relieved that it was over.

By this time, the chef had accumulated an entire bushel of herbs, vegetables and fruits. He plopped the heavy basket down on the ground. "That concludes the garden tour. I thank you all for joining me and hope you enjoyed it as much as I did." One of the women started clapping, and the rest of the group joined in, Rachel included. Roland bowed graciously, then held up a hand for silence. "We still have the cooking demonstration planned for those who are interested. Do any of you want to participate in a hands-on demo in the Saguaro Room's kitchen?"

"Yes!" they all exclaimed nearly simultaneously.

"All right then, let's go make something out of these ingredients we picked." He smacked his lips, smiled, and for some reason his gaze landed on Rachel. "Who's ready for some hot sex soup?"

Lowell and Ryan gave up on the car almost instantly. There was nothing visibly obvious that was wrong, and it was just too damn hot out here to waste time guessing about things they knew very little about. Lowell closed the hood, tried the key one last time, then the two of them walked up to the lobby and strode directly to the concierge. He explained that his car wouldn't start, the battery seemed to be dead, and the white-haired man behind the desk assured him that The Reata would take care of the problem. "I'll have one of our fleet mechanics take a look. If all you need's a jump or a recharge, we can do that right here. I can even have a battery delivered from Tucson by this afternoon if that proves to be necessary. If it's anything beyond that, we can arrange for a tow. Do you have AAA?"

"Yes," Lowell said. "But—"

"Don't worry," the concierge said. "It'll be taken care of. I'll let you know if it's anything more than a battery problem." He opened the drawer of his desk. "Here's a beeper. Keep it with you."

Lowell accepted the device and put it in his pocket. "How much does it cost to have your mechanic look at it?"

"No charge to guests of The Reata. And a jump or recharge would be free, as well."

There was something to be said for staying at a place that treated its guests so royally.

Lowell gave the concierge his license plate and room number, then, with some effort, took the car key off his key ring.

"I'll let you know as soon as I hear something, which I expect will be in an hour or two."

"Thanks," Lowell said gratefully.

The old man smiled. "It's my job."

He and Ryan walked out of the lobby onto the patio, and he scanned the pool area below for the twins. The only people visible were a couple of resort staffers, a too-tanned man with a too-hip bathing suit and a considerable paunch who was sunning himself on one of the lounge chairs, a mother and her infant son in the water, a young couple ordering drinks at the cabana bar—and Curtis and Owen, overdressed and uncomfortable, seated at one of the umbrella-shaded tables near the shallow end of the pool.

"Let's go get them," Lowell said. "Then we'll all go back to the room and change."

Ryan nodded. "Okay, Dad."

They walked down the flagstone steps. The music being broadcast over the loudspeakers was familiar, Lowell realized, and though he hadn't been paying attention, he did so now. They were the songs of his high school years, those one-hit wonders that had been blasting on the car radios as he and his friends cruised Pacific Coast Highway on endless eighties evenings.

This could probably serve well as the sound track of the reunion, he thought.

Why did he keep coming back to that?

They opened the gate, walking into the pool area. Curtis and Owen looked steadily away, refusing to acknowledge the presence of a parent until the very last minute.

"Thurman!"

Lowell turned at the sound of the voice, and his expression hardened as he saw the activities coordinator waving to him from around the side of the faux rock structure that housed the waterfall and slide. He looked away, but the man quickly jogged toward them, arm raised in greeting or invitation. Something jingled as he ran, and Lowell saw that he was wearing a whistle around his neck. "Pure luck!" he exclaimed as he reached them. "The Cactus Wrens are here for their practice session. We've chosen a captain, and I was just going over a few of the ground rules with them."

Lowell ignored him, kept walking.

"Dad," Ryan said. "That man's talking to you."

He stopped. "Look," he told the activities coordinator. "I'm not interested." But then, from the side of the rocks, the members of the team shuffled out, looking lost and unsure of themselves, a group of men in unfashionable bathing suits, some with pale sunken chests, others with overhanging guts. They moved hesitantly toward the edge of the pool, and something about this Bad News Bears of a team touched him, spoke to him.

They needed him.

"The Wrens are still one man short," the activities coordinator prodded.

He wanted to say no, remembered this asshole jock's obnoxious behavior and sophomoric taunts from earlier, but he found that he could not turn down these men if his presence on the team would help them. That was a weird reaction. And totally unlike him. He was not a team spirit kind of guy, was not even a particularly charitable guy, but for some reason he felt compelled to get involved, and he nodded reluctantly. "I'll do it."

"Glad to have you aboard!" The activities coordinator pumped his hand with false bonhomie, and Lowell found himself looking at the man's name tag: *Rockne. The Reata. One hundred years.*

One hundred years?

That couldn't be right; it had to be a misprint. Or a joke. Nevertheless, Lowell experienced a split second of trepidation that reminded him of his initial reaction to their room when Tammy had taken them on the tour of The Reata. He had never been one to put much stock in first impressions—hell, his first impression of Rachel had been that she was a demure and delicate flower, and that was *totally* off the mark—but he was starting to think that maybe his instincts were sharper than his mind and he should start paying more attention to them.

"Now I've got to go round up the Coyotes and the Roadrunners. Why don't I introduce you to the captain of the Wrens, and you can all get started." The activities coordinator—

Rockne. The Reata. One hundred years.

—started toward the group of men standing by the side of the pool.

"Why don't you go wait with your brothers," Lowell told Ryan. "I'll be back in a few minutes."

The boy nodded, heading toward the twins' table, and Lowell followed Rockne to meet the Cactus Wrens.

They were indeed a singularly unathletic group of men. The captain, Rand Black, a firefighter from the small town of Rio Verde, seemed the closest to competent, but there was still something shaky about him, as though he was one of those disaster survivors who spent the rest of their lives looking for catastrophes around every corner. The others did not even seem like they wanted to be here but wanted to just relax and enjoy their vacation, and Lowell wondered how they had been conned or bribed or bullied into taking part in a pool volleyball tournament.

How had *he* been suckered into it?

"I'm glad you're here," Black said after the activities coordinator left. "This is going to be one tough tournament."

"Yeah," a gangly man said worriedly.

"I thought this was just a fun Saturday activity."

"It's supposed to be."

"Then how do you know it'll be so tough? You can't have played against these guys before."

"No. I just got here yesterday."

"Me, too," a short bespectacled man chimed in.

"I didn't even want to be here," said a frail elderly gentleman. "They made me sign up."

"This is our very first practice," Black admitted.

"Then how do you know it's going to be tough?"

"I met their captain earlier this morning. A guy named Blodgett."

Blodgett!

"What's he like?" Lowell asked casually.

"Big. And mean. He looks like he could be a linebacker or something, but I gather he's some sort of bigwig banker or financial analyst. I got the impression that he was a frequent guest here, that he'd stayed here quite often, which means that he's probably been involved in one of these tournaments before."

"Maybe he can't swim well," Lowell offered hopefully.

Black shook his head. "I saw him in the pool yesterday. He's good. He was diving off the side, showing off for some of his drunken buddies." He smiled grimly. "I hated the man then and there. Some people you can just tell are assholes, even before meeting them, you know? And Blodgett is definitely an asshole."

Lowell thought of that rude bullying voice and Rachel's missing panties. He imagined himself getting into an argument with Blodgett during the course of the volleyball game, taking it out of the pool, and then kicking the man in the balls and punching him hard in the face, breaking his nose, an absurd fantasy of physical prowess like the ones that had sustained him through his impotent teenage years. He hadn't had thoughts like that since high school.

High school again?

"So what do you make of this tournament?" Lowell asked. "When the activities coordinator first tried to recruit me, he said that it was just a little activity they set up for people who wanted to compete. But it doesn't seem like a whole lot of fun and, to be honest, it doesn't look like most of your team even wants to be here."

"Damn right," the elderly man said.

Black shrugged. "I don't know. I just . . . I sort of got caught up in it when he was talking, and then I agreed to play. I think I thought it was going to be this little half-hour diversion or something, not something that was going to take up my whole damn day. But I'd already given my word and couldn't back out . . ." He trailed off. "I don't know."

"And did you see his name tag?" the gangly guy asked. "It says he's been working here for a hundred years. Did you catch that? And this is where he's from. His hometown is The Reata. What's up with that?"

There were nods and murmurs of assent.

He wasn't the only one who had noticed! The knowledge made Lowell feel strangely elated.

"It has to be a joke," Black said.

"Maybe," the bespectacled man admitted, but he didn't sound convinced.

"Look," Lowell said, "my boys are over there waiting. I'll go back, put my trunks on, get them set up and then meet you guys here. Is that okay?"

"We're not going anywhere," the gangly guy said glumly. "We'll probably be here all day."

"Go ahead," Black told Lowell. "We'll start practicing. Just jump right in whenever you can." He smiled mirthlessly. "My guess is that we're going to need all the help we can get."

Fifteen

In the bright light of morning, a room service breakfast delivered to their doorstep along with a copy of the *New York Times,* CNN broadcasting reassuringly over the television, yesterday's events seemed like a bad dream. It was impossible to imagine that any of it had happened.

Yet it had.

She knew it.

But somehow Gloria was not as upset as she had been last evening, and her resolve to leave The Reata as quickly as possible seemed to have faded overnight. Ralph, too, appeared much more comfortable and content here this morning, as though he'd taken a sedative to soothe his nerves.

Gloria finished the final bite of her eggs Benedict, the last sip of her orange juice, then settled down to read the paper. Idly, she wondered if that writer they'd met last night—Kevin Phillips? Bob Evans?—had indeed abandoned The Reata for a resort closer to civilization. It was still not a bad idea, but it no longer seemed necessary, and though she remembered why getting away had been so urgent the previous evening, she could no longer muster the passion for it.

"Look at this," Ralph announced from the other side of the table. He was perusing the Welcome folder he'd found on their nightstand next to the phone. "They have spa treatments. All day and half day."

"I could do with some pampering," Gloria admitted. She turned to the right, catching a glimpse of her face in the mirror over the couch. The dryness, the heat, something about the desert did not agree with her. She looked every one of her fifty-three years, and she knew damn well that when they'd left New York less than a week ago, she could have passed for forty. She pushed back her hair, palpated the wrinkles on the sides of her cheeks. "Make me an appointment," she told Ralph.

"Full day or half?"

"Half," she said. "I don't want to have to make friends. If it's nice, I'll do it again tomorrow."

"It wouldn't kill you to talk to someone," he noted.

She fixed him with a look.

"I'm just saying."

Ralph made the appointment for her over the phone, and immediately afterward there was a loud knock at the door. *Who could that be?* she wondered as he went to answer it.

Gloria stood to see, moving around the side of the table to get a better view. A rather elegant and refined-looking man stood outside the doorway of their suite. "Good morning, Mr. Pedwin," he said in a pleasant, slightly formal voice.

"Hello."

"I am The Reata's activities coordinator, and I am here to inform you that you have been nominated to join our sporting league for the duration of your stay. Our *elite* squad is called the Roadrunners, and this is the group for which you have been selected."

Ralph looked doubtful.

"I might add that we have guests who have been attempting to become Roadrunners since they first started making annual visits to The Reata many years ago. The fact that you have been invited to join your very first year is quite an honor."

First and *last* year, Gloria thought, but she could not help but be impressed by their inclusion in the resort's most privileged group. Heaven knew Ralph wasn't much of a sports enthusiast, but judging from the appearance of some of their fellow guests, a lot of them weren't in peak physical condition, either.

The man seemed to anticipate her follow-up question. "It might interest you to know that participation in our league and enlistment as a Roadrunner entitles you to certain privileges not afforded to other guests. You will, for example, be able to dine at the exclusive Starlight Pavilion."

"We didn't know there *was* a Starlight Pavilion," Ralph said for both of them, though that was not something to which she would have admitted.

"That is because ordinary guests are not authorized to dine there and we don't want to offend them by acknowledging the existence of a dining room from which they are excluded," the activities coordinator said with a small smile. "As a Roadrunner, you will also have access to the Winner's Circle Lounge, where free drinks, hors d'oeuvres and entertainment are provided to all players, members and family of the winning team. Granted, that means that the Roadrunners must win their tournaments in order for you to take advantage of this opportunity. But, confidentially, the Roadrunners *always* win."

Ralph cleared his throat. "I'm not . . . particularly athletic."

The activities coordinator spread his hands expansively. "You won't even be required to play. That duty is assigned to the younger, more physically active members of the team. No, just being part of the Roadrunners will be quite enough. There's strength in numbers, you know."

She could sense Ralph hesitating.

"We accept your invitation," Gloria said for him.

"Splendid," the man responded. He held out his hand and Ralph shook it. She didn't like that. There was something official about it, as though they were cementing a deal or ratifying a contract. For some reason, she thought of the resort's manager—

Mr. Cabot.

—and the image of his smiling face left her flustered. But the feeling disappeared as quickly as it had come, replaced by a more familiar satisfaction at the realization that they were now part of The Reata's privileged elite.

"Are you busy right now?" the activities coordinator asked Ralph. "We could drop by the Winner's Circle and take a peek. More than a few of your teammates are there already."

"May I come?" Gloria asked.

"Of course!"

"How's that possible?" Ralph wondered suspiciously. "They're already there? Did you have a game yesterday?"

"Oh no," the coordinator assured him. "This afternoon will be the first."

"Then these are people who just . . . live here full time?"

"Oh, I see what you're getting at." The other man chuckled. "No, none of your current teammates have participated in tournaments before. Well, one has. But the rest are all new guests like yourself. But while the individuals may be different, team privileges still apply. They're allowed to stay in the Winner's Circle until the team loses." The coordinator smiled. "Which it never does."

They were both dressed, a habit Gloria insisted upon for breakfast, but she had not had time to do her hair or makeup. Sensing that the activities coordinator would not be one to wait, she quickly walked over to the closet, withdrew her sunbonnet and put it on, grabbing the appropriate shade of lipstick from the bathroom counter and applying it in the mirror. "I'm ready," she announced.

"Very well then."

They followed the activities coordinator down the corridor, then up the sidewalk to a building she had not noticed before, a modern angular cement-and-glass edifice adjacent to the low Santa Fe–style structure that housed the Saguaro Room and the Grille. Aesthetically, the two complemented each other, but the new building was very much visible, and Gloria wondered how she had not seen it before. She had the unnerving feeling that it was invisible to a lot of other guests as well, that it had been constructed in such a way as to hide in plain sight, revealing itself only to people who were specifically looking for it.

"Here we are. The Winner's Circle." The activities coordinator opened the glass door and held it for Gloria, who walked in followed by Ralph. The interior of the building was one big room, and despite the jutting angularity of its exterior, the room was basically circular, with a few offset window seats. At the far end was a full bar and in between various chairs and couches and futons. There was a large sunken area on the right side of the room in the shape of a crescent, and it was here that most of the people enjoying the lounge's amenities had congregated, drinks in hand despite the early hour of the day.

But that was not the most distinguishing feature of the lounge. No, that honor went to the pole in the center of the room and the six men and women chained to it. They were dressed in the formal attire of waiters and waitresses, but they were tethered to the pole like horses to a children's pony ride, with long chains that fastened to metal belts around their waists. The pole itself, in contrast to the modern design and furnishings, was old and primitive, a single piece of weathered timber that reached all the way to the ceiling and at one time might have been the mast of a ship. Near the base of the pole, two squat, ugly brown men—illegal aliens, Gloria thought—were being secured to additional chains, and as she watched, carpet sweepers and feather dusters were put into their hands, and they were ordered to spot clean the lounge.

At first Gloria was shocked, and for a brief moment she considered leaving the Winner's Circle to protest this gross injustice and clear violation of human rights. But Ralph and the activities coordinator were standing there talking as if nothing was amiss. A smiling young woman with a Middle Eastern accent brought her a complimentary glass of orange juice on a tray, another young woman offered her slices of melon on individual plates of dainty china, and she found that she became used to the situation very quickly. The tethered waiters and waitresses maneuvered smoothly around the large circular room to the ends of their chains, deftly avoiding entangling themselves in a manner that was almost balletic as they served the needs of the seated guests, and Gloria soon realized that this was quite an ingenious way to maintain control of employees and ensure that they remained at their posts.

No it wasn't, she told herself. It would be much more practical to have the staff able to freely move about and perform their duties with ordinary flexibility rather than be tied up like animals.

But that brief aberrant thought fled as a handsome, tuxedoed young man offered her a napkin then adroitly took up the slack in his chain as he headed toward the sunken section of the lounge.

"I could get used to this," Ralph said.

"I thought you'd enjoy it," the activities coordinator told him. He nodded at Ralph, gave Gloria a slight bow. "I have other errands I have to run, other work that needs to be done, so I'll let you two mingle. I'll be back later when it's time to start talking tournament strategy. In the meantime"—he gestured expansively—"enjoy."

Gloria took Ralph's arm, and the two of them walked further into the lounge, past a tanned, fit couple seated on a love seat talking intensely, down the steps into the sunken area where they were greeted by a large fierce-looking man who introduced himself as the Roadrunner's captain. After the initial pleasantries, Ralph began talking shop with the man, who was apparently some sort of financial consultant. Gloria politely extricated herself and looked for a place to sit down. Out of the corner of her eye, she saw a well-coiffed older woman approaching, the deliberateness of obligation in the pace of her step.

"Dana Peters," the woman introduced herself archly. "President of the Springerville Historical Society."

Gloria thought it odd that the woman would announce her occupation along with her name, but she assumed that it was one of those big-fish-in-a-small-pond things, a badge of honor in the hickville she called home, and she merely glanced at Dana Peters dismissively. "Yes," she said, and turned away, gratified to hear a little insulted grunt from the woman.

She found a large comfortable chair and smiled as she sat down, a chained Asian man taking her empty orange juice glass.

She had the feeling they were going to like it here.

Sixteen

His mother and father were gone for the morning, he had the suite to himself, and David lay on his parents' bed, flipping through channels, trying to find a porno movie. Half of the stations they were supposed to get didn't come in, and this morning only Hallmark and Lifetime and a bunch of religious channels seemed to be on this crappy satellite system.

So much of the luxuries of resort life.

He turned off the TV and tossed the remote control on the nightstand. Rolling over, he faced the window. From this angle, he could not see the ground, could see only the top of the next building down and, beyond that, the back of the Catalina Mountains. And the sky. A lot of sky.

He wished they hadn't come here. At home, he'd probably just be playing with his Xbox or listening to tunes and staring into space, but somehow that seemed preferable to being at The Reata. Sure this place was fancy, nicer than anyplace he'd ever stayed before. The pool was hella-cool, and he'd met some kids from California who were a lot more fun to hang with than the dick smacks from his neighborhood. But . . .

But what?

He didn't know, exactly. There was only a formless antsiness in the pit of his stomach, a nagging sense that he should not be here.

He turned his head sideways, one way and then the other, before rolling onto his back and hanging over the edge of the bed to look through the window upside down. No matter what he did, there was something wrong with the sky. He didn't believe it at first, didn't think such a thing could be possible, but the more he looked out the window the more convinced he became that the sky above The Reata was not as it should be. It was as if the ceaseless blue of the sky was painted, or a fake backdrop. The sky was air, constantly moving atmosphere, the life-giving band of gasses that encircled the earth and made it the solar system's only inhabitable planet.

But the sky above this section of desert was just *wrong*.

David sat up.

He was spending too much time alone.

He got out of the bed and wandered around the room, checking the bathroom wastepaper basket for used condoms, looking through his dad's briefcase for incriminating information. He wondered what his parents were doing. As usual, his mom just said, "We're going out, don't wait up," as they left, and his dad chuckled as if that were the wittiest thing in the world and they hadn't all heard it three thousand times before. They'd left their bathing suits behind so they weren't at the pool, and neither of his parents were big on nature hikes, so that meant they were doing something here around the buildings of the resort—although he had no idea what that could be. They certainly weren't able to afford another champagne brunch, but David thought it quite possible that, whatever they were doing, drinking was somehow involved.

He opened the door of the suite and walked outside, thinking he might get some ice and chuck it at little kids if they happened to pass by or steal a room service breakfast if he saw it sitting outside someone's door. Anything to relieve the boredom. Down the corridor to the left, he saw a maid's cart piled high with towels, a canvas bag in the front filled with dirty linen, a bin on the side filled with trial-size shampoos, conditioners, bath gels and lotions. It was being pushed from behind, unoiled wheels squeaking loudly in the morning stillness, and stopped at the next door over.

The Latina maid who emerged from behind the cart with a clipboard was not Jennifer Lopez, but she was young and thin—two rarities in themselves—and there was something sexy about her, a dark doe-eyed sensuality at odds with the deliberately unflattering uniform the resort made her wear. She smiled at him—flirtatiously, David thought—and he smiled back. She looked away quickly, shyly, made a couple of marks on her clipboard and picked up a handful of clean linen from the cart.

The moment she stepped into the adjacent suite he backed up. Their room was next, and his mind sped through a whole host of fantasy scenarios, none of them even remotely feasible. Then he wondered what would happen if the maid caught him masturbating. She was definitely hot, and he imagined that she'd be shocked at first, then . . . maybe . . . interested. She might close the door behind her . . .

It was too much to hope for—but definitely worth a try. He switched the hanger on the doorknob from PRIVACY PLEASE to MAID

SERVICE, then quickly closed the door and ran across the floor, unbuckling his belt and kicking off his shoes. He lay down on the bed, pulled down his pants and immediately started pulling on his penis, hoping to get it long and hard quickly so that she'd see him at his peak. He wanted her to walk in and see him fully erect, stroking himself, thinking she might . . . what? Suck it? Sit on it?

Either.

Or both.

This was stupid, he told himself. This was crazy. But he didn't stop. He tried to imagine what the maid would look like with her top off. Did she have big nipples?

There was a knock at the door, then a pause. He quit stroking, afraid he would come too quickly. "Maid service!" the woman announced in a thick Spanish accent. He remained silent. There was another knock, then the rattle of a key in the lock. The door opened—

—and an overweight, middle-aged lady bustled into the room. She took one look at him lying there, erection in hand, then apologized quickly, her face turning red, and hurried out the way she had come.

David let go of himself, closing his eyes in embarrassment, grimacing as if in pain, and it was all he could do not to let out a raw cry of mortification. He had never felt so humiliated in his entire life. What the hell had he been thinking? What had come over him to make him do such a stupid, ridiculous thing? He tried to retrace the mental steps that had brought him to this point as he pulled up his pants, but the connections were lost, the reasoning no longer clear.

Though ordinarily he would have had to finish, his erection was gone, and he pulled up his underwear and pants. He saw his face in the mirror, and that made him even more embarrassed. What kind of loser doofus was he?

He wanted to get out of the room, *needed* to get out of the room, but he was afraid to open the door for fear that the fat maid would be outside. Or even the sexy maid. He imagined the older woman telling her young coworker about what she'd seen and the both of them laughing at him. He could not bear to face either, and now for the rest of the trip he would have to avoid all contact with the cleaning staff.

But someone still needed to come in here and make the bed. If they didn't, his parents would complain to the front desk and then maybe his *mom* would find out what happened.

This whole thing was just one big spiral of disgrace and mortification.

He had to find something to do. He peeked out the peephole of the door, looking for any sign of the maids or their carts and was gratified to see that the visible section of hallway was clear. Gathering his courage, he opened the door. The maid's cart was still parked in front of the next room over, and he quickly sped outside in the opposite direction, closing the door behind him and leaving the MAID SERVICE sign on the knob.

He hurried up the sidewalk, away from his building, away from any rooms where the maids might be working.

Curtis and Owen were supposed to be in Tucson until at least midafternoon—lucky fuckers—so he was on his own until then. Unless he could scare up that Brenda girl. She seemed to have the hots for Owen, but who's to say she wasn't bored and waiting around, too. Maybe the two of them could get together, have a little fun.

No, he couldn't screw a friend that way.

Besides, he shouldn't press his luck. His batting average with babes this morning wasn't exactly going to put him in the all-star league.

He ended up wandering the grounds of the resort and eventually found himself out by the driving range. He had never been to this part of The Reata before. It was behind the squat building housing the gym and exercise pool, and consisted of a long sloping lawn at least the length of a football field covered by netting supported by tall telephone poles. He saw several men lined up under a long shaded roof at the near end, hitting golf balls onto the preternaturally green grass. A high chain-link fence surrounded the area, the sign posted by the gate stating: NO ONE UNDER 18 ADMITTED.

To David, that was an invitation.

The gate was unmanned, its simple lock accessed by the key card for his room, and he walked inside unimpeded. Glancing toward the covered area where the golfers were teeing off, he saw that one of the men was his father. That was weird. His dad didn't golf. He couldn't afford it. But David sensed almost immediately that this was no ordinary game of golf, no typical practice session. Like the sky above the resort, there was something off here, something not quite right, and while he'd been planning to walk up to his father and find out what he was doing, David held off, stayed back, observing the scene. Wary of being caught by a security guard or spotted by one of the golfers, he kept to the side, moving along the edge of the fence until he was partially hidden from their view by a spiky, cactusy bush.

He examined the scene more carefully. At the far end of the driving range was a series of wooden poles arranged in a straight row across.

Tied to them were women.

One of them was his mom.

David's mouth suddenly felt dry. Was this some sort of game? If so, it was a sick one, and one he did not understand. He saw his father tee off, watched the ball sail through the air. It landed harmlessly on the grass in front of his mother, but the next was a line drive directly into her stomach, and she doubled forward as far as she could with the restraints, wincing in pain. The woman next to her was hit in the head, and there was a sudden gush of blood from the ensuing wound. No one made an effort to untie the woman or tend to her injury. Instead, another golf ball was hit at her, bouncing wildly off the post just above her head.

The woman tied to the far pole was struck on her left hand.

The next one over in her crotch.

None of the women made a sound, there were no screams or cries, no grunts of pain, and the men were silent, too. The only noise in the still, hot air was the thwack of club hitting ball and the sickening fleshy sound those balls made as they connected with their targets.

Confusion and fear. Those were the two emotions suddenly suffusing him, and for several moments he remained flat against the fence, too stunned to move, unable to comprehend what was happening. Then the golfer closest to him, a thin old man in goofy-ass shorts and a matching beret, glanced in his direction, and he thought it was all over. He froze, waiting to be found out, though he was not sure why the prospect should fill him with such dread, especially since his parents were here to protect him.

Protect him?

Yes.

From what?

He didn't know.

The golfer turned to face the green, having obviously not seen him, and David sneaked back behind the bushes, along the edge of the fence, and out the gate. As soon as he was clear, he hurried away, down the path he'd originally come, and did not slow down until the exercise facility was between him and the driving range.

He sat down on a bench in front of a Mexican-style fountain, his legs weak, sweating far more than he should have been. He wiped his forehead with his hand, wiped his hand on his pants. What was that all about? The only thing he could think of was that his parents were into S&M and got some kind of kinky thrill from the game. But while that covered all of the logical bases and explained both what he had seen and why, it didn't ring true. For one thing, there were a whole bunch of golfers there doing exactly the same thing. For another, his parents did not look like they were having fun. No one seemed particularly thrilled to be there, in fact. All of the golfers exhibited a pronounced lack of joy, and their victims were clearly in physical pain. It was more like work than play, as though they were cogs in a machine, performing a specific role or task they had been assigned, and the prevailing attitude was one of grim determination.

He sat there for several moments longer, until he was sweating from the heat rather than from fear and the shaking in his legs had stopped. He still had no idea what he'd just seen—and he wasn't sure he *wanted* to know.

Right now he simply wanted to get his ass safely back to their room where he could lock the door behind him.

He retraced his route and saw the young maid with her cart right outside their door. She was just leaving, having already made up the room, and was about to move on to the adjacent suite. He reddened with embarrassment as he thought about what he had done, and prayed that the fat old woman who'd seen him had not said a word.

The maid glanced up at the sound of his step. He tried to smile as he passed her.

She looked at him, met his eyes, placed her thumb and forefinger about an inch apart.

And laughed cruelly.

Seventeen

It fell from the ceiling while he was getting dressed, a spider as big as a golf ball, and Patrick almost screamed—

like a fairy

—but instead let out a short sharp gasp as it scuttled across the beige carpet and under the bed. He grabbed his shoes and socks, carrying them over to the vanity in the bathroom where he hastily finished buttoning his shirt before putting them on and then gamely trying to search for the creature. He used a rolled-up *Entertainment Weekly* to lift the edge of the bedspread, not wanting to get too close in case the spider was right there, but there was no sign of it. It had moved somewhere else, and that made Patrick uneasy. He'd kept his eye on the spot where it had scurried and it hadn't emerged either from there or from under the foot of the bed, which had been in his sight line as well. The head of the bed was against the wall, so that meant it had gotten out on the opposite side. He walked carefully around the bed and saw nothing in the middle of the floor, but it could have been under the nightstand, under the love seat or even in one of his open suitcases.

That last prospect filled him with fear.

He considered calling the lobby and asking for someone from maintenance to find the spider and kill it or at the very least spray the room for bugs, but he felt too embarrassed and didn't want to admit that he was afraid. He stood there for a moment, uncertain what to do, and finally decided to leave, go to the film festival, and just hope that it got out of the room through whatever crack or hole it had gotten in by the time he returned tonight.

He grabbed his keys and wallet from the top of the bathroom counter where he'd left them, took his briefcase from the closet, checking to make sure he had his tape recorder, notebook and several extra pens, and then turned to go.

It was standing in front of the door, facing him.

Staring at him.

Waiting for him.

Patrick instinctively stepped back. He looked from the spider to the door handle, then glanced frantically around the room. He was trapped in here and could not leave. Well, he *could* leave. But he was afraid to even try. The spider looked much bigger than it had on first sight. *Stop being such a pussy,* he told himself. He could tell, though, that if he attempted to stomp on the creature he would be able to feel it through his shoe, it was so large. The thought made him squirm. And there was no guarantee that he would even be able to kill the beast. This wasn't one of those hairy soft-looking spiders, like a tarantula; its body was shiny and hard, shell-like, and he imagined trying to crush it beneath his soft-soled sneakers and feeling it *move* beneath him, seeing its legs thrash frantically about as it tried to scuttle away, its solid form resisting all of his efforts to squash it.

Patrick backed away, goose bumps on his arm.

Then the spider jumped.

It did not jump far, less than a fourth of the distance between himself and the door, but it was far enough that it made him cry out—

like a fairy

—and stumble backward, almost tripping over his own feet. He kept his eyes glued to the monster, and it leaped again, sideways this time, though it remained facing him. He looked around for a weapon of some sort, something to hit it with. In three or four jumps it could be on him, and he wanted to be prepared.

Two leaps this time, both sideways—it was nearly to the armoire housing the television—and Patrick saw his opportunity. The path to the door was free; he could run over, get out and escape before the spider could even think about changing directions.

He dashed for the door.

There was an instant of panic as his sweaty hand slipped on the handle, but then the door was open and he was out. He stepped away, hoping against hope that the spider would try to follow him and get out of the room, but the door swung slowly shut on its tensioned hinges, trapping the creature inside. He stood there, thinking maybe he'd prop the door open for a few minutes and wait for it to emerge, but then he imagined it leaping at him as he opened the door, landing on his leg and scurrying up his body to his face, and decided against the idea.

It was already touch and go whether he'd make the first screening at the festival, but before taking off, Patrick took a quick detour to the lobby. The clerk behind the desk was the same unhelpful young woman who had been on duty last night when he'd come in to complain about the party next door—*how long were the shifts here?*—and she smiled at him perkily as he walked up. "How are you this morning, Mr. Schlaegel? Did you sleep well?"

He tried to appear as casual and nonchalant as possible. "Fine," he said. "But there seems to be a spider infestation in my room, room 215. Do you think you could send someone over to take care of it while I'm gone?"

"Certainly," she assured him. "All rooms are treated for insects and vermin after each guest leaves and before each new guest arrives, but I will make sure that someone inspects your room this morning just to make sure. Is there anything else I can do for you?" she asked brightly.

He had the feeling no such inspection would occur, and already he was dreading the return, knowing he would have to scour the entire room for spiders when he walked in—in the middle of the night no less. "No," he said. "That's it."

"Have a nice day," she told him.

He started for the front door and was stopped halfway there by a gorgeous blonde of approximately his own age who had the high cheekbones and regal bearing of a fashion model, but the open, friendly expression of an innocent teenager. "I know you!" she said. "I saw you on Roger Ebert's show!"

Patrick was flattered. He'd done an episode of *Roger Ebert and the Movies* after Gene Siskel died, before Richard Roeper came on board, when they were searching for Siskel's replacement. For six months, he'd been the hottest thing in pants to the single women of Chicago. He'd had no conception of how powerful a medium television was until after that broadcast, and it was a revelation. It had been a while since he'd been able to trade on that little bit of transitory fame, however, and this woman was a welcome reminder of those heady days. "Yes," he admitted. "I was on the show."

"I totally agreed with your review of *Death Instinct*! You were so right! I think you were the only person besides me who actually liked that movie! By the way, my name's Vicki. Well, Victoria, really, but everyone calls me Vicki."

"Patrick," he said. "Patrick Schlaegel. Nice to meet you."

"Oh, I'm so excited to meet you, Mr. Schlaegel!" She laughed. "Or can't you tell?"

"Patrick," he said. "Call me Patrick."

"Patrick. So why didn't Roger pick you? I thought you were great!"

It was a question he'd asked himself a million times, and he never had come up with a satisfying answer. "You got me," he admitted.

"I think it's because you were a threat. You were too good-looking for that show. I think they wanted more average-looking people, you know? So Roger wouldn't look bad."

He laughed. "It's a theory."

"So do you still review movies?"

"That's my job," he said. "It's why I'm here, in fact. I'm covering the Tucson International Film Festival." He looked at his watch. "To be honest, I should be there right now. I'm already late for the first briefing."

"Oh. I was hoping we could talk." Vicki appeared genuinely disappointed. She looked around. "Wait here a minute, will you?" She hurried over to the front desk and returned with a pen and a postcard of The Reata. Holding the postcard flat on her palm, she started writing. "Here's my name and room number," she said. "Call me when you get back. Or come and meet us at the pool. I'm here with two of my friends, and we're going to the hotel restaurant tonight for drinks and dinner. About eightish. We'll be there until probably midnight. I'd love for you to join us. I'm sure they'd be thrilled too."

He took the postcard, dropped it into his briefcase. "I'd like that," he said.

She smiled, holding out her hand for him to shake. "Until then."

He shook her hand, nodded good-bye and started across the lobby. One of the two employees—*doormen?*—who seemed to be permanently and pointlessly stationed next to the entrance opened the door for him, and he stepped out into the blinding sunlight, pausing for a moment to put on his sunglasses.

"Hey."

Patrick looked up to see a young man of approximately his own age, with hair and a wardrobe that bespoke urban sophistication, striding toward him across the earth-toned walkway.

"Are you Mr. Schlaegel?"

"Yes," Patrick said warily.

"I'm sorry I didn't catch up with you sooner. It looks like you're ready to take off. I'm The Reata's activities coordinator, and I'm in charge of recruiting players for our volleyball tournament this afternoon, a little shindig we sponsor for the benefit of our guests. Helps to break the ice. Lets everyone get introduced to each other and, at the same time, have a little fun."

"Sounds great," Patrick told him, "but I really have to go. I'm late as it is . . ."

The man didn't seem to hear. "The thing is, we'd also like to have some real sport, keep this thing competitive, for the sake of the onlookers, if nothing else. As you've probably noticed," he confided, "The Reata's summer crowd is not exactly the pick of the litter, athletically speaking. You look like you can handle yourself, though. That's why I was hoping you could join one of our volleyball teams, help bring up our game quality."

"Uh—" Patrick started to say.

"The other two teams are full, but they still need a few warm bodies on the Coyotes. What do you say?"

Patrick shook his head. "I'm really sorry. I'll be in Tucson all day at a film festival. I'd like to, but I can't get out of it."

The expression darkened on the activities coordinator's face. "We were hoping for full participation from our single male guests."

"Sorry."

There was a pause, one just long enough to become awkward, and then the other man was smiling. "Maybe tomorrow," he said. "We have some games planned for tomorrow, too."

"Maybe," Patrick said, remembering that odd, dark expression and not wanting to hasten its return. There was about the activities coordinator a sense of danger and instability, as though the amicable young professional act was just that, an act, a façade hiding the rage-filled lunatic beneath.

How did the man know he was single? Patrick wondered.

He didn't want to be here, didn't want to be anywhere near the activities coordinator, and, besides, he really did have to get going, so before the other man could say a word, Patrick started walking toward the parking lot. He held up a hand. "Later."

He braced himself for a follow-up objection that never came and strode gratefully across the already hot asphalt between the SUVs and yuppie-mobiles to his cheapo rental car. Three minutes later, he was speeding down that awful rutted road through the desert, The Reata in his rearview mirror.

That asshole Townsend had really done a number on him this time, and he thought about how he would get back at the editor. Something this egregious demanded retribution. The Reata wasn't just a boring, off-the-map loser magnet out in the middle of nowhere. It was . . .

Spooky.

Yes. A childish word, a stupid word, but he was man enough to admit that the place weirded him out. His tire hit a particularly nasty pothole, and he glanced back at the gate and guardhouse before both disappeared behind the curve of a hillside. He thought of the angry face of the activities coordinator, the spider in his room, the party last night that supposedly didn't happen, the wolf and snakes he'd met on the path, the angry people at the pool. If he had any sense, he'd just book a room for the night at someplace in Tucson and never return.

But he had to come back.

All of his luggage was still in his room.

And, besides, he wanted to see Vicki.

He had the feeling he might get lucky tonight.

Eighteen

This time, Rachel not only heard but saw something.

It was after the chef's cooking demo. She had struck up a conversation with Laurie Mitchell, a surprisingly down-to-earth corporate executive from San Francisco. Laurie was leaving today, but before she returned home, she wanted to buy a present for her brother's new stepson. Her brother had recently gotten married to a health food store cashier with advanced degrees in philosophy and cultural anthropology, and a twelve-year-old son from a previous relationship. The boy was wild, the mother a flake, and as the kid's stepaunt, Laurie had taken it upon herself to try to be a good influence, to provide a little bit of grounding and normalcy in his tempestuous life. She'd seen a T-shirt in the gift shop that she thought she might buy him as a present and wanted Rachel's opinion on it, since Rachel had three teenage boys. So after they finished watching the demo and eating the soup and salad, they walked up to the lobby.

"Did that sex soup work for you?" Laurie asked as they headed across the flagstone patio.

Rachel laughed. "No," she admitted.

"Me either. I don't feel a thing."

They went inside and passed through the lobby to the gift shop. Laurie showed her the rack full of T-shirts, and Rachel immediately vetoed the yellow one with The Reata's logo and the red one with a striped kachina doll over the word "Hano." She suggested a black T-shirt with a picture of a skeleton rotting into the desert sand next to a barrel cactus and a wooden sign reading WELCOME TO ARIZONA.

Laurie bought it.

Afterward, Laurie had to go to the bathroom, and Rachel accompanied her, feeling an uncomfortable sense of déjà vu as they approached the restroom. She remained on edge throughout their visit, although nothing unusual occurred while they were there.

They were walking back down the corridor to the lobby when it happened.

From around the far corner emerged two men who appeared to be in the throes of a struggle—although the struggle was very one-sided. For a brief moment, Rachel thought the aggressor was the manager she and Lowell had run into yesterday at almost this very spot. It was not the manager, however, but someone who looked very much like him—bearded, portly, well-dressed—and he was dragging a young man down the hallway with him. The young man was wearing a Reata uniform and appeared to be one of the cabana bar waiters. He was crying desperately, unashamedly, his red face wet with tears and snot, begging for leniency, imploring the other man not to punish him. But his bearded antagonist showed no sympathy. The portly man's fingers were digging deep into his underling's arm, and he was yanking the waiter down the corridor with a series of harsh jerks. "Time to pay the piper," he growled, elbowing the waiter in the gut so hard that the cries turned into gasps.

Rachel ducked behind a lodgepole pine pillar designed to look like a totem pole, not wanting to see this, knowing she wasn't supposed to see this, not sure she was *allowed* to see this. Laurie was confused, but she followed Rachel's example, and the two of them watched as the men passed by. Part of her wanted to jump out and confront the bully, call him on his reprehensible behavior and unjustifiable actions. This was no way to treat even the world's worst employee. But Rachel recalled the terrified cries of the girl through the wall and that final sickening thud, and she was afraid to confront the man, afraid of what might happen if he even knew she was a witness to this.

A few feet past them, the two men stopped. Like a child hiding from her parents, Rachel moved around the pillar in an effort to remain undetected, Laurie moving with her. Peeking around the side of the column, she saw that the bearded man was still holding the beaten waiter with one hand and using the other to unlock a door with a key. The door opened, and for a brief second she saw inside. There was no office furniture, no wall hangings, no windows, only a room, its walls and floor and ceiling painted red, with a rusted metal cage in the middle approximately the size of a refrigerator box. Then the waiter was shoved through the doorway with the order, "Get in there!"

"No!" the young man screamed, as primal a cry of anguish and terror as Rachel had ever heard.

And the heavy door slammed shut, cutting off all sound.

The corridor was quiet.

At the far end of the hallway, two guests, a man and a woman, strolled casually around the corner, oblivious to what had just occurred.

Rachel's heart was pounding crazily and she was breathing audibly through her mouth. Someone had to do something! A man was being tortured in there. She looked wildly back toward the lobby, but knew that she could say nothing to anyone there. This wasn't an isolated incident or the actions of a rogue sadist. The resort's management knew about this. They either looked the other way or it was part of their policy.

She could call the police or sheriff's department, but by the time they arrived at this godforsaken location from wherever they were, the crime would have been committed and all trace of it covered up.

In a movie, she would rush forward, fling open the door, expose the dastardly deeds to the light of day and order the couple walking arm in arm down the hall to get some help. They'd rally the guests and the other employees, and the bearded man and any of his accomplices would be apprehended, awaiting the arrival of law enforcement. But this wasn't a movie, and all she could do was stare at the closed door, taunted by the fake silence, and try not to hyperventilate.

"Did you see that?" Rachel asked, barely able to speak.

"I can't believe it." Laurie did not seem nearly as shocked, exhibiting only a mild intellectual outrage miles removed from Rachel's gut-level emotional response, and Rachel recalled that the other woman had not been shocked by the chef's shaved desert rat diorama, either. Looking into Laurie's eyes, she saw a deadened expression that for some reason made her think of the emotional numbness produced by *Brave New World*'s *soma*.

Rachel looked down the wide hallway at the unmarked doors between the clearly marked banquet rooms and wondered what was going on behind their soundproofed façades. She imagined dozens of men who looked like the manager sadistically torturing low-level employees who had reported to work a few minutes late or accidentally committed some minor error. She tried to remember the face of the waiter so she would be able to spot him if she saw him again by the pool, but his features were a blur in her mind. What she remembered most were the fingers digging into his flesh, his whimpering cries of terror.

The first thing they had to do was get out of here.

"Let's go," Rachel said, moving out from behind the column. Laurie followed her as though there was nothing unusual about two grown women hiding in back of a totem pole pillar in an expensive resort in the middle of the day. The two of them headed back toward the lobby.

"Well, thanks for your help picking out Fredrich's T-shirt," Laurie said with a wave as she walked over to the front desk. "I'm going to sort out my bill since I'm here. It was nice meeting you."

Rachel was stunned. She'd expected that at least some of the indignation from the abuse they'd witnessed to remain; she hadn't thought all trace of it would be wiped immediately from Laurie's mind. But apparently it had. She felt some of her own outrage unaccountably dissipating, and though she vowed to hold on to it, by the time she walked back to the room to meet Lowell for lunch, the anger and fear she'd felt had faded and was gone.

Nineteen

It was early afternoon, the hottest part of the day, and though they'd told their parents they'd be spending the next couple of hours before the volleyball tournament in David's room with a PlayStation, they decided instead to hike up the Antelope Canyon trail and check out the hot springs.

Surprisingly, the hike was Ryan's idea. They were lounging around, trying to come up with something they could do—after two days even a resort this nice was starting to feel claustrophobic—when Ryan reminded them about the tour they'd taken when they first arrived. "Weren't there supposed to be hiking trails?" he asked.

Owen thought there was something a little too innocent about the way his brother asked. He'd known Ryan since birth, and that sort of casual purity just wasn't in the boy's playbook. But he had to admit, the idea had merit. Their mom had given them explicit instructions that they were to stay out of direct sunlight in this, the hottest part of the day, and they'd been chafing under those restrictions as they contemplated what to do. Ryan's suggestion was out of the box. Besides, if they got caught, they could always blame it on him.

Curtis clapped Ryan on the back—a little too hard, making his brother wince—and announced, "Pack up some Cokes, boys. We're heading out."

Brenda came with them.

They met her outside the gate of the tennis courts, where she'd apparently been playing with her father. Although only a junior, she was on the varsity tennis team, she said, and her dad wanted her to keep practicing even on vacation.

She was hot and sweaty and to Owen looked absolutely gorgeous. "Where's your racket?" he asked.

"My dad's taking it back. Do you like tennis?"

"I like Anna Kournikova," Curtis offered.

"Highly overrated," Brenda said earnestly. "She's never even won a major tournament."

"We don't watch tennis," Ryan announced.

"But I like to play," Owen added quickly. She smiled at him, and he stared down at his shoes, reddening. "Although I'm probably not in your league."

"We could still volley. It would be fun."

It *would* be fun, and he imagined the two of them hitting the ball back and forth over the net for a while, then her coming over to his side to give him some pointers, standing behind him, her hands over his on the racket, her body pressed tightly against him, breasts flattened against his back. His snake was sneaking out through the elastic legband of his underwear, and he moved his hand to cover it, mashing the cold Coke can against his growing erection to keep it down. He wanted to suggest that the two of them stay behind and play while the others went hiking, but she was probably tired of it, and, besides, her dad was here.

Brenda tapped his shoulder lightly, playfully, then her hand slid down and held his as if it were the most natural thing in the world. Their fingers intertwined comfortably, and he gave her hand a soft small squeeze, gratified to feel one in return.

He had never felt this way about a girl before. Of course, no girl had ever shown this much interest in him before, so part of it was opportunity, but there seemed to be a real connection between them, a deep instant bonding that went beyond mere physical attraction, and it made him feel stupid and smart and happy and expansive and reserved all at the same time. He wanted everyone to see them together and wanted no one to see them, wanted it to be a private affair just between the two of them.

Curtis *had* seen, however, and it seemed to make him annoyed. "Are we going to stand here all damn day?" he asked. "Let's get going."

They followed the gravel path around the tennis courts and the periphery of the outlying buildings, along the edge of the rocky bluff until they came to a breach in the low mountain range. The pathway split, the left fork circling back to the resort, the right winding into the mountains. ANTELOPE CANYON TRAIL 500 YARDS, a small sign announced.

They took the right fork.

After passing over a dry wash and up a slight slope between some giant cactuses, they reached the trailhead. They'd been walking non-stop for the past ten minutes, but they paused for a second at the beginning of the trail, all of them experiencing a sort of collective hesitation. There were two weathered posts to either side of the dirt track. On one of them was a new white-on-reflective-green metal sign: PLEASE STAY ON THE PATH. On the other was a wood and plastic box stuffed with trail guides.

Owen looked at the sign.

PLEASE STAY ON THE PATH.

It seemed more warning than request, he thought. In fact, it sounded almost like a religious message, and he found that a little creepy. He was starting to get the same feeling about this as he had about the exercise pool and that section of the big pool by the waterfall where he and Curtis had seen the body: a fearful apprehension.

Then they were walking, Brenda now in the lead, towing him along while the others followed. He barely had time to think his thoughts let alone articulate them, before they were tramping up the path toward a narrow gorge that looked like one of those places where novice hikers were washed away in flash floods.

"Cool," Ryan said, but it was the only word spoken by any of them. Although they weren't exactly climbing up the cliff, the path was on an incline, and the combination of increasing heat and altitude left them sweaty and winded. They passed through the constricted ravine, which, although twisting, was much shorter than Owen had thought, maybe half the length of a football field. Then the sides of the two cliffs separated, stretching out, and the path wound through an increasingly wide canyon, the rocky mountainsides sloping upward at a gentle angle, the sandy bottom home to an oasis of green bushes and tall trees.

"Pretty bitchin'," Owen admitted.

David had been unusually quiet since they'd met him after lunch, and for no reason, he suddenly blurted out, "I think there's something wrong with my parents."

They stopped walking.

"They're not normal."

No duh, Owen was tempted to say, but instead met Curtis's quizzical eyes with a confused shrug.

"Why?" Curtis asked.

"I saw something. Back at the resort. They have this golf course, not eighteen holes, but one of those places where you practice hitting the ball—"

"A driving range," Brenda offered.

"Yeah. Anyway, there's a sign that no one under eighteen can be admitted, but I snuck in anyway. My dad was playing golf and . . ." He shook his head. "You wouldn't believe it."

"What?" Curtis prodded.

"It sounds crazy . . ."

"What?" Owen and Curtis shouted in unison.

"There were women tied up at the other end of the lawn, to poles, and the men were trying to nail them with golf balls. One of them was my mom. I know this sounds like I made it up, but I watched while my dad whacked a ball and it hit her in the stomach. She just sort of . . . slumped forward or crouched over a little, like she'd been punched. But she couldn't fall down or move out of the way or anything because she was tied to the stake. Her face was all scrunched up in pain, but she didn't cry or make any noise. It was like she couldn't, like it wasn't allowed, like it wasn't part of the game and she'd lose or be disqualified or something if she did." David's voice had grown lower, more grim, and the rest of them were completely silent, stunned.

"The woman next to her was hit in the head," he said quietly. "There was a lot of blood."

Owen wanted to say something, but he didn't know what. He tried to imagine how he would feel if he'd seen something like that with his own parents but couldn't, it was just too alien.

"*Was* it a game?" Curtis asked.

"I don't know. I didn't stick around to find out." A pause. "There's something wrong with The Reata," David said.

Owen looked at Curtis and before he could even gauge the expression on his brother's face, jumped in. "There really was a body at the bottom of the pool. We saw it."

David was still.

"It looked like a stain or something after you told us that, but at first there was definitely something there. A ghost maybe."

Curtis remained silent.

David let out a long-held breath. "I thought I saw it, too," he admitted. "But then it was gone, and I figured it was an optical illusion, so I decided to try and freak you guys."

"What are you *talking* about?" Brenda looked at them as if they were all crazy.

"There are ghosts here," Ryan said matter-of-factly.

Brenda ran an exasperated hand through her hair. "This is the stupidest, most ridiculous thing I ever heard. Did I hike up here with the special class? Come on, people! Our families are staying at like, one of the best resorts in the country. Millionaires, *billionaires,* spend their winters here. I don't know about your rooms, but ours is amazing. And that pool? These hiking trails? All of that other stuff? I don't know where you got these kindergarten ideas, but, trust me, there are no dead bodies floating in the water. There aren't any ghosts, either. Or aliens. Or vampires." She looked at David. "And, no offense, but just because you saw a golf accident doesn't mean people have suddenly gone crazy and are now trying to kill each other with sporting goods." She appealed to Owen. "You don't actually believe this, do you?"

It did seem kind of stupid when you looked at it, and Owen felt embarrassed by his own gullibility and willingness to leap to conclusions. He glanced over at Curtis, who was staring at his shoes, red-faced.

"I know what I saw," David said quietly, but even his voice didn't have the same level of conviction.

Only Ryan held firm. "There *are* ghosts," he insisted. "And they're here."

Brenda smiled at him as though he were a baby. "There's no such thing as ghosts. I'll be honest, I wouldn't come walking down this trail in the middle of the night. But I sure don't think bodies are floating in a pool that dozens of people swim in every day and that's cleaned and inspected each morning. And I don't think golfers are going postal and attacking people for no reason whatsoever."

"The body wasn't floating," Owen felt obligated to point out. "It was lying at the bottom."

She looked at him, and he felt like the world's biggest dummy.

"Just drop it," Curtis suggested. "Everyone's hot and cranky, and we sure as hell aren't going to settle this here. Let's just keep walking."

"Why don't we just head back," David said, desultorily pulling on his earring.

They glanced up ahead to see if it was worth continuing on. Owen saw only more mountains, more trees and brush, more hot sun. He was about to suggest that they turn around when Curtis pointed. "Check it out." Off the trail to the right, atop a small rise, was what appeared to be an old buckboard wagon, half-buried in the sand.

Please stay on the path.

Curtis stepped unhesitatingly over the line of rocks that marked the border of the trail and started across the open ground. David and Ryan followed eagerly. Owen and Brenda remained behind for a few extra seconds, then hand in hand the two of them trudged along after. Brenda obviously did not want to go, there was resistance in the tension of her muscles, but she said nothing.

The five of them stood before the downed wagon, its wood cracked and splintered from exposure to the elements, its yoke and a corner of the driver's seat buried in the sand, broken wheels lying flattened and spoke-shattered nearby. The back of the buckboard was filled with old animal bones and the rotted remnants of burlap bags. Owen wasn't a nature boy or an animal expert by any means, but he thought he recognized among the yellowed bones a cow skull, a horse skull, and the skull of the canyon's namesake, an antelope.

The sight was odd and disconcerting, but it was what lay just beyond the small rise that had suddenly captured their attention.

"Look," Ryan said. "Indian ruins."

Only they weren't Indian ruins. Owen could see that immediately. They were ruins all right: extant sections of wall not more than a foot high that clearly delineated the floor plan of a rather large building, with a smaller roofless but otherwise intact structure built at an angle to its counterpart. But they were cement, not adobe, had traces of light blue paint on their exteriors, and resembled nothing so much as those abandoned commercial buildings they'd seen in dying towns like Wenden and Dry River that they'd passed through on their way over from California.

"It's a ghost town," Ryan said, and Owen could hear the excitement in his voice.

But that didn't seem right, either. The site before them was too small to be a town, and what it reminded Owen of more than anything else was a hotel.

Yes, he realized, that was exactly what it was.

He let go of Brenda's hand and, with his brothers, walked around the downed wagon, feeling chilled but not knowing why. They walked over the barren sand. Sure enough, he was able to make out the walls and doorways of individual sleeping quarters as they approached. The structure still standing appeared to be the hotel's restaurant.

They reached the ruins.

There were more buildings than he'd originally thought. Or at least there *had* been more buildings. To the right, Owen saw the remnants of a wooden structure that had probably been a barn, and a forsaken pile of wreckage that had clearly been furniture before the sun and wind and rain had gotten hold of it. A second set of ruined rooms ran parallel to the first, and between the two blocks was an empty cement pool remarkably devoid of debris.

It made no sense. The Reata had been around since its dude ranch days in the 1920s. He'd seen the photos of old cowboys in the lobby.

So why would there be *another* hotel on the grounds? An abandoned one? Unless . . .

Unless it had been the original resort.

It was the only answer, and for a brief moment he was satisfied, his mind set at ease by the explanation. But then he started wondering, if that was the case, why The Reata was no longer at this location, why the resort had moved out of the canyon instead of rebuilding on the same spot. And why the existence of this deserted hotel had been so effectively hushed up. There was a story here, though he was not sure he wanted to hear it.

Please stay on the path.

The words on the sign now seemed more like an order, an attempt to keep people away and make sure that the existence of this place remained a secret.

They walked slowly through the rubble, stepping over rusted scraps of ancient metal and half-buried pieces of dull purple glass, using broken chunks of concrete like stepping stones. David picked up a sheared length of rebar and flung it against a section of standing wall where it bounced off with an echoing metallic pling that sounded far too loud.

Brenda was still back at the edge of the site, but the boys traipsed through four of the circumscribed squares that had been rooms, reaching the empty pool at almost exactly the same time.

Where they stopped.

Around the pool were makeshift crosses, the kind people put up on the sides of highways to mark the spot of a loved one's fatal accident. But these bore no flowers, and the wood was bare and peeling as though the crosses had not been touched for decades. The effect was not one of respect for the departed but a warning to any who might come across this site.

On the cracked faded cement were the rusted skeletons of lounge chairs.

None of them spoke for a moment. The atmosphere of this place was one of overwhelming solemnity, as though it was the location of some great past tragedy. A massacre, perhaps. Or a natural disaster that had killed scores of innocent people.

There was something else, as well. A sense that everything was off-kilter and slightly strange, like one of those amusement park haunted houses where tilted sidewalks and skewed perspectives created a creepy atmosphere that made even ordinary objects seem weird and unreliable.

He looked at David. David looked at Curtis. Curtis looked at Ryan.

"What is it?" Brenda called from behind them, and that broke the spell.

"Swimming pool!" David said simply, which was true enough but not the half of it.

Owen turned around. "Why don't you—"

"I'm coming!" she announced, leaping over rocks and debris, running around the side of the ruined buildings to meet them.

Owen turned his attention back to the pool. At one time, he supposed, rich carefree people from the East had swum here happily, but that was hard to imagine now. He had never encountered someplace that gave off such an aura of malignity, and he found it difficult to believe that the character of this spot had ever been any different. A new image appeared to him: rich, debauched people engaging in orgies and bloody rituals out here in the desert, far away from the prying eyes of civilized society.

That seemed more believable.

They walked around, exploring, but there was a tentativeness to their investigation, as though they were all looking for something but afraid of finding it.

"Check this out!" Curtis said.

Owen walked over to where his brother was standing. On the right side of the empty pool was a narrow trench with stairs leading to the bottom. They could see from here that it housed a large picture window through which viewers could watch swimmers. The glass was gone, of course, only a few tiny dirty shards remaining in the frame, but like the pool, the trench was surprisingly free of dirt or sand or leaves or windblown rubbish. David started down the concrete steps, and the rest of them followed, one by one.

"I'll stay up here," Brenda said. "Just in case."

Owen looked around. It was slightly wider here at the bottom, and at one time he supposed there had been chairs.

David peeked through the glassless window at the empty pool. "What was this for? To check out babes?"

Curtis shrugged. "I guess."

"It smells like piss down here," David said.

But it didn't smell like piss. It smelled like something else, something none of them wanted to acknowledge.

Death.

There was a crayon drawing on the wall opposite the window, graffiti but remarkably well executed. It was a life-sized rendering of a very old man with long scraggly hair and a skeletal face that seemed at once sad and scary, the portrait of a man so old that he had outlived his humanity. The drawing frightened Owen, and he quickly looked away. If Brenda hadn't been here, he would have mentioned the drawing, brought it up and shown it to the others, talked about how scary it was, but he didn't want to look like a pussy in front of her and didn't want her to think he was any more of an idiot than she already did.

They shouldn't have come here, he thought. They should have obeyed the signs. They should have stayed on the path.

David was already leading the way back up the steps, and with one last fearful look at the crayon portrait, Owen followed.

His ESP wasn't working today, but Ryan was not worried. He'd read enough about psychic phenomena to know that it wasn't as constant or reliable as the traditional five senses, that it had its own timetable and could not be hurried or forced or conjured at will.

Besides, a person didn't need ESP to pick up the vibes off this place.

It was haunted.

They all knew it, though the word itself remained unspoken. They'd had no problem debating ghosts a few moments ago when talking about The Reata, but there'd been physical distance between themselves and the resort, and of course those opinions were subject to interpretation. There could be no doubt while standing amid the ruins of this old hotel, however, that here was a place that was truly and genuinely haunted. Malevolence fairly oozed from the rubble of the old buildings, seeped upward from the ground they walked on, and though the temperature had to be over a hundred, he had goose bumps—and he hadn't noticed anybody else sweating either.

Why, though? What was the cause?

Ryan thought about what David had said about his parents, how there was something wrong with them. He'd been scared by David's golf course story but excited at the same time, and he thought now that it might hold the key. He remembered reading about the Lost Dutchman Gold Mine and how it was located in mountains with high magnetic content and how that affected the brains of all those treasure hunters seeking the gold, making them crazy. They ended up shooting each other and seeing mirages and behaving in all sorts of bizarre ways. The Lost Dutchman was in Arizona, too. Maybe there were a whole bunch of spots like that throughout the state.

That would explain David's parents' behavior, and a lot of other odd things he'd seen people do since they came here.

He wished he'd brought his notebook so he could write all this down before he forgot.

Who was he kidding? He wouldn't forget.

On the other hand . . . maybe he would. If his brain was being bombarded by those magnetic rays, too, it was only logical to think that his memory would be tainted.

Excitement once again took over from fear. He wished he'd brought a compass so he could check out the existence of those magnetic fields for himself and see if that's indeed what was happening. He would have to do some more investigating. Recalling the spooky scenes he'd experienced at the exercise pool, he realized that those could have been either hallucinations caused by exposure to magnetic fields *or* a legitimate psychic experience. He wasn't ruling anything out at this point.

Ryan grinned to himself as he looked down at the empty pool. His book was going to be so good.

They had all split up and were exploring the ruins separately. Well, Owen and Brenda were together, but the rest of them had branched out on their own. That was weird, Ryan thought. Owen had never exactly been a lady-killer, and Brenda was definitely a hottie. What did she see in him? Why wasn't she interested in David, who was older and considerably cooler? Why wasn't she hanging out with those other jocks on the tennis courts?

Something seemed off about that.

Ryan walked slowly around the pool, past the weathered crosses and broken lawn furniture. His brothers were poking through the remnants of individual rooms while David checked out the vestiges of what had been a barn or stable. Ryan's eye was caught by that one standing roofless building, the restaurant, and he made his way through the wreckage to its rubble-strewn entrance. The first thing he noticed when he walked inside was The Reata's logo—a setting sun behind a geometric saguaro cactus—painted onto the side of a counter, the paint faded and peeling but still visible.

The next thing he saw was the mirror.

It was on the wall to his left, or at least a part of it was; the rest lay shattered on the floor beneath. He wasn't sure why his eye was drawn to the silvery object, but it was, and even before he looked into the glass, he knew there was something wrong with it. The shape and angle of the remaining section of mirror was oddly disturbing, but it was what was *in* the mirror that frightened him. For the scene reflected back was not the empty shell of a building in which he stood, was not even the restaurant in its heyday. The room in the broken glass was a dark, expensive-looking chamber with deep red carpet and trophy heads on the wall. In the center of the room, on a thronelike chair, was an old, old man, so skinny that he looked like a skeleton, dressed in fancy clothes that made Ryan think of a cowboy tuxedo. Long, thinning gray hair hung down to the man's shoulders, and his cold dead eyes belied the inappropriately wide smile on his toothless mouth.

The freaky thing was that, despite all this, the mirror still worked; Ryan could see himself in it, superimposed over that ghoulish scene. It looked like he was in that dark room himself, standing in front of the cadaverous man.

He wanted to call his brothers or David, have them check it out and see if they saw the same thing, but at that moment the last segment of mirror wobbled and fell, crashing to the floor. There was no reason for it, no vibration or wind or movement in the room, and he couldn't help thinking that the destruction was somehow intentional.

In several shards on the floor, he thought he saw dark flickering movement.

Quickly, he backtracked and got out of the building.

The others were close by, their individual efforts having led them here to what had been the front of the old hotel. "Find anything?" he asked, and his voice sounded loud even to himself. He realized that it was the first time in quite a while that any of them had spoken. The atmosphere of this place was not exactly conducive to conversation.

"No," David said. "You?"

He wanted to tell them about the mirror, but it didn't seem right to do so here. No, that wasn't the truth. It didn't seem *safe* to do so here. He shook his head. "No."

There was a shadow on the far opposite side of the canyon, a silhouette of the western mountain superimposed imperfectly on the eastern cliffs. They all seemed to notice it at the same time, as though it had suddenly appeared full-blown rather than grown incrementally.

"Anybody have a watch?" Curtis asked, and Ryan thought he heard a trace of fear in his older brother's voice.

A watch! Why hadn't he thought of that? He looked from face to face, hoping that someone had a timepiece and that it had stopped as a result of the magnetic energy, but no one did have a watch, so not only didn't they know what time it was, but he could not test his theory.

"We'd better get back," Curtis said. "We're supposed to be at Dad's volleyball game." He glanced over at David. "Is your dad playing?"

David smiled wryly. "Yeah. He's going to be whaling it at my mom."

Curtis laughed uneasily.

"What about you?" Owen asked Brenda.

She shook her head. "Tennis is our game."

"Well, you can come with us."

"No, I can't make it," she said. "I'm supposed to write postcards with my mom this afternoon."

"That takes all of ten minutes."

"You don't know my mom." Holding Owen's hand, she started walking back toward the bone-filled wagon and the trail beyond. The rest of them fell in behind. "So what about the 'dive-in movie'? Are you guys going to be there tonight?"

"What are they showing?" Curtis asked.

"Does it matter? Some kid's movie. *Finding Nemo* or something."

"I'll be there," Owen promised.

"Mom won't let us out at night," Ryan said, though the prospect of having access to the nocturnal world of the resort filled him with excitement.

"Where'd you get this 'us'?" Owen asked.

"If you don't let me come, I'll tell." He didn't know what exactly he would tell on, the trip to the abandoned resort or the lovey-dovey stuff with Brenda, but the threat obviously carried weight.

"I was just joking," Owen lied.

They passed the buckboard, finally reached the path. Ryan looked back. He could see the wagon at the top of the small rise, but the ruins of the hotel were hidden from this angle. The whole thing seemed like a dream, not like something that had actually happened, and as they started walking back in silence, none of them mentioning what they had just seen, he found himself wondering if there was some way that he could determine the magnetic content of these mountains.

Twenty

They lost in the first round of tournament play, and it was Lowell's fault. He was the one who, as point man on defense, failed to stop a series of spikes when crunch time came, and although everyone else had failed to return the balls as well, fumbling around and splashing in the water like spastic Jerry Lewises, they had not been expected to hold the tide. He was the one charged with providing a real defense, and he'd promised that he could do it. They'd been pretty successful with offense, racking up quite a few points despite the Coyotes' obvious advantage in athletic ability, but they crumbled before the Coyotes' scoring onslaught, and blame for that rested squarely with him.

They'd spent most of the morning practicing, with only an hour break for lunch, and there was a tinge of desperation in their efforts, a need to succeed far beyond the bounds of what this supposedly easygoing competition warranted. Lowell could recognize it, but he fell prey to it, too, and he found himself getting far angrier at both himself and other players for minor mistakes and inadvertent errors than he otherwise would have. It was as if their very lives depended on the outcome of this game, and while he didn't know where or how this attitude originated, he succumbed to it just as much as anyone else.

They lost the match 24 to 20, a much closer score than any of them had expected given the drubbing they'd taken during the last half, and though he blamed himself for the loss, it was clear that his teammates did not. They all congratulated him on a game well-played, and he perpetuated the fiction by praising them as well. Separating to sit with their individual families on the plastic chairs that had been temporarily set up around the perimeter of the pool, they remained to watch the matchup of the Coyotes and the Roadrunners, and as Lowell observed the game from the sidelines, he found himself feeling grateful that their team had not survived to play. They would have been eaten alive. The Coyotes were athletic but the

Roadrunners were *aggressive*. They purposely drove the heavy volleyball into faces and stomachs, yelled taunts and curses and threats at their opponents, splashed and pushed those players closest to the net. Blodgett, the captain, was the worst offender. As Rand Black had said, and as he'd already known, Blodgett was a bully, a big man used to throwing his weight around both literally and metaphorically. He did indeed look as though he could have been a linebacker, and even when smiling his face possessed an expression of arrogant intolerance.

He has a pair of Rachel's panties, was the only thing Lowell could think of as he watched the man, and more than anything else he hoped that someone nailed that asshole in the face with the ball and gave him a bloody nose.

One Coyote actually did spike the ball past Blodgett's head—a pleasant-looking middle-aged man with a track team physique whom Lowell had served against—and Blodgett went crazy, lunging at the man, bellowing like a wounded bull. He hit the net, nearly knocking it over, but the activities coordinator, acting as referee, declined to call him on anything. As he had throughout the tournament, the activities coordinator—

Rockne. The Reata. One hundred years.

—sat on a raised lifeguard's chair in front of the cabana, watching the match with a detached and slightly amused smile, doing absolutely nothing. There was something different about the man this afternoon, Lowell thought. He seemed slightly less jockish than he had initially. But only for brief sections of time. Lowell would watch him, and he'd suddenly seem older, more formal. But then he'd seem younger, more casual, more relaxed. And then he'd be back to his old coachlike self again. It was as if he were a diamond or a hologram, showing different facets and different sides depending upon the angle from which he was viewed.

Blodgett's teammates and their bullying tactics carried the day, unchecked and tacitly endorsed by The Reata's representative, and to no one's surprise, the Roadrunners demolished their competition. Lowell stood with his family on the sidelines next to Rand Black and his wife and watched as the triumphant team cavorted in the water, high-fiving each other. Ironic, he thought. He'd avoided his own reunion only to be thrust into an artificial world with the same hierarchal structure as high school. The Roadrunners were the jocks, the Coyotes were the regular kids and his team, the Cactus Wrens, were the nerds.

Aside from the Roadrunners, no one really seemed to have enjoyed the volleyball games. Not the other players, all of whom, like Lowell, seemed to be participating out of obligation, and not the onlookers, who, judging from overheard conversations, were only waiting for the tournament to end so they could go back into the pool and continue swimming. He didn't know why The Reata would sponsor such an event if no one got any fun out of it, but he had a sneaking suspicion that this result had been known ahead of time and was intentional.

The Roadrunners' victory still did not put an end to the proceedings. Rockne got down from his lifeguard's chair and procured a plain brown box from the snack bar. "It's time for the awards ceremony!" he announced. There were groans from people waiting to get back in the pool and loud cheers from the Roadrunners, emerging from the water. The activities coordinator placed the box down on the cement at the edge of the pool, withdrawing a bright gold statuette of a man with upraised arms holding a volleyball and standing atop a tall Doric column. "The winner's trophy!" he proclaimed. "On behalf of The Reata, I present this to the winning team of our tournament, the Roadrunners! Will the captain of the winning team please step forward!"

The speakers around the pool area, which had been silent throughout the tournament, blared with a triumphant fanfare as rough backslaps and pats on the ass propelled Blodgett forward. He punched the man nearest him in a manner which, under the guise of camaraderie, was clearly meant to hurt, then strode forward, grinning arrogantly. "Thank you!" he said loudly. "This would probably mean more if we had some real competition, but we'll take our wins where we can get them!"

Holding the trophy high, Blodgett returned to his team amid whoops, hollers and laughs of derision.

"Just a minute, there, Mr. Blodgett," the activities coordinator advised. "I think you're due for another trip up here." He reached into the box, pulling out one more gold trophy: a naked flexing strongman standing atop a square block.

And sporting an erection.

"Player of the day!" he announced. "Mr. Blodgett!"

Once again, the big man walked up to accept his prize. This time he said nothing, only emitted a series of apelike grunts that baffled the rest of the crowd but sent the other Roadrunners into gales of laughter. He banged his two trophies together as though they were beer steins at a toast, then returned to his team. Rachel had turned her body in such a way that Blodgett and his teammates could see neither her front nor back, only her side.

"We have one more trophy to give out, our booby prize as it were, presented to the worst player of the tournament!" The activities co-ordinator grinned and set his sights on Lowell, who suddenly knew what was coming. "Loser of the day is—" He paused for effect. "Mr. Thurman!"

"Thank you, thank you," Lowell said, raising his hands in a parody of false modesty. There were some scattered claps and a lot of puzzled looks from the crowd, and loud obnoxious jeers from the Roadrunners' quarter.

He accepted the prize good-naturedly, though he was not at all sure that was the spirit in which it was intended. Still, he felt bad, for his team if not for himself, and he wondered how he had allowed *that* to happen. He was not one of those people who defined himself in relation to a group, who allowed himself to be a cog in the machine. He was definitely not a team player. In fact, for most of his life, he had assiduously avoided joining teams or clubs or organizations, preferring to engage in more solitary, individualistic pursuits. But somehow he had gotten roped into this tournament and against his will and without knowing it had become emotionally invested in the Cactus Wrens. Lowell glanced over at his teammates, saw pained expressions of sympathy, embarrassment and encouragement, and he gave them a wan smile as he walked back to his family.

He looked down at the statuette in his hand.

It was a miniature version of himself.

Lowell nearly stopped in his tracks. His mouth was suddenly dry. He looked up at Rachel, saw a perplexed look on her face, then glanced back at the activities coordinator, who was smirking. Using his finger to trace the contours of the small silver face, he saw a caricature of the visage that was reflected back to him each morning from the bathroom mirror. He couldn't immediately process all of the implications here. One thing he knew was that it had been determined ahead of time that he would be the tournament's designated loser, although how far ahead it was impossible to say. How long did it take to etch a face on a trophy?

And was this supposed to be some sort of joke or a warning?

The pool was opened again, the tournament officially over, and the gathered crowd separated, the Roadrunners heading off somewhere together with Rockne, their wives and their families, other people wandering out of the gate to another part of the resort, swimmers of all ages returning gratefully to the water. Rachel had already claimed a small table and series of lounge chairs with her bag and several towels.

Lowell sat down heavily on one of the lounge chairs, placing the trophy on the ground next to him. Ryan put a tender hand on his drooping shoulder, and he found that extremely touching. "Don't worry, Daddy," he said seriously. "It's just a game."

Lowell smiled. "Come here." He hugged his son, and it felt good. For some reason he had stopped hugging the boys as they approached puberty—embarrassment on both their parts, he supposed—but it was nice to once again feel the warmth of his son in his arms, and he flashed back to when the boys were little and he had picked them up and carried them around and given them piggyback rides and hugged them for no reason whatsoever. Time passed too quickly, he thought, and he wished he could go back in time and do it all over again. Not to change anything, just to once again experience it.

"You weren't *even* the worst player," Curtis said angrily. "Your whole team sucked. You were the best one on there. You should've been on that other team—"

"No," he said, smiling. "I'm glad I was on the team I was."

"That was the guy, wasn't it?" Ryan asked. "The guy who stole our room."

"Yeah." Lowell looked at Rachel. Her face was tight and unsmiling.

"And I saw that other jerk who yelled at us in the parking lot," Owen said.

"They were all jerks," Lowell told them. "But don't let it ruin your afternoon. It's all over now. Have some fun."

David walked up, having found them in the crowd, and Rachel told the twins that, yes, they could swim with David on the other side of the pool if they wanted, but they had to stay out of trouble and had to take Ryan along.

"That's okay," Ryan said. "I'll stay with you. I don't really want to swim right now anyway." He clambered on to an adjacent lounge chair and stretched out, pulling the back up a little so he could watch the people in the pool.

"What about the car?" Rachel asked. "Any news?"

"They're getting a battery from Tucson. It's supposed to be in sometime this afternoon." Lowell sighed. "This is some vacation, isn't it?"

Rachel smiled. "I'll thank my sister when we get back."

"I think it's a great vacation," Ryan said.

Lowell chuckled, messed up Ryan's hair. "Well, I'm glad someone's having a good time."

For dinner, they opted for room service, finding it preferable to order off the highly inflated menu and eat in their suite rather than venture out to the Saguaro Room or the Grille.

Look! I'm on my period!

The boys had hot dogs and hamburgers in their bedroom while watching reruns of *The Simpsons*. He and Rachel ate in the sitting area with the national news on. There was a lot to say, a lot to talk about, but they ate in silence, not wanting to say anything that the kids might be able to hear, or perhaps afraid discussion of their fears and feelings might grant them solidity.

Tomorrow was still up in the air. Once again, they'd been planning to drive to Tucson, but the concierge still hadn't called by five, and when Lowell attempted to dial his desk, all he got was a recording asking him to leave a message. He did so. Twice. Once shortly after five and once at a quarter to six. But neither of his calls were returned, and he resigned himself to finding out about the battery in the morning.

He had a hunch they were going to be spending another happy day stuck at The Reata.

The boys wanted to attend the resort's "dive-in movie," and after they checked it out, Lowell and Rachel reluctantly agreed to let them go. There were numerous families gathered by the big pool, a lot of little kids splashing happily in the water, teenagers and a few adults floating on rafts. They'd shut off the waterfall, and in its place a screen had been lowered on which the movie would be projected. Free popcorn was being offered at the snack bar.

"It looks safe enough," Lowell admitted.

"You take care of Ryan," Rachel ordered as the boys started to walk away, looking for David.

"Don't worry, Mom," Curtis promised.

"And come straight back to the room afterward. Straight back." She looked at her watch. "It's a five-minute walk. The movie ends at nine thirty. If you're not in by nine forty, we're coming after you."

"Okay, Mom. Jeez."

They were making a mistake, Lowell thought. Something weird was going to happen. They'd show a porno movie instead of a Disney film. Or Rockne would come by to organize everyone into water wrestling teams. But he and Rachel had no choice. To huddle in their room, hiding, waiting for daylight, was conceding defeat, was letting them win.

Them?

Who was *them?*

He didn't know.

The message light was blinking on the phone when they returned to their suite, and Lowell checked the voice mail instantly, hoping to hear that the battery had arrived and been installed, that his car was working fine and ready to go. But that was not the message that had been left.

"Mr. Thurman." He recognized the voice of the activities coordinator in his coach mode once again. "I just want to let you know that tomorrow is Sunday, and The Reata is offering nondenominational church services in the amphitheater. Our beautiful sunrise service begins at six a.m." There was a pause. "It is suggested that all Cactus Wrens attend. And pray like there's no tomorrow." A chuckle. "You need all the help you can get."

We're going to need all the help we can get. That's what Rand Black had said, and for a brief wild moment Lowell thought the two were connected, part of some vast conspiracy, that maybe he was the subject of a new reality show where an unsuspecting man was placed in a resort populated by people trying to freak him out. But then reason reasserted itself and he shut that line of thinking down before it grew to global conspiracy proportions.

"What is it?" Rachel asked as he hung up the phone.

"They have a . . . church service," he said distractedly. "A sunrise service at the amphitheater."

He frowned. *Amphitheater?* He didn't remember any amphitheater. "Do you—" he started to ask, but she was way ahead of him.

"I didn't see an amphitheater." Already she was opening up the Welcome pack and looking at the map. She spread it out on the table, then glanced up at him, bewildered. "Right here," she said. "Behind the tennis courts."

"It wasn't there before," he said quietly.

"Maybe it was. Maybe we just didn't notice it."

"No."

They almost talked then. There were no kids around, so they could be open and honest, speak candidly with each other. But something kept them from it, both of them, and she put away the Welcome pack, and he turned on the television, and they settled down to watch a movie as though everything were fine.

Twenty-one

Gloria and Ralph celebrated victory with the rest of the Road-runners, having dinner at the Starlight Pavilion and then drinks at the Winner's Circle.

The Pavilion was amazing. Located in The Reata's main building above the lobby on a hidden second floor, it had a glass ceiling that opened onto the starry night—hence the name—and a menu more exotic and extensive even than the Saguaro Room. A pianist played soft jazz on a small stage, and while Gloria didn't recognize him, she had the feeling he was someone. Although many of the Road-runners ate together at a couple of the larger tables, she and Ralph, along with a few other couples, opted for privacy and sat at smaller booths in quieter corners of the room.

If there was one thing she found less than satisfying about their association with the Roadrunners, it was . . . well, the people. Most of them were a little crude for her taste, a trifle too loud and obnoxious. Of course, that was to be expected for a sporting team, and if membership in the elite crowd required fraternization with some less than desirable companions, then so be it. But she would have much preferred an older, quieter, more staid group of individuals.

At the Winner's Circle, the party really got started, with raucous music blaring from unseen speakers, loud drinking games being played at the bar, and wild dancing from some of the younger women. She began to think that elite crowd or no elite crowd, status was not worth putting up with this. A chained waiter handed her a gin and tonic before Ralph could bring her one from the bar, and she gulped it down, feeling the effects almost immediately. She had a moment of clarity when she realized that they should not be here, that this was all a mistake, that they had been recruited under false pretenses and should be back alone in their room right now. Then another waiter came by, took her empty glass and replaced it with a martini.

She didn't want it, but she drank it anyway.

The tone of the party changed as the evening wore on, became less victory celebration and more saturnalia. Several of the women—including old Dana Peters from the Springerville Historical Society—were suddenly topless, and across the lounge a group of men had stripped down to their skivvies. Someone had somehow removed all clothing from the waiters and servers chained to the post, and Mr. Blodgett and Mr. Snagg were forcing one young Hispanic waitress to urinate in a wine glass.

Gloria grimaced. This wasn't the way they should be spending their vacation.

This was wrong.

She thought of that writer they'd met at the Saguaro Room—

Get out.

—and wished they had followed his advice.

The party antics escalated. A dog had gotten in, and it ran around the lounge barking and tripping people. Two fat men, drunk and laughing, were relaying mugs of beer from the bar and dumping them into the sunken portion of the room in an effort to create a beer swimming pool.

Gloria wasn't sure exactly when she and Ralph became separated—the alcohol made everything a little foggy—but all of a sudden she was alone with an empty glass, and he was on the other side of the pole with two nubile half-naked young women, one of whom had an arm on his shoulder and a breast in his face. Anger flared within her, white hot and burning. It had been many years since she'd had any use for his wrinkled old cock, but it was *her* wrinkled old cock and she wasn't going to let any underage implanted floozy anywhere near it.

She started across the floor toward him but tripped over something she couldn't even see. A tall cruel-looking man laughed at her and dribbled the last of his drink on her head as he walked away. She got to her feet, furious, ready to take on that insensitive jerk, but there'd been a sea change in the room, a shift of mood and focus, and it left her feeling off-balance, not only physically but mentally. She turned around woozily, trying to figure out what had changed.

It was the activities coordinator.

He was standing near the center of the round room, in front of the post, all of the chained workers huddled together behind the wooden pole. The Roadrunners and their spouses gathered around in a semicircle, falling into silence as the obnoxious music mercifully faded. *Where are the children?* she wondered. *Didn't some of them have children?* She didn't like the fact that they weren't here.

Get out.

The activities coordinator was dressed strangely, she saw now, in some kind of dirty cowboy costume rather than his usual elegant suit. "Hail!" he cried.

Most of the other people seemed as confused as she did, but Mr. Blodgett shouted "Hail!" and the rest of them followed suit.

"Hail!"

There was a buzz going through the crowd, whisperings passed from person to person that she couldn't seem to focus on, couldn't seem to hear. She looked around, trying to find Ralph, but he had disappeared.

"Let us give thanks," the activities coordinator intoned. "We have prevailed in tournament play against our lessers. Let us demonstrate our gratitude and appreciation to The Reata by presenting an offering in hopes that our good fortune may continue."

By this time, the Roadrunners were murmuring their assent, like the call-and-response of a church meeting. The activities coordinator would say something and they would reply in unison, though she could not seem to make out what either side said. Somewhere along the line, she became aware of the fact that most of the crowd's attention was on her. Her head felt big, heavy, floppy. She tried to walk away but instead fell into a chair, and it suddenly occurred to her that she wasn't drunk, she'd been drugged.

"Ralph!" she tried to call, but the sound that came out of her mouth was a goofy hiccupped syllable, and several of the people immediately around her giggled.

The activities coordinator was moving toward her while everyone else seemed to be stepping back and away. Even in her altered state, she understood that she was being offered as some sort of sacrifice, and with a grim resignation that was totally unlike her decided that that made sense since she was probably the oldest person in the room and closest to death anyway.

From behind the post, the chained servants untangled themselves and emerged, stepping slowly and in sync. They were still naked but adorned with paint or makeup that made them look like Indians. Each of them carried a hatchet.

"For The Reata!" the activities coordinator shouted.

"For The Reata!" the Roadrunners responded.

The servers said nothing, kept walking.

This was not the way she wanted to die, Gloria thought through the fog in her brain. She scanned the crescent ring of faces for

Ralph, did not see him and tried to call out his name. This time no sound came out, only a dry croak that instigated a coughing spasm.

Standing in front of her, the activities coordinator was no longer the activities coordinator but her mother, her mother as she'd looked on her deathbed, all deep-seated staring eyes and pulled wrinkled skin. "It's time to join your sister," the old woman said with a creaky whine, and there was a spreading stain of blood on the crotch of her flowered dress.

Gloria slid out of the plastic chair onto the floor, closing her eyes so tightly that tears squeezed out of them. She opened her eyes, and her mother was gone, replaced once again by the cowboy-garbed activities coordinator. Next to him, in a queue, the servers waited, hatchets raised at identical levels, blades forward, their chains stretched at angles that made them look like marionettes.

"Prepare the offering!" the activities coordinator cried.

"Prepare the offering!" the crowd echoed.

The servers started forward one by one, chains clanking.

"No!" Gloria tried to scream, but again there was only the croak and cough. She looked wildly around, and the last thing she saw, before the first hatchet sliced off a section of her upper arm and the agony began, was Ralph in the center of the crowd, pressed between two topless women, smiling.

Twenty-two

The film festival was nothing to write home about—although it was Patrick's job to do exactly that. Neither as commercial as Toronto nor as indie as Sundance, it fell through the cracks, with so-called "premieres" of pictures that had not yet hit Tucson or Tulsa but for which critics in New York, LA and Chicago had already received review screenings, and several sophomore follow-ups to debut features that had not made a dent in the marketplace last year. He attended a morning showing of a moderately interesting, sexually graphic thriller, then afterward interviewed the Polish director and the American lead actress with whom the director was now romantically involved. After a lunch of a dry turkey sandwich and Sprite, he watched an interminable coming-of-age story with absolutely zero sense of structure or pacing made by a young African-American woman from Atlanta, but he liked the director for facing off against an overwhelmingly hostile audience for a Q&A session and ended up giving her a moderate rating on his festival scorecard.

He was supposed to see two HBO-financed documentaries this evening, but he found himself thinking of Vicki and her friends, realized how much he'd rather be sitting by the pool, sipping margaritas with them and skipped out on the night's festivities. Townsend would never know and, besides, he had more than enough info for two articles, maybe three.

Familiarity had not made the drive through the desert any shorter or less grueling, and the sun was setting by the time he pulled up to The Reata's guardhouse, creating long strange shadows on the desert floor, reflecting orange fire from the windows of the terraced resort. His parking spot was gone, stolen by a Cadillac SUV—indeed all of the spaces in his lot were taken, forcing him to drive to the next lot down. Here, too, there were no empty spots, and after cruising the small parking area in front of the next building, he decided to head back to the main lot in front of the lobby.

He pulled up next to a light pole, removed his briefcase, locked the car and turned on the alarm. It was a long walk back to his room if he followed the outer sidewalk next to the road, so he took a short-cut through the lobby, hiking down the long steps to the pool area. He opened the gate and heard a familiar voice call out.

"Yoo ho! Mr. Schlaegel!"

It was Vicki. She was where he hoped she'd be—by the pool—and wearing what he hoped she'd be wearing—a thong bikini. The sky was now almost completely dark, but strong halogens in the palm trees bathed the pool area in an artificial daylight, and the desert heat had not yet dissipated, making it perfect for swimming. He walked over to where she lay on a lounge chair between two other equally attractive women in equally skimpy bathing outfits.

"I was hoping you'd come by," she said. "Oh, these are my friends. April and Madison."

The other two women nodded, smiled.

"Hello."

"Hi."

Madison, he thought. There was a whole generation of Madisons out there named after the mermaid in *Splash.* That made her about twenty or so. A fine age. He glanced toward the pool which seemed unusually crowded for this hour. "What's going on here? Some kind of party?"

"They're going to be showing a kiddie flick," April said.

"What's the movie?" he asked.

Vicki groaned at her friend. "You shouldn't have said that. Now he's going to want to stay and watch."

Patrick laughed. "No. No, I won't. I was just curious. I've been watching movies all day. A little quiet time right now actually sounds pretty good to me."

"Some Disney movie," the friend said. "It doesn't start for an hour or two, but I think people want to get good seats."

"There is another pool," Vicki suggested. "It's in the gym or the fitness center or whatever they're calling it." She smiled slyly. "It's nice and private."

"I, uh, need to go back to my room and drop all this stuff off." He held up his briefcase. "And get my swim trunks."

Vicki stood, still smiling. "No you don't."

If this was heading where he thought it was heading, he was more than happy to follow.

She casually took his hand while her friends picked up their sun-glasses and lotion from the small tables between the lounge chairs.

"Are you really on TV?" Madison asked, adjusting her top and then wrapping a towel around her waist.

C cups, he thought. "I was," he told her.

Madison smiled.

Vicki held his hand more tightly, drew closer to his side. "Let's go. It's getting crowded."

The women slipped into sandals and they started walking, passing the snack bar where a line was beginning to form, and maneuvering around the people who were re-arranging their chairs in order to better position themselves for the movie. Patrick unlocked the gate at the opposite end of the pool and held it open as a family of five, all carrying rafts and closed plastic drink cups, passed through.

They headed down the sidewalk. "Vicki's a huge movie fan," April said. "She was so excited to meet you. She's been talking about it all day."

"You have the perfect job," Vicki sighed. "I'd give my eyeteeth to be able to watch movies all day and give my opinion about them. That's just so great."

"What do you do?" Patrick asked politely.

"We're fashion models," Madison declared.

April snorted.

"You could be," Patrick told them.

"Thank you," Vicki said. "But we work at the capital in Phoenix. Madison's an aide, and April and I are administrative assistants."

"That sounds like fun."

"Yeah. Right."

He grinned. "All right. It doesn't. And I *do* have a cool job."

Vicki elbowed him playfully. "You don't have to rub it in."

He was glad he'd skipped out on those documentaries. He was pretty sure he was going to get lucky tonight.

"Do you ever get to meet movie stars?" Madison asked.

They walked through the darkening twilight to the exercise center. Patrick had no idea where it was, but Vicki and her friends seemed to know the way. Which made sense. Judging by their bodies, they probably exercised quite a bit. The three of them kept asking about his job, Madison wanting backstage dish about celebrities, April curious about the perks of the job—like who paid for his trip out here—and Vicki wanting to know his opinion of several recent releases. Although Madison was wrapped in a towel and April had slipped into a pair of shorts and an open shirt, Vicki was just wearing her tiny bathing suit, and he wondered if that was intentional.

He was enjoying himself, on track for a fun flirtatious evening, but the mood died as soon as they entered the pool room. Patrick was not big on vibes or auras or any of that New Age mumbo jumbo but this place had a *feeling* to it, a heavy tangible oppressiveness that blanketed them the second they stepped foot through the doorway. He'd had an inkling of it as they passed through the empty weight room, an almost subliminal impression that he was in the antechamber of some dark lair, but nothing could have prepared him for the feeling of dread he experienced immediately upon entering the pool room. He looked around at the shadowed concrete walls dappled with reflected ripples from the water, at the deep end of the pool, murky and unilluminated by the dim ceiling lights above. Everything was soundtracked by the ticking undertone of the pool sweeper and the humming of its hidden motor.

Cat People, he thought.

He was pretty sure that the plan had been to go skinny-dipping, something he was all in favor of, but that idea seemed to have immediately lost its appeal. Madison re-adjusted the towel around her to make it tighter, April shivered visibly.

"Let's go to the bar," Vicki said, subdued, and turned around without waiting for an answer. They passed back through the empty weight room. There was no argument, no discussion, as though they all knew the reason for the retreat but did not want to speak of it. Which was, Patrick thought, exactly the case.

This time they did not talk as they walked through the night toward the Grille, whose rowdy reassuring sounds of life as they approached seemed to dispel some of the gloomy silence that had settled over them. Once inside, they felt free to speak again, though tentatively at first, like people who had not spoken for a long time and were not sure they remembered how. Patrick found them a table with three chairs and then borrowed another chair from the table of an oblivious couple drunkenly arguing. By the time the waitress finally came—after Patrick had reached out and grabbed her hand, practically pulling her over—most of the psychic residue from the exercise pool had worn off, and they were once again trying to recapture the light flippant tone of earlier, though he found something desperate and hopeless in the effort. He asked for a beer while all three women ordered margaritas.

He looked at them after the waitress left. "You're not old enough to drink, are you?"

"*She* is," Madison said cattily, pointing at Vicki.

Vicki slapped her hand down. "Thanks. For the record, Madison is almost twenty-one, although no one ever cards her. April is twenty-five. And I am . . . a few years older."

"Closer to my age," Patrick offered.

"Exactly!"

They tried to keep it up, tried to get back that easygoing flirtatiousness, but it felt false and fell flat. Insults and annoyances crept into the conversation as the alcohol level increased. He'd been hoping to spend the night with Vicki. Hell, if he played his cards right, he thought maybe her two friends would even come along as well. But he ended up leaving the bar alone and frustrated while the three of them, drunk, giggling and falling all over each other, sang some truly offensive and racist karaoke songs.

He stepped into the night, the air still and warm and vacuum dry, smelling of sand. He'd been drinking only beer and had kept his alcohol intake down, not wanting to impede his sexual performance, but even though that wasn't going to happen, Patrick was glad he wasn't drunk. He wanted to keep his wits about him. He thought of the night before, the snakes and wolves, but the memory was dreamlike and unreal, like something he'd seen in a film rather than experienced firsthand.

He still needed to work on those articles and e-mail them to Townsend before tomorrow's deadline so they'd make it into the Monday edition, and he hurried back to his room, on the lookout all the way for the odd and unusual, but grateful as he hurried down the homestretch that he had not encountered anything along the way. He took out his keycard, unlocked his door.

There was something in his room.

Patrick felt it the second he walked through the doorway and flipped the light switch. His first reaction was to turn tail and run, to get out of that room and head straight for the lobby to ask for help. But he told himself he was being paranoid. He had no proof, only a gut feeling, and not only weren't those admissible in court, they were pretty well discredited everywhere else as well. And after this morning, no matter how casually he'd handled the spider situation, he didn't want to seem like a whiny frightened—

fairy

—child.

The air conditioner was on, had been on all day, but the room still smelled faintly of minty poison, so he knew someone had been by to spray for bugs. Hopefully that had killed the spider—although he could easily imagine the creature escaping through whatever secret hole it had used to get in, remaining outside until the poison dissipated, then returning for revenge.

Revenge?

He'd been watching too many movies, spending too much time in darkened theaters staring at screen fictions and not enough time living in the real world.

There was the sound of crinkling cellophane from the bathroom.

Patrick held his breath, his heart lurching in his chest. "Who's there?" he called, and his voice sounded far wimpier than intended. "Get out of my room." He held his briefcase out in front of him.

There was movement in the bathroom mirror.

He was looking toward the closet at the time so he didn't see what it was, saw only a blur of dark movement from the corner of his eye, but that was enough to make him jump, enough to accelerate the speed of the blood careening through his veins. He did a quick visual swipe of the room, then concentrated on the mirror, but saw nothing.

Alien.

The image came unbidden to his mind, though he knew it was childish and not at all realistic. *Alien* had been one of the seminal moviegoing experiences of his childhood, and while he affected a more blasé sophistication these days, the fact remained that Giger's monster had scared the living shit out of him, had given him intense nightmares for a month, and even now lurked at the edge of his subconscious whenever he was alone in the dark.

There was more crinkling cellophane, the shift of heavy movement.

This was beyond his capacity to handle. He needed to call someone else in here. But still he was loath to cry wolf, and holding the briefcase in front of him for protection, he changed his position, creeping slowly forward and to the left in order to better see around the corner into the other half of the bathroom. There was the second part of the outer vanity and sink, the edge of the inner doorway that led into the shower, tub and toilet area. But that was as far as he could see, and no matter how he adjusted his position, he could not see into the inner room without going closer.

That he was unwilling to do.

He imagined himself creeping silently forward, peeking carefully around the corner—and then grabbed by a slimy bullet-headed monster and eaten.

No thanks.

He took a step backward, and next door the party suddenly

started. Dogs barking and everything. It was just as it had been last night, and the eerie thing was that it arrived full force, not growing in volume as layers were added but starting at its peak, as though it were on tape and the recording had just been turned on.

That was possible, and he wondered if all of this wasn't part of some bizarre attempt to drive him crazy, some *Let's Scare Jessica to Death* situation. But he thought of the wolves and the snakes and that creepy exercise pool, and rejected that idea immediately. There would be no point to it. And besides, he was sure that whatever was happening at this resort was not the result of human intention.

Through the wall, someone screamed, and there was once again that muffled gunshot sound.

The noise of the party gave him cover and gave him confidence, and he took three quick steps forward to look around the corner into the bathroom, ready to bolt instantly if need be. But there was nothing in the tub or on the toilet, and behind the clouded glass, the shower stall looked clear. The only other possibility was that someone or something could be hiding behind the open door, but he could see through the crack next to the hinges that that was not the case.

Emboldened, he walked into the outer part of the bathroom past the vanity and the sink. "Hey!" he called. There was no answer, no noise but the sounds of the party next door, and he poked his head through the doorway, prepared to jump backward should something leap out at him or the door try to slam shut. Nothing happened, however. The bathroom was empty, and he walked inside, still clutching tightly to his briefcase, which was both his shield and sword right now.

He saw here what he could not see from farther away: there was a large black bubble at the bottom of the water in the otherwise clean toilet. It was perfectly round and shiny, like blown glass, and it appeared to have emerged from the hole at the bottom. Patrick had no idea what it was, but the flawlessness of its form frightened him for some reason, as did its jet opacity, and he had no doubt that it was connected to that cellophane crinkle and that heavy shifting sound.

The thing in the mirror had been black.

Had it? He wasn't sure because he hadn't seen it clearly, but it had been dark, and it was only a short leap from that to this. Tensing himself, ready for anything, Patrick leaned over, pressed down on the handle to flush the toilet and jumped back.

The bubble popped, dissipating into crescent-shaped fragments that looked like pieces of fingernails and were sucked down with the water. A foul stench arose from the toilet, an odor of rot and decay that reminded him of spoiled meat. Then it was over and gone, the water was clear again, the bathroom was empty, and there was no sign that anything unusual had ever occurred here.

He breathed deeply, allowing the first full complement of air into his lungs since he'd walked into his room.

The spider had been black, he thought.

The spider was gone. But he could still smell the poison.

Just to be on the safe side, he checked every corner of the room, looked under every piece of furniture and inside every cupboard and drawer before finally putting his briefcase down and setting up his laptop to write.

Twenty-three

He was in love.

Owen knew how that would sound if he said it aloud to anyone. Hell, he knew how *he* would have reacted if anyone before today had told him such a thing. But it was true. Through some chain reaction of fate and circumstances, he and Brenda had ended up in the same place at the same time, and if one thing had gone wrong, if his family had taken their vacation a week earlier or her family had decided to stay at another hotel, even though they lived in the same county of the same state they never would have met.

But they had.

It was meant to be.

He cringed inwardly even as he had the thought. Mush like that was for romance novels and women's TV movies, not real life. But it was what he felt, and there was an electric excitement associated with it, a feeling that he'd experienced in flashes prior to this but that he'd never savored in its entirety.

Love.

He and his brothers had gotten to the pool well before the movie was supposed to start, but the place was already filling up. As soon as their parents left to go back to the room, Owen set about searching for Brenda while Curtis and Ryan took the two chairs that David had been able to save for them amid all of the families jostling for position by moving and scraping the pool furniture across the cement. He finally found Brenda in the water, seated on the steps in the shallow end. There was a light behind her, far away in the deep end, but it was so faint by the time it reached her that it was impossible to tell whether she was wearing a bathing suit or was naked.

She looked naked, though he knew she wasn't.

He wished she was.

He got into the water next to her, surprised by its warmth. It must have absorbed the heat of the afternoon sun and retained it. "Do you have a raft?" he asked.

"No. You?"

He shook his head. "I guess we could just sit on the edge."

"Or stay here in the water." The lights in the palm trees above had dimmed, in preparation for the movie, he supposed, and it was impossible to see her face. The effect was strange, and he found that he was unable to read her emotions from her voice alone. He waded out a bit and turned around so the light from the deep end would make her less of a silhouette and easier to see. She reached for him, took his hand, and the touch of her fingers made him tingle. "Come on. Let's swim out a bit and get away from this crowd."

The steps had been invaded by several fathers with their small children, and Owen allowed himself to be led into deeper waters. In the back of his mind, always, was the location of the body he and Curtis had seen, but he would make sure to steer Brenda away from that area if they got too close.

He needn't have worried. She stopped somewhere around where the water was up to his stomach and her chest. The lights were still dimmed—maybe they were going to stay this way—and out here no one could see what they were doing. They stood close, talking low and tentatively touching, accidental contacts with feet and thighs and arms and elbows that were not really accidental, brushes up against each other that were played off as casual but meant far more, boundary tests that lasted a beat too long, until they were finally and fully kissing. It was the most wonderful thing he'd ever felt, the closest feeling to perfection he had ever experienced. Her lips were soft, her tongue inquisitive, and he wondered how he had gotten so lucky that this should be happening to him.

Owen had no idea where his brothers were at the moment and didn't care. All he knew was that he wanted this night to last forever.

They stopped kissing, pulled away from each other, looked into each other's eyes, afraid to speak, afraid to say anything that would ruin the moment. Feeling brave, he reached out to touch her, then moved his hand down her stomach until his fingers touched the elastic of her bikini bottom. He paused there for a moment, giving her time to object, to move away, to push his hand aside, but she did nothing, and his penis was fully erect as his fingers slid gently beneath the waistband and encountered the downy fibrous texture of her pubic hair. She smiled at him, her lips barely visible in the dark, and then he felt her fingers slipping inside his own suit, delicately closing around his stiff shaft.

He pulled away, not wanting to, but knowing that if he didn't he would explode. She seemed to understand and, rather than taking offense, took his hands in hers and giggled nervously. "Wow," she said.

"Yeah," he breathed, not trusting himself to say more until the physical sensation died down, until his erection subsided and his fingers no longer tingled from the delicious hairiness of her wet crotch.

A kid swam by them, a dark seal-like figure speeding past their legs under the water and splashing noisily to the surface a few feet away. His friend was yelling after him, paddling forward on a raft.

"It's getting too crowded here," Brenda said, and ducked into the water, swimming toward the deep end.

Toward the body.

Owen remained where he was, rooted in place, watching the even rhythmic strokes of her long slender arms. *No,* he thought, *don't let it happen.* But she stopped exactly over the spot, then swiveled in the water looking for him, suddenly realizing that he had not come along with her. "Hey!" she called out.

He could only see the top half of her, but with her hair plastered down, her arms at her sides, she appeared almost bound, mummy-wrapped. She *looked* like the body, and, his skin a field of goose-flesh, he wondered if what he'd seen had not been something that had already happened but had been a premonition of things to come.

Then she was swimming back toward him and the spell was broken. She dived underneath the water as she approached, playfully bumping her elbow against his still stiff erection, and then burst to the surface right in front of him. "Where were you?" she asked, wiping the water out of her eyes. "Why didn't you come with me?"

He didn't have a ready answer and couldn't come up with anything plausible on the spur of the moment, so he remained silent, shook his head.

"I guess this is a good spot to watch the movie," she said. "If that's what you want to do."

He drew her to him, putting his arm around her shoulder, as an overweight woman floated by on an inner tube. "Yeah," he said. "Let's watch the movie. It'll be fun. Maybe afterward . . ." He left the sentence unfinished.

"Yeah."

He smiled at her, kissed her, but over her shoulder his eyes were focused on the spot where he'd seen the body.

Even under normal circumstances, Curtis always thought there was something creepy about hotels at night. Last year, they'd stayed at a Holiday Inn in San Diego, and when he had to go out to get some ice, the interior corridor through which he walked seemed never ending, like the endless hallway in the Haunted Mansion. He hurried past door after door, past the same repeating patterns on the wallpaper, the same geometric designs on the carpeting, and it was spooky, as though he were trapped in some *Twilight Zone* version of hell. He found himself wondering what was going on behind each of the closed doors, in each of the rooms, and the scenes that entered his mind were not of happy families writing postcards and watching television but psychos and sickos carrying out the evil will of unseen presences, committing murders in bathtubs, planning explosive demolitions.

Here at The Reata, all of that was multiplied by ten.

On the screen, Marlin and Dory, two computer-animated fish, were swimming along with a group of surfer dude sea turtles. In the pool, children were laughing. On the chairs, adults were chuckling. But beneath it all flowed a current of dread, a sense that this was ironic icing on a dark and evil cake. He cleared his throat, looking over at David. "There're people swimming where the body was."

"What are you talking about, tube steak?"

But David knew exactly what he was talking about. Curtis could tell from the tight tense expression on his face, from the way the other boy would not look at him.

Neither of them spoke for a moment. Ryan, on the other side of Curtis, pretended to be scanning the pool for Owen and not listening.

"I think something's going to happen tonight," David said finally, quietly.

A jolt, like an electric current, both terrifying and exciting, passed through him. *Yes,* Curtis thought. He stared out at the pool, his gaze stopping on what he believed was the silhouette of Owen and Brenda kissing in midwater. He was jealous of his brother, he could admit that, but there was still something about their relationship that rubbed him the wrong way. He had the same feeling about those two together that he did about The Reata overall: it wasn't right.

Wind began blowing high in the trees, swinging the palm fronds back and forth like whisk brooms, though it did not reach the ground. A few seconds later, the rain started. A drop landed on his bare leg. Another on his chest. There was nothing else for a moment—then the torrent started. Wind-whipped rain suddenly sheeted sideways, hitting his skin like warm wet pinpricks. Lightning flashed close by, followed immediately by a deafening clap of thunder. He, Ryan, David and all of the people immediately around them jumped up from the chairs and ducked for cover, scurrying under shade umbrellas or the overhanging roof of the snack bar, throwing towels over their heads and shoulders. More lightning flashed, and parents were ordering kids out of the pool so they wouldn't get electrocuted.

The three of them stopped next to the snack bar, looking for Owen and Brenda among the fleeing guests. On the screen, Disney's underwater world was fuzzy and wavy behind a curtain of rain. Thunder roared.

Something was wrong. Although Curtis did not know what it was for the first few seconds, he quickly realized that it was the people. Not the guests, not the men, women and children attempting to find shelter in the storm, but the people working for The Reata, the employees. The rain made it difficult to see, gave everything a surreal watery cast, yet with each flash of lightning, Curtis saw shifts in the appearance of the men and women, odd and inexplicable changes that started out subtly but almost immediately grew blatant and noticeable.

"Look at that," David breathed. "Jesus fuck."

The Reata employees, the waiters and waitresses, the maintenance men and security guards, all of the people working around the pool area, were . . . transforming. It was as if the rain possessed some sort of magic, and the water hitting their hair and running down their faces washed off the makeup that hid their real selves. A hot babe in tan shorts and a white Reata polo shirt was suddenly an old woman with varicose veins and an angry lined face. A muscular man shrivelled before his eyes, his teeth falling out as though from years of disease, their bloody roots leaving tracks on his chin as he tried to catch them in his hand. Another man's hair fell out, revealing a red sunburnt head underneath, his cheeks falling into jowls.

"I knew this place was haunted!" Ryan shouted, and there was both fear and excitement in his voice. "I *knew* it!"

Around them was chaos. People were running and screaming, falling into the water as they attempted to escape from the metamorphosing employees. Owen emerged from the melee soaked and shocked, and Curtis grabbed him, pulling him under the eave of the snack bar. For a brief horrible second as the rain pelted his head and shoulders, Curtis thought it might be the *rain* that was doing all this, that there was something toxic in the water itself. But he wasn't affected and Owen was okay, and so were the parents and kids running and screaming toward the exit. Only The Reata workers were altered by the storm, and Curtis half-expected to see them turn into skeletons with each flash of lightning, although at least *that* didn't occur.

"Come on!" David shouted. "We have to get out of here!"

He sounded and looked as scared as Curtis felt, and the three of them followed David as he led them around the edge of the snack bar and along the fence toward the south gate. Only Ryan seemed like he wanted to stay, and although he could see that his little brother was just as frightened as the rest of them, he could also see that Ryan was interested in what was happening, wanted to *watch* it happen, wanted to know *why* it happened. Curtis picked on Ryan a lot, made fun of him for the things he said and the way he acted, but in a way he couldn't help admiring him. There was something different about him, some sort of inner focus that neither he nor Owen possessed, and despite his shyness and whininess and clinginess with their parents, Ryan sometimes seemed like their older rather than younger brother.

A woman came lurching out of the rainy darkness toward them, her face a caved-in mask of wrinkles, her hair streaked gray and black like a monster. She was screaming, although whether in an attempt to scare them or from pain or humiliation, it was impossible to tell.

"Run!" David ordered, and they were speeding along the edge of the fence, squeezing past palm trees, jumping over flower pots. They reached the gate and joined the throng trying to get through. Absurdly, incongruously, Curtis could hear the voices of characters from the movie still issuing from a speaker up above. They had to get away from here as fast as possible, he thought. They had to tell their parents to pack up and leave tonight before—

It happened the second they ran through the gate.

All of his anxiety and fear disappeared instantly. His desperate need to escape washed away like soapsuds with a hose. Suddenly it was not necessary to leave The Reata or even tell their parents. He recognized it as it occurred, even remembered his former passion afterward, but the knowledge was dormant in the back of his mind, there was no urgency to it, all of the emotional and intellectual context having been drained away and leaving only a useless set of facts. A logical disassociated part of his mind reflected that this was like being drugged or brainwashed, and indeed he was suffused with the sort of emotional numbness he'd always assumed came with drug use, but there was no outrage or concern or even curiosity about it.

He could tell from the faces of his brothers and David that the same thing had happened to them, and as a test he stepped back and watched the other guests running through the gate, watched their panic and fear turn to calm acceptance as they passed between the metal fence supports. It was horrible, what was happening. It was unbelievable.

But he didn't care.

He *almost* wanted to talk about the sudden shift with his brothers and David. Almost. But not quite. And then there was a light little fingertip of pressure on his mind and he no longer wanted to talk about it at all, no longer wanted to even think about it.

"Well . . ." said David, wiping the rainwater from his face. "I'd better get back before I'm completely soaked. I guess I'll see you guys tomorrow."

"Yeah," Owen said. "See you."

Curtis nodded his good-bye, and they parted, David running toward the first building on the left, the three of them heading through the storm toward their own suite, as behind them, in back of the fence, the screaming continued.

Ryan lay awake on the made-up couch, listening to his brothers' snores.

This was not the way it was supposed to be.

Curtis thrashed in his sleep, his brain disturbed no doubt by the events of the day, and Ryan thought of what he'd seen at the abandoned resort, what had happened tonight at the pool. He was afraid. Not just in a general little-kid way, but specifically for his life and the lives of his family. For he had no doubt that this place could and would kill them. Whether they had been lured here intentionally or had stumbled into this spider's web of their own accord made no difference. They were here now, and whatever dark force lay at the heart of The Reata was going to do everything in its power to make them stay. Forever. He'd thought up numerous reasons why—because the resort was powered by captured souls or fresh blood, because it needed new employees—but he didn't know for sure and might never know. That was one thing he'd learned from reading all of those paranormal books: there wasn't always an understandable reason. People always wanted a simple cause-and-effect explanation for everything; it made horror easier to take somehow, made it seem more logical. But it wasn't logical. Just as religious people always said that God works in mysterious ways, that the ways of the Lord were unknowable, so, too, he thought, were the ways of the paranormal.

Of evil.

Yes, he thought. Whatever was here was definitely evil.

For his own part, this was now bigger than any book. He no longer cared about writing a haunted travelogue. That suddenly seemed so trivial and unimportant. Maybe he'd do that after this was all over, but for right now his chief concern was figuring out a way to get out of here and get away before they were engulfed.

Owen flipped over onto his back and moaned, a terrified heart-wrenching sound that made Ryan's hair stand on end. He looked over at Curtis, snoring in the other bed. Both of his brothers seemed to access emotions in their sleep that remained capped and under wraps while they were awake, and he wondered if the same thing was true of him. He knew that whatever power resided here had been reaching out to them, had managed to keep the horror of the pool *at* the pool by putting a visibly obvious clamp on the witnesses as they dashed through the gate, and he himself felt the pressure to forget, could not seem to muster the will or the energy to talk about any of this with anyone, although inside he still retained an acute awareness of what was happening and the thoughts in his head were racing a mile a minute.

That was the core of the problem, he thought. Communication. He'd learned in history last year that the first thing dictators usually did when they took power in a country was take over the newspapers. Whoever controlled the means of communication controlled the people. And maybe that's why The Reata had been able to exist untouched out here for so long, because word had never leaked out, because no one had ever told the police or the press or the government or anyone else who could do anything about it. He had no doubt that this was not something new, that it had happened before to other guests, and he figured the only reason the survivors, the people allowed to leave, didn't talk about it or tell anyone was because they'd been silenced or brainwashed.

Like alien abductees.

He thought of that old demolished resort hidden in the canyon. What had happened to it? Why was it there? It was connected somehow to The Reata, but he didn't know how or why, and he had the feeling that if he could solve that riddle, he would be able to figure out what they needed to do to escape.

There was noise from within the bathroom, a low babble, and when he twisted on the couch to look in that direction, he saw a bluish flickering light emanating from around the corner.

The television had switched on in there.

Ryan's heart was pounding, and his first instinct was to wake up his brothers, call for his dad. But he resisted the impulse and slipped carefully out from under the covers, off the couch, creeping stealthily through the darkness toward the bathroom. He wasn't sure why he was being so secretive, what he was trying to prove. There was no one here to impress, and logic said that this was a trap set for him, a way to lure him around that corner into the bathroom so that whatever was there could pounce on him. He *should* go in with his dad and brothers, loud and combative, guns blazing, instead of sneaking in alone.

But his gut said exactly the opposite, told him that was exactly what The Reata wanted him to do, that one quiet kid on his own could slip in under the radar and see things that weren't meant to be seen, things that would wink off and disappear the moment a big group approached.

Maybe the goal was even as simple as wanting him to wake everyone up so that none of them could get a decent night's sleep.

So he kept on, moving slowly and quietly past Owen's bed toward that glowing corner with its low indistinguishable babble. If he had gone first to the other side of the room by Curtis's bed, he could have seen into the bathroom and known what was there. But whatever was in the bathroom would have seen him, too, from far off, and he thought a better approach was to simply peek around the corner and surprise it.

The bluish light fluttered, and from the mumbling chatter he made out the words "mine" or "mind" and "sin." He poked his head around the corner.

And saw on the small television screen that same terrible man he'd encountered in the mirror back at the abandoned resort. It was a close-up of the man's face, framed by that long thin hair: cadaverous sunken cheeks, protruding forehead, cold dead eyes. His toothless mouth was not smiling this time but talking, a continuous rant directed at God knew who. Every so often, he would shift in his position, wobble slightly, and Ryan could see the dark wall of that mirrored room behind him, the red velvet of the thronelike chair. He had the disconcerting feeling that this was live, that a camera was filming something that was happening even as he stood here.

He'd expected to see a scene from a movie—a weird movie, perhaps. A horror film or a porno flick, something that was supposed to have a hidden meaning aimed at him—but he had not expected this.

As he'd half-anticipated, though, the bathroom was empty. There

was no person or monster or ghost or shadow here. The TV had
turned itself on.

And he was going to turn it off.

Ignoring the face and its jabbering, he strode purposefully across
the bathroom and flipped off the television's power switch. The face
disappeared with an anguished cry and the room was thrown into
darkness. For a brief second on the screen there was a glowing after-
image, a white-on-black outline of the face that looked like a Hal-
loween mask. Then it, too, faded, and Ryan was alone.

Behind him, Owen muttered something in his sleep.

Ryan turned, walking back toward his bed on the couch, feeling
his way around the barriers of the dark room like a blind man. He
should be waking up his brothers, he knew. He should be running
into his parents' room screaming about what he'd seen.

But somehow he didn't feel like it.

He reached the couch, crawled under the covers and stretched out.
And though it was a long, long time before he was finally able to
nod off, he remained unmoving, thinking of nothing, as he waited
for sleep to arrive.

SUNDAY

Twenty-four

The wake-up call came before dawn.

Lowell heard the ringing of the phone in his sleep and for a brief second incorporated it into a dream before its outside insistence shattered that illusion and made itself recognized. Three rings later, he had opened his eyes and pushed off the covers. Another two and he was padding over to the phone. "Hello?" he said groggily.

"Who is it?" Rachel called from the bed, and there was a hint of fear in her voice.

"Mr. Thurman!" said the voice on the other end of the line, and he immediately recognized the forced jocklike jocularity of the activities coordinator.

"Hey, Rockne," he said, and was gratified to hear a displeased silence greet his greeting.

"It's time to get up," the activities coordinator said shortly. "The Reata's sunrise service will be conducted in the amphitheater at five thirty. That is precisely one hour from now. So I suggest you shit, shower, shave and do whatever it is you have to do in order to make it there on time."

"I'll think about it," Lowell told him, and hung up the phone.

It made him feel good to hang up on the activities coordinator like that, and he had decided not to attend the service at all, but Rachel had heard his half of the conversation and from those few unrevealing words had somehow been able to deduce what the call was about. Already she was getting out of bed to go to the bathroom. "What time does it start?" she asked, glancing over at the clock.

"In an hour," he said. "But—"

"We're going," she told him. "Sunrise services are fun. And a little religion won't kill you. Besides, we could all use some divine intervention on this trip."

It couldn't hurt, he agreed silently.

The kids didn't want to go. He understood that perfectly. He recalled all the times as a child he had pretended to be sick so he could stay home and play instead of wasting his Sunday morning at church—a plan that invariably backfired because if his mother suspected he was faking he got in big trouble, and if she believed him she made him spend the rest of the day home in bed.

But Rachel was right. They should go. If only to see what kind of church services a place like The Reata offered.

They got ready quickly—two bathrooms definitely helped—and finished off the last of the breakfast pastries they'd brought with them to the resort. Lowell once again checked the map in the Welcome pack, and they trudged through the predawn to the amphitheater, falling in behind a rather devout-looking man and his overdressed wife.

The amphitheater was much larger than Lowell had been expecting. It looked like a concert venue. There were numbered seats and aisles, and the stage was large enough to house an orchestra, with rigging in place for stage lights, although none were in evidence this morning. It was built into the rocks at such an angle that the rising sun would shine upon the performers or speakers on the stage from the right, illuminating them but not blinding them.

The guests were in varied attire: shirtless teenagers in sandals and bathing suits, older couples in suits and floral print dresses, assorted men and women wearing casual summer clothing. The number of people staying at The Reata at one time was surprising. Gathered all in a single place, they could have been the residents of a small town; there was about the assembled throng the same sort of diversity and cohesiveness found in a real community.

Quite a few people had brought their own Bibles, and that surprised him. It shouldn't have; polls always showed that Americans were a very religious people. But growing up and living in Southern California, where none of his friends went to church and Sunday was a day just like any other, he'd come to think of the United States as an almost completely secular society. That clearly wasn't the case, and as a person who would not have dragged his family out here this morning if the word "sunrise" had not accompanied "service," he felt like the odd man out among these people who brought Bibles with them on vacation.

Bibles.

Lowell frowned. He didn't recall seeing a Gideon Bible in their suite, and he was pretty sure he'd gone through all of the drawers and cupboards in the rooms. That was weird. It was the first time he'd heard of a hotel room without a Gideon Bible, and whether it was accidental or intentional, it seemed ominous to him.

They took seats in the center, close enough to see clearly but far enough away that they could sneak out early if necessary.

The sun had risen to the edge of the desert foothills, a crescent wedge of white peeking over a rise, lightening the sky above and casting long shadows that all seemed to point to The Reata.

Emerging from behind a boulder, the minister stepped forward.

Wearing nothing but a black G-string and the head of an elk.

The gasps of the gathered faithful were audible, and people immediately began walking out, the elderly couple in front of them standing indignantly, clutching their Bibles and uttering shocked expressions of outrage, the clean-cut family to their right scurrying to escape the amphitheater as though being chased by demons—which, Lowell reflected, they might legitimately believe was the case.

"Friends, Romans, countrymen," the minister intoned, and though his voice was muffled by the elk head, it could be heard throughout the amphitheater. "Let us bow our heads and pray. Oh, great god Pan . . ."

"Excuse me, excuse me . . ." A mother stepped in front of them, holding a hand in front of her daughter's eyes to block the girl's view of the pulpit as they hurriedly headed toward the exit.

The minister began thrusting out his black-clad, barely-covered crotch at the audience. ". . . sanction our excesses and forgive us our jests as we forgive our jesters. Lead us please into temptation . . ."

"Let me through," an irate overweight man demanded as he shoved his way toward the aisle.

Lowell sat where he was. He wanted to see this thing through. They weren't a religious family to begin with, and he didn't think that anything they might see here would permanently harm the kids. Besides, he wanted to see if this would be taken all the way to the end. More than likely, the shock effect scared everyone off after a few minutes, but he wanted to see if the "minister" had enough additional material to perform an entire service.

Something about his attitude seemed wrong. Despite his agnosticism, he should have been outraged and disgusted by this. He should not have been so blasé about it, so *amused*. But he was. And so were Rachel, the twins and Ryan. All of them seemed to be infected with a benign tolerance, and indeed there was a high percentage of people who remained, many of whom seemed just as curious and uninvolved as they did.

". . . in Pan's name we play! Amen."

From close to the stage, he heard Blodgett's loud rough laugh. "Amen, brother!"

As if on cue, a single ray of sunlight shone from the right, illuminating three furiously chittering rattlesnakes that were arranged head-to-tail in a constant circle on the stage. With great flourish, the elk-headed minister reached down bare-handed and picked one up. It thrashed and flailed about in his grasp while the other two reptiles closed ranks, creating a much smaller circle.

"Rejoice and be glad in it!" the minister announced. He shoved the wildly squirming snake between the elk jaws and bit off the rattlesnake's head. The thrashing of the reptile's long body became more frantic, more intense, blood spraying out from the open neck like water from a hose. He turned it toward himself, the red soaking his chest and stomach, dripping down onto his legs, making him look like an elk that had been skinned and was walking on its hind legs. He spit out the head and then tucked the dying body into his black jockstrap, holding it there until all movement had ceased and it hung down limply like a giant phallus.

Then he began dancing.

And chanting.

The words made no sense. They seemed vaguely Native American but in a superficial, cinematic way, and Lowell had no idea if the words were real or if the man was only going for a mood or an effect. The chanting caught on, though, and soon Blodgett and his obnoxious buddies in the front row were up and dancing and emitting war whoops. At first Lowell thought they were making fun of the minister, but as seconds dragged into minutes, he began to see that they were joining him, not mocking him. He recognized a few other men who were jumping to their feet and starting to dance like evangelicals receiving the Holy Spirit in a tent revival, Coyotes rather than Roadrunners, but what really started to make him nervous was the fact that their families were joining the fray, wives and kids leaping up and going into the aisles while they shouted rhythmic gibberish.

Recognizable words slipped into the minister's nonstop chanting—"death" and "kill" and, unaccountably, "rhododendron"—while the gathered guests continued to spout nonsense. It occurred to him that the people were being hypnotized, something he'd never really believed was possible until he'd seen it a few years back at the Orange County Fair, and he wondered what the minister planned to do or suggest to his faithful once they were all under his spell. A few more individuals stood up to leave, the still-sensible people moving around the oblivious dancers and heading for the exit aisle, and Lowell decided it was time for them to do the same. He didn't know where this service was going, but he knew now that he did not want to find out. "Come on," he said, pulling Rachel's hand.

"Let's—" she began, but she saw the look on his face and nodded. The kids, for once, came along quietly.

Out of the amphitheater, safely on a sidewalk heading back toward the rooms, the rising sun to their left, Lowell made a decision. "I think we should leave," he said. "Today."

He wanted to take back the words the instant he said them, but behind them he heard the rhythmic drone of the minister and his new followers, and he knew that the impulse was not his own. He walked more quickly. "Let's go back home." He expected an argument, was half-hoping for one, but he saw only relief on the faces of his family, and that emboldened him. "I'll meet you guys back at the room," he said. "I'm going to find out about the car."

"Can I come, too, Dad?"

Ryan was looking at him with such hope that Lowell had to smile. "Sure," he said. "Come on."

"Kiss ass," Curtis muttered under his breath, and while ordinarily Lowell would have chastised him for that, today it seemed a welcome bit of normalcy and he let it slide.

They parted by a Mexican fountain at the crossroads of two walkways, Rachel and the twins heading back to the room, he and Ryan traipsing up the hill toward the lobby. Once there, he walked directly up to the concierge. "Is that battery in my car yet? I want it fixed now."

"Good morning to you, too, Mr. Thurman. As it happens, I just received a call from Laszlo, our chief mechanic, and he assures me that it will be ready to go by noon." The old man smiled up at him guilelessly.

"I don't believe you," Lowell said, and it felt good to say those words, to confront this representative of The Reata.

"I'm no mechanic," the concierge admitted. "So I can only go by what Laszlo tells me, but he says the battery is here, and as soon as he finishes maintenance on one of our carts and installs a new something or other in a leaf blower, he's going to pop your battery right in, hook it up, and it'll be good to go."

"Where is this Laszlo?" Lowell asked. "And where's my car? If the battery's here, I can do it myself."

"Can't let you do that." The concierge smiled. "Liability issues."

"I'll sign a waiver."

"I'm not quite sure why you're so all fired up about this. The Reata has bent over backwards to assist you. You didn't have to be towed to Tucson, we got your car fixed right here for you, and you got your battery at the wholesale price thanks to a mechanic's discount. All you have to be is a little patient. Can you do that for me?"

Lowell wanted to punch him in the face. "We are leaving today," he said slowly. "I want my car."

"Check out time is one o'clock," the concierge said, speaking equally slowly. "You will have your car by noon. That will give you plenty of time."

They stared at each other, and finally Lowell turned away. What was he hassling this guy for? The concierge just sat here at this desk and made phone calls; he didn't know what was really going on. What Lowell had to do was find the resort's auto shop, the garage, and talk to one of the mechanics face to face.

Ryan was standing near the front desk, slowly spinning the postcard rack. "Look," he said, pointing to a wooden mail slot on the desk as Lowell walked up. "It says they mail postcards for free for you. Can I get one to send to Gary?"

"Sure," Lowell said, though he did not want to contribute another dime to this place. He felt his anger start to ebb away. There was a *Star Trek* episode like this, he thought. One of the original ones, where after being exposed to the spores of some plant on a planet everyone became apathetic and lethargic and forgot about the things that really mattered.

The same thing was happening here. Though he didn't know how or why.

And by the time he bought Ryan a postcard and the two of them left the lobby, he didn't really care.

Twenty-five

Patrick received his wake-up call, thanked the too-chipper chippy on the other end of the line, then promptly settled back down to sleep. He didn't feel like going to the film festival today, and, goddamn it, he wasn't going to. Fuck Townsend. That prick had gotten him into this mess, had made it damn near a *Wages of Fear* trip just to get to the festival. He could eat shit and die.

He realized that his anger was out of proportion to the situation, and he wasn't quite sure where it was coming from. Frustration from last night, he supposed, and he wondered where Vicki was, what she was doing, whether she'd spent the night in someone else's room. He pushed the thought from his mind. It was none of his business.

He closed his eyes, dozed off again, and when he awoke it was past eight o'clock. He felt good. Playing hooky agreed with him, always had, and he felt the way he had when ditching a class in high school or calling in sick to work: free. He turned on the television for background noise, showered and shaved, then took an orange juice and an apple from the minibar. He wasn't a breakfast person, and figured that would tide him over until lunch.

He had finished eating and brushing his teeth, and was trying to decide whether he should watch a *Dinner for Five* marathon on IFC or spend the morning soaking up some rays by the pool. What he *should* be doing was finishing up his second article on yesterday's festival festivities, but he'd already decided to postpone that until the afternoon. Let Townsend squirm.

There was a knock at his door. He started across the room, wondering who it could be. Someone finally come to check on the party noise that had continued almost all night long? Doubtful, since he hadn't bothered to complain this time. He opened the door. Vicki was standing there, dressed in shorts and a cutoff T-shirt, holding a white piece of paper in her hand. "I've been looking all over for you," she said. "I know you told us your room number last night, but I forgot it, and those jerks at the front desk won't give out any personal information. So I've been walking up and down in front of different rooms, hoping one of the numbers would ring a bell." She smiled sheepishly. "This is the fourth door I've knocked on."

When he didn't say anything right away, she jumped in, speaking quickly. "I'm sorry about last night," she said. "I apologize. I don't know what happened. Things just seemed to get out of hand."

"It's okay," he said stiffly.

Her expression darkened. "I think it was that damn pool. The one in the fitness center. Something about it . . ." She shook her head, forced out a laugh. "And here I am talking in bad movie clichés."

They were clichés, but there was a reason they were clichés. Because they held truth. Patrick stepped aside. "Would you like to come in?"

She smiled gratefully. "Yes." She walked past him into the room, her nipples jutting against the T-shirt. "There's a theater here at the resort," she said. "Did you know that?"

Patrick shook his head. "No," he admitted.

"I just found out about it this morning." She handed him the paper she'd been holding. "This came on the tray with my breakfast, and of course I immediately thought about you."

He scanned the printed sheet. This couldn't be. *The Reata Summer Film Series,* the headline read, and below it was a list of films to be shown in the theater each Sunday for the next two months. Today, at ten and two, were two of his favorite movies, *El Topo* and *Eraserhead,* neither of which he'd seen since his college days. Thank God he had decided to skip the Tucson festival today. "Wow," he said, looking up. "This is—" He broke off.

She had removed her shirt and was standing there topless, looking at him, waiting for him. She met his eyes and then pulled down her shorts.

He took her in his arms.

In the middle of everything, he thought he saw movement out of the corner of his eye, a black scuttling on the floor near the minibar—

the spider?

—but then she was grabbing him where she shouldn't and he was thrusting deeper and harder, and the scuttling thing was forgotten in the mad rush to orgasm.

Afterward, while dressing, he talked to her about *El Topo,* which she not only had never seen, but had never *heard* of, and by the time they were all dressed he had gotten her nearly as excited about the film as he was.

"Now where's this theater?" he asked.

"It's in that main building, down the hallway where those conference rooms are, in back of the lobby."

He glanced at the clock. "The movie starts in twenty minutes, I doubt there's going to be a big crowd for this, but let's try to get a good seat."

She seemed happy just to be coming along with him. "Okay."

Patrick took two Evian bottles out of the minibar, handed one to her, and they stepped out of the room.

"Mr. Schlaegel!"

He turned to see the activities coordinator running down the causeway toward them. Patrick started walking, pulling Vicki with him.

"Mr. Schlaegel! Patrick! Wait up!"

The activities coordinator reached them, out of breath, at the end of the corridor just as they were about to head up the sidewalk. "Mr. Schlaegel! I'm glad I caught up with you. Since you're going to be staying at The Reata today instead of going back to Tucson, I thought you might want to help out the Coyotes. They weren't so hot yesterday in the volleyball tournament . . ."

Patrick frowned. How did the man know he was going to be staying here today? Was his room bugged? Had someone from the resort heard him talking to Vicki about it?

Had someone watched them?

He felt cold.

"It's Sunday. B-ball day. We're going to be playing basketball in the gym this afternoon, and the Coyotes are practicing there right now. I thought you might want to stop by, get in the game, help them out. They're still one man short."

"One *man* short or one *person* short?" Vicki asked.

He spread his arms. "We're open here."

"That's not what I heard."

"If you want to play—"

"I don't," she told him. "I was just checking."

"I don't either," Patrick said, and started walking toward the lobby, his hand around Vicki's, hurrying her along.

The activities coordinator accompanied them, and Patrick remembered the dark expression he'd seen yesterday on the man's face when he'd declined to participate. "I think you ought to rethink—" the activities coordinator began.

Vicki turned on him. "What part of 'no' don't you understand?

We're busy, we have plans, we don't want to play in your stupid game. Get a life. Jesus!"

Patrick kept walking, afraid to look at the man, prepared for any reaction, his hand in Vicki's tightening. The activities coordinator still seemed to him unstable, potentially dangerous, and the last thing Patrick wanted was to irritate or provoke him.

Then, suddenly, he was gone. Vicki's outburst must have done the trick, because when the sidewalk curved, he saw no one beside or behind them in his peripheral vision, and when he turned to look, they were all alone. "Where did he go?" Patrick asked.

"Maybe he took the hint."

If it was good enough for her, it should have been good enough for him, but he felt uneasy as they headed up the sidewalk toward the main building, passing the spot where he'd seen the wolf and the snakes Friday night.

In the lobby, a freestanding sign with magnetized letters announced THE REATA SUMMER FILM SERIES, and an arrow pointed down the corridor to the right, away from the gift shop. Behind the front desk, a cute girl smiled at them, nodded a greeting, and Patrick smiled back. Vicki ignored her. It was quite possible, he thought, that they'd be the only people in the theater. The movie hadn't been well-advertised—hell, he hadn't even known about it until Vicki told him, and his radar was attuned to anything film related—and *El Topo* was not exactly a big draw these days.

They stepped out of the lobby into the high, wide corridor, passing underneath a computer-generated banner that read: WELCOME HOLLINGER AND ASSOCIATES.

"Oh my God," Vicki breathed.

"Wha—" he began. And then he saw.

It stood at the end of the hallway. A small thin man with an overgrown child's head, a simple, innocent, too-happy face wobbling on the end of a long skinny neck. It was a figure out of a nightmare, and it made Patrick stop in his tracks. There was something about the little man that seemed familiar, that rang a bell somewhere deep in his brain, and though he couldn't place it, the association was not a good one.

Vicki recovered her equilibrium almost instantly and kept walking, but Patrick grabbed her hand and held her in place. He could not walk past that thing to go into the theater. There was no logical, physical reason . . . he was simply afraid.

The idiot head bobbled on its impossibly thin neck, smiling at him, and Patrick had to fight the urge to turn tail and run.

"You know," he said, feigning bravery, not wanting her to know how truly frightened he was, "I think I will check out that basketball game. It sounds like it might be fun."

"Are you kidding? I thought this was, like, one of your favorite films of all time. And I've *never* seen it." But she kept glancing over at that odd wobbling figure.

He, too, looked down the hallway. "Yeah, I know. Watching movies is my job, though. I'm taking a break today."

"I thought you wanted to—" The creature took a step forward, and she jumped, letting out a short sharp gasp. *She felt it, too.* Vicki nodded nervously. "Okay, yeah. Maybe it would be fun to, uh, play basketball. Or watch you play. My friends would like it, too."

They turned, hurrying back toward the lobby. Patrick hazarded one last glance behind him and saw the door to the theater closing, the figure disappearing into the auditorium. He shivered, chilled by the thought that they could have been trapped with that horror in the dark. In his mind's eye, he saw himself sitting in a theater seat while that big child's head rose like a moon above the chair in front of him, grinning in the gloom.

And he did not relax until they were through the lobby and out of the building, heading for the gym, that terrible creature safely behind them.

Twenty-six

They were in the Jacuzzi again, seemingly the only safe place in this treacherous resort, and there was no sign of last night's horrors. Pretty women and handsome men went about their duties cleaning the pool, setting up chairs and sweeping the cement. The storm had blown leaves and bugs in the water, and they had not entirely been scooped up, but several kids were still sliding happily down the slide while their mothers staked out preferred seats along the pool's edge.

David reached for his Coke and took a sip. It was watered down, the ice having melted and created a layer of water atop the heavier thicker syrup. The drink felt cool and good, but it wouldn't much longer. A little more time under this sun and it would be the temperature of hot tea.

So why the hell were they sitting in this warm jet-propelled water?

Comfort, habit, stupidity. Take your pick.

He looked across the roiling water at Ryan and Curtis who were staring tiredly back at him, Owen's attention was elsewhere as he scanned the sidewalk outside the fence for any sign that Brenda was on her way.

Where were his parents? David wondered. Back at the driving range? He had the utmost disrespect for his mother and father, and usually he wished them nothing but ill will. That was under ordinary circumstances, however. Here at The Reata, he found himself thinking about them, worrying about them, hoping they were all right.

He stood, getting out of the Jacuzzi. He'd had enough of this. He was starting to feel like a boiled lobster.

"Where're you going?" Curtis asked. Owen finally turned his attention away from the area outside the fence.

David didn't answer. He simply picked up his plastic cup and walked over to a nearby table with an umbrella. After a moment, the brothers followed. "I'm sick of this place," he told them as they sat on chairs around him. "It feels like a fucking prison. I used to think it would be crazy-fun to, like, live at a hotel. You know, have maids make your bed and clean up your mess. Eat out all the time. Have a pool to swim in and cable TV with every channel on the planet."

They were nodding.

"But it sucks. I'm bored. I feel like I'm trapped here. There's nothing to do, just the same old shit day after day, and . . ." He trailed off. *And there's the S&M driving range and the disappearing body at the bottom of the pool and the rain that turned hot chicks into old hags,* he'd been about to say, but something kept him from it.

"I know something we can do," Ryan said.

They all looked at him suspiciously.

"Go back to Antelope Canyon. To the old resort."

Curtis and Owen looked at each other, and David picked up on their frightened reluctance because he was feeling exactly the same thing. Last night, he had dreamed about the old resort, and he'd awakened shortly past midnight drenched with sweat, heart pounding, the images and emotions engendered by the nightmare still fresh and clear in his mind. In the dream, he'd walked alone down the Antelope Canyon trail at night, moonshine illuminating the way ahead, bathing the path in a bluish glow and throwing the mountains into darkness. The ruins of the old hotel had not been off to the side as they were in real life but at the end of the trail, its ultimate destination. He had not wanted to go there, had wanted to turn back, but he sensed a presence behind him, a being so dark and terrifying that he was afraid even to turn around and look at it. So he pressed forward, walking, then running, and soon he was at the empty resort. It looked more like a fortress now, like the ragged remnants of a Wild West stronghold. He walked through the open gates, past a guard hut and a one-room jail, to a large crumbling structure in the center of the fort. There were no windows in the dilapidated building, but a section of the roof had collapsed and moonlight shone through the hole, allowing him to see a shabby throne surrounded by rubble and bones. On the throne was a man so old it was nearly impossible to tell he was human, a skeletal figure with long scraggly hair who looked at him with cold dead eyes and said in a voice like amplified sandpaper, "Bring them to me."

"Who?" David had asked, his voice a fearful, barely audible whisper.

The ancient man pointed behind David and smiled, revealing long yellow teeth. *"Them."*

And he'd awakened.

The dream remained with him even now, but he wasn't about to admit that, especially to a kid like Ryan, and he nodded indifferently. "Sure," he said.

Curtis and Owen, caught in the same trap, acquiesced as well, and in a matter of minutes they were in their tennis shoes, shirts on, walking past the tennis courts on their way to the trailhead. Brenda wasn't with them this time, and for some reason Owen was glad of that. He liked her and all—she was pretty nice, and of course hot as hell—but she was one of those people who belonged in a city, who weren't cut out for the wilderness, and it had been weird to have her along last time. Uncomfortable.

They reached the start of the Antelope Canyon trail.

PLEASE STAY ON THE PATH.

Owen didn't like that sign. He hadn't liked it when he'd first seen it, and he liked it even less now. There was something about that simple, ostensibly innocent message that hinted at a deeper darker meaning and sent chills cascading down his spine. He wondered if anyone else felt the same way, and though he wanted to ask, he didn't.

It had been Ryan's idea to come here, but since David was the eldest, he led the way. They hiked up the incline and between the bluffs. Noise echoed and was amplified in this narrow part of the ravine, and to David it seemed like they were passing through a portal into another time or another dimension. It seemed *symbolic,* this entryway into Antelope Canyon, and he didn't like that either.

"We never found the hot springs," Ryan said. "Last time." His voice doubled back, altered and faint.

Curtis snorted. "What hot springs? If they were there at all, they're dead. That pool hasn't had any water in it since your grandma gave BJs to dinosaurs."

"She's your grandma, too," Ryan pointed out.

"It's just an expression."

None of them seemed to like the strange whispery quality of the echoes, and conversation died out until the canyon opened up before them. *There are ghosts here,* Ryan had said last time, and remembrance of the words made David shiver.

"Why'd you want to come here?" Owen asked Ryan, taking off his T-shirt and using it to wipe the sweat off his face. David had been wondering the same thing.

"Yeah," Curtis said. "It's hot as a bastard in this damn desert." But they all knew that wasn't the real reason for his discomfort.

"I thought we might . . . find something."

Now it was David's turn. "Find something?"

"Remember what happened last night? We're all pretending it didn't happen, and I think something's *making* us pretend it didn't happen, but it did, and we all know it." He paused, took a deep breath, said it fast, "The rain made the people who work at the resort turn old."

Chills surfed down David's arms at him hearing those words said aloud.

"I don't know how it happened, but we saw it and so did everyone else there." He looked at Owen. "Brenda, too."

Owen's voice was quiet. "What does that have to do with this?" He gestured around them, although mostly toward the ruined hotel up ahead and off to the left.

"I don't know," Ryan admitted. "But I think it does."

David did, too. And it was probably why he wanted to turn back around and hide in his room watching television until it was time to go home.

What were his parents doing now?

They walked the rest of the way in silence, none of them wanting to either agree with Ryan or challenge him, all of them wanting to just pretend none of it had happened and they were simply on an interesting nature hike.

They reached the mount with the buckboard, left the trail.

Please stay on the path.

David sucked in his breath as they passed over the rise. His heart started pounding. This was impossible. It had only been a day, less than twenty-four hours, yet the abandoned hotel was no longer in ruins. It was still deserted, still in a state of serious disrepair, but the complete destruction that had previously existed had been tempered somewhat and now there were full-sized walls where before there had been only vestiges of the foundation. The formerly roofless restaurant now had a roof, and the faded paint on the cracked chipped cement looked a little brighter, a little less faded. On a broken wall, he could see two letters: R and E.

Reata.

There had been no construction or improvements made, no one had come here overnight to work on the place. Indeed, the replaced walls and roof looked as old as the rest of the structures, faded and weathered by time and temperature. No, the old resort looked like it had simply gone back in time to a point where it was a little less dilapidated than it had been yesterday. That was impossible, though, and the four of them looked at each other without saying a word. Dazedly, they moved forward, going past the restaurant and walking in and out of the individual rooms, no longer able to pass through them due to the regenerated walls. David even saw a bed in one of the rooms. It was only a rusted metal frame with no mattress, but yesterday there had been no furniture whatsoever.

They walked around the first block of rooms. The pool looked the same, and for that David was grateful. He'd had a sneaky feeling that they'd find it full of water, the hot springs flowing once again and, like the fountain of youth, refreshing everything around, and he was thankful that was not the case.

But what *had* happened here? Something. He didn't know what, but he knew he wanted to leave, did not want to be in the presence of a power that could do something like this. He broke his reserve of cool. "Let's get out of here," he said, looking across the pool at the row of wooden crosses.

"Yeah," Curtis said quickly. Owen was already starting back the way they'd come.

But Ryan said, "Wait a minute. I want to check something out." There was fear in his voice but a focused determination as well, and David did not like that. Owen stopped walking, and the three older boys remained in place as Ryan headed alone down the stairs into that viewing room by the side of the pool. Neither of his brothers made a move to follow him, but David couldn't let the boy go down there alone, so he held tight to what was left of his courage and started down the steps after him.

It seemed cool down here, and darker than last time, but there was still that sick funky smell—

death

—and that huge open space where a window had once been, looking out onto the bottom of the pool. The window had seemed kind of neat last time, the idea of sitting in here looking up at chicks while they swam kind of sexy, but now it just seemed creepy, and he imagined a row of dirty old men hiding down here and checking out hot young babes while their unsuspecting boyfriends sat on lounge chairs up above.

Owen came down the steps, followed by Curtis. "What are you looking for?" Curtis asked.

"I don't know," Ryan admitted. "But I just thought I should check this place out again."

"Did you see that picture?" Owen asked, pointing at the wall opposite the window.

The rest of them turned around, and David's heart began thumping wildly in his chest. It was a life-sized crayon drawing of a skeletal man with long scraggly hair: the man from his dreams. Next to him, he heard Ryan's sharp intake of breath. *He recognizes him too,* David thought, and that frightened him even more.

The drawing was skillfully done, drafted by someone with obvious artistic talent, but it was graffiti, not a formal portrait, and that linked it in David's mind to those makeshift crosses above ground. For some reason, the image that came to him was of worshippers, raggedy people traipsing across the desert to erect crosses to memorialize their loved ones before heading down here to bow before the picture on the wall in some dark ritual.

Only the crosses didn't seem to him like memorials to the dead. They were more like warnings, like the symbols erected in the *Planet of the Apes* to keep everyone out of the Forbidden Zone, and he wondered if they had been put up by the followers of that ancient man wanting to keep people away from their secret spot, or by his victims, trying to save others from their fate.

"Who is *that?*" Curtis asked, and though it was clear he had never seen the figure before, it was also obvious that the form retained its power even through the medium of crayon, that the skeletal face made just as big an impact on him as it had on David in his dream.

And on Ryan.

"Have you seen that before?" David asked him.

Ryan thought for a moment. "Yeah," he said finally.

"Where?"

"I . . . don't want to say," he said carefully. "I need to think about it."

"Do you have any idea who that is?"

"No. That's why I want to think about it."

"Let's get the fuck out of here," Curtis said. "I'm getting claustrophobia."

"Yeah," Owen said. "Let's talk at the top."

It felt liberating to get out of the dark, get away from the stench, and they all breathed deeply when they reached the surface. Curtis and Owen immediately turned on their brother. "So where did you see it before?" Curtis demanded.

"I—"

"Don't give us that crap about how you need to think about it."

"In that restaurant building," Ryan said meekly, pointing. "That guy was in a broken mirror. I saw something moving in the mirror, and it wasn't me. It was him. And he wasn't in the restaurant but some mansion with animal heads on the wall. He looked like an old-time millionaire cowboy, kind of. And he was real scary."

"I had a nightmare about him," David admitted.

"Oh shit," Owen moaned. He turned in a circle, stomped his feet. "So what the fuck do we do?" he asked.

"We tell Mom and Dad," Curtis said.

"Yeah," Ryan agreed.

They were freer here, David thought. The mental and emotional restraints that seemed to be placed on them back at The Reata didn't apply, and that was a new development from last time.

"We need to pack up and go," Owen said. "Get our asses back to California. And tell Brenda and her family to get out while they can, too." He looked over at David. "You think you can convince your parents to leave?"

He shrugged. "I don't know. Not after I saw that golf game." He looked away from his friends, not wanting to face them, absurdly feeling that because of his parents, *he* was somehow part of all this. His gaze landed on a new building behind the second row of rooms. Well, not a *new* building, an old building—but one David was sure had not been there a few minutes earlier. It was wood rather than cement and looked like a barn. He licked his lips, pointing. "Where did that come from?"

Curtis turned. "What?"

"That building."

"I don't know," Owen said, his face pale. "But where did *that* come from?"

He was looking at a carved wooden statue, like a totem pole, standing in front of what had at one time probably been the lobby. The carving was taller than the surrounding buildings and featured a series of grotesque faces, all vaguely human and all imbued with a spark of pure insanity. At the top, like a malevolent father, that skeletal face from the graffiti looked down at them—and it seemed to be looking *right* down at them—the long thin hair forming a sort of frame for the faces beneath him.

"Maybe they *were* there," Curtis said hopefully. "Maybe they were there and we just didn't notice them."

They all looked to Ryan for some reason, as though the boy might have an answer.

"I don't think they were," he said. He walked over to the totem pole thing, looked up at it, gingerly put a hand out to touch the wood, but he drew it back instantly. "Feels weird," he said. "Slimy."

"Let's go," Owen said. David silently agreed. He was feeling more and more nervous the longer they remained here.

"Let's check the new building first." Ryan started walking.

Curtis advanced on him. "Listen, you little dickweed . . ."

Ryan smiled, and the gesture was a welcome sight after the tensions of the last ten minutes. "Too scared, huh? You can wait here with the women and babies, then." He sidestepped his brother and continued on toward the barn.

"Asshole," Curtis growled, but he followed along. So did David and Owen.

The ruins of the barn had been here yesterday, along with what looked like an adjacent corral from the days when The Reata had been a dude ranch, but now everything was restored. Used and worn, but workable. They stepped up slowly, making their way through a maze of collected brush and old broken furniture from the hotel rooms, ready to run at the slightest provocation. The barn door, nearly two stories high, was wide open, and carefully they peeked inside the gloomy interior.

It wasn't a barn, it was a slaughterhouse.

Instead of the stalls and hayloft David expected to see housed within one huge communal room, there was a high narrow chamber with blood-stained walls and floor. Down the center of the room ran a single metal table dulled by use and nicked by knives and hatchets. From somewhere in the dimness above, meathooks hung down, some of them with ancient flecks of dried flesh still clinging to them. On the floor were yellowed bones.

None of them knew what to make of it. They stood there staring, unwilling to go in but unable to turn away. David moved back a step, wondering what lay to either side of the slaughterhouse wall. On each side of the big barn door was a smaller door, also open, though he hadn't registered that before. He moved over to the one on the left, looked in and saw nothing—only empty space. Wooden walls with hay on the floor.

He was suddenly filled with the certainty that if one room contained nothing, the other contained something . . . horrible? . . . important? He approached the door with trepidation, not knowing what he'd find but knowing what he *didn't* want to see inside that room.

He saw it.

The throne from his dream.

David's mouth was suddenly dry, so dry that he started coughing and gagging because he couldn't generate enough saliva to lubricate his throat. Stupidly, none of them had brought drinks this time, so he had to tough it out, and it was all he could do not to puke.

"That's what he was sitting on in the mirror," Ryan said excitedly from behind him. "That was his chair."

Still coughing, David nodded. "My . . . nightmare," he managed to get out.

Whether Ryan or one of his brothers would have walked in there he never found out, because the door slammed shut on them as though on a spring hinge, banging so loud and hard that it made them jump. Curtis reached out to test the door but it was securely closed and unmovable.

David didn't know whether they'd stumbled upon something they weren't supposed to see or whether they'd been directed to see something specifically aimed at them. Either way, the show was over, and even Ryan realized it was time to go. They walked back through the resort, around the buildings, toward the trail.

Please stay on the path.

"We're telling Mom and Dad," Curtis repeated. "We have to tell Mom and Dad."

"If we can remember," Owen said quietly.

"We'll remember," Ryan said. "We just might not *want* to tell them. We might not care."

It was an acknowledgment of what all of them knew but had not until this moment articulated.

"Why does that happen?" Owen wondered.

"Why does any of it happen?" David said. "Why is that old resort fixing itself up? Why did the rain turn those people old?"

"But why are we just sitting there like bumps on a log watching it happen, not doing anything?"

"We *are* doing something," Ryan pointed out. "That's why we're here."

"Not enough," Owen told him. "Not enough."

By the buckboard wagon, now filled exclusively with human skulls from what he could only assume were severed heads, David turned around. From this angle, he could see a square frame looming over the roof of the restaurant, a frame that he would have sworn was not there five minutes before.

It looked like a gallows.

They reached The Reata and stopped in front of the tennis courts, trying to decide where to go next. Some of the urgency they'd felt at the abandoned resort had slipped away, but they still wanted to tell their parents what had happened, what they'd seen, and Ryan thought they should do so right away, before that desire faded away completely. All four of them agreed, and they decided to try to find their parents first, then go after David's, and then try to find Brenda and her family.

He felt like they were the Hardy Boys. Well, maybe not the Hardy Boys because they were kind of boring and lame, but *one* of those groups of mystery-solving teenagers. It was spooky what was happening. Terrifying. But it was exciting, too, and part of him wanted it to last for a while because he knew that nothing like this would probably ever happen to him again.

But that was dangerous thinking, and like too many other things the past few days, it made him second-guess himself, made him wonder if that thought was his own or if it had been imposed on him. Either one was possible, and that was part of the seductiveness of this whole thing.

One thing he wanted to do for sure, after they found their parents, was go back to the exercise pool. Other than his brief encounter with the broken mirror yesterday at the ruined restaurants in Antelope Canyon, it was the only place his ESP had worked, and Ryan needed to find out if that had been a fluke, a rare confluence of circumstances, or if it was a legitimate response that could be counted upon to occur every time, some sort of chemical reaction that happened between himself and the exercise pool. Of course, he could not go back alone. Too dangerous. Besides, he wanted someone else there as a control, to see if it was the pool, himself or a combination of the two that sparked those horrific scenes.

First things first, though. They hurried down the gravel trail, then down the cement sidewalk to their suite. Curtis had one of the keys with him and used it to open the door. "Mom?" he said. "Dad?" There was no response, and they didn't see either of their parents on the bed or the couch, but just in case they checked both bathrooms and the other bedroom. Nothing.

"Where now?" Owen said. "The pool?"

It was as good a place as any, but they weren't there either. They also weren't in the lobby, in the Saguaro Room or the Grille.

"Let's check my room, see if my parents are there."

"Sure," Curtis said.

The maid's cart was outside David's room when they arrived, and as soon as he saw it, David stopped and tried to turn them around. "My parents aren't here if they're cleaning the room."

"We might as well check," Owen said.

They walked in, David first, nervously tugging on his earring as he entered the sitting area. They walked past the unmade bed, around the corner to the bathroom.

There, an overweight maid, her skirt hiked up, was removing a toothbrush from the crack of her ass. She saw them and smoothed down her uniform as she replaced the toothbrush in its holder next to the sink. She should have been embarrassed, but she wasn't. She was defiant. And she swore at them in Spanish as she shoved her way past them and slammed the door on her way out.

They couldn't help it: they all burst out laughing.

"What the hell was that?" Curtis said.

David looked embarrassed, but he was laughing as hard as the rest of them. "Luckily, that's my dad's toothbrush."

"Are you going to tell him?"

He grinned. "No."

Ryan still wanted to check out the exercise pool, though the impulse was much less personal and more rational than it had been a few moments ago, more like wanting to find out the answer to a troubling math problem than anything else. "Maybe our parents, or your parents, are in the fitness center," he suggested.

"Let's check it out," Curtis agreed easily. The search had become fun.

Owen giggled. "Don't use *your* toothbrush tonight either," he suggested to David.

"Or yours," David responded.

As before, the weight room was empty. But there was someone swimming in the pool, a lone fat man who was totally naked and looked like Jabba the Hut. He grinned at them in a suggestive way that made Ryan feel dirty, then rolled onto his back.

"Dude has a boner," Owen whispered.

David and Curtis turned and walked out of the room. Owen started to follow them, but Ryan grabbed his arm. The scenes were coming to him again, superimposed on the real world just as they had been last time, just as they had in the mirror, and an electric thrill went through him, an excited recognition of the power he possessed, as the pool darkened and a white figure appeared against the far wall. "Do you see that?" he asked.

"What?" Owen said, still whispering.

The figure came into focus. It was a man in a chef's outfit, and he was flanked on both sides by a dozen or so well-dressed men and women. This image definitely took place in the past. The men were all wearing old-time suits, and had thick beards and hats, the women wearing big dresses and elaborate hair styles. They all had the same expression on their faces, an excitement that bore a very close resemblance to insanity. They were watching the chef, who was dropping severed arms and legs—*human* arms and legs—into the pool, then using a rakelike instrument to press them down and push them out into the water.

It looked like he was making soup.

The scene shifted, and now there were candles on the cement around the pool and a flickering shadow on the wall that looked like that skeletal, scraggly-haired old man. This, Ryan knew, was the future. He recognized Mr. Blodgett, that asshole who'd stolen their room, and saw a couple of other familiar faces as well. They seemed to be baptizing themselves in the water, using a hand to press down on their own heads, and then popping up with identically deranged expressions that were an eerie echo of their earlier counterparts'.

Why was he being shown this? he wondered. To scare him off or to fire him up? To warn him of what might happen if something wasn't done to stop it?

What *could* he do, though? What could *anyone* do?

Owen grabbed his arm and the visions disappeared. "Come on," he said in an annoyed voice, as though he'd said it several times before to no effect. "Let's go."

The fat man grinned at them, his erection quivering.

Ryan started to turn but caught movement out of the corner of his eye and looked down. The hose of the pool cleaner had snaked out of the water and was touching his shoe. Ryan jumped back, but the plastic tube whipped around his leg, grabbing him. He felt a strong tug as it yanked, trying to pull him in.

"Help!" he yelled, although Owen was already holding on to his arm in order to keep him out of the water. Curtis and David raced back into the pool room, saw what was happening, and reacted immediately, Curtis grabbing him around the middle to anchor him in place, David dropping to his knees, using his pocket knife to cut the hose.

At the first touch of the blade, the hose retreated, like a living creature that had been hurt, snapping back into the water so fast its tapered end drew blood through Ryan's pant leg.

"Go!" Owen screamed, and Ryan was nearly pulled off his feet by both of his brothers as they made a mad dash out of the pool room.

Behind them, the fat man was laughing in a deep booming voice that echoed off the pool tiles.

They ran down the corridor, through the weight room and back outside, where they practically collapsed. Ryan glanced fearfully behind them as they stopped farther down the sidewalk to catch their breath, but the door to the exercise center remained closed. They were not being chased.

"We have to find Mom and Dad," Curtis said adamantly. "We have to tell them what happened."

"Yeah," Owen agreed.

David nodded.

"Let's go then," Ryan said, and started walking. Because he knew that if they didn't find their parents fast, they soon wouldn't care, and everything that had just occurred would be a faint meaningless memory.

Twenty-seven

Patrick sat in the bleachers, watching basketball practice. The teams had uniforms, for God's sake, and if he'd ever needed a metaphor for American society's overplaced emphasis on sports, this was it. Next to him, Vicki watched two Coyotes pass the ball awkwardly before the taller one tried and failed to make a layup.

"Are you really going to play in this stupid game?" she asked skeptically.

He shook his head. "I guess not," he said.

"Then let's go. I don't know about you, but I'm bored already."

Patrick was bored, too, but boredom was welcome after the fear he'd experienced earlier. Never was too soon to see that horrible child-headed man again. Just the thought of that wobbling head on that skinny little neck gave him shivers.

He stood, taking Vicki's hand as they made their way down the bleachers.

"Mr. Schlaegel! Didn't see you come in!"

Great. Patrick looked over at the sound of the voice and saw the activities coordinator emerging from the open doorway of what had to be the locker room. He waved, smiled, hoping they could get out of the gym before the activities coordinator reached them.

No such luck.

He was there when they got to the bottom of the bleachers. "Glad you changed your mind! You can get suited up right in there." He pointed back toward the doorway through which he'd entered. "Got a Coyotes uniform in just your size."

Patrick was already shaking his head. "No," he said. "I need to do some work."

And he did. There were probably fifty e-mails from Townsend queued up in his in-box asking where his articles were. He seemed to have lost track of time here. And he was so unfocused. He wouldn't have thought he could be so distracted by his surroundings, but he had been.

The activities coordinator scowled, and once again Patrick sensed a seething rage that threatened to explode at any second. "I thought you came here to play."

As before, Vicki jumped in. "Well, you thought wrong." She took Patrick's hand and practically pulled him toward the exit. On the court, a player stumbled and fell, knocking over the man guarding him.

"This is your last chance!" the activities coordinator called after them.

Patrick did not bother to answer, and Vicki silently held up a middle finger as they walked out the door. He had no idea why she hated the man so much, but she did and he was glad of it.

It was as if she'd read his mind. "He reminds me of my ex-boss," she said when they were outside, and Patrick thought that explained a lot.

"I really do need to get those articles done," he said, stopping in front of a vending machine.

She nodded, understanding. "April and Madison are probably wondering where I am anyway. I told them I was just going to stop by and apologize to you for last night. I wasn't planning on . . . staying."

He smiled. "Well, I'm glad you did."

"Do you want to get together later?" she asked. "Maybe have dinner?"

"That would be great," he admitted.

She kissed him in a way that promised much more. "Eight o'clock, then. At the Grille. Be there or—"

"Be square?"

" 'Die,' I was going to say, but that's just as good." She smiled and waved, walking backward. "I'll see you later."

The spider was back in his room.

Patrick could practically *feel* his balls retract as he saw the black hard-shelled creature lying in the center of his unmade bed, its body moving up and down as though breathing deeply. It had grown since he'd seen it and was now the size of a small cat. He froze in place, so scared he was unable to move. There was something horribly wrong and alien about a spider that size, a feeling he had never experienced in any of those giant spider movies, but that now hit home in a very visceral, immediate way.

He took a slow step backward, prepared for anything.

The spider remained in place.

He backed up again . . . then he was outside, and he grabbed the door handle, trying to pull it shut, cursing the pneumatic arm that made the door close so slowly.

But the spider didn't move, he was outside and safe, and he started running. He had no compunction this time about going back to the lobby and demanding help. Still, he was unwilling to commit himself fully to the truth and admit to the existence of a monster bug, so he lied and said his bed was infested by black widows, dozens of them, and he wanted someone from maintenance down there immediately to exterminate them.

The clerk called up his room number on her computer. "You complained about a problem with spiders yesterday?"

"Yes. And now they're back."

"Maintenance sprayed for roaches, ants, spiders—"

"And now they're back," he repeated. The girl was young. According to her name tag, she'd been working for The Reata for a year and was from Garcez, Nevada. "I don't expect a resort like The Reata to be overrun with bugs," he told her. "That's not what I pay for."

The girl nodded politely. "I'll just give maintenance a call."

His cell phone rang. Townsend. "Where the fuck are your stories?" the editor demanded in lieu of a greeting. "One fucking piece? That's all you could come up with? If I don't have anything from you by four, I'm running a review by McGrath, you got me? Just because we put you up at a fancy resort doesn't mean you can spend all your time funning in the sun instead of doing your job. Do you understand?"

Patrick had to smile. In Townsend's mind, The Reata had gone from being a joke to a temptation. It served the bastard right for booking him here in the first place. Part of him wanted to calmly inform the editor that he had skipped the festival today and was goofing off, but that was going too far.

"Someone from maintenance will meet you at your room in five minutes," the desk clerk said, hanging up her phone.

"Who was that?" Townsend demanded.

"Nothing. Talk to you later." Patrick clicked off his cell. "Thank you," he told the girl. He nodded a good-bye and walked through the lobby and out the door through which he'd come. A Reata employee wearing clean khaki clothes and carrying a metal toolbox was already waiting for him when he reached his room. "Mr. Schlaegel?" the man said.

Patrick nodded. "Hey there."

Goateed, with a shaved head, the maintenance man looked nearly as young as the desk clerk, but his voice when he spoke was as jaded and mocking as that fat-assed security guard's. "You think you have a spider infestation, eh?"

"Yes I do."

"You know, I'm the one who fumigated your room yesterday."

"You probably killed the ones that were there," Patrick said, trying to be polite. "But now there're new ones."

"You think so, do you? I didn't even see any there the first time." He nodded toward the door. "Why'dn't you just open 'er up there and we'll see what you got."

In the seconds before he opened the door, Patrick knew the spider was going to be gone or it was going to be shrunk down to normal size or something equally humiliating that would make him look like the biggest wimp—

fairy

—on the planet. That's the way these things always worked. But the door swung inward, the two of them walked inside, and the spider was still there, as big as ever and twice as frightening.

Only . . .

Only the maintenance man did not seem to care. He stepped calmly forward, put down his toolbox and climbed onto the bed, standing on his knees. The spider rose to its feet, sensing someone close, but the man moved quickly, pressing down on the creature's back with his right hand, while his left hand broke off a leg. It snapped with a loud crack, and the spider screamed, a harsh screeching sound that hurt Patrick's ears. White viscous goo oozed out of the broken leg onto the bed. The spider was thrashing crazily, screaming, trying to get away, but the maintenance man kept breaking off legs, piling up the black leaking appendages on Patrick's pillow. Finally, he said, "Could you hand me that ball-peen hammer out of my toolbox there?"

Patrick bent down and opened the toolbox, drawing out a hammer, all the while keeping an eye on the legless spider on the bed, its bleeding black form *bouncing* under the maintenance man's hand, that terrible agonized screeching issuing from its unseen mouth. He put the hammer in the maintenance man's outstretched hand, then winced as the rounded end of the tool came down on the spider's head with a sickening crunch that put a stop to the screeching once and for all.

The maintenance man climbed off the bed, put his hammer, still dripping with that gooey white substance, into the toolbox and walked outside. He returned a moment later with a black plastic garbage sack and tossed the oversized spider body as well as the eight broken legs inside. Tying up the bag, he dropped it in the wastepaper basket next to the dresser and went into the bathroom to wash his hands. He emerged a few moments later, looked at Patrick and smirked as though he'd been summoned on a completely ridiculous waste-of-time errand. "The next time you need someone to kill a spider for you," he said derisively, "give us a call."

Patrick closed the door behind the man and nearly gagged as he saw his bed, the sheets and bedspread all covered with bits of black shell and thick trails of that viscous white goo. The smell was somehow less harsh than it should have been and reminded him of lemon meringue pie, but the juxtaposition with that disgusting mess made it that much more revolting.

From the room next door—the *empty* room—came a loud knock on the wall. "Quiet down in there!" a deep voice demanded, and it was followed by a round of laughter.

Patrick ignored the laughing voices and picked up his laptop, taking it outside to write. He sat down on the metal chair in front of his room, placing the computer on the small table before him, but his hands were shaking so badly his fingers kept hitting the wrong keys, and it was several minutes before he could finally type a coherent sentence and get down to work.

Twenty-eight

Lowell was checking on the status of the car, the kids were at the pool as usual, and Rachel sat alone in the exercise center, working out on one of the weight machines, trying to burn off some of the excess energy that seemed to be making her so antsy. Lowell had told her not to come here—they'd had a fight over it, in fact—but she'd refused to let him tell her what she could and couldn't do, and she'd stormed over, determined to spend all morning in here if that's what it took to prove her point.

She wasn't sure now that had been such a good idea. She was alone in here, but every so often it didn't *feel* as if she was alone, and once she thought she caught a glimpse of movement in the mirror that covered the wall in front of her.

She could ignore those occasional moments, though, because she liked using the weights. There was something exciting about it, on a physical level, and the involuntary flexing of her thigh muscles as she pumped iron, the feeling of tension in her crotch, led her to loosen and tighten her vaginal muscles. Loosen and tighten. Loosen and tighten. She was developing a counter rhythm to the lifting of the weights, and soon she was experiencing what she'd been hoping to experience, the sensation building . . . building . . . until, finally, a wave of joyous release passed through her, and she closed her eyes for a moment to savor it.

She opened her eyes, eased up on the weights, wiped the sweat from her face with a towel, and leaned back for a moment, cradled in the arms of the exercise machine. Already her temporary high was fading, and she looked at herself in the mirror, saw her wild hair, the sweat stains on her clothes, the slight indentation where her chest met her belly, the puppet line wrinkles beginning to connect her nose and her mouth. She looked more like her mother than herself, and in that state of disappointment and disillusionment which usually followed a self-administered orgasm, she realized that her life was nearly half over.

I have left the world the way I found it, Rachel thought, and to a person of her time and age and background there could be no greater sign of failure. In junior high and high school and college, she had been told that she could make a difference, and she had believed it, vowing never to knuckle under to the humdrum reality of everyday living. She was going to be someone, she was going to do something with her life. But she hadn't, she didn't. She'd had absolutely no impact on the world around her. Her lofty goals and ambitions had never been reached, had only been so much hot air. She'd planned to do great things and live a fascinating life. Now she was a wife and mother with a boring respectable job. She'd capitulated instantly, giving up without a fight, and she was exactly the type of person she swore she'd never be.

It was deep and dark, the place this thinking could lead her, and it took every ounce of emotional strength she had to keep from going there.

She'd been having a lot of dark thoughts since coming to The Reata.

The flipside was that it was exciting here. Being constantly on the alert, watching out for danger that could befall her husband and kids, keeping a paranoid eye out for the creepy gardener or one of those abusive administrators awakened some sort of primal instinct within her that was, if not predatory, at least as far from complacently nesting as she could possibly be. It was scary, yes, and she wanted to get away from the resort and back to the real world as soon as she possibly could, but . . .

But she felt more alive than she had in a very long time.

And, as strange as it seemed, there was an element of sexual excitement involved as well—which was why she'd just gotten herself off while lifting weights. Maybe it was the constant adrenaline rush, but her desire was up, substantially increased from its usual level, and there was an urgency to it, as though she not only wanted sex but *needed* it. Desperately.

She liked that feeling, though she knew it was dangerous, and in the logical part of her mind she thought it was probably a feeling induced purposefully, somehow, by The Reata to gain her allegiance, to keep her here.

Odd how she had started to think of The Reata as an entity, not as a collection of buildings but as a singular being with thoughts, plans and motivations.

Evil thoughts, plans and motivations.

That was true, and it was what kept her from embracing the experience. Last night, in fact, she'd had a nightmare about the resort, a dream in which she'd accompanied the chef on a midnight tour of his gourmet garden and had come across a plot of black, foul-smelling carrots overseen by a scarecrow made from her stolen underwear. Working the patch, pulling weeds, was the gardener, and he chuckled lewdly to himself as he periodically reached up to stroke the scarecrow's pantied face. She, the chef and the gardener harvested the carrots, which they put in a big basket and presented to a dark figure at the far end of the garden, a scraggly haired skeletal man wearing vaguely western clothes who sat upon a throne. She and the other two men were serfs, she realized, and he was their master. They were presenting him with an offering.

Rachel had no idea what any of it meant, or if it meant anything, but she had a sneaking suspicion that the dream was intended as a message, that it contained some sort of hidden meaning for her to decipher.

She was glad they'd be going home this afternoon.

There was movement in the mirror again, someone or something that ducked behind one of the larger pieces of exercise equipment just before she looked at it, and Rachel decided that it was time to leave. She stood, picking up her towel and tossing it in the wooden bin on the right side of the door. It was midmorning, but hers was still the only towel in there, and she wondered why no one seemed to be taking advantage of this state-of-the-art weight room with its expensive and truly amazing exercise equipment. Then she thought of Lowell's crazed overreaction and the constant feeling that she was not alone in here, and it occurred to her that maybe that was why.

Behind her, on one of the machines, a weight fell with a too-loud clang, and she jumped. Maybe it was a stray bar from her machine that had gotten stuck at an angle on its way down and had only now fallen into place, but she couldn't be certain and wasn't about to check, so she hurried out the door into the hot heat of the day.

She was still sweating from her workout, but though the desert sun was scorching, the dryness of the air actually evaporated the perspiration from her face. Rachel checked her watch. Ten fifteen. They'd promised the car by noon, but maybe Lowell had been able to harass them into getting it done quicker. She'd go by the room first to see if he was there. If not, she'd leave him a note and check on the kids at the pool, make sure they weren't getting into any trouble, make sure they were safe.

She walked down the gravel path between landscaped barrel and saguaro cactus, past a burbling fountain that reminded her that she was thirsty. She quickened her pace. From around the thick trunk of a cottonwood tree up ahead, another woman came toward her on the path, a haughty, ferret-faced woman of approximately her own age whom Rachel had seen cheering fiercely for Blodgett's team yesterday at the volleyball tournament. The woman met Rachel's gaze, then looked disdainfully away. *You're here for the off-season bargain rate just like we are,* Rachel thought, but smiled agreeably as the two of them approached each other, the same way she would smile at any person she happened to meet.

The woman stopped walking for a second as Rachel passed and purposely stuck out a foot to trip her. Rachel stumbled, almost fell, but caught herself and whirled to face her attacker, who was now calmly walking away.

"Bitch!" Rachel yelled, and instinctively reached down to pick up a stone. She threw it as hard as she could, and was gratified when it slammed against the woman's upper back, just above the U of her tank top, and drew blood.

The woman screamed and dropped the oversized bag she'd been carrying, crouching to grab a small rock of her own, which she heaved at Rachel, hitting her tennis shoe. Seconds later, they were in the midst of a full-fledged rock fight, and even as she dodged incoming pieces of sandstone and threw semisuccessful salvos of her own, Rachel wondered how it had come to this. This was insane. Two grown women throwing rocks at each other in the middle of a luxury resort? How could something like this happen?

She didn't know, but as crazy as it was, it felt good, it felt right, and she whaled away with a windmilling arm, going for quantity not quality, aware that many of her throws were missing completely, but certain that enough of them were hitting their target to inflict damage. A small piece of gravel winged the woman's cheek, and a bigger rock smacked into her left breast, eliciting a gratifying cry of pain.

A stone thrown by the woman hit Rachel's arm, a surprisingly solid blow that was felt all the way down to her bone, but then Rachel in her indiscriminate frenzy happened to grab a rather large rock the size of a baseball, which sailed fast and true and connected with the woman's exposed forehead, opening up an instantly bleeding gash. A wave of red gushed down over her right eye, onto her cheek, onto her clothes.

The woman quit, running away, crying and holding a hand to her bleeding head. Rachel dropped the stone she'd been about to throw. "Take that, bitch," she said.

Smiling, she continued up the path toward their suite.

"What do you mean it won't start?"

Laszlo shrugged. "Electrical problem, I think." He gestured around the auto shop. "We don't have right tools here. You must call dealer in Tucson, tow it there."

It was all Lowell could do to keep from punching the man. "I was told my car would be ready by noon today! Why couldn't you have told me this earlier? Why didn't you know yesterday?"

He held up his hands in a gesture of defeat. "We don't have right tools."

"Have you tried . . . everything you can?"

Laszlo nodded, wiping greasy hands on a rag.

Lowell stared at the open hood of his car, wondering what could possibly go wrong next. He supposed he should thank the mechanic for trying, especially since he only had to pay the wholesale price for the battery and nothing at all for labor, but the truth was that he didn't feel very grateful. In fact, deep down, he blamed The Reata for the problems with his car.

How had it come to this? How had one of the Southwest's most famous and exclusive vacation spots shifted in his mind from the beautiful exotic luxury resort they'd seen on the Internet and in brochures to some sort of haunted hotel responsible for tampering with his car?

Because.

It was as good a reason as any and better than most. Sure he could cite examples of weird experiences they'd had here—this morning's "church" service was exhibit number one—but it wasn't empirical evidence that had convinced him there was something fundamentally wrong with The Reata. No, that was knowledge he possessed on a gut level, something he just *knew,* not merely something he believed.

"We can keep it here until you call tow truck," Laszlo said.

"Thanks," Lowell told him, though he didn't really mean it.

Rockne was waiting for him outside the auto shop. The activities coordinator was wearing a red baseball cap, and had a whistle around his neck and a basketball in his hand. He threw the ball at Lowell, who caught it easily.

"Good reflexes," he said. "Are you signed up for our basketball tournament?"

Lowell threw the ball back. Hard. "I'm busy."

"Too busy to help out your team?"

"They're not my team, and yes, I am."

"Busy doing what?" The activities coordinator spun the basketball on his finger.

"We're leaving this afternoon," Lowell said. "We're checking out today."

"That's funny. I thought the schedule said you were booked for five nights." He didn't sound in the least concerned, and that made Lowell think about his car again—and think that it most likely *had* been sabotaged.

But sabotaged just so he would have to stay here and play basketball?

That was too much of a stretch even for him.

"Not interested," Lowell said and pushed past the activities coordinator.

"We'll be practicing in the gym!" Rockne called after him. "Hope to see you there!"

Their suite was still empty when he returned. His anger flared for a second, but beneath it lurked an unfocused fear and the nagging feeling that he should go over to the exercise pool and make sure Rachel was there and that she was all right.

A moment later, she walked into the room, sweaty and safe. "Is the car ready?" she asked. Apparently they'd both decided to ignore their earlier argument and pretend nothing had happened.

"It wasn't the battery," he told her.

"What does that mean?"

"The car won't start. The mechanic thinks it's something to do with the wiring or the electrical system. We'll have to get it towed to Tucson."

The blanched expression on her face probably mirrored the one on his own when he'd first heard the news. "You mean we're trapped here?"

"No. I'm going to call Triple A right now, get someone to tow us to Tucson. We'll stay there tonight."

"There are five of us," she pointed out. "We can't all fit in the front seat of a tow truck."

"We'll figure something out. Where are the kids?"

"At the pool. Where else?"

He met her gaze. "Do you think that's . . . safe?"

For a moment it appeared she was about to argue with him, to tell him nothing had happened to her, he was just being paranoid, the kids were fine. Then that defensive shell cracked and she shook her head helplessly. "I don't know. I'm going to go over to the pool and check on them."

He nodded. "I'll find out about the car."

Lowell thought for a second that she had something else to tell him. She paused, opened her mouth as if to speak, but then changed her mind and turned.

"What?" he said.

"Nothing."

After she left, he unplugged his cell phone from the recharger and called AAA. He gave the representative on the other end of the line the required information, but after an unusually long wait, the man informed him that a tow truck would not be available for several hours.

Lowell sighed. "I'm not going anywhere," he said.

He clicked off, and a second later the room phone rang. His heart lurched in his chest. *Something's happened to the kids,* was his first panicked thought. But when he answered the phone it was Rand Black. After a desultory greeting, Black awkwardly announced, "We're practicing for the basketball tournament right now." The Cactus Wrens' captain sounded weary and discouraged. "I already talked to that jackass who calls himself the 'activities coordinator,' so I know you don't want to do this, but I thought I'd give it a shot. We really need a center."

"We were planning on leaving today . . ." Lowell began.

"Yeah, he told us you can't get anyone to come out here and tow your car until later this afternoon."

How did he know?

"Yeah," Lowell admitted.

"I know you don't want to do this, and I don't blame you. Hell, most of us don't either. But we could really use your help. Again." Black paused. "I don't know if you've heard, but there're prizes for the winners this time. Real prizes. Comped vacation, the entire stay. Dinner at the Saguaro Room." And here the man's voice sounded wistful—or was it only Lowell's imagination? "Night on the town at Tucson's hottest spots."

Lowell chuckled. "What about a prize for my usual place? The loser?"

"Consequences," Black said shortly, and there was a soberness to his tone that wiped the smile off Lowell's face.

"What does that mean?"

"I'm not sure. That's all we were told. Winners would get prizes and losers would face consequences. That's why we need your help."

Lowell didn't know what to say.

"We're afraid of the consequences," Black said softly.

A suffocating feeling of entrapment and obligation settled over him. He didn't want to be drawn into this. But he couldn't let the Cactus Wrens suffer . . . consequences . . . if he could do something to help them. He was pretty good in basketball. He might be able to push them to a win. "Okay," he agreed.

"Thank God." Black's sigh of relief was nearly audible.

"You're at the gym?"

"I'm calling from the phone outside, but, yeah, we're practicing right now. We get another hour, then it's the Roadrunners' turn."

"I'll be there in a few minutes," Lowell promised. "After my wife and kids get back."

"Thank you," Black said honestly. "I appreciate it."

"I'll meet you there," Lowell said.

They were lost.

Curtis didn't know how it had happened, or how it *could* happen, but somehow they'd gotten turned all around and had ended up on a sidewalk that took them to a laundry and storage building. From there they'd only gone further astray, walking down paths that meandered around desert brush and trees and wound up at locations with which they were completely unfamiliar.

Like now.

They stared at the fenced-in garden.

"This is impossible," David said for the fifth or sixth time, and for the fifth or sixth time he was exactly right. The Reata wasn't that big. The resort was not a mazelike warren of interconnected buildings, it was a terraced hotel, with everything spaced out far enough to be easily distinguishable. And no matter where one was at the resort, bearings could always be taken from the mountains behind it.

But . . .

But the buildings didn't look right somehow. It was as if they were always coming in from an odd angle that made even familiar sights unrecognizable. Each time they went down a sidewalk or one of the gravel paths, they always wound up either turned around and back at the same location where they'd started, or at a spot where they *didn't* want to go.

Twice they'd found themselves at the exercise center, once in the front of the building, once in the back.

Now they were staring at this garden, probably the same one where their mom had taken her cook's tour, and the full fruit trees and heavy tomato vines only served to remind them that it was nearly lunchtime. "I'm hungry," David said, looking through the bars of the metal fence. "I'm gonna get me an apple."

That sounded good to all of them, and since there was no one to kick them out, they quickly found the gate and slipped inside. A lot of the plants growing here were weird, Curtis thought as they walked down the slight slope to where the fruit trees were. He saw a bush with black leaves and a vine with some sort of triangular vegetable that smelled like fish. Ryan must have sensed the same thing, because when he spoke his voice was low and worried. "Let's hurry up and get out of here."

They reached the apple tree, and he, Owen and David each picked a piece of fruit. Ryan stood nearby. "I'm not hungry," he said.

David took a bite, then heaved the rest of the apple as hard as he could toward the back of one of the buildings. It fell far short of its mark and bounced on the dirt.

"Rotten?" Curtis asked.

"No. It tasted good." David grinned. He picked another apple, took a bite and threw it. Soon all three of them were flinging fruit as far as they could, and it felt good, felt like they were striking a blow against . . . something. Ryan stood by quietly and watched.

"What do you boys think you're doing?"

They all whirled around at the sound of the rough voice. A man was standing in the middle of a bunch of tomato plants. He couldn't have walked in there without them hearing or seeing him, Curtis thought. He must have been sitting in the plants all this time, watching, before deciding to stand up and confront them. He looked like a farmer, with his checkered shirt and cap, and Curtis wondered if this was his garden.

"We're—" David started to say. And ran.

The rest of them were caught by surprise, but before they could follow suit, the man shouted "Stop!" in an angry authoritative voice that made David halt in his tracks.

The man pushed his way through the tomatoes onto the open ground. He was old but powerfully built and probably could have kicked all of their asses at once. "I asked what you boys thought you were doing."

"Nothing, sir," Owen answered for them.

"I saw you picking those apples. I saw you throwing them away."

He looked from Owen to Curtis to David to Ryan, glaring. "Those were perfectly good apples."

"I'm sorry," David said.

"You'd better be." The man withdrew a rag from his back pocket, using it to wipe the sweat from his forehead. Only it wasn't a rag. It was a pair of women's underwear. Curtis had a queasy feeling in the pit of his stomach.

"Boo!" the man screamed at the top of his lungs, and they all jumped.

He laughed, a deep rumbling laugh that sounded like the noise a tree would make if it could express amusement. The man suddenly turned and shoved his way back through the tomato plants. He crouched down for a moment, then stood again, holding a trowel in one hand and a pair of clippers in the other. He banged them together over his head, then leaped up, dancing.

The man was insane, Curtis realized.

He looked at David, at Owen, at Ryan, saw from their faces that they understood his plan instantly, and with a nod, they all started running.

There was no shout to stop this time, no angry pursuit. As far as he knew, the man just continued to dance. But he did not turn around to check. None of them did. They stared straight ahead, slammed open the gate and dashed out, still running, not slowing until they were sure the garden was far behind them.

Twenty-nine

There were women in the game this time, and while Lowell had always considered himself modern and open-minded, he didn't think women *should* be here. Play or no play, fun or no fun, this was a man's sport, and if bitches wanted to get involved, well then they should start their own tournament. Luckily, Rachel had no interest in participating. In fact, she looked very feminine this afternoon, sitting in the bleachers wearing a tight top and a short skirt that showed her off to best advantage. She may have had three kids, but she still looked damn good.

Lowell stopped himself. *Bitches?* What was he thinking? This train of thought was not even remotely connected to his own beliefs and opinions.

Only these *were* his own beliefs and opinions. They may not have been before, but he certainly believed them now.

How was this possible? How could he suddenly start thinking things that he never would have considered before? The only conclusion he could come to was that his mind was not his own—and that was the scariest notion he could ever conceive. Physical restraint or intimidation was one thing, even that strange emotional damper that had been placed on him since arriving at The Reata he could deal with, but to have his thoughts altered, to be corrupted from within so that his core convictions were no longer his own . . .

What was the next step? he wondered. Not *caring* that he was harboring idiotic opinions? Not *knowing*?

Maybe he would become a totally new person living in the outer shell of his old body.

The idea made him want to kill himself to keep it from occurring.

That was a completely alien thought.

The stands were full, and Lowell recognized a lot of people from the sunrise service. People who had walked out offended, people he would have thought would check out and leave immediately afterward, were in the bleachers waiting enthusiastically for the first basketball game to start.

The two teams—the Wrens and Coyotes—had been warming up at opposite ends of the court, but at the sound of the buzzer, they broke for their respective benches. "We can do it," Rand Black said as the team gathered around him, and the funny thing was, Lowell thought they really could. Black had said the same thing before the volleyball tournament and was obviously saying it now to boost their spirits and give them confidence, but Lowell had been eyeballing the other team and the truth was that the Coyotes didn't seem to have any really strong shooters, and the Wrens easily had them on height. Most importantly, the Coyotes team was half chicks this time out, many of their other players having quit or checked out this morning. The Cactus Wrens were all men.

If they played their cards right, this could be a blowout.

As the center, Lowell was called upon for the tip-off, and he found himself facing an old lady who glared at him with beady eyes. "Fuck you, Mr. Fuck," she said softly, the words all running together. "I call you Mr. Fuck, you fucker. Fuck you. Mr. Fuck."

Rockne, holding the basketball and acting as referee, grinned.

The whistle was blown, the ball was thrown, and Lowell jumped as high as he could, feeling a strange and unwelcome sense of satisfaction as he hit the ball to Black and bumped the old lady to the ground. The cries of the crowd that accompanied his action were not of outrage but approval.

That seemed to set the tone for the game.

There were elbowings and kneeings, trips and punches, but Rockne, the lone ref, did not call any fouls. Lowell himself the high scorer for the first quarter, got involved, delivering a hard elbow to the tit of that old bat who'd jumped against him, and she went down in a hail of obscenities to the delight of the roaring crowd. In the front row, he spotted an elderly couple who had left the sunrise service shocked and horrified by the so-called minister's shenanigans screaming at the top of their lungs, cheering him on. "Kick her!" the old lady yelled. "Kick her in the twat!"

Something snapped within him, like a rubber band stretching and then whipping back to its original shape. Seeing that old couple screaming crazily brought him back to reality like a slap to the head.

He was himself again.

That didn't mean he went soft on the court, however. His game was on today, and though he hadn't played basketball in quite some time, he was a lot more coordinated and in a hell of a lot better shape than most of his opponents. Not to mention taller. He and Black, the two best athletes on the team, developed a kind of rhythm, and by halftime they were up by twenty points. By the end of the game, they'd beat the Coyotes by forty-eight, and it was Lowell's idea to retire as champions.

"We're not playing," Rand Black declared when the referee announced the beginning of the second game. All of the Cactus Wrens stared defiantly at the activities coordinator.

"You . . . have to." For the first time, the man appeared flustered; he'd obviously never encountered a refusal to play before.

"We don't have to do anything!" Garrett Reynolds piped up. The gangly man had scored ten points in the last quarter and his confidence was high.

"The Roadrunners would have an unfair advantage," Black said calmly, logically, offering a rationale Lowell wished he'd come up with. "We've just been running around, playing our asses off for the past forty minutes. They're all rested and ready to go."

The activities coordinator—Rockne—did not have a comeback.

The crowd was starting to disperse, rows of spectators carefully making their way down the aisles at both sides of the bleachers, and more than anything else it was the defection of the audience that seemed to signal the true end of the tournament.

"We want to play!" Blodgett bellowed from midcourt.

It was the perfect opportunity, and Lowell couldn't resist. "Play with yourselves!" he shouted. "You're good at that!" There was laughter from the departing spectators, a response that seemed to diminish the activities coordinator and enrage Blodgett.

"Right now!" Blodgett yelled. "Right now!"

Calmly, dismissively, Lowell turned away. He saw supportive grins on the faces of his fellow Wrens.

"The Cactus Wrens forfeit!" Rockne announced. "The Roadrunners are our basketball tournament champions!" But no one was listening, no one cared, and his voice barely carried above the varied conversations of the dwindling crowd.

Lowell found Rachel waiting for him by the home team basket. "Take off that ridiculous uniform," she told him, "and let's get the hell out of here."

The kids were still out when they returned to the suite, and though the boys might return at any second, Rachel wanted sex. Once more, she was aggressive in a way that Lowell found disturbing and more than a little off-putting.

"My pussy's dirty," Rachel told him, and she flipped up her skirt.

She wasn't wearing any underwear. She spread her legs wide. "Lick it," she ordered. "Lick it clean."

Dutifully, he lowered his face between her legs and began swirling his tongue in the circular motion he knew she liked. Her hands held his head down hard, and she ground her crotch painfully into his face until she achieved satisfaction. Afterward, she sucked him with a fierceness he had never experienced before, and though it was arousing on a purely physical level, inwardly he recoiled. Grunting like an animal, she sucked harder, faster, more furiously, and then he came, exploding in her mouth, and she greedily gulped it down, holding him between her lips until he was completely spent. She squeezed out the last few drops then let him go, licking her lips like a cat and smiling, a look of complete satisfaction on her face.

Who is this? he thought. It sure wasn't the Rachel he knew.

Then he was pulling up his pants as she walked over to the dresser, took out some underwear and put it on, and suddenly she *was* the Rachel he knew. She seemed embarrassed by what had just happened, though neither of them mentioned it, and he thought of his own suddenly reactionary reactions at the beginning of the basketball game. They were being played by whatever force or power lurked in this resort, and the feeling was extremely unnerving. He felt as though they were stepping across a minefield, never sure when their next movement was going to blow off a leg or kill them dead.

He had still not heard back from AAA, and he called back to complain. They should be leaving here by now, halfway on the road to Tucson. The representative on the phone looked up his name and number, then explained that a series of accidents in Tucson had taken up the resources of the towing service that was supposed to pick up his car. As his situation was a low priority, and The Reata was so far out of the way, it would probably be tomorrow morning before a truck arrived to tow their vehicle.

They were trapped here for another night.

The boys returned shortly after. They didn't say where they had been, and neither he nor Rachel asked, but their manner suggested they had seen something they did not want to talk about, something that had made a profound impression upon them.

They all spent the rest of the afternoon together, playing cards on the patio of their suite. They should be talking, Lowell thought, opening up with each other, communicating, but he didn't know how to get them to do it and, besides, the impulse was more of a general notion than a conviction.

They ate dinner early, room service again, and stayed inside after dark, the boys in their room, he and Rachel in theirs, each of them watching their respective televisions. It felt to him like they were hunkering down in their bunker, hiding from whatever was going on outside their door and hoping it would not touch them until the sun rose again in the morning.

He supposed to some extent that was exactly what they were doing.

By ten o'clock, Rachel was already asleep next to him, and out of curiosity, he used the remote control to turn down the sound on the TV and flip to the resort's information channel. He didn't know what to expect, but what he saw was an infomercial for The Reata that was far more honest and realistic than anything on their Web page or in their brochures. There was a shot of today's basketball game, with one of the Coyotes gleefully headbutting a Cactus Wren, and a scene of a bottomless woman in a Reata T-shirt singing karaoke at the Grille. He turned the sound up slightly: "Here at The Reata you can play all day and party all night in our luxurious surroundings amid the natural beauty of the Sonoran Desert." The picture shifted to what appeared to be a vulture pecking the eyes out of a dead human baby lying motionless in the sand.

Lowell turned off the television. They needed to leave. They needed to get out of here.

Tomorrow, he promised himself.

Come hell or high water, tomorrow they were getting away from The Reata and never looking back.

MONDAY

Thirty

Lowell awoke early. He sneaked carefully out of bed so as not to disturb Rachel, grabbed the cell phone and took it into the bathroom to call AAA. A beep and a message told him that the phone was out of range, but he didn't see how that was possible since he'd just used it yesterday. Another try in the bedroom and another outside yielded exactly the same results. Rachel was still sleeping—snoring, in fact—so he was quiet as he lifted the handset of the room phone to call out.

The phone was dead.

Lowell hung up, tried again, jiggled the little catch in the cradle, but there was no dial tone, no noise, nothing.

He had a bad feeling about this, and he quickly dressed and put on his shoes.

"Wha—?" Rachel said groggily.

"Nothing," he told her. "Go back to sleep. I just need to check on something."

There was no newspaper on the welcome mat outside their room, and while the world was usually quiet this early in the morning, today it seemed *too* quiet. He wasn't sure what that signified, but he didn't like it, it worried him, and he hurried down the steps and up the sidewalk toward the lobby. Something was wrong. He could feel it. No, more than feel it, he could see it, although it took him a few moments to realize what it was exactly he was seeing.

Empty parking lots.

He stopped walking. He'd reached the first group of rooms above their own, and the parking lot in front of the building was empty. Either everyone had checked out and gone home or everyone's car had been stolen. He continued on, sprinting up the cement to the next building and the next until he reached the lobby and the main parking lot.

Jesus Christ. All of the cars were gone. Overnight, each of the lots had been emptied. Even the little carts that the staff rode around in were nowhere to be seen.

He walked across the bare asphalt to the guardhouse to find out what the hell was going on, but the little shack was abandoned, its doors locked, the gates blocking the road closed.

Now he really was worried. He ran back across the parking lot to the main building, opening the door himself since no attendants were there to do it for him. The lobby was empty. Not only that, but it appeared to have been empty for some time. He felt like Rip Van Winkle, as though he'd fallen asleep and a great amount of time had passed. There was dust on the front counter, and the ornate mirror behind it was cloudy, the carpeting on the floor worn and threadbare. Looking through the windows at the patio outside and the pool below was like looking at a ghost town: chairs and tables were overturned, the cabana bar boarded up, the pool filled with visible debris. Only the well-landscaped grounds gave any indication that this was not the way it had always been, that yesterday this had been a thriving luxury resort with an extensive staff.

Since there was no one around, he placed his hands on the dusty countertop of the front desk and hopped over. The computers were gone, all shelves and drawers empty, but the phones were still in place and connected. He picked up one. Then another. And another. Until he'd tried all five.

The phones were out.

Just in case, he tried his cell again, but it still didn't work, and he had the feeling that the same would hold true for all of the guests' phones.

If there *were* any other guests.

The anxious feeling within him was not panic, not yet, but it was on its way, and he quickly left the lobby and hurried down the sidewalk to the closest set of rooms. He knocked on the door of the first one he reached. Putting his ear to the door, he heard the welcome sounds of movement and voices from inside.

He and his family were not the only people who had been stranded here.

He breathed an inward sigh of relief, and when the door opened a moment later and a tired man in a bathrobe squinted at him and said "Yeah?" Lowell could have kissed him.

"Sorry," Lowell said. "Wrong room." He'd considered telling the man what had happened, explaining that they'd been abandoned here, but decided against it right now. There'd be time for that later. If it really did turn out that there was no way to leave, all of the guests would have to get together and map out a strategy. Until then, he wanted to make sure he made every effort to find a way out.

The helicopter!

He'd forgotten about that, and once again he found himself running down a sidewalk, this time toward the heliport.

As he'd feared, as he'd known, it was empty. Well, not exactly empty. There was no helicopter on the target-shaped landing pad, but on the flat ground next to it was a burned and twisted hunk of metal that looked like it could have come from a crashed chopper.

From this vantage point, Lowell could see the backs of several of The Reata's main buildings, and he glanced from one to the other, trying to think if there was something that he'd missed, some other means of escape or communicating with the outside world that he was overlooking or had forgotten, but he was all out of ideas.

There was only one conclusion to be drawn: they were inexplicably stranded here.

He made his way back to the suite, walking along the rear of one of the buildings, gratified to see open drapes behind the patios and balconies, with lights and movement in most of the rooms. One of these, he realized as he passed by, was their original room.

Blodgett was still here.

panties

It didn't matter. The man might be a jackass, but he was in the same boat as the rest of them.

Lowell emerged from behind the building to see a crowd gathered on the road next to the pool gate. The waterfall was turned off, and he could hear the voices of angry guests. The throng was fifteen or twenty strong, many of them with sleep-tousled hair and wearing Reata bathrobes. They'd obviously discovered what had happened and seemed to be quizzing someone in authority. Had they found a remaining Reata worker?

They had, but it was a janitor, and he was apparently as much in the dark as the rest of them. Moreover, he possessed limited English skills, and most of the demands and queries made of him seemed to go right over his head.

Lowell felt sorry for the janitor, who was coming under increasing verbal fire. *Leave him alone,* he wanted to say. *The man doesn't know any more than you do.* But the crowd was angry and vociferous, and he wasn't brave enough to stand against them. He searched the faces of the crowd, hoping to find Rand Black or one of his fellow Cactus Wrens, someone he could appeal to, but while some of the faces seemed vaguely familiar, there was no one he actually knew.

His gaze stopped on the face of a dark-haired woman approximately his own age.

No. It couldn't be.

Lowell squinted, cocked his head, moved around the edge of the gathering, examined her from different angles, but no matter what he did, the woman still looked like a grown-up version of Maria Alvarez, his first girlfriend from high school.

Maria Alvarez.

It didn't seem plausible that she was avoiding the reunion, too. And that she'd chosen the exact same resort as he had in order to get away from Southern California . . . but *was* it possible?

Who was he kidding?

He watched her face carefully. Maybe it was someone else, someone who just happened to bear a resemblance to Maria. But she shouted "Where is everyone?" at the janitor, and it was her voice. Even after all these years, he still remembered that voice, and when he saw the way she folded her arms across her chest in an expression of dissatisfaction, the déjà vu was complete. "I want an answer!" she demanded.

He thought about Rachel's recent aggressive lovemaking.

Lick it clean!

Fuck me! Fuck me hard!

Those were the types of things Maria used to say.

A shiver of cold passed through him. He didn't know why he hadn't remembered it before, but he recalled now her assertiveness, how she would coordinate their sexual encounters and make specific demands of him in the backseat of his car. She'd been the school slut, and he'd been the envy of all his friends. A motherless girl from a poor neighborhood off Main, she had zero self-confidence, was ostracized by many of the other girls, and made up for it by being aggressively sexual. All she needed was someone to believe in her, someone to care about her, and then everything would be all right. Or at least that was his theory. But she'd ended up fucking half the junior class, including his then–best friend John Murdoch. And when he dumped her, she laughed at him.

The thing was, he hadn't really been interested in Maria until she had practically thrown herself at him. He'd had his eye on someone else, a girl from P.E. named Brenda, and even after he and Maria had become an item, he still secretly longed for Brenda. But that had never come to pass, and by the time he was free she was already with another boy.

Something was going on here that defied explanation. A haunted hotel was one thing. Ghosts and strange occurrences and an evil power permeating everything? That he could accept. But these constant allusions to his own life, to his high school days, on the very weekend of his dreaded twenty-year reunion . . .

It wasn't possible, it didn't make any sense, it didn't fit into any theory or framework he could envision.

He was staring at the woman, watching her, and for no reason her head swiveled away from the janitor and turned toward him, her eyes locking on his. She smiled, a lewd promising smile he remembered well, and instinctively he glanced away. But he recovered instantly and looked over at her again.

She was gone.

It wasn't Maria, he told himself. It wasn't anyone. Just a figment of his imagination. But he knew that wasn't true. People had looked at her when she spoke, the janitor had tried to respond to her question.

Another low-level employee, a maintenance man of some kind, emerged from the walkway that led to the generating station, and the janitor told the crowd "Wait!" and ran off to see his coworker.

"Get back here!" a man called.

"Where are you going?" a woman shouted.

Lowell turned away. There were no answers to be had here. He doubted there were answers to be had anywhere. The thing to do right now was go back to his suite, talk it over with Rachel and the kids and decide what they should do next. He felt a little better that they were not completely alone here, but not as good as he had a few moments before. The mood of that crowd was ugly, and he had the feeling that if they turned out to be stranded here for any length of time, tempers would get even shorter, people angrier.

He started down the sidewalk, passed a set of rooms, took the fork that led to their suite and saw, standing between two saguaros on the upslope ahead and to his left, the activities coordinator. The sight chilled him to the bone. He did not know why, but the activities coordinator was the last person he wanted to meet on an empty walkway in the deserted resort. He sped up, quickening his pace, looking only at the sidewalk. Out of the corner of his eye, he saw the man moving down the slope toward him, and he realized with sudden dread that their paths would cross a yard or so up ahead.

Lowell walked even faster, looking over at the man, and suddenly he was no longer the activities coordinator.

Rockne. The Reata. One hundred years.

He was the coach, Coach Hendrie, the P.E. teacher who had made Lowell's life a living hell in high school for dropping out of varsity baseball.

No. It was an optical illusion. His mind playing tricks on him. Stress. *Something.*

"Thurman!" the man yelled in the coach's perpetually hoarse voice.

Lowell kept walking, ignoring him, hoping he would go away. Instinct was telling him to run, but he had too much pride for that, did not want to act like a complete candy-ass pansy, as the coach would say.

They did meet on the path, and the coach spoke only a few words before moving on.

"The Roadrunners against the Cactus Wrens," he said, smiling, his beady eyes boring into Lowell's. "This afternoon. At the driving range. Be there or else."

Then they were both continuing on their respective paths and Lowell, his heart pounding, had to force himself not to run back to the suite and slam and lock the door behind him.

Owen answered the knock at the door, and his heart soared within him as he saw that it was Brenda. He suddenly felt ten pounds lighter. Ever since his dad had explained that they were trapped here, that everyone who worked at The Reata had disappeared, Brenda had been on his mind. The noble self-sacrificing part of himself hoped that she'd gotten away and was on her way back to California safe and sound. But the larger, selfish part of his being wished that she was still here, trapped with them. He'd even come up with several plausible scenarios all of which ended with the two of them alone and naked together.

Now she stood before him, and he was grateful. "Hi, Owen," she said, and it was like none of the insanity was happening around them, as though they were the only two people in the world.

"Hi," he said. He didn't know whether or not to invite her in. Curtis and Ryan knew Brenda but none of them had even mentioned her to their parents and it would be kind of weird to suddenly just announce, "Mom and Dad, this is my girlfriend Brenda."

This was his chance to introduce her to them, though, and he stepped aside to let her in. He'd just call her a friend at first. Then once they were back in California and they got to know her a little better, he'd let them know that it was a little more serious. "How are you doing?" he asked.

She didn't answer, just walked on by him toward his father, and something in the way she moved made him think everything was not as it should be. He glanced over at his brothers, saw puzzlement on Curtis's face, worry on Ryan's.

They'd noticed, too.

"Mom?" Owen said. "Dad?"

His parents, talking in the sitting area, turned to look. His dad's face suddenly turned pale, as though he'd seen a ghost or was about to puke or both.

"Lowell?" his mom asked worriedly.

Brenda chuckled, and the sound raised the hackles on the back of his neck, turned his veins to ice. It was a horror show laugh, unlike anything he'd ever heard in real life, and issuing from the mouth of a teenage girl, it seemed obscene and horrendously frightening. The expression on her face was sly. "Long time no see, Lowell."

Lowell? What the hell was this?

"Brenda?" Owen said, confused.

"Brenda?" his father echoed.

"Do you two know each other?" his mom asked, and at least the hint of anger and suspicion in her voice was normal, had some grounding in reality.

"He wanted to fuck me. But I fucked his son instead." Brenda sidled next to Owen, snaked an arm around his midsection, and somehow it felt *slimy*. He wanted to pull away from her, but he couldn't seem to move. This couldn't be happening. This had to be a nightmare.

His mom's face was set in stone, and his dad's was drained of all color, frozen in open-mouthed shock.

"She was in my P.E. class," his dad said lamely. "She went to my high school."

Brenda giggled in a way that made Owen want to run for the hills. What his dad said didn't make any sense . . . but he knew his dad: the man was telling the truth. And right now Owen didn't know Brenda at all.

"What are you talking about?" his mom said in a voice filled with righteous anger, and once more she cut through the craziness and brought it back to the here and now.

Brenda held him tighter, fingers slipping beneath the belt line of his pants, and that was the last straw. He pulled away from her, moving closer to his parents. Curtis and Ryan had retreated back to the doorway of their bedroom.

"Brenda Hafer was a girl in my P.E. class my junior year in high school." His dad spoke slowly and clearly. "I had a crush on her. That was twenty . . . twenty-one years ago." He paused, looked at Brenda and took a deep breath. "This looks like her." Another pause. "I think it *is* her."

She smiled cunningly. "You wanted to get in my panties, didn't you, Lowell? You wanted to fuck me."

"Stop it!" Ryan screamed, and for a brief second, everything was still. Even Brenda's horrible smile was momentarily wiped from her face.

And then their mom took charge. "Get out," she told Brenda, and advanced on the girl. Surprisingly, Brenda backed up. Owen exhaled, realizing he'd been holding his breath. His mom crowded his girlfriend toward the open doorway, where she backed outside onto the porch before the door was slammed in her face.

His girlfriend?

No, she was not that anymore. She never had been. He still didn't know what was going on, if this was some ghost from his dad's past returning to take revenge (although she'd seemed awfully solid for a ghost) or if some look-alike—the real Brenda's daughter perhaps—was playing some sort of elaborate practical joke. Neither of those seemed likely, however, and Owen realized that he now thought of her as part of The Reata, part of the weirdness that had been swirling about them since they'd arrived. He remembered how she hadn't wanted them to leave the path in Antelope Canyon, had tried to keep them from seeing that other, long deserted resort, and he thought now that that might be important.

The filters were off, he realized. Whatever had been dampening their interest in what was happening around them, keeping them from speaking out about what they saw or heard or felt, was gone. No longer needed, probably, and that idea scared him.

"That was the girl from your high school?" his mom asked.

His dad nodded. "Yeah."

She turned to Owen. "How do you know her?"

"He met her by the pool on Friday," Ryan offered, and though it was the truth and needed to be said, Owen was a little put off by his brother's tattletaler tone. "They like each other."

"*Liked,*" Owen said, attempting to inject a little humor into the situation.

His attempt was not appreciated. "What did you do with her?"

His face reddened. "Mom!"

"Was she telling the truth?"

He looked at his shoes.

"Well?"

Reluctantly, he nodded. Glancing over at his brothers, he saw respect and a tinge of jealousy in Curtis's face. Ryan looked disgusted.

His mom turned back to his dad. "What *is* she?"

"I don't know," he admitted, and his voice was quiet, frightened. "I really don't know."

Thirty-one

Vicki got out of bed, wincing. Her ass still hurt from the vigorous bout of anal sex they'd engaged in last night, and she crouched down and hurried awkwardly across the room toward the bathroom.

She was getting too old for this.

Conventional wisdom said that women were at their sexual peak during their thirties, but Vicki had desired sex much more often in her early twenties than she did now, a decade later. Back then, she'd been up for almost anything, and if her night didn't end with an orgasm she felt as though she'd wasted an evening. But these days, once or twice a week was plenty, and sometimes even that was too much.

She closed the bathroom door, sat down on the toilet.

To top it off, she had diarrhea.

She didn't know if it was related to the sex, but she assumed it was and she vowed that next time a guy wanted to use the back door, she was going to tell him that entrance was closed for business and steer him around to the front.

Even if he was someone famous.

Vicki smiled to herself. It *was* kind of cool to have been bedded by someone like Patrick, although she'd practically had to throw herself at him to get him to do anything. He was smart, cool, cute, and his celebrity status was the icing on the cake. She wasn't a groupie by any means, and she certainly wasn't shallow enough to sleep with someone just because they'd been on television, but she had to admit that having seen him on TV before meeting him had probably raised his standing in her eyes.

From her right, from the bathtub, came a thump, a noise as if something had fallen, followed almost immediately by a scratching, scuttling sound. The image in her mind was of a rat falling into the tub from a hole in the ceiling and scrambling to get out. Though she wasn't done and hadn't even wiped, she stood before turning to look.

"Oh my God!" she cried. "What's that?"

A naked little man, completely hairless and barely bigger than a Ken doll, was trying in vain to scale the rounded slippery sides of the bathtub. He was craning his neck like a baby bird and the strained expression on his face reminded her of the terrible visage of the human-headed fly in the original version of *The Fly,* that tiny toothless horror who screeched, "Save me! Save me!" before Vincent Price crushed it with a rock.

She didn't pause to look longer or to think about what was happening but bolted from the bathroom, grabbing her underwear and pants from the floor, putting them on as fast as she could while she kept one eye on the lighted bathroom. Patrick was nowhere to be seen, and she couldn't remember if he'd been next to her in bed when she'd gotten up; she'd been too groggy and preoccupied to notice or care. It was conceivable that that thing in the tub *was* Patrick, and she looked around until she found her top and then dashed out of the room, still slipping her arms through the sleeves.

Outside, the grounds were quiet. Too quiet. She didn't know why, didn't know how, but while the world was usually hushed this early in the morning, there was a different quality to it today, as though some underlying buzz, some subliminal noise that was always there but never recognized, had been taken away.

She hurried as fast as she could down the sidewalk to her room, trying not to think of that little hairless man in the tub, trying not to imagine him creeping over the bathtub's edge, running through the bathroom and bedroom and dashing out the door to race crazily along the pathways of The Reata.

Had she closed Patrick's door?

She couldn't remember.

Vicki increased her speed. She didn't see a single soul on the way back to her room, didn't hear any noises other than the slap of her own bare feet on the cement. Small rocks dug into her heels and soles and she wished she'd stopped to put on her shoes, but that would have taken too long and, besides, her shoes were next to the dresser . . . which was against the wall right next to the bathroom.

She made it back to her room, took the keycard from her pants pocket and unlocked the door.

Her friends were gone.

Their clothes still hung in the open closet, suitcases lay on the floor, but neither bed appeared to have been slept in, and the room had an unfamiliar air of emptiness. She had a bad feeling about this. "April?" she called. "Madi?" She checked the bathroom—even the tub, although she was prepared at a second's notice to leap out of the way and run—but it too was unoccupied.

Vicki sat down on her bed, looking over at her friends' suitcases. April and Madi were gone. Not just gone as in left for home, but gone as in dead. She didn't know how she knew this but she did, and it suddenly occurred to her that she might be next.

There was a knock at the door. A single loud rap that sounded like a baseball bat striking the wood.

Silent, holding her breath, she waited for a follow-up, the giggles of her friends, perhaps, or a call of "Maid service!" but there was nothing.

The knock came again, even louder this time, and there was something threatening about it. Vicki was suddenly filled with the conviction that if she opened the door, she would meet the same fate as April and Madi.

Death.

Another loud bat-against-the-door crack.

There was no other way out of here. The room did not have a rear exit, and all of the windows opened out in the same direction as the door. Why hadn't they gotten a room with a patio? Why had they been so damn cheap?

The sound came again, and it was not just the loudness and suddenness that terrified her, it was the absence of any other noise, the fact that there was no accompanying shout or cry.

Only the sound of the door being smacked by something powerful.

Again.

And again.

And again.

Vicki started to cry. She couldn't help it. She wanted to remain silent, to try to fool whatever was out there into thinking the room was empty and no one was here, but she couldn't stop herself, and one stifled sob turned into a series of hiccuping cries that sounded especially loud in the morning's strange silence.

Crash!

Whatever was out there was no longer just hitting the door, it was slamming into it, trying to break it down.

Crash!

She screamed, releasing a torrent of pent-up fear that manifested itself into uncontrollable shaking and sobbing.

Crash!

The door flew in on its hinges, and the big black thing that burst into the room was not at all like the creatures she had imagined.

It was worse.

It was much, much worse.

Patrick returned to his room confused. He was even more confused when he found his door open and Vicki gone. What the hell was this? *The Quiet Earth*? He called her name, checked the bathroom, even checked the closet just in case she'd had some sort of panic attack and retreated in there, but she was nowhere to be found.

No one was.

He'd gone out to get breakfast when he discovered that the phone didn't work, thinking he could pick up a couple of croissants or bagels and some coffee and juice from one of the resort's restaurants as a surprise for her, but everything had been closed and looked abandoned. He hadn't seen any guests or employees anywhere along his route.

He was going to be so happy to get back to Chicago and the real world and get the fuck away from this godforsaken desert once and for all.

The next time Tucson had a film festival, McGrath could cover it.

Patrick was trying to decide what he should do when the door opened behind him. *Weren't those things supposed to lock automatically?* He turned to see the activities coordinator standing in the doorway, silhouetted by the morning sun. "You have some explaining to do, Mr. Schlaegel." The voice was different than it had been, more authoritative, more villainous, with the same sort of overenunciated semirobotic creepiness as Hugo Weaving in *The Matrix* movies.

"I'm busy," Patrick said, knowing his reply would not make the man go away but attempting to retain some control over the situation and pretend, outwardly at least, that everything was normal.

The activities coordinator walked into the room, and his face looked slightly different, too, more clearly defined, more lined and angular. Menacing. "I think you need to come with me."

Patrick was about to decline or disagree, when to his surprise the man reached out and with a vicelike grip grabbed his upper arm, squeezing the muscle. "Hey!" he said, but allowed himself to be led out the door, afraid of what might happen if he resisted. The asshole was strong. *Too strong,* a part of his brain said, and it was true, but in the litany of strange things that had been going down lately, excess strength was not exactly something that stood out.

"Where are we going?" he asked, speaking so as to not let intimidation take over completely.

"Victoria Shanley's room."

He was filled with an apprehension so intense that it nearly stopped him in his tracks. If it wasn't for the sheer brute strength of the activities coordinator pulling him forward, he would have dug in his heels and refused to continue on. But he knew that if he did so, that painful pressure on his muscle would increase, and it was not hard to imagine the man yanking his arm out of its socket.

As with his earlier trip to the restaurants, they passed no one else on the way. The resort appeared to be abandoned, and he wondered with a growing sense of horror whether he and the activities coordinator were the only two people left at The Reata. His feeling of dread magnified tenfold.

Then they reached another building, walked halfway down an open corridor and stopped before room 561. The activities coordinator opened the door to the room, and Patrick's heart shifted into overdrive. There was blood everywhere, on the floor, on the walls and especially on one of the beds. There was meat on the bed too, or something white that looked vaguely like rent flesh, and Patrick thought of how the maintenance man had killed that monster spider. In his mind he saw the same thing happening to Vicki, saw a uniformed Reata employee hold her down on the bed with one hand while he ripped off her arms and legs with the other, blood splattering every which way.

"Wha—?" Patrick cleared his throat, tried to blink away his suddenly watery eyes. "What happened?"

The activities coordinator shrugged. "Someone killed Victoria Shanley. And in a very messy and gruesome way, I might add."

There was almost a pattern to the spattered blood, or at least that's the way it seemed, and it took Patrick a moment to realize why he thought that, what it reminded him of. It was a children's toy, one so old he didn't even remember the name of it, where a kid placed a piece of paper in a machine with a recessed spinning disc and then dropped paint onto the paper. The paint then exploded outward in op art ecstacy, creating firecrackers of color.

This was almost like that, and the horrible thing was that there was so much blood, the gore was so completely overwhelming, that it was almost abstract. It was nowhere near as disgusting or abhorrent as it should have been because the overpowering extent of it robbed the scene of any sense of intimacy or connection with the victim.

The victim.

Vicki.

"We know you left the Grille with her last night." The accusation hung in the air, unspoken but as clear as if it had been announced over a loudspeaker.

Patrick didn't know what to say, so he didn't say anything in order not to accidentally incriminate himself. He'd been set up, framed.

He expected to be told that the police were on the way and that the resort's security staff was going to hold him for them, but instead the activities coordinator said, "Can we count on you for the game today? The Coyotes are still one short."

It came out of nowhere, and he stared dumbly at the man, stunned into silence.

"They could use your help this afternoon."

The implication was obvious if insane: he would not be considered a murder suspect, the resort would suppress all knowledge of his connection to the dead woman—

Vicki

—if he agreed to participate in their stupid tournament.

"I thought those games were just on weekends," he said stupidly.

The activities coordinator grinned. "Not any more." There seemed to be a resonance to that remark that he did not get, an intended meaning too subtle for his numbed brain to comprehend.

He nodded, as if in a daze.

"Then I think we're through here." The activities coordinator put an arm around his shoulder, and while the gesture was more familial than the arm-pulling that had brought him here, the intent was the same: to force him to go where the man wanted.

Patrick hazarded a last look back at the room, saw the blood on the rug, the walls, the furniture, the bits of flesh on the bed. From this angle, he could see into the bathroom, and though he expected to see the shadow of something big and menacing in the frosted glass of the shower stall reflected in the mirror—

Alien

—the bathroom was clear and clean.

"Let's go." The activities coordinator led him outside, closing the door behind them.

And he allowed himself to be led.

Thirty-two

Rachel stood in front of the picture window, staring down at the manicured grass below. Behind her, the TV was on and working, a CNN entertainment report about advances in computer-generated animation issuing from the stereo speakers, and it was this symbol of normalcy from the outside world that made everything happening here at The Reata seem that much more strange and surreal. She recalled when she'd stood in this exact same spot the first night they were here, when she'd seen that horrible face in the monsoon cloud and the gardener doing his deranged dance on the lawn. If only she'd spoken up then, if only she'd said something to Lowell.

But would he have believed her? Would he have agreed to leave the hotel?

It was a moot point because, as they'd clearly established, something had *kept* her from speaking up, something had kept *all* of them from sharing their individual experiences, although that imposed restriction had now been lifted.

Somehow that worried her more than anything else.

Lowell had returned from a second trip out discouraged and disheartened. He'd hoped to talk to some of the other remaining guests or employees and find out what was going on, see if any of them had any plans or ideas. But the few brave enough to come out of their rooms when he knocked had all suggested with frightened desperation that they practice for the tournament.

The golf tournament.

She thought about what the boys had said about their friend David's parents and shivered.

The kids were still trying to convince Lowell to go with them to the abandoned resort they'd found off one of the hiking trails. "It's the key!" Ryan argued passionately. "I know it is!"

Curtis nodded. "You gotta come with us, Dad!"

"No!" he said angrily.

"I'll go with you," Rachel announced. They looked from one to the other, not quite sure how to respond.

Old stereotypes died hard.

"Mom can handle it," Ryan said, defending her against unspoken doubts, and she smiled at him, her heart filled with pride. He was such a good boy, such a nice boy, and while he had always been kind and thoughtful, he had also proved to be much tougher, stronger and more resilient than she would have expected. Sometimes crises brought out the best in people.

All of her boys were special, and her eyes teared up as she looked at them.

"If anybody's going, I'm going," Lowell said. "But I don't know what you think we're going to find there or what good it's going to do. Going farther out into the desert is not going to help us escape."

"Neither is sitting here in our room," Rachel said.

He glared at her. "At least it won't get us killed!"

Killed.

The word had been spoken, and though it had been in the back of her mind, in back of *all* of their minds, probably, it sounded different when spoken aloud. More real. More immediate.

Even the kids were quiet.

"We'll all go," Rachel said firmly, and she shot Lowell a look, letting him know not to scare them again—although part of her thought it was probably good for them to be afraid. *Scared is prepared,* her father used to say, and those were words she still believed.

"Okay," Lowell agreed. He took a deep breath. "I don't think we should go anywhere alone. Any of us."

Curtis nodded sagely. "That's what happens in horror movies. That's when people start dying."

It seemed strange to be putting on walking shoes, gathering water bottles and preparing for a hike. It seemed . . . frivolous. But they weren't pretending everything was normal and going on with life as usual. They were going on what was essentially a fact-finding mission, hoping to discover something they could use.

For what?

She didn't know. She doubted that any of them did. But at least they were trying to do something. At least they hadn't given up and weren't hiding here in the room waiting to die.

Waiting to die.

She tried to push the thought out of her mind, but it was there, front and center, and wasn't about to go anywhere. Tears welled up in her eyes again as she looked at Lowell and the boys, but even as her outside was softening and fuzzing up, her insides were growing firm and steely. Maybe it was inevitable and maybe it wasn't, but there was no way she was going down without a fight, and if something was going to go after her family, it would have to go through her first.

"I think it was the original Reata," Ryan was saying excitedly, "and if we put our heads together, we might be able to figure out how the two of them are connected."

"It won't bring anyone back," Curtis told him.

"No, but maybe it'll help Dad figure something out." He looked admiringly up at Lowell, and Rachel's heart swelled.

"We should find David first," Curtis suggested. "See if he's all right." He caught Lowell's skeptical look, obviously remembering Brenda. "David's real."

"And his parents are acting weird," Owen said. "I think he might need us."

"Do you know his room?" Rachel asked, walking over.

The boys nodded.

"We'll go by and make sure he's okay."

David was in his room, alone, and oddly enough he didn't know anything was wrong. Or that anything was any more wrong than usual. His parents had never come back to the room last night, and while he was worried about it, he wasn't *that* worried. It wasn't until Curtis and Owen filled him in on the fact that almost everyone who worked for The Reata had disappeared and the lobby looked like it had been abandoned for decades that he seemed to realize the seriousness of the situation. He turned off his television. "Wait," he said. "Don't leave me. I'm coming with you."

"We won't leave you," Lowell promised, and Rachel took his hand and squeezed it.

It was a much longer walk to Antelope Canyon and that other, older resort than she'd thought. On the way, they passed close by the walkway that led to the driving range, and from that direction came the thwack of balls and cries of pain. They hurried on.

"I thought you weren't supposed to go off the trail," Lowell said when the boys stopped and explained that the old resort was just behind the rise off to their left.

"We just wanted to see what that was," Curtis said, pointing at the buckboard wagon deteriorating into the sand.

Owen's voice was small, nervous. "Brenda didn't want us to go there. She tried to tell us to stay on the path." He reddened as he mentioned her name, looked away from his father.

"I think they were trying to hide it," Ryan said. "The old resort. I don't think they want people to know where it is."

"Then why would they have a trail out here at all?" Lowell wondered. "Why go so close to it?"

That was a good question, and it made Rachel nervous. She felt like a pawn in some unseen power's unknown game. They walked over the rocks that bordered the trail and slogged through the shifting sand up the small rise to the wagon.

She nearly screamed when they reached it.

"Oh my God," Lowell said.

David backed up, looking like he was going to be sick. Curtis, Owen and Ryan turned quickly away, looking up at the sky or down at the dirt, breathing heavily.

Bodies lay piled in the buckboard. Male or female, it was impossible to tell because the heads were missing and what was left was so hacked up as to be unidentifiable. Blood covered everything, like ketchup poured upon meat, and sand had blown into the blood, mixing with it, making red mud.

Rachel saw all this in the split second before averting her gaze, as she tried to ignore the combined smells of ground metal and excrement that assaulted her nostrils.

"Who are they?" Curtis asked, his voice hushed, still looking away.

"I can't tell," Lowell admitted. He swallowed hard. "I take it this wasn't here yesterday."

"There were skulls," Owen said. "Old skulls."

"We can't even call the police," Rachel said, but she was only stating the obvious. Whatever happened from here on in they were going to have to deal with it themselves; there would be no recourse to authority. She looked ahead at the buildings of the old resort. They weren't nearly as rundown as the boys had led them to believe, and she had the feeling that was new. "Is that what it looked like yesterday?" she asked, pointing.

Curtis shook his head. "It's . . . different," he said. "It's changing."

"It's fixing itself up," Ryan offered, and at that David and his brothers nodded enthusiastically.

Rachel stared at the old hotel. Painted words across the blank wall of one building read THE REATA, and it bore more than a little resemblance to the existing resort. Except that the faux western theme was a little more cowboy than Indian, even down to the barn and corral at the north end, and the place was smaller, more compact, more primitive. Typical of its time, she assumed, and she estimated that time to be somewhere around 1900. This would have been one of those early dude ranches built to attract rich adventurers from the East, and while it seemed quaint in comparison to the present-day Reata, it would have been the height of luxury in this place during that era.

She looked over at Lowell. "What do we do?" The idea of walking into an abandoned resort that over two days had transformed itself from a pile of ruins to a reasonable facsimile of the place it had been over a hundred years ago did not sit well with her.

But it was why they'd come here, and they didn't exactly have a host of options from which to choose. So when Lowell said, "We go in and look," she simply nodded.

"I'll show you the restaurant where I saw the mirror," Ryan declared. "And that little lookout room by the pool."

"But we stay together," Lowell reminded them, and his voice served to temper the boy's excitement.

Good, Rachel thought. Ryan was enjoying this a little too much. He needed to be careful out here. They all did.

The air seemed to grow colder as they walked through the desert to the old Reata, although Rachel thought that was probably just her imagination. They stopped first by the lobby. In front of it stood a totem pole nearly twice as tall as the building, an intricately carved post of lodgepole pine, and like the kids said, there were terrible faces carved into it, horrible demonic visages filled with rage and pain. But the figure at the top was missing, the old man, and in his place was a fierce-looking but very realistically rendered wolf, which made no sense to any of them and which none of them could understand.

They walked inside. Though it had no door and the glass in the windows was broken, the lobby seemed remarkably well-preserved. The front desk looked even more like a saloon bar than the one in their Reata, and there was a guest book on top of the counter, though the writing in it was faded and illegible. They spoke not a word but walked through in silence, pointing to items of interest, as though afraid that to speak would announce their presence to . . .

To whom?

Rachel did not even want to speculate.

They walked out of the lobby through the same broken doorway they'd come in, and she expected the oppressive feeling that had settled over them inside would dissipate outdoors, but it did not. Ryan led them over to the restaurant, which had the long tables and simple kitchen of a cowboy mess hall. The Reata's setting-sun-and-stylized-cactus logo was painted onto the side of the counter, the paint fresh and bright, and it looked oddly anachronistic here in these primitive surroundings. It wasn't supposed to be here, Rachel thought. Whoever—*whatever*—had put it here had made a mistake, and that gave her hope.

The mirror was on the wall to their left.

Rachel understood immediately what Ryan had meant when he said there was something wrong with it. At the moment, it reflected back only the scene before it: the dining room and themselves. But its silvery surface hinted at hidden depths, and even its shape seemed unsettling, the angles slightly off.

They stared at the mirror for several moments, all of them, as though waiting for it to change, waiting for a glimpse of that old man Ryan said he saw. But nothing happened.

"Maybe I should break it," Ryan suggested. "It was broken when I saw him."

"No," Lowell said, shaking his head. "Leave it alone."

From there they went to the pool. As they'd probably all known or suspected, it was filled with water, dirty brackish water that should have smelled like sulfur but had no odor whatsoever. On top of the water floated brown cottonwood leaves and a dead palm frond. On top of the palm frond, like a Viking being sent off to Valhalla, was a skinned rat. The crosses that the boys said had been placed around the pool were gone.

"The glass must be fixed!" Curtis said, pointing down a set of stairs that led into a trench next to the pool. "No water's getting in."

"The picture of him's on the wall behind that bench," Ryan said, letting his dad go down first.

But Lowell did not look at the wall, and as Rachel walked down the steps, bringing up the rear, and gazed out the observation window to the pool beyond, she saw why.

People were swimming in the pool. Five or six of them at least. Men with handlebar mustaches and full-body bathing suits, women in flapper swimwear. They splashed and played in water that was light blue and perfectly clear, and every so often one would swim up to the glass, tap on it and wave at them.

Curtis dashed behind her and ran up to the top of the steps. "It's still the same up here!" he shouted. "All dirty and no one's in it!" He rushed back down just as a plump woman planted her lips on the glass and then, smiling, swam for the surface.

"The graffiti's gone," Owen said, pointing at the wall.

Indeed it was, and in place of a crayon caricature of a spooky old man there was only The Reata's logo, the same brightly colored modern version they'd seen in the restaurant.

"The smell's gone, too," Ryan said.

David grinned. "Maybe they're connected," he responded, and even that small joke was welcome, helped cut some of the tension in the air.

They remained in the viewing room for several more minutes, watching the swimmers, Lowell or one of the boys occasionally darting to the top of the stairs to verify that nothing had changed, bandying about ideas on how this could be happening, all of them instantly and unanimously rejecting the logical, hopeful theory that they were watching images on a large television screen.

Finally, they went back up.

"Where next?" Ryan asked. "The barn?"

"No," Lowell said, walking.

"The throne's there. We saw it."

But Lowell had seen something else, a sight that meant something to *him,* and Rachel caught up to him, took his hand. "What is it?" she asked quietly. Then she saw it, too.

A gallows.

David had said he'd seen that last time, but none of them had noticed it on the way in, not even David, and she chose to believe that was because it had been hidden behind other restored buildings, though she doubted that was the reason.

They all saw it now, though.

There were bodies hanging from two of its three ropes.

"Stay here," Lowell ordered.

"No," David said, and she expected him to add, *You're not my father,* but instead he repeated Lowell's mantra. "We need to stay together."

No one argued with that, and as gruesome as the sight before them was, as much as she wanted to protect her babies from seeing something like this, she knew that those days of innocence were long gone. They were all in this together, and they would likely see a lot worse before it was all over.

Before they died.

Once again, she was unable to push the thought away, unable to put even a slightly positive spin on their situation. They moved slowly forward, as though treading over ground that had been planted with land mines. Ryan had been following his father up in front, but now he fell back, slowing his pace until he was next to her. She felt his soft hand creep into her own, and she held it tightly, re-assuringly. Curtis and Owen, too, seemed worried, scared, tentative, and they dropped their pace to be nearer to her. If she'd had three arms, she would have used all three to hug each of them close.

They shouldn't be here, she thought. They shouldn't be seeing this.

Scared is prepared.

"Oh my God!" Curtis exclaimed as they drew close enough to see the bodies. "That's the woman who checked us in!"

Indeed it was. Her name tag still pinned to the torn and blood-stained remnants of her blouse, Tammy—

New Haven, Connecticut. Six Years.

—was swinging from a heavy rope, eyes white and staring in her dirty purple face, her mouth open almost impossibly wide. A fly crawled over her bottom teeth, then onto her cheek and into her ear. A trio of wasps lazily buzzed out from beneath her torn skirt.

Next to her was the waiter Rachel had seen being dragged down the lobby hallway when she'd been hiding with Laurie behind the totem pole pillar, the beaten man who had been pushed screaming and fighting into that manager's office. He had clearly been sub-jected to even more abuse behind closed doors. One arm hung at an awkward angle, and the young man's face was swollen so hideously that his eyes were not visible and his mouth was pulled up by his cheek.

The queasiness in her stomach was like nothing she had ever ex-perienced. Only part of it was due to the actual physical grotesque-ness before her. Most of it was from being in the presence of death, from looking at two people she had seen alive who were now corpses, hanging murdered in front of her.

Lowell turned away from the gallows, grabbing Curtis's and Owen's heads and forcibly pointing them in the opposite direction. "There's nothing here for us," he said grimly. "Let's go back."

"There is!" Ryan insisted. "We just have to find it!"

"Find what?" Lowell said.

"This whole place is changing, fixing itself up!"

"And how does that help us?" Lowell shook his head. "I don't want you to be here. I don't think any of us should be here. It's dan-gerous."

"But—" Ryan said.

Lowell held up a hand. "I'll tell the others back at The Reata what we found. Maybe together we can figure something out. But for now we need to leave." Unconsciously, he gestured toward the two hanging bodies. "We're risking our lives by even being here."

But there was no one around when they returned. Even the noise from the driving range had been silenced, and they walked down empty pathways searching for someone, anyone. From the open door of the Saguaro Room, a bird flew out, followed almost immediately afterward by a small bobcat that dashed through the door then sped around the side of the building heading for the rocks.

"Maybe everyone left," Curtis said. "Maybe a bus came and got them all."

"Maybe they disappeared into thin air," David said, and though Rachel didn't say anything, that seemed far more likely. She met Lowell's gaze and saw the same awareness there.

She thought of that hanging waiter on the gallows, a sight she would never forget, a sight she would carry with her to her dying day, and that made her think of the corridor where she'd seen him last. "Maybe they're in one of the banquet rooms," she suggested, "having a meeting."

"I haven't checked those rooms," Lowell said, and his tone of voice made her realize that he was thinking about what he might find in there. It was not their missing fellow guests. She shuddered, wishing she'd kept her mouth shut. "Come on."

The lobby was just as Lowell had described it, and the spooky thing was how eerily similar it was to the lobby they had explored back in the canyon. This was the natural evolution of that smaller room, its more sophisticated descendant. They walked across the worn carpet and down the hallway. The totem pole pillars were no longer high class kitsch, had lost their sophisticated politically correct sheen. They were instead just like the totem pole at the old resort, covered with intricate carvings of malevolent faces: monster mouths and demon eyes.

They walked past the door to the manager's office, and Lowell tried the knob but it was locked. On the opposite side of the corridor were the closed double doors to the first banquet room. The Santa Fe Room, according to the plaque on the wall. These were unlocked, and the six of them stepped inside.

It was a torture chamber.

Rachel had never seen anything like it, had never read or heard of anything so completely and totally devoted to the infliction of death and pain. *Stay outside,* she wanted to tell the boys. *Don't come in here, don't look at this.* And she knew Lowell was thinking the same thing. But they had to stay close together. She knew that if the kids were in the hall while she and Lowell toured the torture chamber, the doors would suddenly swing shut and by the time the two of them got the doors opened again the boys would be gone.

Rachel walked slowly forward. Everything here was old and well-used. To her right was some sort of iron maiden, but one with a distinctly American bent, the outside of the device resembling a cigar store Indian, the spikes' spear-ends tipped with arrowheads. In a wood-and-glass display case were dozens of straight razors with elaborate exotic handles, nearly all of them tarnished with dried blood.

But that was just the beginning.

There was a primitive treadmill onto which was affixed sharp stones, shards of broken glass, spurs of metal and spiny pieces of densely needled cactus. Rusted meat hooks alternated with heavy metal balls on chains hanging from a frame roughly the shape and size of a garage door. An enclosed bench that resembled a church pew with dark discolored pegs of various lengths and diameters protruding from its seat was next to a human-shaped cage with a wicked-tipped tightening screw at the top. Other mechanisms of torture, featuring ever more Byzantine architecture and design, continued on throughout the large room.

"Is this for us?" Owen asked in a hushed voice.

"No," Rachel rushed to assure him. "These are for . . . uh . . ." She trailed off, unable to come up with an alternative.

What the hell were they for? These instruments had obviously been used in the past, but were they now here as a warning, as part of some museum, or because they *were* intended for use in the near future? Despite her words to the contrary, she suspected the latter.

David reached out and put a hand on the iron maiden.

"Don't touch that!" Lowell ordered him, and the boy yanked his hand back as though jolted by an electrical shock. "We don't know what these can do," he explained. "We have to be careful."

They all stood close to each other, unsure of what to do next.

"Well, the people aren't here—" Curtis began and was interrupted by a noise from behind them.

The activities coordinator poked his head around the corner. His face was covered with dirt. Black and green lines had been painted onto his cheeks and forehead, making him look savage. "Get ready, boys and girls." He grinned. "It's game time."

Thirty-three

Lowell stood beneath the awning with the rest of his team, staring across the driving range at the Coyotes. The bushes that had ringed the green had been cut down, and to the left and right, outside of the fence, scores of people were pressed against the iron bars—all of the guests who were not playing in the tournament as well as maids and maintenance men who seemed to have been left behind by the mysterious exodus. Rachel and the kids were in that crowd somewhere, and while he didn't want them to be here, on balance they were probably safer in public in the company of others than they would be alone in their suite.

Rockne the activities coordinator stood before them at the center of the driving range in all his savage glory. He was still wearing his coach's whistle and name tag, but other than that, the man bore no resemblance to anyone who could ever be gainfully employed. His shirt was a ripped polar bear pajama top, he wore a black skirt instead of pants, and around his neck, like Superman's cape, was safety-pinned a white towel sporting the monogrammed "R" of The Reata dyed with a red that could have been paint, could have been blood. All of his exposed skin had been smeared with dirt and emphasized with camouflage makeup.

The activities coordinator was attempting to explain the rules of the upcoming game, which was apparently a cross between golf, polo, soccer and dodge ball, but his words were hard to follow because the man kept facing east then west, addressing every other sentence to each opposing team. Lowell had a sneaking suspicion that the confusion was intentional. He got the gist of it, though. The Cactus Wrens and the Coyotes were to square off, each side supplied with a bucket of balls, and use the nine irons provided to hit the balls at each other, the intent to incapacitate their opponents. The team with the most men and women standing at the end of the game would be declared the winner.

There was a lengthy pause as two old men recruited from the audience carried out buckets of golf balls, placing one by each member of both teams. The Coyotes had a numerical advantage, Lowell noticed, counting. There were only fifteen Cactus Wrens as opposed to eighteen Coyotes. Glancing toward the onlookers on the other side of the fence, he saw women, children and quite a few men. How had they gotten out of this? he wondered. Hadn't the activities coordinator said that all male guests were required to participate? He was about to speak up and say something, when Rockne suddenly ran off the green to the side, standing in front of the closed gate.

The activities coordinator raised his hands, blew his whistle. "Go!" he yelled.

Balls began flying.

Lowell placed two on the tees before him and hit them randomly, haphazardly, unsure if they found a target and not really caring. He started to put down another ball, when one of the Coyotes' balls slammed into his side, nearly knocking the wind out of him. He fell to the ground, clutching his midsection, and another ball smashed into his shoe so hard that it stung his heel through the rubber sole.

Though he knew it was wrong, though he knew he shouldn't, though he knew he was behaving exactly as the activities coordinator wanted him to behave, he was filled with anger, hate and a sharp desire for revenge. Despite the pain in his side, he stood amid the hail of golf balls, placed two of his own balls on the tees in front of him and let fly. He did it again. And again. Repeating like clockwork, not watching where the balls went but aiming for the densest group of Coyotes, hoping by virtue of volume to hit one of them. He remembered what David had said about seeing his parents on the driving range and wondered if they were here somewhere among the players. Had they and the others David saw been given advance warning and a chance to practice? If so, it was an unfair advantage, and the thought of that made Lowell swing all the harder, the metal edge of his club striking the dimpled balls with a strength born of rage.

Will, the oldest man on the Cactus Wrens, cried out in pain but Lowell did not stop to see what had happened. He put two more balls down, sent them flying, then grabbed two others from the grass next to him and hit them as hard as he could.

They were soon out of balls, so they started scrambling around on the grass to gather those that had landed about them.

"Tully!" Black called to their smallest and skinniest teammate, the one who would be the hardest target to hit. "Get a bucket and collect as many balls as you can!"

Tully scrambled around, gathering all he could and parceling them out to Black and the nearest Wrens while the rest of their team-mates continued to grab their own from the ever-shrinking amount out there. If there were fewer balls around them, Lowell thought, that must mean that fewer were being hit at them, which meant that they must be winning. He paused for a moment to look across the green and was gratified to see several Coyotes nursing injuries and others hiding behind the net next to the far fence, given up. The bas-tards may have been given the advantage of an early warning, but through some freak stroke of luck, the unathletic collection of men who made up the Cactus Wrens seemed to have far superior luck in hitting their targets.

"Time!" the activities coordinator announced, and all activity sud-denly ceased.

Lowell looked around. Two old men were rolling on the grass and moaning, the unlucky Tully had been knocked unconscious in a final volley, and a few people like himself had been hit and hurt. But for the most part, the Wrens had emerged from the encounter relatively unscathed. *Was this it?* Lowell thought. *Was this the end of it?*

He should have known better.

"Clubs only!" Rockne cried, and before Lowell knew what was happening, an angry mob of Coyotes was racing toward them, golf clubs raised, mouths open in primal screams of fury.

Maybe it was because they were stationary rather than moving, maybe it was the luck of having fewer injured members, but despite their outwardly geeky appearance, his teammates whaled on the madly rushing Coyotes, taking them down. The Coyotes' aggressive screams turned into cries of pain and moans of agony as irons were slammed into their legs and midsections, and they fell hard on the grass. To his left, one big guy took a swing at Rand Black's head, missed, and Black returned the favor, his golf club connecting with the man's skull. The accompanying thwack of metal against flesh and bone sounded sickeningly satisfying, and a few seconds later, Lowell swung his own club into the breast of the old bitch who'd jumped against him in the basketball game. He felt more than heard her ribs crack, a woof of air escaping from her lips as she fell.

He expected her to hiss some invective at him, to use her iron to try and hit his feet from her prone position. He *wished* she would. But instead she merely looked up at him. "I know," she said, and there was such sadness in her eyes that he had to turn away.

He backed up, moving under the awning away from the struggle, no longer having any stomach for this imposed institutionalized aggression, horrified at the damage he had wrought.

"Time!" the activities coordinator announced.

The adversaries on both sides quit save for two men in the center of the driving range who were furiously trying to take off one another's heads. The activities coordinator watched mildly until the Cactus Wren successfully felled the Coyote, who dropped to the grass and remained still.

It was now possible to see the extent of the carnage. Broken bleeding bodies lay all about the green, many with limbs posed at odd angles, quite a few unmoving and silent, presumably dead. A ragtag collection of survivors remained, and as though acting on instinct the Wrens retreated under the awning while the Coyotes limped to their original position at the opposite end of the field. Outside the fence, the onlookers were quiet. Lowell tried to spot his family among the devastated faces in the crowd but could not see them.

"For the second time in a row, the Cactus Wrens are declared the winners!" Rockne announced. There were a few halfhearted claps from the standing Wrens.

The air was heavy with tension. Everyone remained silent, waiting to see what would happen next.

"We're doing things a little differently now!" the activities coordinator said loudly. "The Roadrunners are not going to play against the Cactus Wrens! That final matchup will be saved for the next tournament! For now, the Roadrunners will administer punishment to the losing team!" He gestured theatrically toward the battered men and women in the center of the driving range. "Boys? Have at 'em!"

From a breach in the fence behind the small shed that stored the golf equipment, the Roadrunners ran out screaming, bodies covered with dirt, faces painted like the activities coordinator, weapons raised high. They were wielding golf clubs and baseball bats, spears and knives, and the expressions on their faces were of joy and excitement, a wild exultation at being allowed to finally run free and do what they wanted to do.

What were these men in real life? Lowell wondered as he watched with numb horror. Rand Black had said Blodgett was some sort of financial analyst. Did the others have equally innocuous jobs? Dentists? Realtors? Computer programmers? What did it take to turn someone like that into someone like this? Was the potential always there, lurking beneath the surface, waiting for the opportunity to

emerge? He remembered Blodgett's hostility on the night he'd
stolen their room . . . and Rachel's panties.

Yes, he thought. The potential had always been there, and once
more, his mind brought it all back to high school. He had sometimes
wondered in the intervening years how the practically sociopathic
kids who'd terrorized the hallways had been able to dial it down
enough to get along in regular society, how they'd managed to find
jobs and wives and a life in the real world when, deep down, they
were the same assholes they had always been.

Because they covered it up, he thought now. Because they pretended to be people they were not.

Here, they were allowed to be themselves, their ids granted free
rein.

The first Roadrunner reached the first Coyote. And bludgeoned
him to death. Lowell watched it happen, watched as the bigger man
took his baseball bat and swung it at the man's head as though it
were a ball. The Coyote went down, bits of bone and brain flying.
The others arrived and made contact, swinging golf clubs, thrusting
with spears. Some of the Coyotes attempted to fight back and were
quickly overpowered by their bigger, stronger and more combative
adversaries, but most chose to run for it, and the air was filled with
the whooping delight of the Roadrunners chasing down their prey.

The Coyotes' punishment for losing the game was death, and
though deep down Lowell had known that from the beginning, it
nevertheless terrified him. He felt at once relieved that they'd won
the game and guilty that doing so had resulted in death for others.

They were spearing the injured on the ground, and Lowell
scanned the driving range until he found the old lady. Blodgett himself was pounding on her head with a baseball bat. Not content with
merely crushing her skull, he kept pounding until her head was little
more than a pulpy red spot on the grass. Another woman, trying to
flee, was taken down with a golf club to the stomach, and she
shrieked in pure agony as a good-looking well-built man with a
knife grabbed her hair and hacked off her scalp.

The Coyotes, Lowell realized, was the only team to have women
on it.

He was not sure what that meant.

The fight, if that's what it was, was mercifully short. Part of it was
the fact that so many Coyotes were already injured and the able-bod-
ied Roadrunners simply overwhelmed them, although even if the
Coyotes had been in peak form the outcome still would have been a
foregone conclusion. In a matter of minutes, the Coyotes were either

dead or had fled, and several Roadrunners climbed the tall fence to go after those who had escaped the same way.

The activities coordinator had been watching from the sidelines, and he strode purposefully to the middle of the grass. He raised his hands for silence but didn't get it this time. The Roadrunners were out of control and some were still beating on the dead bodies while the others laughed and high-fived each other and patted each other on the back, moving impatiently and excitedly around the center of the field.

Lowell did not like where this was going, and he quickly and surreptitiously backed up against the fence and made his way along the inside of it toward the gate, praying it was still unlocked.

"That is the end of today's tournament!" the activities coordinator announced. There was very little response. *Would he be giving out awards this time?* Lowell wondered, and shuddered to think what they might be for.

"Tomorrow—" Rockne began.

And was felled by a blow to the head.

"Shut the fuck up!" yelled Blodgett, and a cry of triumph went up from his fellow Roadrunners.

The activities coordinator collapsed in a spray of blood. Lowell tried to watch what happened to the man, but after he fell, Lowell could no longer see his body. He thought at first it was due to all the movement—Blodgett's angry pacing, the other Roadrunners' back and forth jostling—but it became clear almost instantly that Rockne was no longer there. He had disappeared.

Somehow Lowell was not surprised. On some level, he supposed he had even expected it.

Rockne. The Reata. One hundred years.

He crept along the edge of the fence. What was going to happen now? He was under no illusion that the activities coordinator's disappearance meant an end to The Reata's reign of terror—whatever power lay at the heart of this evil place was still here—but Blodgett and his minions no longer had any checks on them, and Lowell had the feeling that was intentional. The Reata was using them all as pawns, playing with its guests to see how this would turn out.

Lowell knew exactly how it would turn out. Mob rule, a Darwinian nightmare. The Roadrunners would run roughshod over everyone else and turn the place into their own private playground, an anarchic melee.

Was that The Reata's goal? He thought of the abandoned resort in Antelope Canyon and the way it was changing. "Fixing itself up," as

Ryan said. Maybe the boys were on to something. Maybe that was the key to everything that was going on. Maybe *that* resort was the real power and was somehow feeding off this one. As the current Reata devolved, the old one in the canyon strengthened, growing younger, like some architectural Dorian Gray.

There were too many possibilities to consider, and all of that could be done at a later time. The priority now was getting out and getting away. He reached the gate and, keeping his eye on Blodgett and the Roadrunners immediately about him, opened it, sneaking through. There was no outcry, no one chased after him, and he was suffused with gratitude that he'd made it. Rachel and the boys had obviously been watching him, and they were there to meet him, taking him quickly back out through the crowd. Other Wrens were sneaking along the edge of the fence behind him—he obviously hadn't been nearly as secretive as he'd thought—and their families were silently motioning for them to hurry up. For now, the Roadrunners remained oblivious.

Lowell wished them well as he and his family, David still with them, crouched down and sped up the sidewalk away from the driving range, using the standing crowd of onlookers as cover. Once around the corner of a building, he hastened them back to their suite, locking the door when they arrived, using the chain and the deadbolt though he knew that neither could keep out a determined mob. He propped a chair under the doorhandle. David was silent and pale, and he wondered if the boy suspected his parents were dead. Lowell was almost certain of it.

"So what do we do now?" Rachel asked. Her voice was low and frightened.

Everyone was waiting for his answer, but he didn't have one. "We wait," he said, closing the drapes and turning on the television. CNN was airing a White House press conference, and he was grateful for this window to the outside world.

Sometime before dark, the electricity went out.

Patrick hid in the limbs of a cottonwood tree, peeking through a screen of fluttering leaves, safe for the moment. The Roadrunners were still roaming the resort grounds, looking for stragglers, and he knew that if one of them caught him he would be killed.

He'd seen Tony Lawson, the Coyotes' captain, beaten to death with a spiked club.

Violence in real life was nothing like it was in movies. He'd known that on an intellectual level, of course, and like most of his

friends he'd deplored war and aggression from a purely philosophi-
cal perspective, but seeing how quickly people could devolve into
bloodthirsty beasts, he understood in his gut how deep-down horrible violence really was.

When the activities coordinator had announced that the Roadrunners were not to play against the winners but punish the losers,
Patrick had fled, deserting his team, worried only for his own safety,
caring only about preserving his own life. He hoped some others got
out as well, but he wasn't going to risk his own life trying to help
them.

"I stick my neck out for nobody," Bogart said as Rick in
Casablanca, and although he'd renounced that philosophy by the
end of the film, Patrick still thought the sentiment one to live by.

Live being the operative word.

So he'd jumped the fence, darting between cactus and behind
palm trees until he'd reached the building that housed his room.
Only he'd lost the key. The magnetic card had been in his shirt
pocket, but it had obviously fallen out during the "game" or when
he'd leaped over the fence, so Patrick quickly walked the pathways
searching for someplace to hide. From around the corner of a building, he heard an old man cry "No! No! Please, God, help me!" and
then the rough laughter of several other men, and that was when he
climbed up the cottonwood tree, going as high as he could without
venturing onto branches too weak and thin to be safe.

And here he remained, silent, unmoving, hiding.

Beneath the tree passed a young boy and his father, the same two
he'd run into on his first day here.

Fairy

"Don't worry," the father was saying. "We'll get them all and
bring them to justice."

Patrick held his breath, not daring to breathe.

"Are they all faggots?" the boy asked.

"Every last stinking one of them."

And then the two of them were gone, walking around the corner
of the building toward the spot where Patrick had heard the pleading
of the old man.

Both father and son saw something that made them laugh uproari-
ously.

Time passed. He grew hungry and his stomach growled but luckily no one was around to hear it. One unusual noise as they passed
by would cause people to look up and discover him—and that would
be the end of it.

Thunderheads rode into the desert on an unfelt wind, and though they blocked out the sun, they did not bring lower temperatures but only served to make the air more humid. For his part, Patrick was glad. It felt more like Chicago, more like home, and he was grateful for anything that could take him away even momentarily from this hellish place.

The storm arrived just after sundown, and he crept out of the tree under the cover of night and rain, knowing he needed to get away from here but not knowing where. He took a quick piss, then ran quickly down one of the gravel paths, the noise of his passage covered by the rain and occasional thunder. He stopped at every corner, peeked carefully around every building, but came across no one else. For all he knew, The Reata could be completely abandoned by now and he the only one left, but he didn't think so and couldn't count on it.

He still had money in his wallet, and he used the last of his one-dollar bills to buy two Cokes from a vending machine near the tennis courts.

He still didn't know where to go, but he thought of the hiking trails that led into the surrounding desert and decided that might be a plan. He'd be exposed to the elements and anyone who followed the trail would be able to find him, but his gut feeling was that it would be safer to be away from the resort itself.

Completely soaked by the now torrential rain, he hurried up a trail that led into the mountains behind The Reata. The path led over a short hilly section of desert before disappearing between two closely aligned bluffs. For all he knew, this was a flash flood area, but at the moment it looked like a good hideout, somewhere he might be able to catch a few winks without fear of being discovered and beaten to death. He started thinking of ways he could booby-trap this entrance into the canyon or how he could hide in a place that would allow him to see anyone approaching from a long ways off. His brain was ticking off endless scenarios from classic westerns. He should write a book: *Everything I Need to Know I Learned from Movies.*

To his surprise, the downpour slowed to a drizzle as he passed between the sandstone walls, and by the time the canyon had opened out around him, and he found himself in what looked like a wide desert valley between two mountains, the thunder and lightning had stopped.

He could have halted here, but the trail kept going and he knew he'd feel safer the farther he was from The Reata, so he continued walking. The cans of Coke were feeling heavier in his hands, and as he was both thirsty and wanted to have a hand free, he popped open the top of one and drank it. He hated to litter, but he wasn't about to carry an empty soda can around with him. But he couldn't just drop it on the trail because someone might be able to track him that way, so he cocked his arm and heaved it as far as he could to the left of the path.

Where he saw an orangish glow coming from behind a low rise.

Could it be a ranch or a farmhouse? Could someone else live out here? It was possible, and though he knew he was being overly optimistic, he left the trail and slogged through the wet sand toward the source of the light.

The rain started up again, altering perspectives and playing games with distance. Patrick kept his eyes on the now flickering shimmering light, and it was not until he was almost upon it that he realized the source of the light was an old hotel.

Another resort.

The blood turned cold in his veins. From up ahead, he heard the sounds of a party. In fact, it sounded like the same party that had been going on each night in the empty room next to his. His brain and whatever instinct for survival had gotten him this far were telling him to turn around, to hide in the canyon behind a rock or bush somewhere between the two resorts. But he had to know what was there, had to discover the cause of those noises, had to find out whether there really was a party going on and whether it was peopled by humans or ghosts.

He passed a spooky-looking totem pole and, seeing no lights in the lobby, continued on toward the source of the light and noise.

He found it by the pool.

Torches—not kitschy tiki torches but primitive burning branches that smelled of creosote and looked vaguely Native American—had been placed in wrought iron holders next to the doors of the rooms and were embedded in holes in the cement around the pool. There was a party underway, and the participants were doing what any normal person would do at a pool party—swim, drink, talk—but the men and women were ancient, almost mummified. By torchlight, they appeared monstrous. But when they jumped into the pool they became young again. An overweight man with the wrinkled face of a dried apple went into the water, emerging with a hundred years shaved off him, and Patrick recognized the creepy security guard he'd met Friday night after his encounter with the snakes and wolf. Once out of the pool and in the rain, the man shrivelled and turned old again, a transformation so real and recognizably organic that it could never be mistaken for a special effect.

They all turned old when the rain hit them, Patrick noticed now, and he backed up to make sure that he remained in the shadows and did not accidentally reveal himself.

By the deep end of the pool, where the diving board should have been, was an elaborate throne upholstered in red velvet upon which sat a tall skeletal figure with long white hair. He did not do anything, did not move, simply watched over the party like a king surveying his subjects. There was an aura of power about the figure, a deep sense of authority and ancient evil that made the hairs on the back of Patrick's neck prickle.

The Roadrunners, those runaway thugs who now had control over The Reata, no longer seemed so frightening or formidable.

At least they were human.

He backed up, moving as stealthily as possible around the corner of the building, intending to get the hell away from here as quickly as he—

A wrinkled bony arm whipped around his neck from behind and caught him in a headlock, squeezing so tightly he could not breathe. A voice like scratching sandpaper whispered something in his ear he could not understand. He smelled dust and rancid meat.

At least it will be quick, he thought as he was dragged toward the pool.

But it wasn't, he found out.

It wasn't at all.

TUESDAY . . . AND BEYOND

Thirty-four

They awoke in the morning sweaty from the uncirculated air in the stuffy room. The smell of rotting food from the minibar permeated the atmosphere, mixed with the odor of morning breath. Lowell was the first up, and he opened the slat of the shutters slightly and peeked out. He saw nothing unusual, nothing suspicious, but that in itself was suspicious, and he didn't trust the tranquil morning view before him. He opened the slats a little wider and stood as close as he could to the window, trying to look down at the spot directly below, but still there was nothing out of the ordinary, only some flowering desert brush and an expanse of manicured lawn.

Rachel got up and went to the bathroom, and while she was in there the boys and David came out of their room. "Anything for breakfast?" Curtis asked.

"I don't think so," Lowell said. "But see if you can find anything to scrounge."

Rachel emerged from the bathroom. "That water's out," she said. Lowell went in and checked the toilet. It had flushed properly, but there was only a small bit of water at the bottom of the bowl and the tank was practically empty. He stopped up the sink, turned on the faucet, and the only thing that came out was a small trickle and then a series of decreasing droplets.

Great.

"Everybody try to hold it," he said, coming out. "If you have to pee, use the sink. Anything else, use the toilet in the other bathroom. We might be able to get two flushes out of it if we're careful."

Sometime in the middle of the morning, Rand Black came by with a small group of men, two of them Cactus Wrens and a couple of others he didn't recognize. Lowell did not invite them in.

"They're gone," Black said. "Blodgett and his crew. No one's seen them all morning."

Peeking at them through a crack in the still-chained door, Lowell was not sure he bought that. Where would they go? *The other resort,* a voice in his mind said, but he refused to believe it. No, it was more likely that they had put Black and the other men up to this, threatened or intimidated them into trying to draw out Lowell and his family.

"We're getting a search party together to see if we can find them," Black said. "Wanted to know if you'd come along."

"Why would you *want* to find them?" Lowell asked.

"So we can keep tabs. So we know where they are and what they're doing. So we won't be caught off guard."

It was logical, made sense, but Lowell still didn't believe it. Besides, there was no way he'd leave Rachel and the kids alone. "Sorry," he said, and closed the door, locking it again.

He expected more knocking, pleas for him to join them, appeals to his team spirit, but there was nothing, and when he peeked out again a moment later, they were gone.

What the hell was wrong with him? There was safety in numbers. He'd had a chance to get out of this suite and see what was happening in the company of five other men, and he'd chosen to stay cooped up in here, hiding. Was he now so paranoid and suspicious that he could no longer tell the good guys from the bad guys?

Rachel was obviously thinking the same thing. "What are you doing?" she cried. "Go with them!"

"I can't leave you and the boys here alone."

"We'll be fine," she said in a manner that brooked no argument. "In case you haven't noticed, we can't eat or go to the bathroom. We're going to have to get out of this room anyway if we're going to survive. At least we should know where those killers are."

"It could be a trap."

"It's not," she told him, and although he didn't know why, he agreed with her.

"Okay," he said. "But if I'm not back within two hours . . ." He trailed off, unsure of how to finish the sentence, not knowing *what* she should do if he didn't return.

"You'll be back," she said, and gave him a quick kiss. "Go!"

He caught up to Black and his crew just down the sidewalk. "Hey," he said. The five of them looked at him suspiciously. They'd obviously been talking about him, and the fact that they didn't trust him made him pretty sure he could trust them. "Sorry," he said. "About back there. The electricity's off, the water's off, we have no food. It's a bunker mentality."

Black nodded, satisfied. "Glad to have you." He introduced the other men. Scott and Rick, the other Cactus Wrens, he already knew.

Elijah, a CPA from Wisconsin who seemed befuddled by everything that was happening, had somehow avoided getting drafted into the tournaments, but Mike was a former Coyote, although Lowell could not recall having seen him before.

Strange, Lowell thought, how he had started classifying people by their team affiliation. He didn't like the fact that he was doing that. He thought it was something The Reata probably wanted.

"Glad you're okay," Black said after introductions had been made and hands had been shaken. "A lot of people aren't."

"How many . . . ?" He couldn't bring himself to complete the sentence.

"A lot," Black said. "Too many."

"And some of them either aren't in their rooms or aren't answering their doors," Rick said. "So we don't know what's up with that."

Black nodded.

"Well, where are we going now?" Lowell asked.

"We've divided the resort into quadrants and are making a systematic search of each area, starting with this one." Black held up a map of The Reata he'd taken from his Welcome packet and marked up with a pen. "Now we're going over to the physical plant and employees' quarters. After that, we'll go down to the next set of buildings and check each room."

"Okay."

"But we're not splitting up. We stay together. It'll take us longer, but there's safety in numbers."

As always, the morning was hot, but the heat and sunlight and blue skies did nothing to dispel the atmosphere of darkness and death that hung over the resort. Even animals seemed to have abandoned the place, and the circling of hawks, scuttling of lizards and other sounds of the desert that Lowell had almost gotten used to over the past few days were nowhere in evidence. Following Black's map, they walked down a sidewalk running next to a narrow service road that wound behind a block of guest rooms.

"What the fuck?" Rick said.

A small city of tents made from linens and towels stretched along both sides of a man-made ditch in front of a series of small duplexes. The doors to the duplexes had been ripped off their hinges and thrown into the ditch along with clothes, furniture and other personal belongings. Windows to the apartments had been shattered and tendrils of smoke curled from most. It looked like The Roadrunners had ransacked the workers' lodgings, taken what they wanted, burned the homes and then fled, leaving the employees to construct makeshift accommodations out of whatever they could find in the maids' supply closets.

This was confirmed when Laszlo the mechanic emerged from one of the makeshift tents, holding a heavy wrench in his hand. A man crawled out of another tent clutching a hammer. Two standing Hispanic women carrying mop handles thrust them forward as though they were spears. From behind them, Lowell heard a loud bang, and he turned to see two strong, dark men holding metal trash can lids and barring the way they'd come.

"We want no trouble," Black announced. "We're just taking a tour of the resort to see what's what. We're not here to fight with you."

"You destroy our homes," Laszlo said angrily, his eyes narrowing to slits. "And for that you must pay."

"We didn't destroy anything," Elijah tried to explain.

"We don't even know what you're talking about," Lowell said.

"You not know? You burn out our homes, wreck our furniture and you don't know?"

"Those were the Roadrunners," Black said. "We're the Cactus Wrens."

"What's that to me? You're guests. You're all guests."

"But we're looking for those guys, too," Lowell told him. "And all guests are not the same. Those guests *killed* some of us. They're looking for the rest of us. That's why we're here. We're trying to find them first."

Some of the belligerence dropped. "Why you try to find them?"

"So we know where they are. So we can hide from them or fight them or do whatever we need to do to protect our wives and children."

Laszlo looked at the man with the hammer, then glanced back at the women. Other people were peeking curiously out of their tents but had no weapons in their hands and did not appear eager for a confrontation. "They are probably in the Winner's Circle," he said.

"Don't trust him," advised Scott. "He works for The Reata. He's part of it."

Lowell ignored him. "What and where is the Winner's Circle?"

The man with the hammer spoke up. "It's a private club for the winners of the tournaments. A lounge. My wife worked there." A catch in his throat made Lowell realize that the man's wife was probably missing. Or dead. "I can take you."

Laszlo shook his head. "Jose . . ."

"I have to know."

The mechanic looked from Lowell to the other five guests. "You have no weapons?"

Black pulled out a pocket knife.

"We go with you." He nodded at Jose, who turned and spoke rapidly in Spanish to one of the maids, a young girl in her teens whom Lowell assumed was his daughter. The girl nodded, then glared at the guests and spit angrily on the ground.

"Some workers gone too," Laszlo said.

"Did the Roadrunners take them?" Black asked, and Lowell knew what was going through the man's mind: if they had, those people werc probably dcad.

"Some," the mechanic said. "Others . . ." He fluttered his fingers in the air as though imitating smoke.

"Others disappeared with management," Jose explained.

Laszlo nodded. "They are one of them."

The Winner's Circle was in a building Lowell did not remember seeing, though he had walked past this spot dozens of times the past few days. A tall modern structure adjacent to the low southwest-style building that housed the Saguaro Room and the Grille, it would seem impossible to miss, but he could tell from the expressions on the men around him that they had not noticed it before, either.

Jose led them to a door of smoked glass which, surprisingly, was unlocked, and they walked into a huge round room. Loud music assaulted their ears, though there'd been no hint of it a second before, so good were the soundproofing qualities of the lounge. It seemed to be the backing track of a popular song, and Lowell thought of the karaoke in the Grille. The electricity obviously wasn't off in here.

Maybe it had its own generator.

The place was empty, save for the bodies. The nude forms of several men and women, all chained to a central post, lay in twisted positions about the floor, blood on their buttocks and genitals indicating that they had been sexually abused before being killed. There were other bodies here as well, and Lowell recognized a Coyote he'd played against in the basketball game tied to a chair, eyes bulging from his head, and tongue lolling as though he'd been strangled. His brown hair was coated with semen. A sunken section of the floor, a smaller crescent within the larger circle of the lounge, was filled with blood, and in the red liquid floated a woman's head and several writhing rattlesnakes.

Next to him, Elijah let out a frightened moan, obviously recognizing the other Coyote as well. "Jackie," he said.

They moved carefully around the perimeter of the room before circling toward the center, on guard for boobytraps or ambushes. From the opposite side of the lounge, near the bar, Lowell saw a karaoke screen. On it was one word, scrolling over and over again: *Fuck Fuck Fuck Fuck Fuck* . . . Behind the counter, the bartender lay among a pile of broken bottles, his head pummeled into something that resembled a squished pumpkin.

"My wife's not here," Jose said when they finally reached the post in the center of the room, and Lowell could hear the relief in his voice.

"What *was* this place?" Black wondered, looking around.

"I told you," Jose said. "It's a club for winners of the tournaments."

Scott turned toward him. "Did *you* work here?"

"I cleaned the floors sometimes. After."

"After?"

"It was never like this," he said quickly. But Lowell could see that Scott did not believe him, and Lowell himself was not sure the maintenance man was telling the whole truth. He thought of those ordinary German citizens who supposedly saw the trains leading to the concentration camps, who smelled the black smoke that belched out of the incinerators, but asked no questions. Rick, Elijah and Mike remained cowed, shocked into silence by the gruesome depravity on display.

"They're obviously not here," Black said.

Jose nodded grimly. "But they *were* here."

Laszlo cleared his throat. "Maybe they . . . disappear." He made that fluttering motion with his fingers once again.

As strange and horrible as that prospect was, Lowell wished it was true. But he had the feeling that Blodgett and his buddies were still around somewhere, waiting, biding their time.

"It's gonna be a hot afternoon," Black said. "It's hot out there already." He gestured around the Winner's Circle. "These bodies are going to be pretty ripe by this evening. And by tomorrow . . ." He shook his head.

"What do we do?" Scott asked. "Bury them all?"

"That'd be tampering with evidence," Lowell pointed out.

Black nodded. "Assuming the law ever makes it out here." He sighed. "I guess we just seal this place up and hope for the best, tell everyone to stay away."

Rick said what Lowell was thinking. "What about all those bodies on the driving range?"

"It's not my call to make," Black said. "But I'd say leave them there."

"We have turkey vultures here," Jose said. "And crows and coyotes."

Black shrugged. "Let nature take its course." And Lowell realized that he was right. They'd tire themselves out and waste several days if they tried to provide a proper burial for all of the corpses that littered the resort grounds.

"The authorities better get here fast," Elijah mumbled. "That's all I can say."

They were silent as they bisected the round room on their way to the door, and Lowell felt the bile rise in his throat as he got a closer look at one of the dead chained employees and the damage that had been done to the man's genitals. He kept himself from throwing up by concentrating on the rectangle of light that was the door outside.

In the open air, he breathed deeply. All of those people in there, he realized, as well as all of those dead bodies on the driving range and elsewhere, had families and friends, coworkers and acquaintances, other people in the outside world who cared about them. In a day or so they'd be bloated beyond recognition or picked apart by scavengers, while their loved ones would be going on with their lives, blithely assuming they were having a fun relaxing vacation and would soon be home. The thought made him feel incredibly sad.

"So what's next?" he asked. "Where do we go from here?"

"Any ideas?" Black took out his map to show Jose and Laszlo. "We've divided The Reata into quadrants and have covered this area here and here. We were going to go this way next. But if you have any other ideas . . ."

The two men looked at each other. Laszlo shrugged and Jose shook his head.

"Then I guess we'll continue on. You're welcome to join us."

"I think we'd better get back," Jose said. "Just in case."

They parted, the employees promising to find them if the Roadrunners showed up again, Black promising to let the employees know if they discovered where the Roadrunners were staying.

"That's weird," Mike said, and they all turned to look at him. It was the first time he'd spoken.

"What's weird?" Black asked.

"The way we're all acting. We should all be banding together. Instead, we're—" He moved his hands apart. "We're still the guests and they're still the hired help."

He was right. In movies, in fiction, people always came together against a common enemy, putting aside personal differences. But it didn't work out that way in real life, and again Lowell thought that The Reata had known that . . . maybe even counted on that. The resort was playing them, and their only hope was to thwart its expectations and behave in ways that were unexpected.

Black seemed to realize the same thing. "You're right. We need to stick together."

"Besides," Elijah added, "they know more about this place than we ever will. We should be able to do something with all that information if we put our heads together."

They were walking, heading down a gravel path toward the next block of rooms. Lowell saw something large just off the path ahead. "What's that?" he asked, pointing.

It was a man sleeping under a bristly bush, practically curled into a fetal position. He whimpered when he saw them, and when they tried to pull him to his feet, they saw that he was wearing only bloodstained jockey shorts and tennis shoes. His skin was intentionally covered with dirt and on his face carefully applied war paint had smeared, making him look like a retarded clown.

A Roadrunner.

The men next to him stiffened, and Lowell felt his own muscles clenching. He expected the man to yell for help at any moment, to call for reinforcements, while they were attacked from all sides by savage Roadrunners, and his first instinct was to take offensive action and make sure that cry for help never got out of his mouth. If he'd had a weapon of some sort he probably would have used it.

But instead of alerting his companions, the man burst into tears. "I'm sorry," he wailed. "I'm sorry."

Lowell's heart softened, and he saw the man not as a Roadrunner, but as some poor schlub who'd come here for a luxury vacation at a bargain price and wound up playing sports that were supposed to be fun but instead ended in death and destruction.

The man looked at them, tears rolling down his face, unwiped snot dripping from his nose. "I didn't mean to . . ." he cried. "I didn't *want* to . . ." He reached out for the closest person, who happened to be Lowell, and threw his arms around him, hugging him tight and sobbing into his shoulder. Lowell heard the remorse in his cries, felt the desperate need to reconnect in his unstinting hug.

Maybe there's hope yet, he thought.

Thirty-five

The survivors pooled their food and water. Rachel made cold Cup Noodles soup for the boys, who gagged down the crunchy noodles and freeze-dried vegetables only because they were starving, while she and Lowell had a Butterfinger apiece. Their dinner might not have been the world's most nutritious, but at least they had something in their stomachs. The maids and maintenance men and other on-site workers had had efficiency rooms with stoves and refrigerators, so there would have been more food, but The Roadrunners had cleaned out the pantries and iceboxes when they trashed the help's homes, stealing it for themselves.

Rand Black's original idea had been for all of them to move into a single block of adjoining rooms, circling the wagons as it were, but when he, Lowell and a couple of other men went up to the lobby to see if they could find keys, the building had been sealed shut—doors bolted and windows covered with wood from the inside.

Rachel had the feeling the killers had barricaded themselves in there.

Maybe they were even using the torture chamber.

So the survivors had been forced to spend the night in their existing rooms, although the remaining workers agreed to move their tents in the open spaces near inhabited rooms for security. Most of the guests had offered to let employees sleep on the floors of their rooms, but there remained suspicions on both sides—the workers not comfortable with the idea of sleeping in a Reata room, the guests not comfortable with the idea of sharing space with Reata employees—and they'd decided to stay near each other but not together.

Rachel stood by the window and looked down, comforted by the sight of three white tents on the grassy area below. She remembered the first night when she'd seen the gardener there, carrying his rake like a weapon and then doing his psychotic little dance.

They should have left the next morning.

While they still could.

Did she really think they would be trapped here forever, that they would die here? Surely someone had to be looking for at least one of the guests who hadn't called or come home when he or she was supposed to, surely someone's boss or friend or spouse or parent or child would get worried and call the police, who would then come out to investigate. But how long would that take? And would they still be alive when it happened?

Or would they be dead, their ghosts trapped here for eternity, a part of The Reata?

She shivered. Hokey as it might be, the thought was a little too close for comfort.

Rachel looked out, above the tents. From their room, she could see an orangish glow behind the buildings farther down the hill, a gentle radiance that threw the southern portion of The Reata into reassuring silhouette, making it appear once more like a bastion of civilization in the wilderness.

Lowell noticed it, too. "It's coming from the amphitheater," he said. "They must be doing something there."

They.

How had it come to this? Us versus Them. Shouldn't they all be in this together? Shouldn't it be all of them against the resort?

Lowell came over, stood next to her, put an arm around her shoulder. From their room, she heard the boys talking in low worried voices.

"We should go there," she said, pointing toward the orange glow.

She felt the reluctance in his stiffness next to her, and the fear. She experienced the same thing, but she felt even more strongly that unless they all pulled together they would not make it, they would not live to be rescued. Another day as hot as today, with no food or water, and they'd become sick, dehydrated. A day later . . .

She could not allow that to happen to her sons. She would not.

"They're assholes," she said. "But they're people."

"People who slaughtered dozens of other people."

"Because they were forced to," she said. "Because they'd been influenced or corrupted or whatever word you want to use."

"And you think we can just walk up to them and say, 'Hi. Let's make up. We're all people here, after all.'" He shook his head. "Appeals to our common humanity are not going to work."

She glared at him. "Do you have a better idea? I know! Why don't we just sit here and starve to death! Or we could hide out until we're too weak to move and *then* try to negotiate a truce!"

"What truce? You saw what they did in the tournament. They *killed* people."

"Would you have done any different?" she asked, and from the expression on his face, she knew that she'd gotten to him. She took a deep calming breath, placed a hand on his arm. "Maybe you wouldn't have enjoyed it as much, but you would've done the same. You wouldn't have had a choice. That's all I'm saying. Maybe . . . maybe they regret what they did."

He nodded slowly, and she knew he was thinking of that man they'd found sleeping under a bush. "We could . . . look," he said. "But we're not just going to walk into the middle of their camp. We'll check out the situation first, watch them."

"I don't want the boys coming," she told him.

"The boys? You're not going either."

"The hell I'm not."

He held up a hand as if getting ready to lecture her, then apparently thought the better of it. "All right," he said. "We'll just make sure the kids stay inside. There are people around. Jose's in one of the tents on the lawn. I'll tell him to keep an eye out."

Ryan wanted to come along—he seemed strangely energized by everything that had happened—but they made it clear he was to remain in the suite with his brothers and David and not open the door for anyone other than themselves. The other boys seemed listless and depressed to Rachel, and showed no interest in leaving the room. Owen, in particular, looked devastated, and she wondered if he was still thinking about that girl.

Brenda

Rachel glanced over at Lowell. She was still unsettled that a figure from his past would appear here at The Reata and attach herself to their son. She wondered how that had happened.

And why.

Lowell went downstairs, told Jose where they were going and asked him to watch the suite, make sure no one entered or left. Then the two of them started off across the grounds.

She'd been cooped up for so long that the world outside seemed like hostile territory, the landmarks by which she'd navigated The Reata for the past few days unfamiliar. She felt rudderless and disoriented, and though she knew they were walking down the slope to the lower portion of the resort, it felt as though they were traveling in the opposite direction. It would be very easy to get lost here, and she knew that she had to be extremely careful outside of their suite or she might end up wandering in some remote area of the property, easy pickings for whatever lurked out there in the dark.

The moon was out and full, providing illumination, and they made their way toward the amphitheater, Lowell leading the way. They stuck to paved pathways, afraid of being out in the open and drawing attention to themselves but more afraid of what might lurk in the shadows.

The back of the amphitheater was empty and unguarded. They approached with caution, peeking around the corner to make sure no one saw them before crouching low and sneaking into the last row of seats, hiding in the shadows thrown by a skinny palm tree. At the front of the amphitheater, the first four or five rows had been torn out, chairs tossed aside to make room for the chaotic revelry that was taking place. There were scores of people here, far more than merely the Roadrunners and their families, and Rachel realized that they must have attracted converts. She thought of the Biblical tale of the golden calf. She had never believed that story, had never bought that after enduring two thousand years of slavery and waiting to be delivered from Egypt only to escape through a spectacular series of miracles, Moses' followers would start worshipping a golden calf because he was a little late coming down from the mount.

She believed it now, though. Watching the frenetic bodies downslope from them, she could feel the chaotic energy of this place, the pulsing power fueling this lawless confusion. She felt its pull as well, the powerful attraction, and a part of her wanted to jump up from her hiding place and join them. It was only the thought of her kids and the solid presence of Lowell next to her that kept her from dancing in the hot night with wild abandon.

The glow they'd seen from their suite was from a huge bonfire at the back of the stage, a conflagration fueled by dried brush and broken wood furniture taken from various rooms. In front of the blaze, in silhouette, half a dozen men and women were performing some sort of crude play, and Rachel was reminded immediately of *Hamlet* and the performance put on by the traveling players for the benefit of Hamlet's uncle. She couldn't tell exactly what was happening on stage, but it appeared to be a reenactment of the molestation of another resort guest. On the flat area below the raised stage, still illuminated by the bonfire, she saw several people scurrying about under the command of a large dominant figure barking orders.

Blodgett.

They'd caught someone, a uniformed Reata employee, a maid or laundress who had been hiding on the grounds or in the surrounding chaparral, and they'd tied her with wire and connected the wires to a series of broomsticks and branches held by different men. They were making her dance like a marionette, jerking on the wires, which dug into her flesh and generated sheets of flowing blood. Above the singing and screaming and orgiastic cries of the other celebrants, she heard the chilling sound of Blodgett's rough booming laugh.

It was dangerous to be here. If they were caught, they would be killed. She grabbed Lowell's sleeve, pulling on it to indicate that they should leave, and he followed her out from under the palm tree shadow, out of the amphitheater's last row and into the anonymous night.

There was no peace to be made with the Roadrunners.

On their way back, they took a different route, a shorter route, and passed by the pool. Torches were burning, jammed into cracks and crevices in the fake rock by the top of the slide. In the pool, dead bodies bobbed, their black shapes visible only against the orange reflective torchlight shimmering on the gently rippling water.

"I was wrong," Rachel said. "They might be people but they're not like us."

"No," Lowell told her. "You were right."

They didn't say anything after that, simply continued walking. Rachel was suffused with a numbing deep despair. They were doomed. She could see the black shapes of the bodies from the corner of her eye, floating on the orange-dappled water. She thought of the boys. *What would happen to them?* she wondered. *How would they die?*

Suddenly Lowell started running.

"What is it?" she asked, panicked.

"The rooms!" he shouted as he ran, and she could see in the moonlight strewn towels and flattened sheets where the tents had stood. "They're on fire!"

Ryan sat on the floor in front of the dead television, wishing it was on, wishing they were anywhere but here. David, Curtis and Owen were sitting silently at the table, nibbling on Necco wafers. One of the hotel workers had given them a candle and some matches, and they huddled around that feeble flickering flame, grateful for its light.

They needed to return to Antelope Canyon. Ryan knew it if no one else did. He'd brought it up to his dad, his mom, David and his brothers, but his parents were too focused on the here and now, on what was happening at The Reata, and David and his brothers were too scared to go back there again.

Not that he blamed them.

Ryan was scared, too. More scared than he had ever been in his life. More scared than he ever thought he could be. But unless the Rescue Rangers suddenly appeared and whisked them all back to civilization—a possibility that seemed increasingly unlikely—they were going to have to find their own way out of this horror. And that meant putting a stop to the rejuvenation of the old resort. He didn't know whether there was some special ritual they had to perform or whether they could just blow the place up, but he knew they had to act before the hotel in Antelope Canyon was fully restored.

What would happen when the old resort *was* fully restored?

He had no idea.

But it was something very, very bad.

Ryan stood and stretched. In the car, he had an old Gameboy that ran on batteries, a toy that accompanied him on all their long trips. If he'd only taken it out and brought it into the room, at least they'd have something to do. He walked up to the table, held his hand out for a Necco wafer, and got a brown one. Popping it into his mouth, he glanced through the open doorway into his parents' room.

And saw movement.

Ryan's heart lurched in his chest. He motioned for the others to turn around and look, afraid to speak aloud and not sure if he could do so even if he wanted to.

Something emerged from the gloom, a thin white figure with a blurred blank face that he recognized from his vision at the exercise pool. It floated rather than walked, gliding past the bed toward their room. He remembered his certainty that its touch meant death.

Acting fast, almost without thinking, he ran across the room, slammed the door and with fumbling fingers locked it. "Quick!" he yelled. "Get over here! Push something in front of the door! The dresser!"

Neither Curtis, Owen nor David had seen what he'd seen or knew why he wanted them to blockade the door, but they were there instantly. "The fucker's bolted down!" David called, trying to push the dresser.

"It doesn't matter," Owen said, and Ryan suddenly realized he was right. "The door opens out."

"What is it?" Curtis demanded. "What's there?"

Ryan didn't know how to describe it. "A ghost, I guess," he said quickly, backing away from the door and keeping his eye on the handle in case it should turn. "A weird white thing that was floating through their room. I saw one of those things before," he added quickly. "By the exercise pool." He thought now that if he ever lived through this to write anything it would be a harsh story of survival rather than an entertaining travel book.

Their candle suddenly flared, the flame turning blood red and shooting high into the air, its tip flicking against the vaulted ceiling like a serpent's tongue.

There was a knock at the door. Not a loud crash or a demanding boom but a mild, almost polite rapping that was somehow far, far worse. It paused, then started again, paused, then started again, and then there were no more pauses, only that light insistent tapping, the wordless plea of that faceless being asking to come in.

"Go away!" Ryan screamed.

The rapping continued, and the tall thin flame not only flicked at the wooden ceiling but spread across it, not burning it exactly but multiplying along its surface. The room was suffused in a red glow. The slats of the upper right shutter were opening and closing on their own, resembling nothing more than the winking of an eye, and there was a pulsing beneath the covers on the bed that made it appear as if the mattress was home to some type of monstrous amoeba. A persistent shadow in the corner, roughly the shape of a monkey, danced hyperkinetically, although there was no figure in the room to which it even remotely corresponded.

"Fuck," David breathed. "Oh fuck."

The floor *rolled*, as though it was liquid and they were atop it, riding the wave. The building itself was changing around them. Everyone had been so focused on the Roadrunners and finding food and matters of practical survival that they'd almost forgotten the real reason they were in this mess—the resort. Whether it was haunted by supernatural beings or whether it was alive and creating such creatures itself, this place was far more evil and far more dangerous than any human ever could be.

"We have to get out of here!" Curtis shouted. His voice sounded like he was trying to communicate over a jet engine, though despite all of the activity, the only noise in the room remained that maddening gentle knocking.

His brother was right, Ryan knew, but the door outside was

through their parents' room, and their own windows were hidden behind that terrible winking shutter and could not be opened. They'd have to be smashed, and the four of them would be forced to leap to the ground, quite a jump even under ideal circumstances.

David took charge. Picking up the chair on which he'd been sitting, he lifted it above his head and ran toward the shutters, throwing it as hard as he could against the winking upper corner. The slats cracked and fell, the frame jerked loose from its hinges, and both the upper and lower shutters fell away from the window. There was no residual movement, the wood was only wood, and David threw open the left pair of shutters, picked up his chair, hefted it and slammed it into the glass. The pane must have looked a lot thicker than it really was, because it shattered instantly beneath this onslaught, and David awkwardly manuevered his body around in order to clean the glass from the edges of the window with a chair leg.

The room was suddenly filled with the overpowering smell of smoke, but since that strange red flame was still expanding over the surface of the ceiling and not touching the wood, the fire had to be coming from outside. Was the building burning? Or was there a fire down below on the grass into which they'd be jumping?

It didn't matter. They had to get out of here, and David went first, screaming as he leaped out of the open window into the night. The rest of them were hot on his heels, not speaking, not needing to speak, as they attempted to escape that hellish room.

Ryan hit the ground hard, landing on his feet but immediately falling over from the jolt. Rolling, he had time to see that the building housing their suite *was* on fire and that the tents on the grass around him had been torn down, their occupants nowhere to be seen. He tried to stand and was grateful that he was able to do so. Curtis, Owen and David were on their feet as well, as surprised as he was not to have any broken bones. They looked up at their room. Through twin tendrils of smoke curling down from the roof, a white figure could be seen standing in front of their shattered window, the ceiling red with heatless flame behind it.

Ryan felt tired, empty, hungry, scared. He wished this was all a dream, a nightmare from which he would awake, but it wasn't, and his brain and body were overwhelmed by everything he had seen and experienced. He might have read a lot of books, and maybe he had some insights that might help them handle the situation here, but deep down he was just a kid, and he didn't want to have to deal with this. He *shouldn't* have to deal with this.

A familiar shout caused him to turn around, and his heart swelled as he saw his parents speeding toward them across the lawn, calling their names, their faces an alternating mixture of terror and relief. His father reached them first, and Ryan fell gratefully into his welcome arms.

"Dad," he sobbed.

Thirty-six

Other buildings had collapsed during the night. They saw the destruction from Rand Black's window when they awoke: an entire block of rooms that had imploded, crumbling into itself; the Santa Fe structure housing the Saguaro Room and the Grille now a jumble of faux adobe, exposed wooden beams, broken plumbing and snapped wiring; the modern building next to it that had been home to the Winner's Circle completely gone, not even a foundation remaining. Smoke or dust issued from the piles of rubble, polluting the air outside and giving the rising sun a brownish cast.

Despite the boys' story, Lowell would have still probably assumed the Roadrunners were behind it all had he not been to that other resort in the canyon. For that is what The Reata now resembled. And if the kids were right about the symbiotic relationship between the two, that other resort was probably in tip-top shape right about now.

But he could not convince the employees or the other survivors of any such thing. Black was stirred up and energized, and going room to room, tent to tent, he gathered a large band of angry men nearly thirty strong to chase down the Roadrunners and their supporters. Lowell accompanied them, but more out of obligation than conviction. Black had offered to share his room with them last night after their own suite disintegrated before their eyes, and the firefighter and his wife had been gracious enough to provide sleeping space for their boys and David in the limited area they had. He owed them.

How many people were here at The Reata right now? he wondered. Even if only two-thirds of the resort's rooms had been occupied—and the full parking lots had indicated it was probably more than that—that left approximately fifty rooms. An average of two people per room made a hundred. And as far as employees, between managers and support staff and maintenance services there were another thirty.

And how many were left? It was impossible to say, and he only hoped that their side outnumbered the other side.

Not that it would make any difference in the long run. The Reata was pitting them against each other and no doubt had plans of its own for whichever side came out on top.

They marched up the sidewalk to the rooms that were left, gathering recruits. On the gate by the pool, they found a note, written in blood on a white queen-sized bedsheet. The message consisted of two words: TOURNAMENT TONIGHT.

None of them knew exactly what that meant. Obviously the Roadrunners wanted a match of some sort, but what sport they intended to play and where it was to be held and all of the other practical details remained unstated and unknown. The note was aimed at them, however, so obviously they'd been expected to come here and find it. That easy prediction of their movements didn't sit well with anyone.

"They were at the amphitheater last night." Black turned toward Lowell. "How many would you estimate?"

"I don't know," Lowell admitted. "All of the Roadrunners. What's that, fifteen or so? Plus their families." He paused. "I saw some recruits, too."

"Let's figure fifty to be on the safe side."

"That sounds about right."

"The question is: what do we do when we find them?" Black sounded just as angry as he had before, but a sense of pragmatism seemed to have entered his thinking. "I doubt we could overpower them even with the element of surprise. Do we watch them, follow them, take them out one by one when we get the opportunity, or—"

"*Take them out?*" Jose said.

Lowell was thinking exactly the same thing. If the firefighter had said "capture them" or something along those lines, he would have been right with him. But Black clearly had no problem with killing Roadrunners, with murdering each of them individually, irrespective of their culpability in any of this.

"Yeah," Scott said defensively. "Take them out." He motioned around at the battered resort. "You see what they're capable of. Hell, we all knew it before that first volleyball game. Now it's kill or be killed, and unless we want to be the victims here, we've got to strike hard and make it count."

"It's stooping to their level," Lowell said quietly, though he was not sure he believed his own argument. He, too, felt the pull of violence, understood the satisfaction to be gained by taking that sort of action.

"I came here for a vacation with my family," said a clean-cut young man Lowell didn't know. "I'm not going to end it by murdering someone."

"I suppose it's against your religion," Scott sneered.

The man faced him. "As a matter of fact, it is. Do you have a problem with that?"

"Okay, okay," Black said wearily. "Let's not fight among ourselves." He turned back toward Lowell. "Any suggestions?"

He didn't have any. He agreed with the religious guy, he wasn't willing to kill anyone—

not yet

—but he also thought they should be keeping tabs on the Roadrunners, especially if Blodgett and his crew were expecting them to participate in some sort of tournament. "Let's find them first," he suggested. "We'll see how it plays from there."

They could see from here that the lobby was still sealed shut, and Lowell was sure that was where the Roadrunners were hiding, but just in case, they set out for the amphitheater, approaching it cautiously in three split groups, one from the rear, one from either side. As expected, the amphitheater was empty save for several nude and broken bodies strung from the rigging above the stage. The bonfire had burned itself out without causing too much damage, but all of the seats had been ripped from their moorings and piled in front of the stage in obvious preparation for another bonfire. Graffiti marked the walls all around, and on a big boulder in back of the stage was a frighteningly realized depiction of an ancient scragglyhaired man who had to be the same figure the kids had seen. As the other men prowled the aisles and backstage area of the amphitheater looking for Roadrunners or any living victims, Lowell studied the drawing. It was in ash or charcoal, and portrayed a man so thin and desiccated he looked almost like a corpse. Only his eyes were alive, and even in this rough amateur sketch their irredeemable darkness shone through chillingly.

There was nothing else to be found here, and they made a quick tour of the remaining resort, including a short trip to Laszlo's garage, where the battery bought for Lowell's car still sat forlornly on a metal cart next to an open bay, before returning to the main building that housed the lobby.

According to a waiter, the building was also home to the Starlight Pavilion, a secret restaurant catering exclusively to winners of the tournaments. Lowell had not realized before how integral these tournaments seemed to be to life at The Reata. He'd known before the first volleyball game that it wasn't just the casual diversion the activities coordinator had made it out to be, but he hadn't understood until now just how much importance the powers that be attached to these competitions.

They stood under the awning by the front entrance, which had been sealed shut with plywood onto which had been painted a childish red skull and crossbones. "Any ideas on how to get in?" Black asked Jose and the other employees.

"There's a service entrance around the side," Jose said. "But it's probably boarded up, too. It's worth a shot, though."

As if on cue, a spear shot out from an unseen opening, hitting Laszlo in the arm. It pierced the skin and carved a slash above his elbow that immediately started gushing blood, but the mechanic merely pulled off his T-shirt and clamped it against the bleeding wound as the rest of them retreated. Jose thought to grab the spear.

The wound obviously hurt, but it wasn't life-threatening, and Laszlo didn't seem too concerned. He appeared to be more angry than anything else, and he pulled the spear from Jose's hand as the entire group continued moving farther out into the parking lot.

"Still think we shouldn't strike first and ask questions later?" Scott demanded.

They looked slightly ridiculous, Lowell thought, thirty or so grown men cowering in a huddle in the middle of an empty parking lot, and he, too, thought they should be taking some kind of action, but he didn't know what and didn't know how.

"So I guess our tournament this afternoon is the javelin toss?" someone said dryly, and the laughter that greeted his remark at least alleviated some of the tension.

Black, standing next to Laszlo, looked at the spear, as did Lowell. It looked old, like something taken out of a museum. "Where—?" Lowell started to ask.

"They sell 'em in the gift shop," Jose said, and Lowell remembered seeing a display case with several overpriced pots and Native American artifacts.

"At least we know where they are," Black said. He thought for a moment. "Okay. We'll station someone here, rotating shifts, to keep an eye on them. Two people," he amended, obviously thinking of the spear. "Just in case. If there's any movement, anything unusual, come and get the rest of us. I suggest we do like they do today, remain all in one place for safety's sake."

"We have walkie-talkies," Jose said. "They run on batteries and don't have much of a range, but they'll work anywhere in The Reata.

We could give one to the people standing watch, and spread the others around."

"Why didn't you tell us this before?" Black asked, exasperated.

"I'm telling you now," Jose said coolly, and Lowell realized that the employees still did not completely trust the guests. The feeling, he supposed, looking at Scott, was mutual.

Two men volunteered to take first watch, Jose and a custodian, while the rest of them returned to pick up their families and meet on the grassy area in front of the last set of rooms, the building farthest away from the lobby. Lowell wasn't sure if it was real or just his imagination, but the entire resort now seemed to have a sickening putrid smell, like spoiled meat, and he could not help thinking of all those dead bodies bloating in the desert heat.

They spent the rest of the morning worrying and talking, the afternoon practicing and making weapons out of the few materials they had on hand. Lowell sharpened a broom-handle spear, and the boys made smaller shivs from broken branches. Laszlo and another mechanic raided the garage and came away with quite a few wrenches, screwdrivers and tire irons.

The tension and close quarters caused them to get on each others' nerves, and a fistfight broke out between one of The Reata's custodians and one of the guests, a former Coyote who, before all this started, had complained to the front desk about an overflowing litter basket, a complaint that had resulted in a reprimand. People immediately began taking sides, and it would have turned into a huge ugly brawl with employees versus guests had Lowell not interceded and reminded them that they needed to work together against a common enemy. The men grudgingly gave it up, going back to their respective tasks.

"What kind of tournament do you think they want to have?" Lowell asked Black.

The firefighter shook his head. "I don't think it's a ball game."

"If you had to guess?"

He looked at Lowell. "Hand-to-hand combat. To the death."

Lowell looked out at the awkward guests and the only slightly more agile employees, running around a makeshift obstacle course, weapons in hand. "You think we'll be ready?"

"No."

The Roadrunners came out at night.

The crackle of six walkie-talkies across the crowded parking lot and a message from the two most recent volunteers jolted everyone into battle stance. "They're out," Scott whispered. "They're dressed dark and going down the stairs. They'll be coming out the pool area."

That was closer to the lobby than where they were.

"Go!" Black shouted. "Go!"

Lowell squeezed Rachel's hand, gave her an extra spear, told her and the boys to protect the others who were staying. "Keep an eye out. Watch all sidewalks and trails, keep checking behind that palm tree; it's a good hiding place. We'll be back."

But he wasn't sure if they would, and as he ran with the other men up the hill, he realized what an untrained, unprepared, ragtag group of fighters they really were. The Roadrunners would crush them.

At least they had the advantage of surprise. The Roadrunners didn't know where *they* were, and they had spies keeping close track of the Roadrunners' movements. An ambush was still possible.

He *could* kill, he realized now.

He could and would.

It became quickly clear that they would not reach the pool area before the enemy, so Black stopped them in an easily defensible area near the employees' quarters, closing the gate that offered the only entrance here, deploying men to every side of the open space, stationing some in trees and in buildings, leaving a small volunteer contingent on the road out front as bait, telling Scott and the other watcher their exact location so they could be forewarned of the Roadrunners' approach.

Lowell stood next to Black inside a storage room, peeking out of the partially open door, feeling scared but strangely excited.

The walkie-talkie crackled. "They're on their way. They're almost there."

The first few Roadrunners through the gate—not Blodgett—were bludgeoned with tire irons by custodians stationed to either side of the entrance, but then one of the custodians went down, and the two sides came together on the narrow sloping stretch of ground, clashing like armies on a battlefield. Lowell and Black sped out of the storage room, attacking from the side. Lowell stabbed the buttocks of a feral woman in bloody rags who screamed and ran away, then swung at an older man in a dirty summer suit, hitting him across the face. The man fell down, clutching his head and crying out in pain, and Lowell moved on. Should he have stayed to finish the job, stabbing the man through the heart? Maybe so, but he couldn't do it, and his goal became not to kill but to injure and incapacitate.

He was pretty successful at meeting his goal.

For a while, it seemed that men and women were coming after

him right and left. He felt like the hero of an action movie as he swung and stabbed, tripped and kicked. He received a few blows himself, including one on the left shoulder that rendered that arm nearly useless, but overall he gave far more than he got, and somewhere in the middle of the skirmish, Lowell realized that individuals were escaping, dashing over the fence or around the buildings, running into the night. Whether they were pursued or pursuer, he could not tell.

At some point, the action wound down, he was no longer fighting all comers, and he looked around, thinking the fight was over, wanting to see which side had won. But the battle had merely moved out into the road, and he took the opportunity to stop and catch his breath. He sat down on a rock for a moment, hoping his brief respite would enable him to get a second wind, praying that it didn't cause the deaths of some of his fellow Cactus Wrens. He breathed deeply and started coughing. They should've carried water with them, he thought, and then he was throwing up, puking onto the dirt. He wiped his mouth, went out over the collapsed fence, and found not the concerted focused fighting of only a few moments before but a wild free-for-all that seemed to spread over the visible area of The Reata before him, individuals chasing each other down trails, around cactus, wrestling on the sidewalks, darting around and in and out of the extant buildings. He'd been planning to join the fight, but there was not really a fight to join, and wearily he made his way down the road toward the bottom parking lot to make sure Rachel and the kids were all right.

They were gone.

All of the families left behind were gone, in their place a broken walkie-talkie, and some bloody clothing and the speared body of a man he didn't recognize. "Rachel!" he called at the top of his lungs, not caring if he drew attention to his whereabouts. "Ryan! Curtis! Owen!" The Roadrunners had split up, he realized, and somehow Scott and the other watcher had missed that. They'd been battling only a partial contingent, which explained the easiness of the fighting. The rest had been dispatched elsewhere.

Here.

And it had cost his family their lives.

No. He couldn't think that way. And he set off, spear in hand, down what he considered the most likely trail, which led toward the chef's garden.

The garden was trampled, but no one was there. He picked up a stone-headed tomahawk from the ground that had to be from the gift shop. The moon gave off more than enough light to see by, but there were still plenty of shadows, and he moved carefully past each one, looking for hiding combatants or dead bodies, praying he found neither.

The Reata seemed bigger than it had before. The resort was set on sixty acres, and he thought he'd been over most of it, but he found himself on trails he hadn't known existed, walking past burning rubble that had been buildings he didn't recognize. He heard screaming from somewhere—sound carried strangely here—and shouts of single words in unison, but there were other screams from other directions, other shouts, and he had no idea what was going on out there. Somewhere on the east end of the resort, standing on a tall boulder so he could see as far as possible, he spotted a group of men and women traveling up a nearby service road. The two in front were carrying torches, and there was something in the angry march of their walk that made him hop down off the rock and head immediately in the opposite direction. There was shouting from this area, too, invectives and words of anger, and he quickly stepped off the trail, ran down the slope to an oleander bush and hid.

Not a moment too soon.

They passed by, shouting their desires and demands, Roadrunners and Coyotes and Cactus Wrens and others. They'd come together in the brush, these various factions, and like all anarchic crowds they'd decided to turn on their leaders, no longer blaming their opponents for the wrongs visited upon them but blaming their own commanders for the situation in which they found themselves. They'd turned savage in the night, and whatever their original classes or occupations—rich or poor, janitor or stock broker—they were now children of the desert, spawn of The Reata, and they returned to the ruined buildings looking for scapegoats, looking for blood.

He waited until they passed by, then headed back down the path the way they'd come.

He found Blodgett in front of what had been the Grille.

The man was whimpering, and even Lowell felt sorry for him. He'd been stripped and doused with gasoline and set afire, and though he'd managed to roll out the flames, a large portion of his body had been charred and there was about him the sickening smell of burnt skin. He was lying on the ground, curled up in a fetal position, and he looked up at Lowell with eyes that begged for release or absolution or help or . . . something.

Blodgett was not the enemy, he realized. The man was just another victim.

As was the mob that had turned on him.

But that mob was uncontrollable, and Lowell knew that if those people found him they would attack him, too. Stone him to death, perhaps. Or string him up.

Maybe they'd already done so to his family.

He hurried on, growing increasingly frustrated as he realized that he was on a trail he had already taken, that this was an area of the resort he had explored extensively. Stopping where he was, he made a beeline for the spot where he knew the tennis courts were. He had not been anywhere near that area tonight.

He found Rachel and the twins huddled together in the shade of a cottonwood tree, hidden from the moonlight in a puddle of darkness. Rachel called his name, sobbing, and he ran to meet her, giving her a hard hug, almost weeping with gratitude as he saw that she had no scratches on her face, that her clothes were still on, that her limbs were not broken. Curtis and Owen, too, gave him big hugs, both of them crying as they hadn't cried for years, like little children frightened of the dark and grateful for the saving grace of a parent.

But . . .

He stepped back, met Rachel's dark haunted eyes, and a bolt of cold shot through him.

"Where is Ryan?"

Ryan saw the old man. The one from the mirror, the soulless cadaver with the scraggly hair. He didn't know at first whether he was dreaming or whether it was real, but the fact that he was even asking that question gave him the answer he needed because he never questioned the reality of a dream while he was in it, no matter how absurd the scenarios became.

This was real.

The old man was striding up the nearby sidewalk like he owned the place, walking fast and sure for someone who looked like a corpse, a gait that only served to make him seem even more frightening. He'd come from Antelope Canyon, and though Ryan had no idea why he was here, the thought in his mind was that the man had arrived to survey his new acquisition. Ryan turned to his mom and brothers, but to his astonishment they were asleep, his mom leaning against the tree, his brothers on the ground. They'd been awake only seconds previously, and Ryan was filled with fear as he took another peek toward the sidewalk.

The scraggly-haired man—the Owner, as Ryan had come to think of him—had left the sidewalk and was walking purposefully across the gravel toward him, eyes trained directly on his own. Ryan wanted to run and get away, but his mom and brothers were here, and before his brain had time to do more than acknowledge that conflict, the man was here and reaching down. He grabbed Ryan, and with one hand as strong as a vice and just as cold, jerked him to his feet and dragged him away from the tree, toward the sidewalk. Ryan was too scared to even scream. His heart seemed to be beating somewhere up near his throat, and before he knew it they were down the desert trail on their way to Antelope Canyon.

He was going to die, he realized as he was dragged across the gravel, his feet stumbling over themselves to keep up. He didn't want to die. There were things he wanted to do, places he wanted to go. He wanted to be with his parents and brothers. He wanted to see his friends again back in California. He wanted . . . so much. He started crying, though no sound came out. Between the darkness and his tears, he couldn't see where they were going, but he didn't need to see. That vicelike grip held him fast and guided him surely, and he knew exactly where they were headed.

They reached it far faster than he would have thought possible, and he could see it even from the trail, so bright were its lights. The old resort had been fully restored, and when he wiped his eyes with his free right hand, he saw entire buildings that had not been there before. It looked different than he would have expected, more modern in some ways and more antique in others. It was a mixture of a lot of different eras, and Ryan had the impression that it had taken bits and pieces of other Reatas over the years, combining them all in one.

They passed by the buckboard wagon, fully restored and standing on four perfect hub wheels. In its driver's seat, staring forward with reins in her hand as though waiting for a team of horses to arrive, was a white figure, a lithe, nearly naked girl whose pale form looked ghostly in the moonlight.

Brenda?

It looked almost like her but not quite. She said nothing, did not even look in their direction as they passed, but he saw her, and he saw the load she was planning to drive as well: the dead bodies of children, all stacked like cordwood in the back. On top of this ordered arrangement was David, naked and bloody and crumpled into a ball like a used piece of scratch paper.

Then they were at the bottom of the rise and at the resort. Ryan saw lights in rooms, and though some of them looked electric, others looked like candles. The man—the Owner—dragged him to one of the buildings he had not seen before, one that looked like a haunted mansion and stood at the northernmost end of the resort, the focal point of all other structures. The two of them passed through a creaky old front door into a dark room of wood and red velvet, with trophy heads of both animals and humans on the walls. In the center of the room was a throne that was also cushioned with red velvet but was framed with bones. It was *his* chair, and Ryan expected the old man to sit down and make him do some freaky sex stuff to him, but the Owner pulled him past the chair, into another room, this one all black from floor to ceiling. There was a bed in the center of the room. Or kind of a bed. It was made out of wood, but to Ryan it looked more like an altar, like a Wild West version of those old stone tables where humans were sacrificed.

"Prepare him," the Owner said, and from the blackness another figure emerged.

"No," Ryan said. It was the first word he'd spoken since his abduction and it came out small and terrified, exactly the way he felt. "No," he said again, whimpering.

Silence greeted his plea, and he knew then that he was doomed.

Thirty-seven

The lobby was open.

It was the first thing Lowell noticed as they approached the pool. He saw the uncovered doorway at the top of the steps, the wide square entrance black and yawning like an open maw, and though he'd been planning to first comb the pool area and check the bodies in the water to make sure none of them were Ryan, he decided instead to go straight to the lobby, hoping against hope to find his son or some evidence that he was alive.

Walking up the steps and across the flagstone patio, his family right behind him, Lowell felt like a primitive tribesman visiting the home of his god. There was about this mission the same kamikaze sense of daring and foolishness, the same feeling of being in the presence of a great cosmic power.

"Stay close," were the only words he spoke before they walked in.

He did not recognize the room. Everything that had made it so initially impressive upon arrival was gone, leaving only an open space that looked like it had been gutted and abandoned decades ago. The only evidence that the Roadrunners and their converts had recently used this room for their headquarters was a single burning torch crammed into a hole in the floor.

Lowell heard crying from off to the right, the forlorn weeping of an old man, a sound that seemed particularly eerie in this setting under these circumstances.

It was the concierge.

He was at his desk to the side of the doorway, almost the only thing left standing in the ruined lobby, and the floor around him was littered with broken bottles of whiskey.

Lowell looked back at Rachel and the twins, as much for support as anything else, and stepped up to the desk. The old man had obviously been here through the Roadrunner occupation, but that petty rivalry seemed more inconsequential than it ever had before, and the first question out of Lowell's mouth was: "Where did everyone go? What happened to the people who worked here?"

"Gone," he cried. "All gone." He looked up in anguish, sniffled. Lowell could smell his breath from here. "They were supposed to take me with them."

"Where did they go?"

"I don't know."

"But you knew they were going."

"Oh yes." More sniffles.

"And you wanted to go with them."

He wiped his eyes. "Of course."

Rachel jumped in. "What *is* this place? What's happening here? Our son—"

"Shhh." The old man put a finger to his lips. "They can still hear you."

"Who?"

"Them."

Lowell was growing frustrated, was starting to think that the old man was more than a little touched. "Look—"

"They know things about you. About everyone. They use it against you."

Lowell stopped. *They know things about you.* He thought about the last few days and all of the subtle and not-so-subtle references to his high school years. Whatever power was here—*it* or *them*—knew about his high school reunion, knew that he had taken this trip at this time chiefly to avoid going there, and had used that information to try and break him down.

"What is this place?" Rachel asked again.

The concierge stood. He was wobbly but not too wobbly, and though he obviously had been drunk he did not appear to be so any longer. "Have you been to The Reata Museum?"

"I didn't even know there was one."

"It's usually part of the tour. The introductory tour when you first arrive? It's right next to the gift shop." He paused, frowned. "Or what *used* to be the gift shop."

Lowell's heart skipped. "What is it now?"

The concierge did not answer.

Lowell thought of that torture chamber in the banquet room down the corridor. He glanced in that direction, saw only darkness beyond the perimeter of the torchlight.

Rachel took a deep breath, and he heard the threat of tears in her voice. "Our son disappeared, our youngest boy. He's thirteen. We just want to find him. We just want him back."

The concierge's voice softened and he suddenly sounded more lucid. "Let me show you the museum," he said. He pushed a wisp of hair off his forehead. "My name's Jim, by the way. Jim Robinson."

"What's in the museum?" Lowell asked.

"I'll show you what you're up against."

"I thought they could hear us."

"They can. But it doesn't matter any more. Not to me, and probably not to you."

Rachel seemed to have edged away from the verge of tears. "If it's so horrible, why did you want them to take you with them?"

"I have cancer," he said.

Lowell frowned. "I don't understand."

"I could live forever."

The twins had said nothing through all of this, and they said nothing now. Lowell glanced over at their devastated faces and wanted nothing more than to tell them that everything was going to be all right, but that would have been a lie. None of them had any idea where this was going, and Lowell thought it was quite possible that they'd all end up dead in the desert, their corpses rotting in the heat and sinking into the sand until such time as the authorities figured out something was amiss and made their way out here. It was a gruesome image but one made unavoidable by the events of the past few days. He had never in his life imagined that all of them would die together, certainly not this way. While he'd allowed in his more pessimistic moments for the realities of car crashes and random violence, he had always assumed that he and Rachel would live to a ripe old age, get to see their sons married and maybe have a few grandchildren. But thoughts about how they would all end up here, now, made him realize how fragile and fleeting life really was.

He only hoped the resort was content with their bodies and didn't take their souls.

The concierge withdrew a flashlight from his desk. "I've been saving this," he said, switching it on.

Lowell raised his eyebrows. "I'm surprised the Roadrunners didn't take it."

Jim smiled wanly. "They were afraid of me. They wouldn't dare. Come on." He led the way over the torn-up floor. They passed the spot where the front desk had stood and walked toward the open doorway of the gift shop. The concierge would not shine his light in there, and although Lowell tried to look, he could see nothing. He felt a slight suction in the air as they walked by, though, and heard what sounded like wind whistling through a great distance. It frightened him, that empty blackness, and he moved to the right of Rachel and the twins, blocking them from it as best he could.

Jim led them into the room next door, shining his light on the walls. It was a small square chamber filled primarily with framed photographs. In one corner was an antique chair and writing desk, along one wall a glass display case housing old documents, but that was it.

The concierge quickly summarized the history of the resort and its founder, Jedediah Harrison, a scoundrel, con artist and land speculator distantly related to President Harrison, who'd had a small cabin in Antelope Canyon—a "getaway house," Jim called it—since right after his first fraud conviction in 1801. In the late 1800s, he became obsessed with buying up all of the land around the area, though at the time it was considered all but worthless. He used his political connections to subvert the Homestead Act and, like the villain in an old western, bullied and bought out the farm families and ranchers who had tentatively settled this wild section of what was then New Mexico Territory. His goal was to set up a dude ranch for wealthy Easterners and to pocket both the money they'd pay him to work his ranch and the money he'd earn from the sale of the cattle and crops they'd be tending. He built his dude ranch and ran it with some success for one season but then quietly closed it down, reopening two years later as a luxury resort, The Reata, billed at the time as the West's most remote and luxurious hotel.

"Jedediah Harrison was a hedonist and a sadist," the concierge said, "and he was ecstatic about being able to practice his, uh"—Jim glanced at the twins—"*proclivities* free from the prying eyes of law enforcement. He also thought he'd found in the waters of The Reata the fountain of youth, and that was the big draw for his victims or partners or whatever you want to call them."

"I didn't know there *were* waters at The Reata," Lowell said.

"Oh yes. The original resort was built over a natural mineral spring that continuously fed the swimming pool. Harrison was convinced that these waters would not only keep a man looking youthful but would make him immune to all diseases and allow him to live forever."

The original resort.

"In Antelope Canyon?" Lowell asked.

"Come here." He led the way over to a picture opposite the door, shining his light on it. "That's the original Reata." It was a photograph taken in front of that old wagon, only in the photo it had been in working condition, and in its back was a sign stating: THE REATA. Behind it stood a series of buildings that resembled the abandoned resort in the canyon but looked different somehow, more quaint, more innocent.

The old resort *was* the key. That's what the kids—

Ryan

—had tried to tell him two days ago, only he'd been too stubborn and stupid to listen until it was too late. He believed it now, though, believed it utterly, despite the fact that he still had no idea what any of them could possibly do that would put an end to the horrors occurring around them.

"Guests to the resort were by invitation only, and most of the top politicians and big industrialists were on the invitee list. One or two of them died here, under mysterious circumstances, and quite a few others perished later in accidents or unusual incidents. Rumors grew that the place was cursed, but that did not stop people from coming. Because the waters *did* appear to have curative powers and aid in longevity. Harrison was well over a hundred and still going strong when The Reata opened in 1890, although his stated age at the time was sixty-five, itself almost unheard of. Supposedly, he'd bought the cabin when he was in his early thirties, which actually made him somewhere around a hundred and twenty. By 1929, when the first Reata was destroyed, he was still the same. He would have been a hundred and fifty-nine."

"So how did he die?"

"He didn't."

Rachel reached for Lowell's hand. Her fingers were cold. "What do you mean, he didn't?"

"He disappeared after this new resort was built, but no one ever found a body, and technically he's still the owner of The Reata. The people who work here, the people in management, the ones who left and were supposed to take me with them, claim he still comes around. They say they've seen him." Jim shifted his flashlight and the beam landed on another photo. It was a tintype of the founder and was one of the spookiest pictures Lowell had ever seen. It was indeed the scraggly-haired man depicted in the graffiti at the amphitheater.

Rachel gasped.

"You've seen him before?"

"I had a dream about him."

Jim was suddenly interested. "You dreamed of him?" There was a wistfulness in his voice that Lowell found almost as frightening as the story he'd been telling. "Then he called to you. He only calls to the ones he wants."

"No," Owen said in a scared, small voice.

"He can't have me," Rachel said firmly and grabbed both of her boys' hands.

He was a hedonist and a sadist.

"You said the first Reata was destroyed," Lowell prompted.

"I'll get to that."

For Harrison was only the middle chapter in a much longer story. He had cheated the homesteaders out of their property, but the homesteaders had taken the land from the Indians before them, and the Indians no doubt had displaced whatever dominant animal had held sway before that.

There wasn't exactly a *curse* on the land, the concierge said. But all of the killings and betrayals had created a place that was *unclean*, as the Bible put it. He looked up at Lowell. "It's like the land absorbed all of those bad feelings and bad deeds and—" He cut himself off. "No, that's not really it at all." He sighed. "History just keeps repeating itself here. This isn't the first time something like this has happened, and I'd be willing to bet that it won't be the last. I don't know why, I don't think anyone does. Or ever has. It just happens, it just is. Like the ocean is just there and the birds just chirp and the wind just blows. It's a fact of nature. There really was a fountain of youth here—Ponce de León should have been looking farther to the west—and whether that's a good thing or a bad thing, I don't know. But I do know that the land around it is bad. It attracts bad people and it does bad things to people who are otherwise good." His voice dropped. "Like me."

"Maybe that's why they didn't take you," Curtis suggested. They were the first words he'd spoken, and they were music to Lowell's ears. The boy was not only paying attention, but thinking. He would be okay.

"Maybe," Jim said doubtfully, once again pushing aside that stray wisp of hair.

"You said there *was* a fountain of youth," Lowell reminded him. "And the first Reata was destroyed."

"The waters ran out. Or at least that was the story. No one's ever known if that was true or if Harrison simply diverted the spring through a pipe or something for his own personal use because he didn't want to share. That's what a lot of people think. The only thing we know for sure, though, is that one day the waters were gone. And The Reata . . . fell apart. It was like the resort needed the waters to stay fresh and the buildings just deteriorated without them. It happened all at once—two of the boilers exploded, starting a fire. Ten people were trapped and crushed under falling brick and mortar. The survivors were rescued, the victims buried, the place was condemned and Harrison disappeared." He looked at them. "What do you think happened next?"

Lowell shrugged. "They built *this* resort?"

"Wrong. It *appeared*. Sprung up overnight. Pool and all. And the pool was full, mind you, though the waters aren't spring fed and never seemed to have any powers at all. Managers were here and in place, and they immediately started interviewing for the other positions. There've been improvements over the years, improvements made the usual way with contractors and plumbers and electricians. But . . ." He shook his head, gestured around him. "It just popped up."

There were a million questions Lowell wanted to ask, but all of those could wait. What was important now was finding Ryan, and none of Jim's talk of history was bringing them any closer to locating the boy. Lowell's head was filled with horrible scenarios in which Ryan was murdered in various gruesome ways by the wild mob outside, by ghosts and hellish creatures, by The Reata itself, and the longer they stayed here, the longer they waited, the more likely it was that such a thing would come to pass.

"It *protects* itself," the concierge went on. "I'm sure you've noticed that. Or at least it does until it doesn't have to anymore. If people see things or hear things, it makes them forget, it makes them not care, it kind of . . ." He paused, trying to think of the right word. "It casts a *spell* on them. Of course, now everything's almost over. And everyone's trapped here; you can't escape. So it doesn't need to waste the energy."

"We need to find our son," Lowell reminded him.

"I'll tell you something weird," the old man confided, shining his light. "See that picture there? See that cloud? The one that looks like kind of a sideways mushroom? Well, I saw that cloud two days ago, drifting overhead while I was taking a nap outside."

"A lot of clouds look the same."

"No," he insisted. "It's *the* cloud. I've looked at that picture enough times to know."

Lowell didn't argue.

"And do you know when that picture was taken?"

He shook his head.

"July 14. Two days before the first Reata was destroyed." He met Lowell's eyes. "That's today."

They had not yet killed him.

Ryan lay in the silent darkness of . . . wherever he was . . . thinking. He had no doubt that he would be killed. He had been stripped of his clothes and rubbed with some kind of grease that smelled like bad meat before being redressed in a white sheet and bound so thoroughly with harsh twine that he could not even wiggle his hands or feet, let alone try to escape. But the fact that the Owner was drawing it out, turning it into such an elaborate ritual, made Ryan think that there was something special about him, that he was *needed* in some way to complete the transfer between the two resorts.

Maybe that's why his ESP had kicked in, why he'd been granted those glimpses into The Reata's past and future.

What could he do with that information, though?

It stood to reason that if he was needed for a specific purpose, if there was something special about him that the Owner required, that he also had the potential to stop this climactic event from occurring. But how? There was no way he was going to escape. But if there was truly something special about him, maybe he could change that aspect of himself so that he would no longer be a catalyst, so the Owner's plans would be thwarted and go unrealized. What made him special, though? Was it his age? He could not modify that. Was it his lack of sexual experience? No hope for that now. Whatever it might be, he was gagged and tied tightly and had no opportunity to alter anything.

He was willing to sacrifice himself for his family but he was not willing to sacrifice himself for The Reata. Ryan was surprised by how calm he was, by how rationally he'd thought that through. The prospect of imminent death did that to a person, he supposed.

And if he was going to die, he wanted to die for a good cause.

There was sound in the darkness, rhythmic noise from another part of the house getting louder, drawing closer.

Bootsteps on wooden floor.

He held his breath, shut his eyes tightly.

The Owner was coming.

A light was switched on, its incandescence so bright after the complete blackness that it burned even through his eyelids.

The bootsteps stopped.

The Owner was here.

Thirty-eight

The concierge refused to go with them, and they didn't have time to sit around and try to persuade him, so they took off on their own, making their way through the darkened minefield The Reata had become, listening for any sounds of the mobs, going to the place they all knew they had to go.

The old resort.

They clutched their primitive weapons, as well as the concierge's flashlight, and hurried up the trail through the open desert into the canyon, speaking only when necessary, staying quiet, keeping low. Rachel's feet hurt, her head was pounding with an excruciating headache unlike any she had ever experienced, and her bowels felt as though they were about to explode at any second, but she kept her body under control and kept her mind focused on her son, on Ryan.

What had happened to him? Where had he gone? How had he disappeared? One minute all four of them had been huddling together, hiding behind the tree, and the next she and the twins were waking from a nap they didn't know they were taking, to find that Ryan was gone. David they had lost somewhere along the way, running that gauntlet from one parking lot to another as the hordes descended, but she and the boys had made it safely to this upper area of the resort. She chose to tell herself that Ryan had left of his own accord, that he had seen something and decided to check it out, that he was following someone. But that fiction became harder to sustain after Lowell arrived and they started searching, and whether or not it had started out with Ryan inquisitively searching out information, it had doubtlessly ended with him being captured.

Or killed.

She pushed that thought away, though it refused to leave.

One thing she had always admired about her youngest son was his inquisitiveness. Curtis and Owen weren't like that. They did well in school, got good grades, but they lacked Ryan's spark. The twins would no doubt be successful in whatever endeavor they eventually chose, but Ryan was special. He would do what she'd always wanted to do. He wouldn't have just a job, he'd have a career, and it would be something interesting and offbeat, something that he would come up with on his own and pursue tenaciously. He was shy but focused, and while that combination did not serve him so well as a child, as an adult it would lead him into places his brothers could not go. Her eyes teared up as she thought about him, and she tried to concentrate on the task immediately before them, on finding Ryan.

They heard the noise before they saw the lights: screams and laughter, the festive sounds of a wild party. As they'd known, the old Reata was fully restored and repopulated. Even standing on the rise by the now-new buckboard with its filigreed sign, they could see scores of men and women enjoying the high life, strolling about with drinks in hand, engaging in randy pursuits about the grounds. Between two buildings they could even see people swimming in the well-lighted pool.

"What do we do?" Rachel asked. "Try and sneak up?"

Lowell held tight to his tomahawk. "Walk over there, I guess. Try to blend in."

They moved across the darkened desert toward the lights and activity of the resort.

Four totem poles stood in a semicircle in front of the lobby, the tall posts carved with demonic faces, terrible visages filled with rage and hate. At the top of each, smiling not-so-beneficently down was the skeletal countenance of Jedediah Harrison. Rachel looked up at him once, then quickly looked away, afraid in a primal, instinctive way of his terrible ancient face.

A couple strode past them, the woman in petticoat with parasol, the man in waistcoat with watch fob. They would have looked like extras in an old western, or historical society volunteers peopling a pioneer village museum, were it not for the mottled green of their rotting skin and the sickening stench of death that lingered around them.

Still, the couple took no notice of either Lowell, herself or the twins, and that gave them confidence. They stepped past the lobby, peeking in the windows just in case, then walked purposefully toward the pool area. They'd agreed that they would start at the pool—they all instinctively *felt* that it was the focal point of the re-sort, though that feeling had no basis in fact. Heading between two rows of rooms, they passed a man in a 1950s-style business suit slapping a dirty woman in rags and face paint, and a crowd of obnoxious guffawing hoodlums dressed in cowboy garb and kicking a dead dog.

Outside a room that looked like a playhouse or theater stood a small man with an oversized child's head, a grinning idiot aberration that stared at her with such complete lack of comprehension that it frightened her. Next to the bigheaded creature, slumped in a chair to the right side of the door like a guard or a ticket taker, was a dead man who looked awfully familiar. Rachel thought she'd seen him before on TV.

They reached the pool, and here they stopped. Gaslight and torches aided old-style electric lights in illuminating the area, and they could see men and women in full-body striped bathing suits cavorting in the water. But that was not what made them pause. No, it was the flayed bodies lying on the antique lounge chairs, the nude woman writhing against a saguaro cactus past the deep end, the well-built man copulating with a skull-headed scarecrow next to her, the myriad examples of unfathomable horror scattered throughout this surrealistic scene.

Three women, their pale bodies marked with red whiplashes that made them look like living candy canes, dashed out of a nearby room screaming and giggling, and jumped into the pool. "I'm on my period!" one of them shouted to the delighted cries of the others, and Rachel's blood ran cold as she remembered the karaoke crowd at the Grille.

"Ryan's not here," Curtis said next to her, and Rachel turned to look at him, impressed with the levelheadedness of his tone. She hadn't been sure what type of reaction a teenage boy would have to such a spectacle, but he had clearly ignored the unnatural goings-on, scanning the area for any sign of his brother before concluding that he was not there. She grabbed his hand and squeezed it with the sort of tender fondness she had not exhibited since he was in preschool.

"Join us," a squat man with a handlebar mustache said, walking up to Lowell. He was wearing a Reata T-shirt but no pants, and his erection pointed out obscenely. "We would have your woman."

Lowell kicked him in the crotch, and Rachel felt a small thrill of satisfaction as he fell to the ground, clutching himself and wailing. She expected to be set upon after that, expected his cries to alert the others of intruders in their midst and to have a swarm of Reatans attacking them, but they moved forward without incident or notice, Lowell leading them past the shallow end of the pool and around the edge of a block of rooms.

The gallows were empty this time, the bodies of the punished em-

ployees taken down and . . . what? . . . buried? . . . eaten? She didn't
want to know. They walked past the unpainted scaffolding toward a
building that had not been here last time. A chapel. She had no idea
why Ryan would be there, but it was as good a place to look as any,
and silently following Lowell's lead, they walked up the steps and
through the open doorway. It was packed with parishioners, all of
whom turned to look as they entered. They were all ancient, closer
to living corpses than human beings, and the air was suffused with a
sweet, overripe flowery smell that nearly made her gag.

The chapel was lit by candles placed in wrought iron holders
along the walls. At the head of the church, in front of an altar of
bones, stood a preacher. It was the same minister from the sunrise
service, only he was not *wearing* an elk's head this time, he *had* an
elk's head. He was neither animal nor human but some ungodly
combination of the two, and his voice when he spoke had a dis-
turbingly guttural beastly sound, as though words did not flow naturally off his tongue.

"It will be reborn anew after the sacrifice!" the minister intoned.
"The Founder will create from him a new Reata impervious to the
ravages of time—"

"What sacrifice?" Lowell demanded, and though Rachel would
not have spoken up, would not have said a word, she realized that
time was getting short and they needed to take concrete action if
they were ever to find and save Ryan.

"What sacrifice? Why, your son, Mr. Thurman! Please . . ." The
minister gestured toward an empty pew, his head wobbling. "Sit
down and join us. You have earned a place of honor, in this the
house of our Founder."

Lowell ran up the aisle, tomahawk upraised. "Where is he?" he
bellowed. "Where's my son?" He jumped onto the dais. "Goddamn
it, you tell me now or I'll bash your fucking head in!" The boys had
run after him, their own spears outthrust, but Rachel remained where
she was in case the parishioners came after them and they needed
rearguard support from this area.

The corpselike men and women remained seated, passive, and if
she hadn't seen their heads turn to follow the action, she would have
assumed they were dead.

The minister raised his hands as though he were being robbed by a
bandit, but she had the feeling that the pose had some sort of religious significance to him and his flock. "The boy is consecrating the
waters, the waters of life, the waters of The Reata that bring forth
such bounty and such pleasure . . ."

"Where?" Lowell demanded, thrusting the tomahawk forward and catching the minister at the base of his elk-haired neck. The sharpened edge of the weapon drew blood, and a red trickle passed over the thick brown hide before dripping down the white skin of his human chest.

But the minister did not stop in his oration. ". . . He whose heart is pure will be revered by The Founder and will reside within him for all eternity . . ."

"Where is my son?" Rachel screeched, and she was shocked at how loud her voice was, but she kept screaming anyway. None of the parishioners even looked at her. "Ryan!" she called. "Ryan!"

Lowell knocked the minister down and turned on the seated flock. "Where?" he demanded, but they stared up at him blankly, and he grabbed Owen's arm, running back down the aisle, both boys in tow.

All four of them ran out of the chapel. *Sacrifice.* They were going to kill her boy, her baby, in some stupid primitive ritual in order to keep Jedediah Harrison and his hellish resort alive for another hundred years or so.

But it wasn't stupid, it wasn't primitive. The ritual worked, they all knew it, and that gave their quest an even greater urgency.

"Ryan!" she continued to cry at the top of her lungs. "Ryan!"

The twins took up the cry as they hurried down the chapel steps. "Ryan! Ryan!"

"Waters . . ." Lowell said, thinking aloud. "We were just at the pool, so that's not it. Where—"

They were no longer being ignored. In the time it had taken them to run in and out of the chapel, seemingly every being at the resort had been gathered together and now stood in a crowd before them, filling the open area in front of the church and spilling over into the pathways between the rooms. At the front of the mob was the manager, still fat and bearded but nowhere near as jolly, flanked by five nearly identical men who could have been clones, impersonators. They were glaring at the four of them, and though their faces weren't rotting or disintegrating, there was something very old about the eyes of the men, something very unnatural in the stillness of their positions. Elsewhere, she saw members of the office staff she recognized, as well as the hostess from the Saguaro Room. The gardener, standing by himself, grinned at her, holding up a pair of pinking shears.

Managers, desk clerks, hostesses, gardeners. She was being tortured by service employees. There seemed something appropriate about that, but she had neither the time nor the inclination to think about the irony. She briefly noted that none of the workers at the bottom of the totem pole, the maids or janitors or laborers, were here. They were all back at the other resort. Like the concierge, they had been left behind. Harrison had used them to take care of the day-to-day grunt work of The Reata, but they were not part of it. They were not *of* it.

Behind the managers and the few people she recognized were scores of others, not only the original guests and employees of Harrison's Reata but the people who had come after, generations of individuals who had worked here, who had stayed here, who had somehow become part of the Founder's flock.

Where was Harrison himself?

Sacrificing Ryan, she thought, and she looked quickly over at Lowell, met his gaze, and saw in his eyes the same despair she felt.

They both glanced around, searching for a way out but not finding any. The crowd before them did not move, did not change, and neither did they. Both sides remained frozen. She saw Lowell glance back into the chapel to make sure no one was coming out from there.

All of a sudden there was screaming and shouting from the area in front of the lobby, great war whoops and gratifyingly modern cries of "Let's roll!"

It was the cavalry. Rand Black and too many others to count, all streamed into the resort, weapons at the ready, led by the concierge. The old man was clutching what looked like a broken bottle on the end of a stick. Anger limned his features, granting him the appearance of an avenging angel. The Reatans turned at the sound of the ruckus, but too late. They were already being hacked and stabbed, attacked from behind and on the right flank, and those capable of doing something about it were in the wrong position, awkward locations.

"Go!" Black yelled at the top of his lungs, and though they had no idea at whom the command was directed, Lowell grabbed Rachel's hand and they ran.

They left in the thick of it. In the midst of the fighting, in the chaos of battle, Lowell grabbed Rachel and the twins and herded them off to the side, around the edge of the chapel. He had no idea where they were going or what he was doing, but they'd been given a break, granted a reprieve, and if they were ever to find Ryan—

the sacrifice

—he was going to have to act fast and act now.

The desert was dark behind the chapel. The lights stopped here.

The moon had temporarily disappeared behind a cloud, but he remembered from the last visit that there was a barn and corral out this way. A slaughterhouse was inside the barn, according to the kids. And the Founder's throne.

Rachel and the kids moving right with him, Lowell hastened over the shifting sand, using the concierge's flashlight to avoid the desert pitfalls of cactus and rock. The moon reappeared from behind the clouds, and he saw the barn, saw the corral next to it, holding horses that weren't *quite* horses, but there was another building illuminated as well. A house. Not a small cabin or low ranch-style home, but a tall gabled mansion bathed in darkness that not even the moonlight could penetrate.

It had to be Harrison's, and Lowell increased his speed, heading straight for it. *Yes,* he thought. The man would build his home directly over the spring that brought forth the water that kept him alive. And if the spring needed to be rejuvenated with some sort of ritualistic sacrifice, this is where it would occur.

Ryan was in that house.

He glanced up as he ran at the black façade.

They know things about you.

Lowell thought of what the concierge had told him and was grateful for the knowledge. Forewarned is forearmed, as the old saying went, and he knew that he was ready for anything they were planning to throw at him. Old girlfriends, bullies from his school days, his parents . . . Whatever Harrison and his minions conjured in order to throw him off track, he would ignore. He would remain focused.

They reached the house and stormed up the porch steps, but the front door was locked. Lowell threw his weight against it, motioned for the twins to do the same, and all three of them slammed sideways into the wood at the same time. The door did not budge.

"Lowell?"

They were about to take another run at the door when he heard Rachel's voice, heard the fear in it and the confusion. He turned. She was looking back toward the lighted buildings, and when she saw that she had his attention, she pointed to one he hadn't noticed before, one situated between the chapel and a series of stand-alone bungalows, one that didn't match at all with the others, one not in the primitive style of the original Reata or the hodgepodge of ersatz western structures that had been incorporated into the restored resort around it.

The exercise center.

Lowell stared at the low squat building. That was the first place he'd experienced the supernatural at The Reata, and from the beginning he'd had a bad feeling about the facility. But why was it here? How had it gotten here? What made it so important that it, out of everything from the new resort, had been saved?

The waters.

He put an ear next to the door of the house, listening. There was no noise inside. It could have been soundproofed, but he thought not. The house was empty.

Ryan was in the exercise center.

Again, they were wasting valuable time. "Come on!" he yelled. They could see a gravel pathway now, and the four of them ran quickly, no longer having to negotiate the unstable sand. The fight was still raging, and though there were bodies on the ground, most of them appeared to be old and decrepit.

The good guys were winning.

Lowell was surprised. A ragtag group of hotel guests and low-level employees wielding homemade weapons made from sticks and stones and broken tools would seem to be no match for supernatural creatures a hundred years old, but perhaps the recuperative powers of the waters were waning even now, leaving the recipients of their magic in weakened states with fading health. He would not have guessed that to be the case after seeing the Reatans frolicking in the pool and massed before him in front of the chapel, but *something* had to account for their surprising ineffectiveness before their attackers.

Still, he cut a broad swath around the combatants as he led his family to the exercise center. He had mixed feelings about this. He had no doubt that it was dangerous, and he worried about exposing Rachel and the twins to unnecessary peril, but at the same time he was wary of leaving them by themselves.

Besides, they wanted to get Ryan back as much as he did.

So they approached the building together. And at the last minute, they were joined by the concierge. The old man appeared out of the darkness to their left, breathing raggedly and sweating profusely. "I saw you," he managed to get out between gasps of breath. "I came to help."

Lowell wasn't sure how much help he would be, but the concierge was carrying a new weapon, obviously something he had taken from someone else: a rusty sword. *That* might be some help.

"Where'd you get it?" Lowell asked, nodding at the weapon.

"Took it off a dead man," he panted. "It's one of theirs."

One of theirs.

Lowell was not sure if that was good or bad, if it would help them or hinder them. But a steel blade, no matter how old and rusted, was bound to be more effective than their own pitiful sticks. "Let me have it," he said.

Jim shook his head, drawing back. "It's mine."

"That's my son in there!"

The concierge looked at him. "Then let's go get him."

There was no time to argue, so Lowell let out a frustrated "Shit!" and opened the smoked glass door, leading the way into the building.

It smelled differently than it had before. That was the first thing he noticed. Before, there'd been the strong modern odor of rubber mats and newly unpacked equipment overlayed by the scent of pine disinfectant, a subtle whiff of chlorine beneath it all. Now there was a musty smell as of old attic trunks, combined with the aroma of . . . some type of food. Stew, maybe? Wafting about was another fragrance nowhere near as pleasant, a gaseous rotting odor that could come only from something dead. Not something recently killed or something that had been dead a long time, but something intermediate, when decay had started to set in and the flies were buzzing.

The fat man was in the weight room once again. *Had he come with the building?* Lowell saw him instantly, on the same machine as before, and he gave a small start as he entered the exercise area, thinking for a moment that there was an army of obese men waiting for him as he saw the multiplied images in the mirrored wall. But there was only the one man, and he grunted and grinned as he lifted an amazing amount of weights. Behind him, the twins gasped.

They recognized him, too.

He didn't know how or why but he didn't have time to find out.

"Guard him," Lowell ordered Curtis and Owen. He didn't want the fat man following him into the pool room, cutting off his only avenue of escape. "Yell if he moves. Stab him if you have to." He met his sons' eyes, saw them nod, noted the look of grim determination on each.

"I'll stay with them," Rachel offered, and for that he was grateful. She motioned toward the doorway and the corridor beyond. "You two go."

Lowell and Jim moved forward quickly without another word.

He should have told her he loved her, Lowell thought. He should have told the boys. Just in case. That's what people did in movies and books when they went someplace from where there was a very real possibility that they might not come back. But real life was

messier than fiction, and in it you didn't always have time to do or
say the right things.

There was noise up ahead. And both the stew smell and that disgusting odor grew stronger, competing and combining in a way that
made him afraid he'd vomit. Lowell was in the lead by a single step,
and he moved sideways to block the concierge, wanting to make
sure the old man didn't just barge in. If they were to have any hope
of success here, they would need all of the advantages they could
get.

The light in the pool room was even more wan and sickly than it
had been before and nowhere near as constant. Candles or torches,
he assumed, and as he crept forward he saw the weird way the flickering light reflected the movement of the water, making shadows
and shapes on the wall directly in front of the doorway that looked
like creatures, monsters, beings that had never existed or had lived
so long ago that their forms were not even recorded in genetic memory.

The sounds inside the pool room were louder, clearer than they
had been a moment earlier, but they made no sense. He heard mumbling and chuckling that seemed to be coming from a crowd of people, accompanied by liquid gurgling and occasional clicks.

He poked his head carefully around the corner of the doorway.

Well-dressed men and women surrounded the pool in a framing
rectangle. The Reata's elite. Not the people who worked at the resort—no matter how high their station, they would not have been allowed in *this* company—but the moneyed men and society matrons
who'd kept it alive financially, who'd brought Harrison the cash he
needed to expand his holdings and supplied him with the bodies he
needed to satisfy his unnatural cravings.

At the head of the pool, surrounded by these ladies and gentle-
men, was The Reata's chef, dressed in a stereotypical white apron
and puffy hat. The water was roiling and heat steamed upward, making the inside of the room almost unbearable. Lowell saw vegetables
bubbling up in the pool: carrots, cauliflower, zucchini. He saw, as
well, parts of human bodies: fingers, legs, hair. He pressed forward,
Jim at his side, still unseen by the gathered Reatans, who were completely focused on the pool in front of them. He wasn't sure what he
was going to do, but he moved ahead with careful steps along the
dark edge of the wall, keeping his eye on the chef, who was pinching
salt onto something directly in front of him.

A woman with a pearl necklace shifted slightly away from her
husband, and it became clear what was being prepared.

Lying at the chef's feet, ready to be rolled into the water, was Ryan.

Lowell felt as though he'd been kicked in the gut, as though all of the life and air had been instantly sucked out of him. His eyes were watering, but not enough to block the view of his son, bound like a pot roast, apple stuffed in his mouth, waiting to be thrown into that hellish soup. He could no longer see Ryan's eyes through the onrush of tears, but he would be seeing them in his mind for the rest of his life, wide open and staring, hurt and terrified, filled with the knowledge that his parents had not arrived in time to save him, that he was going to die alone.

He was not going to die alone, though.

He was not going to die.

If Lowell had a machine gun, he would have killed them all at that moment, would have swung the weapon around the room, spraying bullets until every last damn one of those worthless fucks was too dead to ever come back. But he didn't. He had only a gift shop tomahawk. And the concierge had only a rusty sword. They'd be overpowered before they'd taken out more than three or four of them.

But it would be worth it if they could give Ryan a chance to escape.

Wiping his eyes angrily, he turned back toward Jim, and his blood ran cold. The old man was staring raptly at the water, and Lowell realized that the concierge was where he wanted to be. He'd expected to be taken to this place with the rest of the senior staff in order to stave off his inevitable demise, and had drunk himself into a state of almost complete despair after finding himself abandoned in the lobby. But though he'd been left behind, he'd finally gotten here, he'd finally arrived. By hook or by crook, he'd made it, and now he had the chance to join the rest of them, to partake of the waters and live for a long, long time.

That was why he hadn't wanted to give up his sword, that was why he'd accompanied Lowell here.

A shudder passed through the room like a wave, a physical tremor that palpitated the air about him and caused the gathering to gasp as one. Lowell swiveled around. Jedidiah Harrison emerged from the darkened area behind the chef as though he'd stepped through some hidden doorway or portal from another place. He looked as terrifying as he had in his various portrayals—only more so. For this was no mere rendering, no two-dimensional drawing or inanimate carving. This was the living, breathing Founder himself, a man more than two hundred years old, an evil entity so powerful and focused that he had singlehandedly created this community out of the desert, attracting America's wealthiest and most self-absorbed to his sick cabal, offering them lives lengthened immeasurably in exchange for their participation in his sadistic revels. There was a grisly smile on his face, the inexplicably joyous grimace of a skull, but his eyes were dead and cold, satiated with the years of violence and debauchery, jaded beyond measure and incapable of feeling love or joy or even fear, so far beyond the range of ordinary human emotion that it was impossible to fathom the terrible desires in that depraved brain.

Lowell thought about his first experience at the exercise pool, Rachel's encounters with the psychotic gardener, all of the bizarre incidents they'd experienced at The Reata. He and Rachel had come to think of the resort as an entity unto itself, as a sentient being. But it was not. It was an extension of the Founder. Whatever *he* was, *it* was, and while Jedidiah Harrison may have discovered the fountain of youth here two centuries ago, he had corrupted it and it had corrupted him, and the two were now so inexorably intertwined that it was impossible to tell where one left off and the other began.

The steam was suddenly thicker, stronger, the candles lighting the pool room dimmer, more faint. White figures emerged from the murk, skinny wraithlike forms with no discernable faces, only strangely blurred visages where their features should have been. Conjured from the waters, they were gliding across the top of the shiny black liquid, back and forth, forth and back, across the length of the pool, and Lowell knew instinctively that if any of them touched him, he would die.

The men and women began chanting, and, though foreign, the words they recited sounded familiar. He'd heard them before.

At the Grille.

Yes. They'd been part of one of those strange karaoke songs, and even as he thought it, the Founder started singing. He had a horrible voice, harsh and raspy with no hint of rhythm. But that was not what made it so difficult to hear. No, it was the age of his voice, the endless years and the terrible knowledge that that voice held, the aural manifestation of the man's evil unnatural existence.

The white wraiths in the steam began to move faster, picking up speed, and with the acceleration came increased clarity. For flickering seconds of time, faces appeared on those blank blurry visages.

The chef stepped aside with a small formal bow, and Harrison, still singing, took his place at the head of the gathering, his dusty boots stepping directly in front of the spot where Ryan's body lay.

He raised his hands as if to exhort his followers to chant even louder—

—and Ryan rolled into the pool with a splash.

There'd been no warning, and Lowell had been so distracted by the Founder that he did not see it happen. His gaze snapped quickly down, but he was too late. Ryan was gone. His son was somewhere in that roiling water, which had now turned black.

"Ryan!" he screamed, but his voice was lost in the din and no one heard his anguished cry.

His son had probably been watching him as he rolled his bound body into the pool, hoping for some last contact, some connection or acknowledgement, but Lowell's eyes had been elsewhere and he'd missed it. Ryan *had* died alone, and he hated himself for that, knowing that no matter how long he lived, he would always have to live with the knowledge that he had failed his son.

This was clearly unplanned. The chanting faltered, and Harrison stopped singing entirely, his face a mask of incredulous rage.

Ryan had prevented the ritual from being concluded.

His son had known that, Lowell realized. He had intentionally sacrificed himself in order to put an end to the Founder's hopes of revivifying the waters, knowing that if he did so at the wrong time, the ceremony could not be completed.

Tears stung Lowell's eyes. The boy was a hero. Ryan had not only been smart enough to figure out what he needed to do in order to throw a wrench in the works, but he'd been brave enough to carry it out. He had sacrificed himself instead of allowing himself to be sacrificed, and in doing so had hopefully put an end to Jedediah Harrison's centuries-long reign of evil.

The Founder stepped forward, glaring down into the agitated black water, his cowboy boots stepping on the spot where Ryan's body had lain. Lowell stared at those boots and the section of cement on which they'd stopped. Grief and fear hardened into anger within him.

That old fuck had lived for far too long.

His grip tightened on the tomahawk. He wouldn't get out of here alive, but if it was the last thing he did, he was going to take that monster down and bash in his head until there was no way he could *ever* be revived. He felt a brief tinge of sadness and regret, the faces of Rachel and the twins passing before his eyes, and he wished there was some way to tell them how much he loved them, how much they meant to him. Then—

Jim moved in front of him, sword extended. Lowell thought that the concierge was going to try to stop him, and he was filled with a bleakness so complete that his weapon arm dangled limply down in defeat as he prepared to be sliced through. But the old man had not turned on him. Either his desire for revenge was stronger than his desire for life, or he wanted to somehow make up for his previous collaboration with The Reata, because he pushed Lowell back, and it was clear that the concierge knew exactly what Lowell had planned to do.

And was going to do it himself.

"I'm dying anyway," was the only thing he said as he rushed forward, and next to Ryan's sacrifice, Lowell thought it was the most heroic act he had ever witnessed. He wanted to object, wanted to tell the concierge that he didn't have to, that it wasn't really his battle, that Ryan was *his* son, but there was no time for that mealy mouthed posturing, and they both knew the truth of the situation: Jim was old and dying of cancer; Lowell was young with a wife and two boys.

They saw him coming, but none of them were prepared for it. And though these people were old enough to have seen it all and nothing really fazed them, their instincts for self-preservation remained intact, and they scattered, breaking their chain, one old dowager falling into the water, her companion toppling backward in the opposite direction. Jim made a beeline for Harrison, and before the Founder could lift a hand to save himself, the concierge was hacking away at those ancient arms, at the sunken chest. The clothes were rent, the sallow skin beneath them sliced, but there was no blood, only a feeble trickle of liquid that looked uncomfortably like the black water in the pool.

With a mighty roar decibels higher than should have been possible, the Founder swatted at the sword. The move cost him his brittle right forearm, which was sliced by the blade and dropped into the water with a loud plop, but he managed to knock the weapon out of Jim's hand, and the rusted weapon clattered ineffectually onto the cement. The ancient man looked more monster than human as he continued to roar with rage, his features distorted with fury, but before he could act again, the concierge leaped upon him, knocking him to the ground and grabbing his skinny bony neck in a last desperate attempt to finish him off.

Lowell wasn't about to just stand by and watch and, tomahawk raised, he sprang forward. The men and women awaiting the return of the waters, and, presumably, the birth of a new Reata, had backed against the walls, terrified, trying to stay out of the way and protect their own hides. Lowell jumped over the concierge, whose own neck was being throttled by a strong hand that looked like that of a skeleton covered in parchment, and raised his tomahawk above the exposed head of the Founder. For a fraction of a second, he saw into those cold ancient eyes, saw in them dark depths that he could not even fathom. Then he was bringing the stone edge of the weapon down on the scraggly-haired head as hard as he could again and again and again until the body was no longer twitching and the skull was crushed beyond recognition.

He stopped finally, sweating from the steam and the passion and the exertion, breathing heavily through his mouth. The chef was whimpering, cowering in a corner, and some of the other men and women were still alive too, hiding their hideous faces with their hands or their hats, but most of them had gone the way of all flesh and were little more than rotting corpses and dried dead husks of the people they had been.

Those white wraiths were gone, too, returned to whatever hell had spawned them.

And Jim was dead.

Somehow Lowell had not expected that. He'd thought he'd arrived in time to save the old man, but Harrison's grip had been strong and sure, and it had probably taken less than a minute to crush the life out of the concierge. Lowell felt sad but at the same time grateful, although he could not help wondering if the two of them would have been able to get away with such a slapdash harebrained attack if the ritual had been completed and the waters had been restored. He had the feeling that at full strength, the Founder could have dispatched them both with ease. It was only the fact that the spring had not been revived that had saved them.

Ryan had saved them.

The steam dissipated, the water stopped bubbling, and vegetables and body parts bobbed to the dark surface of the pool, but there was no sign of his son. He was down there at the bottom with the bones, Lowell thought, but as if in response, the brackish water began to be siphoned away, the pool level shrinking inches before his eyes until it was down one foot, two, three, four. . . .

There was no shallow end, Lowell saw now. The entire pool was of a uniform depth well in excess of a hundred feet. At the bottom was a black hole, and somewhere down that hole was Ryan.

He didn't want to think about that now, he *couldn't* think about it, and in a daze he lurched out of the pool room, meeting Rachel and the twins halfway down the corridor. They'd come to tell him that the fat man had dissolved before their eyes, and when Lowell passed through the weight room on his way out, he saw what looked like drips of cooked fat on the metal bars of the weight machine.

They stepped outside.

He told them what had happened.

The resort was dark, all of the lights and torches out. Dead bodies were everywhere, in various stages of decomposition, and among the corpses wandered stunned guests and exhausted employees, confused and frightened.

The sky was lightening in the east, above the mountains, the sky fading from black to dark blue. He knew he should try to find Rand Black or Jose or Laszlo, one of the other Cactus Wrens or one of the employees, knew he should search the once again dead resort for survivors, but he just couldn't do it. Supported by his family, he stumbled across the sand, past the dark lobby and the downed totem poles toward the sunken buckboard wagon. All four of them holding tightly to one another, they trudged back to The Reata, or what was left of it, and when they emerged from the canyon, a helicopter was hovering over the ruins of the resort. On the ground, between the rubble and the palm trees, were the flashing lights of emergency vehicles in the parking lot.

They were saved.

Rescuers had finally arrived.

Other men and women, and more than a few children, were already in the parking lot awaiting transportation, having told their stories to disbelieving policemen, firemen and paramedics. Lowell, Rachel, Curtis and Owen joined the crowd, and when a clearly stunned police officer asked them what had happened, Lowell discovered that he could not speak. Though crying, Rachel jumped in, starting to explain from the beginning, from the night Blodgett stole their room and her underwear, and Lowell sat down hard on the ground. The tears came then, tears that threatened never to stop but to go on forever. Great sobs wracked his body, and he cried as he had never cried in his life. He cried for himself, for Rachel, for the twins, for everyone here at The Reata.

But most of all he cried for his son, his youngest, his hope for the future, the light of his life.

A smart and quiet boy named Ryan.

Born in Arizona shortly after his mother attended the world premiere of *Psycho*, Bentley Little is the Bram Stoker Award–winning author of fourteen previous novels and *The Collection*, a book of short stories. He has worked as a technical writer, reporter/photographer, library assistant, sales clerk, phonebook deliveryman, video arcade attendant, newspaper deliveryman, furniture mover, and rodeo gatekeeper. The son of a Russian artist and an American educator, he and his Chinese wife were married by the justice of the peace in Tombstone, Arizona.